S. J. NAUDÉ

THE THIRD REEL

SALT

CROMER

PUBLISHED BY SALT PUBLISHING 2018

2 4 6 8 10 9 7 5 3 1

First published in Great Britain in 2018 by
Salt Publishing Ltd
12 Norwich Road, Cromer, Norfolk NR27 0AX United Kingdom

The poem on page 259 is by DJ Opperman and is reproduced
with the permission of NB Publishers.

www.saltpublishing.com

Salt Publishing Limited Reg. No. 5293401

A CIP catalogue record for this book is available from the British Library

ISBN 978 1 78463 150 5 (Paperback edition)
ISBN 978 1 78463 151 2 (Electronic edition)

Typeset in Neacademia by Salt Publishing

Printed and bound in Great Britain by Clays Ltd, St Ives plc

For Pierre

Du warst mein Tod:
dich konnte ich halten,
während mir alles entfiel.

You were my death:
you I could hold
when all fell away from me.

—PAUL CELAN, *Fadensonnen* (1968)

THE THIRD REEL

I.
REVOLUTION OF
THE CHILDREN

(London, April–December 1986)

Chapter I

WHEN ETIENNE WAKES up, a world map has been imprinted on him. Then the continents start moving and disintegrating: the shadows, it turns out, of cobwebs moving in the morning sun. Above him a ladder leads to a platform and large bronze bells hanging between beams. Next to him lies a sturdy body, hair spread over the pillow. He has kicked off the sheet; one knee is pulled up. Frank the New Zealander. Twenty-five, three years older than he.

In Pretoria, the city of his youth, Etienne used to visualise his awakening in a New City as a Blake drawing. An explosion of light and muscle power. Sunbeams fanning out, lightning shooting from dragon horns. At night, in the silence of the suburbs, he would open his book of Blake pictures across his knees. While the city was sleeping – bodies struck down in airless rooms like plague deaths – he wanted to fling open the curtains and invite visions of other cities into his bedroom.

Only in the military base outside the city was there life. He would close the book and think of soldiers on sentry duty. Of the intimacy of glowing cigarette tracks approaching each other in the dark, crossing and moving apart. As a child, he once visited the base's hospital with a school friend whose father was a landmine victim just back from the border war. Etienne wasn't allowed in the hospital room. He walked through the corridors and looked down at the anonymous barracks while trying to imagine his friend's father without legs. At night in his room he would henceforth visualise rows of sleeping soldiers. Blake's light, he reckoned, had the same temperature as the air around their grey beds.

That kind of heat was what he'd felt on his skin last night. In the morning hours, he and Frank had climbed the ladder to the wooden platform. Etienne leaned over towards a bell, touching the bronze. They were both naked. Frank – much larger than he – was behind him.

Frank stretched his fingers towards the bronze too, the hair in his armpit brushing against Etienne's shoulder. 'There are far more impressive ones. As a continent of bells, Europe is young. Eastern civilisations were far ahead of the West.' Frank elaborated: about the Chinese history of bells, about Continental village festivals to inaugurate newly cast bells. About how, in England, casting pits would be dug in the church itself. Etienne was listening with his skin, to every little puff of breath in his neck.

Frank knocked against the bronze. 'The waist.' He flattened Etienne's hand against the bell. 'Made of copper and tin.' He moved Etienne's hand higher up. 'The shoulder.' Their hands slid down together. Etienne's chest was now pressed against the bell; their fingers slipped underneath the lip. 'And the clapper.'

By the time Frank was explaining bell-tuning methods, Etienne's cheek was touching the cool metal. Frank was saying something about second partials, but his words floated in the tower like down. Etienne hardly heard Frank's definitions of terms like 'tierce' and 'quint'. Only the tone of his voice registered. Dense and dark, like the New Zealand soil of which Frank had told him earlier that evening. The clapper knocked against the bronze, made it sing. Etienne's teeth and bones sang too.

Etienne and Frank had met earlier in the evening at the Royal Vauxhall Tavern. Amid the throng they spilled beer on each other, then, laughing, tried to wipe the drops from each other. Before long they were outside. Away from the drag queens on the little stage and the currents of men flowing as smoothly as honey inside. Only the pumping bass of Frankie Goes to Hollywood's 'Relax' could still be heard. Frank led him to a lawn behind the Tavern. 'Vauxhall Pleasure Gardens,' Frank said. On the railway viaduct nearby, train wheels screeched against tracks. The smell of garbage drifted over from the Tavern's bins. 'In the nineteenth century, everything looked different here: walking lanes for lovers, tightrope walkers, hot-air balloons, fireworks . . .' Frank looked around with rising intensity, as if he could see right through 1986. 'Women with umbrellas. Dandies with pencil moustaches. Rococo and chinoiserie . . . And now? Just the trains. And parched grass.' He took Etienne's cheeks in his hands. 'And you and I.' Frank's hands were callused; his hair fell over Etienne's face as he kissed him. It didn't surprise Etienne, the insistence of a man's lips against his own for the first time.

They entered the tunnel under the viaduct, turned right in Lambeth Road, amid the fumes of buses and taxis. After ten minutes of walking, they stopped at an old church. 'I live in the tower. And no hunchback jokes, please. I'm a campanologist.' Frank read the question mark on Etienne's face. 'A bell-master. Someone who knows bells, who fixes and tunes them. And sometimes rings them.' His hand was on the back of Etienne's neck; he swung open the church door. 'Welcome. And don't be overcome by Protestant guilt. It hasn't been a church for a long time. A museum of gardens these days.' Etienne wasn't too sober. He looked at the little hairs on Frank's knuckles. They

5

walked up the steep tower steps, the smell of church mould in his nose. Frank's quarters consisted of a small room with a stone window. And, above their heads, the bells. Below them, the Thames: a black highway dividing the city.

Etienne exits the church, inhales the traffic fumes. Like the sulphuric smoke, he thinks, of Blake's heavenly fires. Further down the street, he realises: Frank hasn't rung the bells. Neither last night, nor this morning. And it *is* Sunday, after all. Not much of a bell-master, our Frank. Lying there spread-eagled while the sun draws musk from his body's creases, the bells motionless. Wouldn't it be simpler to mechanise the bells? Etienne wonders. It is the '80s, after all.

A bell-ringer, nevertheless, with the loveliest round buttocks of all bell-ringers. When a shockwave of sound hits Etienne from behind, he stops. It is pure, like a bird singing for the first time. He turns around. The sound is emanating from the sun, which is shining fiercely behind the tower. Is Frank looking down at him while doing the ringing? Etienne smiles, lifts his hand in a blind salute, fist clenched.

He walks further. 'A campanologist,' he says out loud in the wind, shaking his head. The sun warms his shoulder blades; the bells keep ringing. Is this the kind of pealing that might once have welcomed a king back to London after a hunt in the countryside? An image appears in his mind's eye: a procession of coaches entering the city and, behind them, horse-drawn carriages stacked with deer, slick with blood, horns interlocked like a primitive shelter of branches.

He closes his eyes, smiles as he walks. The bells keep sounding. At Vauxhall station, he turns and passes underneath the tracks, then turns right. He turns left in Vauxhall Grove, walks down to Bonnington Square. The bells' rhythm is slowing in the distance. He opens No. 52's front door, takes the stairs to the top. One by one the bells fall silent. Morning sun is pouring into his room. With his eyes fixed on the skylight, trying to recall if the tower can be seen from the roof, he crashes into his drum kit. 'Fuck,' he says in Afrikaans, silencing a resonating cymbal with his hand. He undresses in front of the mirror, looking at his new body. It might *look* like his old body, but every cell has been displaced. Silvery blood is pumping though his veins. There are bruises on his chest. But when he rubs them, they come off: bell soot. His skin is excited by the merest touch. Even when he *almost* touches it. His nerves are picking up the slightest distortions in the air.

His old flesh has had to yield to something harder, bronze-like. Something that can be polished to a cold sheen. He is ready for the New City. His body is a radar, his skin a new country, his heart a shiny machine.

Chapter 2

WHEN ETIENNE ARRIVED in London in late April, fresh from the plane and Tube, suitcase in hand, he headed directly to the offices of The Committee on South African War Resistance, or COSAWR. He had no contacts in the city. In South Africa he had known no one else who would consider dodging the draft. For his school and university friends, two years in the army were an opportunity to become a man, to do your part for the fatherland.

During his last year in university, Etienne wrote a letter to the End Conscription Campaign, or ECC. *I would do anything to avoid going to the army. Do you have any advice for me?*

The evening after he had posted the letter, his father summoned him to his study. Etienne got a scare, convinced his letter must have been intercepted. It turned out to be a vague conversation, amid gleaming wooden panelling, about Etienne's future. Etienne was in his final year of engineering studies and was still living with his parents. 'Remember, not only your own interests are at stake where career matters are concerned. A man must be able to support his family *and* be valuable to his country. The time has come to shake off the things of a child.' His father referred to his own studies as an agricultural economist 'in times when agriculture was decisive for the Afrikaner's upliftment'.

Etienne looked his father in the eye. He wasn't thinking of agricultural history, but of his history teacher. A Mister van

Rooyen. Of his moustache and the knob in his nylon slacks. His buttocks sweating while he barked orders during cadet hours.

School cadets: a joint project by the military authorities and education department. Etienne had attended a school for boys. For years he and his classmates had to drill in the heat every Wednesday. The school grounds were temporarily militarised. Teachers were now in uniform, acutely aware of their rank. They had to march across the sports fields in shorts and shirts of brown canvas, sweat darkening armpits and buttock clefts. Van Rooyen was the leader of the pack, stars and stripes on his epaulettes. Afterwards he would shower and dress with the boys. 'I'm with you all the way, guys. It's looking good. Soldiers-in-training.' Little muscle man, Van Rooyen: sweat smelling of conspiracy, bare feet on a concrete floor, scrotum being soaped up under a cold shower.

Now Etienne averted his gaze, mumbled something about skinny cows and rusty ploughs. His father ignored him. 'What I'm saying is that one must have vision. Idealism running like a golden thread through everything you do.' His father began his career as a lecturer at the University of Pretoria, but, after his years of student leadership and an early professorship, started making swift political progress. He was elected a member of the Volksraad, and later appointed deputy minister of agriculture. A young star in the Party.

Before he could be appointed a cabinet minister, his political career was nipped in the bud. The press release spoke about *other opportunities that I could not refuse*. Etienne knows there were murkier reasons. A letter was slipped under their front door one evening. When his father returned from a late meeting, there were whispered conversations, his mother crying. The light in the study shining all night. His father's voice, urgent on the phone. Etienne never got to the bottom of the matter. In any event, this hardly broke his father's stride. He was appointed head of the Land Bank, later chairman of an agricultural cooperative. Esteemed and successful, he now serves on various boards of directors: a bank, a life insurer, a tobacco company.

'You would, of course, first have to complete your conscription after finishing your studies. That's an honourable way of contributing to the greater good. You'll quickly work your way up to officer status. I'll whisper a word in the right people's ears. But you'd have to show your mettle too. And after the army, I would urge you to do your master's degree in business administration. A good start for the business world. And, in the long run, you'll learn that whom you associate with is critical. The Organisation remains important.' On his father's desk was a bronze sculpture of a leopard pouncing on an impala. Like an action photo. 'I shall introduce you to people. In time. Remember,' he added, 'clever young Afrikaner men have a special responsibility. Our freedom and survival in this country were bought at a high price, and are increasingly under pressure.' Etienne became aware of the shape his bare soles were imprinting on the carpet's deep pile. *Bought at a hiiiigh price*, he mocked in his mind, but resisted rolling his eyes.

'One thing you now have to let go of is this nonsense about rock music.' His father shook his head. 'All the drum-playing. Child's play. It doesn't fit in with your future.' His father looked up at the shelves, as if he was trying to find his next sentence in a book. For a few moments he closed his lids, his eyeballs moving behind them. He stroked his hair, smiling stiffly. He opened his diary, found a date a few months ahead. 'How about you and I go hunting for once? Go and shoot ourselves a few springboks. In the Kalahari. I have a friend with a farm.' His voice had become hoarse; he cleared his throat. 'We'll get to know each other again. Out there in the veld.' It wasn't the first time his father had tried to arrange a hunting trip. Etienne gazed at him past the fine engravings in the bronze where the leopard's claws were tearing into impala skin. He was taken aback by the hunger in his father's eyes, the neediness with which he was trying to find something recognisable in his son.

The ECC didn't write back. A man called Etienne: 'Better not to write things down.' First there were a few suspicious questions; his Afrikaans surname - Nieuwenhuis - didn't help. An explication of the principles of pacifism followed. And of available options. How it would help others if he stayed on in the country as a conscientious objector. 'It started with a few courageous individuals, but the ranks are growing. Ultimately they won't be able to prosecute everyone; the whole system will start collaps—'

'Practical advice,' Etienne said, 'is all I need. I want to go to London. As soon as possible.' The man lost interest. He provided COSAWR's London contact detail, wished Etienne the best and ended the conversation.

In one respect his father was right. It *was* time to grow up. A month later Etienne was in the departure hall of Jan Smuts airport.

He thinks back to his arrival in London, like an orphan with his old-fashioned suitcase. He went directly to COSAWR's office, where Ben, a beautiful Jewish Johannesburger, referred him to one Miss Jackson when Etienne told him that he had brought very little money with him. She had a rambling old Victorian house in Kilburn, Ben explained, where she let rooms for a song to young South African men. Everyone in her boarding house was a draft dodger. Not one of them could go back home.

'She almost never turns anyone away. And for the first month or two one stays for free.' Ben also gave him information about applying for asylum; they would assist him. And he handed Etienne a small-format magazine: *Resister*, the paper of the anti-conscription movement.

He took the Tube to Kilburn. Miss Jackson opened the front door in a free-flowing tie-dye dress, linen scarf around her neck, breasts like pendulums. He complimented her on the scarf. 'Mexican,' she said. She didn't invite him in; they kept standing in the entrance hall. Young men came and went. One or two greeted him in passing. Etienne glanced at them. He could see how Miss Jackson gauged his gaze. He gauged her too, this mother for sensitive souls who had escaped Angola and the burning townships: young bodies from the south, their fresh skins still sun-darkened for their first few months in the north.

Etienne enquired about accommodation options. She remarked: 'What an interesting accent!' She looked at his pale stalk of a body, at his straight black hair. 'It is unusual, but I'm afraid every room here is currently occupied . . .'

As consolation prize she introduced him to one of her lodgers. Brent. A Capetonian, a sociologist who had studied at UCT. The only trace remaining of the southern sun was a spray of freckles over the bridge of his nose. His hair was thin and dull red, his chin long. Brent took him to a little café in Kilburn High Road. Brent spoke to him about 'the Cause', about the illegal occupation of South-West Africa (Namibia, as he referred to it), about the war. The militarisation of South African society. The sacrifices of courageous individuals. He wanted Etienne to become involved in the London anti-apartheid structures.

Etienne looked at Brent's loose T-shirt, at the drooping corners of his mouth. 'Do you perhaps know of a place where I can stay?'

When the waitress brought their cups, she spilled milky tea on Etienne's suitcase. Brent looked intently at Etienne. 'Do you agree that we, with our privileges and our education, have a duty? That we are uniquely positioned to effect change? The world's eyes are on South Africa. Now more than ever.'

Etienne looked at Brent's Adam's apple. He hadn't slept in thirty hours. His eyes were hardly focusing; his skin was sticky. 'Education?' He thought of Mister van Rooyen's buttocks, of his physics lecturer's golden-framed spectacles. 'I've barely had one. And, in any event, hardly gained any wisdom from it.'

They walked back to Miss Jackson's place. Under Moroccan light shades in the lounge, Brent made a phone call to an acquaintance in a squat in Vauxhall. 'You'll like him. Patrick. A Jamaican. He says there's always room at their place, especially for someone who's escaped the South African fascists' clutches.'

When he arrived in Bonnington Square, south of the Thames, No. 52 in Brent's handwriting on a piece of paper in his hand, the front door was wide open. He knocked nevertheless. No sign of life. He entered. The house smelled of stale incense and boiled vegetables. In a communal living room, there were cushions on the wooden floor. He went up the stairs. On the first floor a door was standing ajar. Sweet vapours emanated from the room, and reggae from a boom box. Etienne peered in. 'Hey, man,' someone said from a cloud of smoke. Etienne just nodded. 'I'm Patrick. Make yourself at home. Try the attic room. There's a bed. I think.' He didn't move from his mattress. 'And by the way, respect, man.' The respect, Etienne realised after a few moments, related to their shared disdain for the fascists in the distant south.

In the top room there was a futon under a sloping ceiling with a skylight. Etienne opened it, stuck his head out. Outside was a flat roof and, a few storeys down, a little park or public garden. There was no cupboard, but there was a corner for his drums that he had shipped before his departure from South Africa. He could now, at last, provide a delivery address to the shipping firm. He rolled his shoulders in their sockets, loosening up. Soon he would feel the drumsticks against his palms again.

When he returns from Frank's church tower, two weeks after his arrival, there is a letter on his futon. Protea stamps, the address in his father's handwriting. Strong upward lines, kinks crossing and twisting like lightning. The line under *United Kingdom* almost cuts through the envelope. He curses his mother. Shortly after his arrival he had sent her a telegram with his address. It started with DONT SHOW TO DAD STOP. His father must have put her under enormous pressure.

Etienne closes the door, sits down on his futon in the morning sun. He opens the letter. It will not affect him, he resolves. But as he reads, something starts twisting in his chest. The closing paragraphs read:

> And I won't send you a cent. If you want to go and live
> in a grey city, far from your own people, don't expect

sympathy from me. If you run away like a coward from your duty to defend your country – after I'd paid for your studies, and in your final year! – let the British support you. Go and queue for the dole. Or do some manual labour. Go and work with your hands, like a Bantu.

Do you have any inkling of the damage you are doing to my reputation? What a scandal it is to have you as my son? If I had known what you were planning, I would have handed you over to the military police myself.

Now, Etienne thinks, I am on my own. 'Good,' he says out loud. He doesn't recognise the sound of his own voice. He has the sense of something plunging inside him, like in a house where things are toppling from shelves and cupboards.

Chapter 3

APART FROM PATRICK, there are two Brits and a Belgian in No. 52. Etienne rarely sees them. He has had to get used to doors that don't lock, and to residents of the Square drifting freely through rooms. Here you have no property. You don't belong to anyone, and no one belongs to you. Everyone has access to everyone else, and to each other's possessions. Nothing is forbidden or compulsory. No one has any claims. He likes it. One big free-floating body. A pond in which one can swim around unencumbered. No one making rules, no one in control.

The drum kit has arrived. *That*, he hopes, will remain his. And his passport, as long as he needs it. His application for asylum is in process. It is scorching him, the green booklet he carries around in his underpants. A tainted document, a brand mark next to the scrotum. As soon as he can, he will cast off his origins like a worn piece of clothing.

He concentrates on shaking off his accent. Soon he starts succeeding. He pricks up his ears, imitates others. Patrick remarks that he hardly sounds like a South Londoner, rather like a BBC newsreader. In the evenings Patrick's marijuana smoke drifts up to him where he is practising his sentences under the skylight. Words and syllables. Phrases. Over and over: pronunciation, tone, cadence.

He has to get *past* things – this is how he thinks of his project here. Like overtaking vehicles on a highway. Past Mister van Rooyen with his sweaty buttocks, past the chunk of bronze violence on his father's desk, past his mother's eyes and past the people of the ECC and COSAWR. Not to say anything about Miss Jackson and Brent. And he wants to empty his mind of his studies in South Africa: the proofs he could always memorise so easily, the plans and diagrams he could draw so precisely. How strange that, despite all the years spent bent over his engineering textbooks, such a deep rift kept yawning between him and the signs on those pages. They are like a strange machine in his hands, those terms and formulae. He wants to drop that machine, let it shatter into solenoids and resistors.

The week after their first meeting, Etienne spends hours with Frank in his tower. The summer afternoons are long. Silver sweat soaking the sheets inside, the silver river flowing outside. The Thames's currents alternate rhythmically, violently with the tides. And in the cool early evenings they wander through the city. Everywhere Frank elaborates on how things once were. In 1850. Or 1750. Places where pontoons used to cross the river. Or where executions once took place. The site of the city's first sewage works. He strips the city away, layer by layer.

Soon Etienne realises: he is not the only one for whom the bells are tolled. He hears them ringing at other times. A sound like a flare in the night. 'Jesus,' Patrick says one morning, wandering around in a dressing gown, hands covering his ears. 'That fucker in the tower again. Can't he stop announcing his conquests to the entire world?' A dagger in Etienne's side. Patrick observes him with a sly eye. 'You too, hey? You're also a tower visitor?' He shakes his head, the dreadlocks swaying.

'For you it's a summer of first loves. That guy . . . He's known lots of seasons, man.' He inhales smoke. 'He's gathering a congregation. To worship his arse.'

Etienne starts withdrawing in Frank's company. He observes him, listens to his damp voice. Everywhere the monologue accompanies him; everything in the city is secret code for something else. Etienne is tiring of all the information about bygone things. There is enough that is *new* here. Frank – his New Zealand rugby legs and wealth of black hair – is here; the rest of him is dispersed over the centuries. As the enthusiasm of Etienne's reception starts waning, the speeches become fewer.

There are other noises in London, Etienne thinks, than those emanating from Frank's tower. The two of them still sometimes intertwine in the tower. But Frank is like a parent killing a child in its sleep with sheer body weight, like someone in a violent coma. When the bells ring, Etienne's heart no longer kicks fiercely in response.

The houses in the Square vary in their degrees of dilapidation. The inhabitants are constantly at work. Basins, tiles and cement are bartered. Old gas ovens and fridges rattle on trolleys in the streets. Trees are planted: in little gardens behind houses, in the community garden, on pavements. People build wooden sculptures and set them alight when parties end. Everywhere violins and flutes sound. Bands practise: late punk, British or Irish folk, guys whacking engine parts. There is a café where inhabitants, now including Etienne, take turns cooking. Ingredients come from gardens in the Square. Anyone may eat there for free.

No. 37 is used as a bar. The house was grazed by a German bomb in the '40s. Part of the roof is missing; of most interior walls just wooden skeletons are left. In the back garden, amid the tall grass, there are rusty sculptures, welded together from car parts. Late at night, No. 37 is a refuge; here you will always find people drinking beer. A fire burns constantly in the black marble fireplace, irrespective of the weather. You are simultaneously inside and outside. Under the greenish London sky, drinkers project their silences at each other. Or talk incessantly through the night. The conversations have an undercurrent of revolution. The parliament building across the river is the focus of anger and resistance.

Nothing is stolen in the Square. Things circulate, though, flowing from high to low concentration. Some houses are densely packed with canvases, found objects, rubbish, pots of paint, clay, photographs, old newspapers. Works of art don't survive for long. They are given away, or taken. Briefly exhibited in rooms, taken apart, sawn into pieces. Lovers make pieces for each other, then destroy them with fire or a garden fork when the relationship sours. Or leave them in the rain until the paint washes away.

One afternoon Etienne hears music outside. He looks out: people congregating in the community garden. All women. An orchestra playing medieval music, people singing and picnicking. He darts down the stairs, goes outside and joins them. A German woman with reticent shoulders offers him cheese and bread. The cheese is from the Bavarian village that she hails from. Her name is Hilde. She wants to know where Etienne comes from, what brought him here. His accent, he realises, is still betraying him. He gives a vague answer.

She tells Etienne about Bonnington Square. In the '70s, she explains, the Square was cordoned off; houses were to be demolished. She and her lover were among the first people to move into a house here. They cut the wire fencing and slipped in. It was an inhospitable place: windows had been bricked up, pipes and cables pulled out, sewage pipes blocked with concrete. It looked like German cities after the war. Houses often had no doors; just a few had electricity and water. Gradually places were made more habitable. Brick by brick, window frame by window frame. 'In the beginning,' she says, 'there were only a few of us.' She tells about smoke rising through collapsed roofs on winter days. About rooms in which people would sleep in rows on mats. Like rats. 'Now it's home,' she says. 'Or almost.'

He moves on, past herb and vegetable gardens. He speaks to Glenda. She is from Glasgow. She is agitating; her voice is vehement, her R s brutal. Even though she is speaking loudly above the orchestra, he has to strain his ears to decipher the accent. 'We'll secede! Decolonise the Square, shut it off against the chaos. And when Thatcher sends her henchmen, we'll block the streets. And then it's fucking war.' She imagines the scene out loud: barricades of furniture and mattresses, shouting, petrol bombs. 'Total resistance,' she says. And in the same breath: 'We'll make a forest of this place.' She looks at the garden. 'I've been planting trees for years. Look at my palms.' She shows her calluses, speaking softly now. 'We wanted to bring intimacy,' she says, bending down and touching the leaves of a sapling. 'Tenderness and filtered light.' The trees will envelop the Square in shadows, that she swears: 'Like the shade of my lover's body, like her inner thighs in the London spring.' They will make the Square invisible to the exploiters, to the enemies in the parliament and the City. These promises aren't made only to Etienne but to the entire city. Etienne imagines a furious forest from a Scottish woman's fingers: tree roots that crack open the streets and lift foundations, branches pushing at walls. Breaking *and* protecting. A revolution of the plants.

Hilde joins them. She has an unusually long upper body, Etienne notices. She is Glenda's lover, it turns out, of the tender spring thighs. In her gentle German village voice she tells how they are mobilising, how they are resisting eviction. 'Do you want to get involved? Help us to fend off the wolves?' Etienne smiles evasively.

Chapter 4

EVERY DAY, IN the early afternoon, a 1960s social housing block casts a long shadow over No. 52. When the column creeps closer, Etienne's room smells of wet concrete.

In such a shadowy hour he clambers through the skylight onto the flat roof. In the community garden people often practise street art: juggling, unicycle riding, acrobatics. Today a dark-blond man is sitting in front of a bed of herbs, sketching. Etienne observes him. The shadow shifts, moves along; the sun bakes down on their shoulder blades. The draftsman takes off his shirt, Etienne too. The man's pencil stops. He looks up at Etienne; Etienne grins and goes inside. For a while he sits on his futon, his heart beating wildly; then he goes down the stairs.

'May I see?' Etienne asks, approaching the man in the garden. He hesitates, then holds out the drawing. A herb plant, freshly extracted from the soil. Precise, photorealistic. Each hair on the stem is reproduced, each grain of sand on the roots.

Etienne asks his name. 'Aodhan.' An Irishman, judging by the accent. Blue eyes. Glacier blue, the light of a dead planet. Aodhan closes his sketchbook. They look at each other, walk out into the street together. At the turn-off to Vauxhall Grove they vacillate. The corners of Aodhan's mouth move. Come, he indicates with his head.

They stop in front of the very block that casts a shadow over Etienne's room in the afternoons. The front door has been kicked off its hinges. Aodhan enters, Etienne follows. The ammonia smell of urine enters his nostrils. They climb the stairs to the sixteenth floor, walk down the corridor. Etienne looks into empty flats; through the windows one catches glimpses of the city.

'The Council has condemned the place,' Aodhan says. 'It's supposedly unsafe. There are only a few of us here. Junkies, mostly. Not a happy hippy circle like you guys in the Square.' From the corridor an electrical cord leads into Aodhan's space. Inside are a mattress and cardboard boxes, a television in a corner. The floor is bare concrete. Below them lies the city. A bird of prey against a cliff, Etienne thinks, looking at Aodhan.

Against one wall, there are huge drawings of architects' schemes. Buildings, city plans. On the opposite wall there are dozens of A4 sheets with botanical sketches. Seeds, leaves and flowers. In striking detail. 'Do you work as an architect? Or a botanist?'

'My work is what you see on the walls.' Aodhan points through the window to office blocks on the Thames's north bank. People are streaming across Vauxhall Bridge. 'Who wants to work with the briefcase and umbrella zombies?' He turns to Etienne. 'So, what do you do?'

'Music. Drummer. Looking for a new band at the moment.'

Aodhan approaches the architectural drawings. 'The best music,' he says, 'is the silence of concrete.' He fetches a book, opens it. Pictures of massive buildings in cities that Etienne didn't even know existed: Tbilisi, Yalta, Belgrade, Kagawa. All the photographs were taken in winter. Bunkers. Fortresses. Government offices. Abandoned hotels. Snow against concrete. Close-ups of concrete seams, of veils of rust and damp. Aodhan's eyes are becoming ever bluer. He starts talking about brutalist architecture. About crushing weight, shapes that erase the sun. He is trembling, Etienne notices, while telling Etienne about concrete cities so heavy that they push the earth out of its orbit . . .

Aodhan stops mid-sentence. His fingers lock around Etienne's arms, pull him closer. Aodhan's hands are hard, as if he is digging for a stony secret. Up here, all obstacles fall away. It is as if all the city's doors and windows are being blown open by a sudden blast.

When they are spent, they stand naked in front of the plant drawings. Aodhan presses a finger on the pencil drawings, uttering the Latin name of each. Etienne asks about a few that remain unnamed. 'New sketches. Plants that only exist on paper. Without names. I make them up.' The detail is as precise as before, as if drawn for a botanical encyclopaedia. Hard to imagine, Etienne thinks, that there is no source species. A while ago he started drawing plants that he had never seen, Aodhan explains. A visual imitation of the sound of the Latin names. And then he started making up his own species. He takes out more sheets of paper from a box. 'Here's my latest series. A collection of carnivorous plants. They exist only in sketches.'

Etienne touches the rough paper, looks at the menacing plants. Here, leaves and stems have transformed into traps and jaws. He should introduce Aodhan to Glenda with her compost fingers, Etienne thinks. Aodhan could provide the fictitious plants for a green dome covering the Square. A seam of meat-eating flowers as bulwark against the wolves of capital.

Aodhan wants to take Etienne on a tour of the world's most brutal architecture. 'But,' he says, 'let's begin in London.'

When they meet in Vauxhall Grove at dawn, the church bells are tolling. Etienne's fingers are itching. He remembers the dampness underneath the thick hair on Frank's neck.

Sometimes they take the Underground; mostly they walk. They go up to concrete colossuses, look up: Finsbury Estate, the Barbican, Hyde Park Barracks, Brunswick Centre, Sampson House, Balfron Tower. Etienne shades his eyes with his hand when gazing at Trellick Tower's grey cube houses high up in the sky. The lift tower is set apart from the building, just lightly connected with it by means of concrete bridges.

'The material is *refusing*,' Aodhan declaims. 'It is repudiating *everything*. Cities in the sky,' he continues. 'Foundationless.' Etienne isn't sure he is following any longer. 'Hanging clusters. Suspended over nothing. Staircases and walkways to nowhere . . . The material as god,' Aodhan says. 'Emptiness in density. No interior space. Cool exterior, absolute compression on the inside.' They walk until late in the evening. Aodhan's eyes gleam like steel. Back on the sixteenth floor in Vauxhall, he sits studying his Polaroid photos of the buildings. 'Temples,' he mumbles, but not to Etienne, 'that are denying birth and death, and heaven and hell . . .' Etienne is so tired that he hardly hears the church bells when he slips into sleep.

Another concrete tour. Birmingham this time. And then on to Gateshead. All in one day. At daybreak they are sitting on a train. Aodhan is trembling. 'One has to *touch* the structures,' he says. He goes on about the New Street train signal building, which geometrically renounces the world. The Birmingham Central Library, which cheats gravity. And then the highlight in Gateshead: Trinity Square car park. Here they will secretly spend the night. Etienne thinks of the condemned building in

London where he now spends his nights with Aodhan. Before long it will probably be imploded while they are sleeping . . . What is he getting himself into?

Aodhan notices nothing but the blunt buildings. Etienne tires of all the concrete, keeps his eye on Aodhan's swarthy body instead: short and compact, almost hairless. Unreceptive like a chunk of stone. There are moments, during sex, when Etienne reaches the moister parts of Aodhan's body, and possibilities glisten in the dampness. But overall he remains hard and closed off, like his beloved concrete.

They complete their tour of hulking buildings, and, unexpectedly, Etienne also falls under their spell. Aodhan takes them back to the station; they board a train to Gateshead. During the three hours or so of the journey, neither of them speaks.

When the two of them approach the Trinity Square car park late afternoon, Etienne's hands start trembling. In the dusk, the black structure towers above everything else. They enter, walk up the helix of the access ramp to the very top.

They sit down on the concrete edge, feet dangling over the edge. It is the last place in England where anyone would want to sleep, Etienne thinks. Even the homeless avoid it. Aodhan's voice is unsteady. 'It's as ugly as I had hoped, this place. And so hostile. It's fucking with my head, giving me a rock-hard fucking erection.' They wait until it is emptied of cars, until the concrete echoes quieten down and the city lights shine brightly. Then they walk around. Aodhan almost breaks Etienne's arms when he suddenly pins him against a pillar. Etienne shoves him away, but Aodhan fights back. They struggle out of their trousers. Aodhan's body spasms; their semen simultaneously splashes against the raw concrete. They sit down, feet over the edge, look breathlessly out over the city. Aodhan drags a finger through a trail of semen, tastes it, rubs it into the concrete.

When Etienne seeks warmth from Aodhan a little later, he pushes him away. 'Don't spoil everything,' Aodhan says and gets up. He keeps walking under the fluorescent lights, from one pocket of light to the next. He moves around all night long while Etienne is trying to sleep with his cheek against a cold wall. From time to time Aodhan switches on his flashlight, lets the beam slip against grey walls.

Etienne finds consolation back in the Square, in this green hollow within the city's vortex. Here where seeds germinate and herbs grow almost audibly, where one always smells fires. Where you can seek out other inhabitants' silences in front of No. 37's marble hearth.

When he returns after his and Aodhan's tour, an envelope with his mother's handwriting on it is waiting in his room. He holds it for a while before opening it. The tone of the letter – her first – is odd. As if nothing is wrong, as if Etienne is on holiday. He looks closely at the handwriting. It *is* hers. He reads on. There is news about plants in his parents' garden that have succumbed to frost. About a cousin's baby. A high-school rugby match. She doesn't ask a single question.

He frowns. She knows he has no interest in rugby.

The next day there is another letter, bearing the stamp of a different post office. From his mother again. More recognisably her: breathless, full of short or half sentences. Like a hunted animal. She had written three previous letters, she explains; she gave them to his father to have his secretary post them at the office. She started suspecting his father was intercepting them. One afternoon she discovered the unmailed envelopes in his study. She confronted him. (He probably blamed her for his escape, Etienne thinks.) Now he has undertaken to actually post the letters, but she is convinced he reads them first. Henceforth, she will send parallel streams of letters: official ones for his father's eyes, and secret ones for Etienne's. The latter she will post herself.

The secret letter explains that she wants to send him money, but doesn't have access to the bank accounts. And currency control is a problem too. *Nobody and nothing can get out of here*, she writes, *not even money. My heart is broken about all of this. About you.* She wants to come for a visit. His father is refusing to fund it. She doesn't really know whether Etienne would welcome this either. She probes, asks the questions mothers ask: does he have a decent place to stay? Is he warm? (Doesn't she know it is summer in the northern hemisphere?) Is he eating healthy food? And *enough* of it?

Something is amiss in her explanation of the double stream of letters. Is she in fact writing the 'normal' letters for her *own* sake? Is she finding consolation in the correspondence that pretends everything is just fine?

From now on he will create two piles. One for the false letters, another for the real ones. He will no longer open the former. And he will decide in due course whether to respond to the latter.

Chapter 5

SINCE THE ARRIVAL of Etienne's drums, he has been increasingly aware of the band scene. Everywhere bands are looking for members: in the Square's café, in the Vauxhall Tavern, in the bar at No. 37. There are handwritten advertisements on noticeboards: for guitarists, vocalists, drummers. Bands practise in the community garden or in musty Victorian pubs. Etienne jams with a few of them. Shortly before his departure from Pretoria, Etienne started hearing folky rock everywhere. Spiced up with political protest lyrics in Afrikaans. There it was a novelty. Subversive. Here, such music is considered mainstream American, middle-aged. In Pretoria he was in a band with university friends. Sometimes they tried to sound like Bruce Springsteen, then again like Bob Dylan or Rodriguez. They were the only band on campus. At night they would practise in a laboratory – the vocalist was majoring in plant sciences. Etienne's fellow band members had no desire to listen to his obscure British bands. He had to import the albums that he read about in foreign music magazines, at great expense. In the afternoons – wandering across his parents' dead winter lawn, Walkman headphones covering his ears – he searched for new sounds.

Here pretty much everyone joins a band at age thirteen. There are folk singers. Wannabe punk rockers. Monotone synth-pop types. Folk one has to have in the genes. Punk rock isn't synchronised with Etienne's speed. Too frenetic, although he likes the notion that it requires courage rather than talent. The electronic brigade he admires from a distance – the synthesisers remind him too much of the piano playing of his school days that he gave up so resolutely. This is what gets the most playtime in the Vauxhall Tavern, where he now spends his evenings: the New Romantics. Japan, Ultravox, Soft Cell, Bronski Beat, Kraftwerk, Depeche Mode. And anything angry or experimental. The Smiths is a favourite. Morrissey's 'The Boy with the Thorn in His Side' always features.

One evening he talks to a man in the Tavern. He has a heart-shaped face and shiny lashes. He is small, with perfect skin. Someone else approaches Etienne shortly afterwards, asks breathlessly: 'How do you know him?'

'Who?'

'Marc Almond.' So *that's* who he was talking to, the singer of the band Soft Cell. The next day he goes out and buys two Soft Cell records, containing songs that are often played in the Tavern: *The Art of Falling Apart* and *This Last Night in Sodom*.

On another night he speaks to a man who introduces himself as Jimmy Somerville. *Him* Etienne recognises. Formerly the vocalist of Bronski Beat. These days The Communards. 'Where are you from?' Somerville asks. He looks like a teenager, his face sharp and intense. The devil-may-care shrug of his shoulders demands attention. His head is tilted in sullen vulnerability.

'Finland,' Etienne says on the spur of the moment. 'We are decades behind you when it comes to music.' They stand in each other's breath, drinking beer. The music is becoming louder. Somerville presses a palm against Etienne's lower back when leaning in to talk to him. His lips brush against Etienne's ear; he hooks a thumb in Etienne's belt. Somerville looks him straight in the eye. His expression is in turn teasing, challenging. He is dancing and wriggling while he speaks. Etienne asks questions. About music, the scene in London.

Somerville starts asking his own questions. 'Your accent doesn't quite sound Finnish to me,' he says.

'I have to go,' Etienne says abruptly. 'I'm flying back to Helsinki early tomorrow.' When Etienne extracts himself, Somerville pouts. When Etienne looks back from the exit, he is standing there among the men, hand stretched out towards Etienne. Etienne's heart keeps racing on his way back home.

The next day he buys Bronski Beat's album *The Age of Consent*. On the inside cover, in a kind of treatise on gay rights, he reads that the legal age for sex between men in Britain is twenty-one, for heterosexuals sixteen. He is a criminal in South Africa, Etienne thinks, and would have been a criminal here too had he arrived a year or two earlier. It excites him, makes his scrotum tighten.

He is lying on his futon, sweating. On a turntable that was left behind by a housemate, the record is playing. He holds his ear close to the black blade of the edge. He should have stroked Somerville's buzz cut when he had the chance. Should have pressed himself against his restless hips and buttocks.

Etienne hones in on the forlornness of Somerville's song 'Smalltown Boy'. He returns the needle to the beginning of the track. Over and over again. In the electric moments before the first notes, Somerville's boyish face appears before him. With both hands resting on his kicking erection, Etienne listens to the ominous falsetto while the shadow of Aodhan's building is creeping across the skylight. The needle drifts to the end. Each rotation makes it jerk back into the groove: scratch, scratch, scratch.

There are guys who want to start gay bands, and are looking exclusively for gay musicians. Etienne likes the idea, but the canvassers' talents are limited. Bands come and go, sometimes within days. Names change, members change. It is like ancient slime from which something still has to emerge and take shape, this pond of South London amateur bands. In the spirit of punk, everyone can play or sing. Etienne envies them their blind self-confidence. But perhaps, he thinks, greater doubt would improve the music. He keeps his options open.

Etienne studies the buildings and city projects on Aodhan's wall. Strips within old Continental cities are razed to the ground, replaced by new schemes. Buildings span rivers and highways, are erected on pillars over old buildings: cities above cities. Aodhan dreams of parallel cityscapes, imposed on existing ones. There are cross sections of floating concrete masses, networks of invisible steel rendering it weightless. Etienne smiles. The drawings have exquisite detail, but they defy physics. He looks at Aodhan in front of the window, only his profile showing. A kind of dictator, one who wants to supplant flesh with the weight of other materials, who wants to reign supreme over form, flout gravity.

Aodhan hardly possesses anything. He does have a video-cassette recorder and a television. The latter's wires are hanging out; the light tube is exposed. Sometimes the image disintegrates. Aodhan then rummages about inside the television box, hits the screen, bends the wire antenna. Sometimes there are sparks, or electrical buzzing noises. But if one can tolerate the intermittent white flashes on the screen, and Aodhan's eruptions, it is possible to watch videos.

'I want to show you a film,' Aodhan says one afternoon. 'I think you'll like this. Russian.'

The director is Tarkovsky. *The Mirror* is the name of the film. They lie watching on floor cushions. Chains of images from a child's perspective roll over the screen. In one sequence a mother is bent over, her head in a bowl of water. She lifts out her dripping hair; it keeps swaying like seaweed in front of her face. All in slow motion. Water runs down the walls and pours through the ceiling, which is caving in. On a gas stove a huge flame is burning . . . There is a kind of eruption inside Etienne; he is completely hypnotised.

Aodhan, lost in the drawing he is working on, hardly registers Etienne's departure at the end of the film. Etienne walks through the city in a daze. Everything looks different, more sharply drawn. Images have been burnt into his retina; highways have been rerouted in his brain.

Scarcely an hour later he returns. 'What else do you have?' Aodhan gets up from his drawing board, distractedly inserts a new video. A film by director Werner Herzog. *Fitzcarraldo*. Aodhan sits down, continues his drawing. Etienne watches on his own. It is about a man who wants to build an opera house in the Amazon. He is alone in his wild obsession. In his rage he decides to have a team of Indians heave a boat over a mountain. He wants to harvest and ship out rubber from the other side of the mountain and use the profits to build his opera house. Etienne is amazed that lunacy can be translated into visual images in this way. Halfway through he looks up at Aodhan. The glow from the television catches his cheeks and forehead, his eyes like frozen stars. Aodhan turns his head. His gaze pins

Etienne down at a distance. He has a lover, Etienne thinks, who wants to cast him in cement. He feels his own pulse. His heart is pumping cold blood.

Etienne is now constantly watching films. He borrows Aodhan's videocassette recorder, goes and sits in the only room in No. 37 that still has all four walls and where there is a television. He connects the machine to it, closes the door, stays in there for hours. He borrows videos from squatters, or takes them out from film libraries. And he frequents cinemas. After three months in London, the money he has brought with him from South Africa is running out. Somebody makes him a fake student card. He gets discounts everywhere: at the new Renoir Cinema in Bloomsbury, the recently renovated Gate Cinema in Notting Hill, the British Film Institute's cinemas in the bunkerlike building on the South Bank. He spends his life in the dark, sees four, sometimes five films per day. One by one he discovers the European auteurs. Pasolini and Visconti. Fellini and Antonioni. Godard and Truffaut. Herzog and Fassbinder. Wenders and Schlöndorff. In the mornings, when he is still half-dreaming, projector light merges with the scent of saliva on hungry skin.

Etienne's interest in the band scene has been waning. The drum kit has been abandoned in a corner of his room. It would hardly bother him if someone welded it into a piece of sculpture. Henceforth he will dedicate his life to images on the screen. Of that he is certain. How exactly he doesn't know. How disheartening that he had been cooped up in such a small cage in the distant south – how much there is to catch up with! He thinks of how he would slip his Blake book under his mattress when he heard his father's footsteps in the corridor, of the smell of glue when he and his father used to build model aeroplanes on summer afternoons.

It is late in the evening; his skylight is wide open. He has recently traded his Sony Walkman for a neighbour's record collection. He is listening to the Communards album, to Somerville's insistent falsetto in the cool night sky. Should he ever come across Somerville again, he would swiftly hook his thumb into his belt. But Etienne rarely goes to the Vauxhall Tavern any more. And Somerville hasn't made an appearance again.

Aodhan no longer seeks Etienne out. Etienne is, in any event, done with those hard hands. How he fits into Aodhan's schemes is impossible to know. Aodhan with his eyes like the arctic night, with his concrete heart in which hallucinatory plants germinate: new species for a new kind of city.

Chapter 6

ETIENNE EXITS THE British Film Institute. He blinks against the afternoon light. The river is grey, the afternoon muggy. He has just seen another Tarkovsky film. *Stalker.* Three characters travel together through a forbidden zone where the rules of physics have been suspended. Their destination is a mysterious room where desires become reality. The takes last for minutes; hardly anything happens. But what techniques of hypnosis were employed? Why does he keep wandering in circles through London's streets?

He walks and walks. His armpits are itching; streams of sweat are running down his sides. When he approaches Tower Bridge, he smells something sharp. A vinegar factory, according to a sign. He walks down Tanner Street, turns towards the river on Bermondsey Street. He has been here before with Frank, who educated him about the cramped fur factories that had once operated here in backyards and leaking attics. Etienne peers into alleys and dim spaces, vaguely hoping to encounter carcasses and piles of untanned hides.

He crosses Crucifix Lane, enters a tunnel beneath the train viaduct. There is moss on the vaulted Victorian ceiling; the pavement is crusty with pigeon shit. His eyes adapt to the gloom. He stops next to a man sitting on his haunches. In a dark niche in front of them, under a warning sign with a yellow lightning bolt, sits an angel. Etienne widens his eyes. A *picture* of an angel, in fact, freshly stencilled against a black door.

Bright white. Wings folded behind the shoulders, wearing jeans and boots. Buttocks on the pavement, arms around the knees. The angel's head hangs forward; he has a cigarette between his fingers. There is a bottle of poison in front of him, marked X.

It feels to Etienne as if the city outside the tunnel is ablaze. He switches his gaze from the angel to the man below him. Tree roots trail out of his white vest, creeping over his neck: a tattoo. The man's intensity is like a blade; he reaches forward, towards the poison.

'There he is. Cast out. Raped by the head angel, perhaps by God himself. And then thrown to the wolves.' As the man says this, he gets up abruptly. He is taller than Etienne, and so close that Etienne can smell him. Sweat, with an undertone of cordite. He doesn't turn around; the tree roots on his neck are right by Etienne's face. He leans back against Etienne's chest, lifts his knee. Etienne can see past his shoulder; his Doc Martens boot strikes the angel. The counterforce makes Etienne stagger. The lock breaks, the steel door clangs open, the tunnel echoes.

He pulls Etienne through the door by his wrist. There is a black buzz of electricity in the air. Etienne's trousers are stripped off in the dark. Something takes hold of Etienne; he forces the man's shirt over his head. There is the sound of tearing. The chest in front of him is smooth. A cool tongue moves over Etienne's stubble like wind through burnt grass. In the fumes of bat piss they count each other's knuckles, feel the tendons in each other's wrists. Their bodies lock. It is as hot as hell. Etienne couldn't care less where there are transformers in the dark, or live cables. The volts have entered him already; he is plugged into the city's grid. His cheek is against the rough brick; he is reduced to muscle and sinew and power. A thick

37

current is flowing right through him, to abattoirs and factories.

Thundering trains cross above them. White flames erupt in the dark. Etienne hears the man's teeth clatter, wonders whether he has bitten off his tongue. He can't make out the man's face. Sweat is glistening on his Adam's apple.

They disentangle. The man doesn't bother picking up his shirt. He fastens his belt, walks out. Without a word, his upper body bare. By the time Etienne has come to his senses and stepped out onto the pavement's pigeon shit, the man has already walked some distance down the tunnel, approaching a half-circle of light. On his back the tattoo is exposed: an uprooted tree, crown branches fanning out across the lower back. On the middle back, a knotty trunk. Roots grow over defiant shoulder blades, and up his neck.

The man leaves the tunnel; the tree dissolves in light. Etienne looks down at himself: he is standing stark naked there on the pavement. He is surprised that no bark is clinging to him. His hands are trembling. He smells of the sweat of a stranger.

He involuntarily thinks of his father's study, of the smell of stale pipe smoke.

Six weeks earlier, just after Etienne had started working his way voraciously through the catalogue of European auteur films, like a caterpillar, he encountered Brent on a pavement in Soho. After a back-and-forth of a few polite questions, Brent's face became solemn. 'The country is burning, you know. It's time to tighten the screws. We could make the regime falter. We have the ears of everyone who counts.' He spoke about Matthew Goniwe and the other Cradock leaders, of the peace conferences in South Africa.

'Are you talking about Thatcher's ears?'

Capillaries shone through the skin over Brent's temples. 'Well . . . everyone except Thatcher and co. The opposition, in fact.' He leaned forward. The light was catching fine strawberry-blond hair on his upper cheeks. 'There's so much to do. Protest actions to organise. Posters to distribute. All small contributions will—'

'I'm going to film school.' Etienne was surprised. The realisation that this was exactly what he should do had coincided with his utterance. 'I don't have the time.'

'That's a first, that excuse.' Brent turned his face away from the sun. He rattled off a list of names, a moment of silence between each. 'All in detention in South Africa. Conscientious objectors. Here *we* are, safely ensconced in London. Don't you feel *any* sort of responsibility?' His freckles disappeared in a flush of indignation.

Etienne just kept shaking his head slowly. Brent mumbled something about 'bigger issues' and walked away.

If this guy had been a real player, Etienne thought, he might have been more amenable. Someone with authority, who was proposing something spectacular. Something that required imagination, and that would capture *Etienne's*. An offer, for instance, to let him travel to the Soviet Union for revolutionary training. Or to coach him in the art of disguise. To smuggle him to South Africa to blow up pylons and train tracks. Or to let him pose as the prodigal son who ostensibly returns chastened, but in truth intends to extract information from his father. And who then plants a bomb in the boardrooms of companies who are in cahoots with the regime. Or even better: an assassination. Etienne who shoots one of his father's senior politician friends in the forehead in his parents' lounge. Or slips an explosive device in aforementioned politician's briefcase, thus succeeding in blowing up the entire cabinet. Or what about a scheme entailing that Etienne must prove his loyalty by strangling his own father in his bed? A lightweight, our Brent, an amateur. Didn't even attempt to address Etienne as 'comrade'. Hasn't done any research about Etienne's family connections. No strategy, no vision. An utter lack of dramatic instinct.

Anyway, Brent and his judgements were immaterial to him. With absolute clarity he now knew: his calling had always been to make films.

He went knocking on COSAWR's door again. When he had first visited, Ben had offered help: 'We have contacts in many spheres. Institutions here are very receptive to apartheid exiles.' Ben received him hospitably again this time, updated him on the progress of his asylum application. Etienne explained his film-school plans, enquired about scholarships. Ben undertook to take the matter further, sent him away with a new copy of *Resister*. Mindful of his earlier reception at Miss Jackson's, Etienne didn't have much hope.

The meeting in the tunnel stokes turmoil in Etienne's chest. His ears are now attuned to the city's electrical hum, and the silence of all things subterranean. The things Frank would elaborate on: tunnels, sewage canals, crypts. Abandoned Tube stations and catacombs with their stacks of bones. Sweat trickles down his spine when he thinks of the electrical substation in the tunnel; blood pulses in his lower abdomen. He *has* to find him, the man with the tree on his back. But how?

Every afternoon he returns to the tunnel, waiting at the angel's grimy shrine. People walk by, start when they notice

40

Etienne and the angel. The tattoo-man doesn't make an appearance. Etienne tests the door. The destroyed lock has been replaced. He has to find a way in. He prods the angel with his foot. Gingerly, to start with – perhaps there is a secret unlocking mechanism. He pushes with a finger on the X of the flask of poison, places his palm on the largest wing feather. He stands back, kicks the angel in the head. Nothing. He has been excommunicated, expelled from the oily nether-city of which the tattoo-man is surely the mayor and the angel the gatekeeper. Pedestrians gather behind him, watch him kick and push. His soles are marking the white wings, his fingers dirtying the poison flask. The angel isn't budging.

A clue comes sooner than Etienne had expected. Late one night he is sitting in No. 37, on one of the half-rotten velvet sofas. There is a fire in the hearth; drizzle is sifting through the roof. Hilde and Glenda are sitting in the firelight, each with a beer. Etienne joins them. Hilde is wearing a batik dress that makes her upper body look even longer, her shoulders even warier. She is telling Glenda about southern Germany's lost oak forests, of the last bison being shot there in the 1920s. She doesn't seem to mind that Etienne is listening. She is talking about a centuries-old hunting lodge near her parents' Bavarian village. Once it was in the middle of a forest, she says. Now it is crumbling in the yard of a factory. She turns to Etienne. 'I haven't been back to Germany in years. I want to visit my parents. But I'm afraid that I'd lose my home. That I'd find, upon my return, that the Square has been razed to the ground. Everything under the rubble . . .' She looks down at her flat leather sandals.

'That's absurd,' Glenda says, wiping beer from her mouth

with the back of her hand. 'They'll never bury *me*.' She hits her own chest with her palm. 'I'll fight until my last breath. That much you know.' Glenda has ginger hair. Short sides, curls piled on top.

Hilde tells how she and a childhood friend used to play around the old hunting lodge. They would dig up bones and deer horns. She still has dreams about the interior of the lodge. They had wanted to peer inside, hoping to find stuffed animal heads mounted on the walls. But the windows were too high. 'The smell of old wood is what I miss. My southern German heart is really made of oak . . .' She looks into the flames. 'And I'm not the only one. I know of a German in London who has an oak tree tattooed on his b—'

Etienne sits forward; the flames in the hearth are burning high. 'Who?' His voice is urgent. 'Where?'

'I don't know him well . . .' Hilde says hesitantly. She frowns.

Etienne's heart is beating wildly. 'Please,' he says, 'I've met him myself . . . I want to – *have* to – get in touch with him.'

'I've only seen him once, at a squat party. Somebody challenged him to strip off his shirt. And then a massive oak tree appeared . . .'

'Where is he?'

'All I could think was: I too want such a tree on my b—'

'Where *is* he? What's his name?'

Glenda puts down her beer. Hilde's voice is cool. 'That I don't recall. He's a child nurse. That's all he told me. At St Thomas Hospital, I think.'

The women get up. Etienne is left behind, sweating in the glow. Three half-empty beers are standing on the little table.

For three days in a row, Etienne has waited outside St Thomas. For hours on end each time. On the first day he asked for a list of paediatric nurses at the hospital reception. He was refused. Today he attempts to enter the paediatric section. A nurse stops him, wants to know where he is going. 'I'm from Finland. I'm trying to find a long-lost friend.' She frowns. Only family members of patients are allowed in, she explains over her reading glasses. She looks as if she is on the verge of calling hospital security. Or the police. He retreats, resumes his waiting outside. He looks at the parliament building opposite the river, at the water accelerating around bridge pillars. The currents are fatal, Frank once told him; they will suck you into the mud. He went on to explain the history of river crossings, ferrymen and bridges.

It suddenly occurs to Etienne that the hospital may have different exits. At that very moment the German tattoo-man walks out the main entrance. He immediately sees Etienne, casually walks up to him, takes his hand and feels every knuckle. Etienne feels *his* knobbly knuckles too. One by one. They start walking.

'I'm Axel.'

'I'm Etienne.'

There are fine hairs on the tops of Axel's fingers. Etienne sniffs the air, greedy for a hint of sweat. He looks surreptitiously at the green uniform hiding the tattooed tree. An antiseptic smell rises from the gown, or that of burnt skin. Etienne wants to press his face in the gown. He remembers the armpits, the kneecaps, the spine like a snake skeleton. Saliva tasting of soot and electricity.

Axel doesn't ask how Etienne has managed to find him. While they are walking, Etienne extends his hand, feels Axel's pulse. Unlike his own, it is beating strongly and steadily. His heart is not made of wood.

If it is so easy to find Axel, Etienne thinks, nothing can ever escape him again.

A mid-August afternoon. When he returns to his room, two letters await him. One is from the Home Office: asylum has been granted. He opens the other envelope: COSAWR has managed to arrange a scholarship for him! Also, an exception has been made for late admission to the London Film School. A Labour Party MP had personally taken up the matter with the film school. Etienne will be starting his studies in barely a month's time.

He takes the Underground to Covent Garden, heads to the film school. The soot-black buildings are keeping him out for now, but soon his northern life will start properly. His feet barely touch the ground. He is travelling at the speed of light.

In his room, again, there are two envelopes: his mother's parallel letters. He opens only one. *Do you have proper accommodation? Are you earning something to live off? Why am I not hearing from you?*

He lies down on his futon, thinking of the face-brick walls and steel windows of his parents' home, the swimming pool with its blue mosaic tiles, the German Shepherd in its cage. The slate-tiled veranda, the smell of freshly mown grass. Of himself practising piano in the heat. His father never openly disapproved of the piano playing, but wasn't interested either. After Etienne had completed his last music exam, he never touched the keys again. For months he pleaded with his mother for drums. Then she bought him a set. She had asked his father for money to buy a new lounge set, chose a cheaper set and spent what was left on a drum kit. This is it, his father decided a month later: the drums had to go. Only a swift glance from Etienne was required for his mother to intervene. Etienne never said a word. His mother had to fit in her arguments quickly before she was interrupted by her husband. The drums stayed. In the corner of his bedroom, like a war monument.

Etienne only resisted his father once. He was fifteen or sixteen. A Sunday afternoon. Etienne had thought his parents were asleep and was too engrossed in his Blake pictures to hear his father in the corridor. Before he knew it, his father was in the room and grabbed the book. With one hand, so that the spine bent the wrong way. 'And what is *this?*'

Etienne grabbed the book back. 'Give it back, it isn't yours!' His father reprimanded him for his cheeky tone. Etienne put the book down on the bedside table, picked up a school textbook. He pulled up his knees and pretended to be studying, keeping a furtive eye on his father. His father retired to the corner where the model war planes that they had built together were hanging from the ceiling. His breath made the planes move; his shoulders bumped against them. The bombers started sweeping in a chaotic formation, making his father duck. Etienne kept his nose in his textbook. His father approached the bed, moved the Blake book so that the edge neatly lined up with the bedside table's. His fingers momentarily rested on the cover. Then he walked out into the corridor.

Henceforth the Blake book would stay under Etienne's mattress, except when his parents were asleep.

His mother's letter continues: *Your father is not as merciless as you might think. He cannot help himself; his sorrow sounds like anger. He is making plans to help you. Give him a chance.*

Etienne sits up on the futon, writes a letter to his mother. He has everything he needs. Accommodation, food to eat, clothes to wear. He is relieved that he has managed to escape South Africa. *I am renouncing it, that Republic of Dust. I'm glad I'm now a criminal there. Never again do I have to set foot there.* He is rewiring himself, he continues. He doesn't need help, whether from her or his father. And he doubts whether he will ever write again.

Chapter 7

SEPTEMBER. ETIENNE IS taking introductory courses in camera techniques and cinematography, directing, script-writing and film editing. He has a choice between film theory and history. In addition, he is taking a seminar entitled Lost Continental Films.

A film narrative is a series of constantly changing images that depict events from a variety of viewpoints. According to his American textbook, that is. He reads about visual planning. About storyboards. Objective and subjective camera angles. The determination of camera height and angles. How to alternate close-up, long- and medium-distance shots. And about more complex camera movements, on dollies or from cranes.

He likes the ultra-long shot, the wide lens taking in epic scenes. His textbook demonstrates this with frames from cowboy movies: three lonely riders in a wide-open landscape, a herd of bison thundering ahead of a cloud of dust. Or a battlefield littered with dying soldiers. His other favourite is the 'Dutch tilt' – a low camera aiming upwards at an oblique angle to the player. It disorients the viewer, his textbook explains, and also suggests that the character is disoriented, drunk or agitated. In extremis. One day, Etienne thinks, he will make a film in which every shot is taken from such an unsteady angle.

'In whichever space the cameraman finds himself,' Etienne's camerawork instructor says while acquainting them with 8 mm and 16 mm cameras, 'he's moving in a world of dotted lines.

He is constantly seeing viewpoints like vectors, calculating every permutation of angle and distance. The lines resemble the trajectories of bullets flying everywhere. He is caught up in a violent skirmish. Constantly measuring and estimating, aiming at soft targets in the best available light. Gradually it all becomes second nature.'

In film theory the lecturer explains hypotheses about film, the eye and the brain. Etienne's notion that the brain simply merges static frames by inserting after-images in between is clearly naive. The lecturer elaborates on complex theories regarding the illusion of movement in film - physiological, psychological, technological. He uses terms like 'phi phenomenon', 'iconic memory' and 'shutter frequency'. The students become restless; they are here to make films, not to philosophise about the interaction between neurology and the film frame, or to express flicker fusion rates in hertz.

As a practical project that cuts across disciplines, each student has to make a 16 mm film. Equipment is provided. Etienne has already decided on his subject matter: Axel and his world.

Axel lives south of the river, across from the City's towers. The squat is in a dilapidated Georgian house in Bermondsey Street, close to the tunnel with the angel. A revolving set of friends and wanderers lives there with him. Axel's fellow squatters don't know he is a nurse. They only know him as an artist. In the backyard there is an old well. Contaminated water glistens at the bottom. Frank once elaborated about the residue of centuries of malodorous industrial activities here - tanneries, fur factories, paper and textile manufacture. And, of course, the vinegar factory, which is still active. The soil is soaked with previous centuries' toxins.

Axel lives as if it is 1930. In the kitchen there is a cast-iron Dover stove. Coal is delivered from time to time. There is no central heating, though most rooms have a fireplace. Bathing happens in a tin bath on the kitchen floor. Walls have been removed between some rooms; sagging ceilings display water stains. There are a few broken chairs and mattresses. On the walls are crusts of paint and brittle wallpaper. Just a stone's throw away, beyond the viaducts of London Bridge station, there are rows of glass buildings north of the river where financiers lead the kind of existence that was once laid out for Etienne in South Africa. Before he became a criminal.

It is here, just out of reach of the City towers' morning shadows, that Etienne makes his first film. He doesn't ask anyone's permission. He takes the camera in his hand, switches it on, lets the film roll.

Guys come and go, unperturbed by the camera. They move in and out of focus at the edge of the lens. They smoke and sleep, drape their naked selves over shared mattresses, sing and play guitar through the night. Take pills, gulp wine from bottles and stroke each other's backs, drink saliva from each other's lips. Sometimes one will run down the street with wide pupils, or stare down the well for hours. It is possible, at any time, to encounter a shiny naked stranger in a steaming tin bath.

Etienne focuses his lens on one of Axel's art projects. Wallpaper torn away in concentric circles. Painfully precise. Like the growing circles of a sawn-off tree trunk. One of the drifters, a Brit, interprets the circles while the camera is rolling. In the centre there is a dot of wine-red Georgian paint. It is surrounded by Victorian wallpaper, which yields to a wider circle of Morris motifs. This is followed by mustard-coloured

1950s patterns, then psychedelic 1970s zigzag. A tunnel through which one may travel back in time, or through which the past ripples out into the present. Etienne switches off the camera, pictures Axel, nose against the wallpaper. Tearing with the hand of a surgeon, painfully slowly, all through the long winter.

He directs his lens toward the smokers around the well. 'Right here below us,' one of them declares in a Spanish accent, 'there is enough arsenic to wipe out the entire fucking City. We just have to get it in the drinking water.' Now Etienne turns the camera towards two Swedish guys. They are leaning back, shirtless, planning a revolution, joints between their fingers. He zooms in on tiny hairs on their ears. Or fingers scratching at a scab or cupping around a scrotum. He focuses on the one Swede's abdominal tattoo: THE REVOLUTION IS MY BOYFRIEND, it reads amid the upper trail of pubic hair.

Like a half-grown litter, these Bermondsey Street striplings, Etienne thinks. During the day they doze contentedly; at night they copulate clumsily and indifferently.

When Etienne and Axel are alone, the camera is switched off. The hairs on Etienne's arms are constantly raised. They writhe and ejaculate. They poison each other, are at the same time each other's antidote. They contaminate each other, inoculate each other. Outside the clouds are urgent and the sky blue.

This afternoon Axel is lying on Etienne's futon. He smokes slowly while Etienne is examining his body. He throws Axel off the futon, turns him over, studies the tattoo. Axel smells of dry wood and hot stones. There is no sound in his eyes. The attic room becomes a vacuum. Their mouths lock, their temples are streaming with sweat. They half-suffocate each other, spill seed. They sit in opposite corners, stare at each other, charge at each other.

The next day they are in Bermondsey Street. Guys are hovering in the kitchen and by the well. Etienne and Axel are in an upper room. They are noisy. Now and then someone comes and watches them in silence. No one dares interrupt their copulation; their bodies have grown into each other. After a while the watchers leave.

They are dissolving in an ever denser thicket of images, Etienne thinks: branches becoming entangled in a storm, bones intertwining. They grab and attack and tear, breathe fire and spit it out. They were electrified when they met in the substation. Etienne is waiting for the short circuit, for the current to be interrupted.

Tonight they are in Etienne's room again. Axel tears himself away, throws his head back. Etienne lets go of Axel's neck, startled by the marks across his throat. Axel makes a noise, as if he is gargling with blood or seed. 'Look,' he says and points at the pale green sky beyond the skylight. 'He is tired of the cold stars. He is coming down . . .' Axel is listening intently, watching the door with widened eyes. 'He is *here*.'

'Who?' Etienne's body is a slippery carcass among wild dogs. 'Who's here?'

Axel is whispering now, his eyes shiny. 'God. He is jealous; he is looking through the keyhole. He wants to come and taste the fiery saliva. These bitter juices that are seeping from us like wolf's blood.'

Axel's irises turn toxic green. It is dizzying to Etienne, the fact that he and the German are driving each other to such raving, such visions. In the outer corner of his eye a white flame is burning constantly.

Chapter 8

ATOP THE BERMONDSEY Street house's three brick storeys is a wooden attic: 18th-century, with factory windows and high ceilings. Once a workshop, now Axel's studio and gallery. In the ranks of the squatters, Axel is honoured as an art hero. In a rough-and-ready, casual sort of way, but still. Sometimes his eyes become hard and black, and then he shuts himself off in the studio. Guys wait around the well. All day long. In between his film-school classes, Etienne and his camera are there too. They sniff the air, the young men. They want to *smell* what is going on up there. Now and then an assistant or two are summoned upstairs. Some come just for the day. Others spend the night. Some keep coming back, others quickly lose patience. Those whom Axel invites up are sworn to silence.

Axel leaves clues. A sliver of a photo is found on the stairs one morning: an underwater scene. On a hot afternoon a fragment of yellow satin wafts down to the well from an open window. A soiled child's glove appears in the toilet (crusted with blood?); snippets of fur appear next to the oven. These things are snatched up. They prompt speculation, or disappear into trouser pockets, where they are silently fingered. Materials, the well-sitters imagine, that betray something about the work that is taking shape upstairs. Axel is full of tricks, Etienne reckons. He is carefully construing secrets: the scraps are dispersed to throw the hungry ones off his scent, to still their appetite briefly and then heighten it again.

Etienne looks past the false signs, focusing instead on those Axel summons from outside. Squatters' children, and the offspring of council-flat dwellers. Young boys or teenagers. They knock on the front door, are shown the stairs to the studio. Some are accompanied by parents. One child arrives with a yapping dog; others bring toys. Dead-eyed children, some of them, and frightened. Others are swift as lizards, with sly lashes and couldn't-care-less shoulders. Magnesium flashes flicker in the afternoon light: Axel is taking photos. A bedroom is used as a temporary darkroom. The hours when Axel isn't working in the attic or the hospital, or spending naked with Etienne, he is holed up there. And no one is allowed in.

Axel sends out squatter assistants on blind expeditions. They are instructed to arrive at a specified place at a given time, where a stranger then hands over unknown items. They come back laden with props: chairs and side tables, velvet cloths and candelabra. And costumes – Victorian children's outfits. It is as if the whole of South London is in Axel's service. Everyone responds when he invisibly snaps his fingers. They are all made to feel as if they are becoming part of his art, slotting into an inevitable pattern. He is a perfectionist, perhaps a tyrant.

The installation has been completed. The assistants are dispatched to distribute pamphlets for the opening. Axel takes Etienne upstairs. *Only* him.

The windows are wide open. On one wall there are rows of photographs in sepia. Dozens of them. Tacked on with inch nails, trembling in the breeze. Etienne approaches. Boys, all of them. Dressed in their Sunday best, hair combed or slicked back with oil. Some of them have a sailboat or a ball in their hands. They sit uncomfortably in chairs, or on the laps of sombre parents. Something is amiss. Etienne moves along, looks at more photos, trying to unravel his discomfort. A little dog is pulling away from one boy; a cat is arching its back.

A train rumbles in the distance; something is dawning upon Etienne. He steps back. A baby is sleeping on velvet, naked like a cherub. Children are sitting bolt upright next to brothers or friends. Or in a family group, head resting on a mother's or father's lap. Some children are holding hands. Some have their eyes closed, others are gazing mercilessly at the viewer. 'These children . . .' Etienne casts his eye over the rows, his gaze settling on identical twins. With identical caps and knickerbockers. One is looking into the camera, his likeness is sleeping on his shoulder. 'Are they *alive?*'

Axel smiles, shaking his head slowly. 'All dead. Shortly before the photos were taken. They're Victorian post-mortem photographs.' Axel presses his finger on the twins. 'Photography was expensive in those days. After someone's death there was a last chance for a photo. Usually the only chance . . .' He steers Etienne by the shoulder, presses his nose up against the photographs. 'Look closely. Some have their eyes closed; the lids of others have been painted over with eyes. See how they *stare.*'

Etienne retreats to the middle of the room. He knocks against something, turns around: a glass case on a pedestal. A silver teaspoon is floating inside the glass (upon closer inspection, it is suspended from silk threads). The spoon is filled with a milky fluid.

'Is that . . . ?'

Axel nods. 'Semen. Fresh every morning.' The corners of his mouth move. 'My own, in case you were wondering . . .' He takes Etienne by the arm. 'Come and see the other side.' More photographs in rows. The neighbourhood children who have recently been coming and going. The Victorian images are echoed, picture by picture: boy with dog, naked baby on velvet, identical twins with caps. But these models are alive.

Etienne switches on his camera, turns the lens towards Axel. 'What do you call your installation?'

Wake up the Children, the title turns out to be. There is a party, a kind of opening – wine bottles scattered about, a band playing next to the well. South London squatters swarm down Bermondsey Street and up to the attic. They study the photographs raptly, linger by the quarter-ounce of fresh semen hovering behind glass. Everyone wants to be close to Axel. They stand in his sphere, brush against him, utter his name. Letter by letter: A-X-E-L. Hands rest on the glass case; it is collecting vapour and fingerprints. Every day, Axel explains, one pair of photos – old and new – will be removed and disposed of in the well. Etienne picks up his camera, points it at Axel, immediately switches it off again. The attic is jam-packed; there is hardly room to move. People cluster ever more densely around Axel. Later Axel, and then some of the other men too, strip off their shirts. Axel is slick with sweat and surrounded by the leanest men and women of the tribe, the ones with the darkest hearts. They want to touch his skin. Like Jesus's robe.

They want to drag Axel off with them, these South London squatters, but it is Etienne whom Axel chooses. They spend more and more time in each other's company.

Tonight they are in Etienne's room in the Square. There are white flashes outside: a neighbour welding rusty sculptures. Electrical crackling noises, as if something is being shocked to death. They are lying on the futon, leafing through the pages of the Blake book. The evening is cool; their clothes are scattered on the floor. Axel doesn't know most of the Blake works. Etienne is relieved to be showing him something new. Axel is saying more than usual, muttering something about 'no-man's light' and 'prophetic radiance'. The glow, he explains, that would emanate from Etienne's chest if he were to rip it open. Light in which they could pray to each other in the nude.

They let the book slip to the floor, try to rip each other open. They don't stop before the room is smelling of raw flesh. Then they start again, slowly and tenderly.

'It's the only thing I brought with me,' Etienne says when he leans back against the wall and lights one of Axel's cigarettes. 'This book.' He doesn't add 'from South Africa'. He puts it down on Axel's chest, keeps turning the pages.

Axel drops glowing ash on the page; it burns a hole in a choir of angels. They hastily extinguish it. 'And your drums. I brought almost nothing from Germany; I make everything from scratch,' he says and falls asleep against Etienne's shoulder. Outside welding sparks are flying. Once, just after they met, Axel mentioned that he had lived in Berlin at some point, even named a few cafés and gay bars that he used to frequent there. Etienne figured that he must have been well-known in Berlin's night streets. Other than that, tonight's conversation is the closest they have ever come to sharing anything about their origins and previous lives. They don't usually ask each other questions. They don't talk about parents, family or places of birth. About schools, homes or childhood friends.

They are comets in deep space, falling smoothly. They grant each other the oxygen-free universe. And all the light of all its suns.

Etienne still has Aodhan's video recorder. He rarely watches films at the film school. His Belgian housemate has rewired an old television for him. At the film-school library he borrows work of underground American directors. Kenneth Anger films from the '40s and '60s, with sailors, motorcycle gangs and undertones of S-M. And Andy Warhol's *Empire*. A static camera focusing on the Empire State Building for eight hours. All that changes – ever so gradually – is the light. He lies back on his futon, watches it right through the night.

When the video stops automatically, the shape of the Empire State Building has been burnt onto his retinas. Next to him on the floor is one of the *Resister* magazines that Ben at COSAWR so solemnly hands over every time he goes to their offices. Axel, on his last visit, used it to wipe semen spatter from the floor. Etienne slings it into a corner, under the drums. On the television there is the buzz of digital snow.

A Sunday evening. Bermondsey Street. Just the two of them. Axel is heating water on the Dover, filling up the tin tub. He makes Etienne sit in the steaming water, washes him from head to toe. Axel pours another kettle of boiling water into the bath. He slips in behind Etienne. Etienne's jaws slacken.

At night the wind blows through cracks in the windows. In bed Etienne examines Axel's back: muscle and sinews like bark and knots. He seeks out Axel's wrist under the blankets. Axel, insistent and half-asleep, reaches for Etienne's knuckles, then lets go. Etienne dreams of child ghosts. Slave boys. They have returned to the dank workhouse in the attic, where they used to tan hides until their hands were raw, and used to thread and stitch until they were almost blind. Not the kind of children whose lifeless bodies would ever have been posed for post-mortem photos. They are circling Axel's glass case. Their fingers, despite the half-moons of soot under the nails, leave no marks.

Etienne wakes up, lays a palm on his chest. His heart is beating erratically, emitting Morse code. The ghost boys are still slipping from behind peeling wallpaper, through cracks in the plaster. They are following the heat signals being exchanged by Etienne's and Axel's bodies, like insects that can see in the dark. Etienne switches on his camera, aims it at the ghosts. They don't respond to the shutter's whirring. Are they feeling it too? he wonders: the sorrow in this room that is so deep, one would drown in it if it were water.

Etienne gets up early. A long day of film-school classes lies ahead. He gets up, goes up to the attic and takes a photo off the wall. A seated mother. Her son is standing next to her, his hand on her shoulder. Good work by the photographer: nothing betrays the fact that he is dead. Until, that is, you look at his feet and see the base of something akin to a hatstand, propping him up. Etienne switches on his camera, zooms in on the mother. He swivels, takes a long shot of the teaspoon behind glass. Shortly Axel will come and fill it with freshly harvested semen, warm and fragrant in the morning glow.

If Axel could lay his hands on the ghost boys, he would incorporate them in his installation, Etienne thinks. When Etienne later develops the film he took of them, there is nothing on it.

Chapter 9

ETIENNE HAS BEEN in London for almost six months. Twin letters from his mother arrive every week, one of them usually a day or so after the other. The postmarks show they are posted simultaneously in different places. Why does *every* letter need a false counterpart? Is she just soothing herself? he still wonders.

It is troubling him, these cracks through which South Africa remains visible. He stops opening any of the envelopes.

In their editing classes Etienne and his fellow students learn how to select and arrange shots. And the art of timing. 'The editor,' the instructor droned in the first class, 'recreates rather than reproduces the filmed event, so that the cumulative effect exceeds the sum of the actions in the individual scenes.' It sounded as if he was repeating it for the thousandth time. A failed director? Etienne wondered. 'Editing of images,' he continued, and a flame momentarily sprang up in his eye, 'is the only art that is unique to filmmaking. The best auteurs – artists like Kurosawa – always edit their own work.'

Today the editor's eyes are glazed over. He explains in monotone that editing is mainly about the optimisation of dramatic possibilities, but that prosaic on-set editing is also required to correct continuity faults and other camera errors. Etienne pricks up his ears. He likes the idea that gaps and faults can be transformed into something beautiful.

The instructor's voice is becoming even more subdued, his eyes even glassier. He explains the stages of commercial editing. The editor's cut that is refined to the director's cut, which is then polished further to become the final cut. He uses phrases like 'the codification of film grammar'. He rattles off the names of older directors. Kuleshov and Eisenstein, Buñuel. He talks about the jump cuts of the French Nouvelle Vague, and non-narrative films from the '60s.

Etienne's thoughts start wandering. He thinks of Axel, his silent throat, his cheekbones. Of his long fingers, the cloudiness behind his pupils. Of his dark gullet.

For the second hour of the class, they go to an editing room for practical instruction, to enable them to complete production work on their own 16 mm films. It is a lesson in basic techniques: how to synchronise image and sound, how to cut and splice film. The students stand in a half-circle around the instructor, who is sitting in front of the editing machine. He is demonstrating and explaining. Sound and image rolls are loaded onto the motorised plates. Everyone tries to keep an eye on the tiny screen, but the room is too crowded. Expertly, and with bored movements, the instructor feeds the rolls through the cogs. He feeds, cuts and joins, feeds, cuts and joins.

Etienne has had the material for his film developed, and spends his evenings editing at the film school in Covent Garden. He is clumsy with the machine, struggling with the visualisation and arrangement. He tries to recall the demonstration. A few times he cuts the film in the wrong place, once or twice he tears the perforated film edges with the cogs' teeth. He swears out loud, gets up and swings the window open. Cobblestones are gleaming in the street, polished by feet over centuries. A group of drunkards loudly leave a pub. It is after eleven. He forces himself back, gritting his teeth. Gradually he cobbles something together from the frames and scenes. He had something other in mind than what is taking shape. Directors like Kenneth Anger or Bruce LaBruce are his inspiration. But each image follows the preceding one too swiftly; there is too little variety in camera angles and light conditions. A storyline isn't necessary. But there is something else that just won't fall into place. Patterns are evading him. Deeper structure.

At least he has a title now: *Waking up in Axel's World*.

The seminar about lost films grips Etienne from the outset. He has to start acknowledging that he feels more at home with the history and philosophy of film than with the camera or editing machine.

'Lost films,' the lecturer started in the first seminar, pausing for effect. 'Ghost films. Images that have become nebulous shadows. Or films of which only fragments remain. Silver nitrate that has bubbled away to black powder, or been sucked up into firestorms as toxic fumes.

'Before the 1950s,' he continued, 'few people thought films were worthy of preservation. They were viewed as short-lived entertainment. Prints were made of negatives and distributed to cinemas. Cinemas didn't have storage facilities. And after being shown, the prints were destroyed.' The lecturer took a round steel case in his hand, took out a film reel. The vinegary smell tickled Etienne's sinuses. He sat forward, dizzy, nostrils flaring. 'And on top of that,' the lecturer continued, 'silver nitrate is highly unstable and very flammable. At production studios – which *did* have storage facilities – entire warehouses often went up in flames.' Light reflected on the lecturer's glasses, making him seem blind. 'Films that were stored at high temperatures often combusted spontaneously. Or simply disintegrated.

'Or sometimes, when a fire had to be filmed, the studios would stoke it with stacks of old film reels.' The lecturer looked straight at Etienne. 'Think of those thousands of images, withering and seeping into the atmosphere. The filming of the destruction of film . . .' He lowered the reel. 'Many films were destroyed in the war, of course. Of the tens of thousands of shorts and feature films made before 1950, at least half are forever lost. Of the pre-1930s silent films, around ninety per cent have been lost. Even of the most popular films, so many copies were printed that the negatives often wore away and faded.' He slipped the reel back into its steel sheath, fastened the catch; his eyes darkened.

'These films only exist in descriptions, posters and stills. Occasionally, copies *are* still found. In attics. Old cinema storerooms. Archives in the Eastern Bloc. Often only fragments, though. There is an entire movement here in the UK to find such films. The British Film Institute has a long list.'

For the next seminar a projector was set up. While the lecturer was threading the film through the cogwheels, he explained: 'This work dates from 1920. Only in 1970 was a copy found again. In a Moscow archive. A Weimar-era work, made by Bertolt Brecht.' Etienne didn't want to ask stupid questions; he would do some reading about Weimar and Brecht afterwards. It was a short film in which a barber shaves someone's hair to look like a traditional Chinese man, and in the process accidentally cuts off another client's head. The barber's assistant reattaches the latter's head with a needle and thread. There is a sword fight and two characters kissing at the end. What a magnificent piece of flickering nonsense, Etienne thought.

In subsequent sessions, the lecturer shows them film posters. Also stills, originally used for promotional purposes. They watch fragments on the projector. Worn, bleached prints from the '30s. Films that are drifting away, dissolving.

Restoration techniques are discussed. The students are sent to the archives to do some digging. Their assignment is to select a lost film from the list, research its history and put together all remaining material relating to it. To build a sort of puzzle *around* the film, with just one piece – the film itself – missing.

'If you wish,' the lecturer says, 'you could even embark on a bit of a search. But don't spend too much time on it. It isn't every day that masterpieces are dragged from the shadow into the light.'

Now that Etienne no longer reads his mother's letters, he is visited by events – apparently meaningless moments – that he thought he had forgotten forever. It happens at night, just before he dozes off. In one such half-dream, he is five or six. They are travelling, he and his parents, somewhere in the Free State. They stop at a picnic spot with a little cement table and benches. Next to a tarred road, under some bluegum trees. A dusty side road disappears into the veld. Telephone wires are singing overhead. His father is wearing shorts and long socks. He is young; his body is loose, even careless, amid the cosmos flowers. Etienne is wearing a child's safari suit. His mother hands him a hard-boiled egg. He walks some distance into the long grass; it closes up almost entirely above him. Then he freezes; his legs simply won't go any further. He has the sense that he is stepping outside time. Slowly he lets go of the egg, drops his arms by his side. The egg keeps hanging in front of him, floating like an oval moon. There is nothing but him and the grass and the silence.

The next moment his mother jumps out of the grass, scooping him up, laughing. The cotton of her dress is cool; she smells of orange juice. The memory never goes beyond that. Dreamless sleep arrives to claim him.

Etienne is working on an essay about montage techniques in Soviet film art. Axel is lying next to him on the futon, shirtless. A video is playing a scene from Eisenstein's film *Battleship Potemkin*: people being shot and trampled by Cossack soldiers. Intermittently, Etienne pauses the image, approaches the screen to study the trembling frame from up close. The television is temperamental. It makes hissing sounds, smells of scorched rubber. Sometimes, when Etienne presses the pause button, the screen wavers and flickers as if subliminal images are being flashed in between, then continues obstinately. As if the video is refusing to disrupt the rhythm of the scene. It happens now, and Etienne throws down the remote, goes looking for his housemate who originally fixed the television. He is not in.

When Etienne returns, Axel is standing with the remote control aimed at the television like a weapon. The image has finally frozen, stuck at the well-known frame of the old woman who has been wounded by Cossack soldiers. Her pince-nez sits askew over her nose, her bloody face contorted in a shout. When Axel gets up and slaps the television with his open palm, the image breaks up and disappears. Etienne throws his hands in the air. 'Leave the fucking thing,' Axel says. 'I brought you something that will interest you far more. Something I've been meaning to give you for a while.'

A few nights ago they'd been lying on the roof in Bermondsey Street, under clouds that were reflecting the city's lights. Etienne told Axel about the thousands of missing film reels. Axel didn't say anything. Even so, he *was* listening.

'Here's a film for you,' he now says. He takes out a file from his backpack, offers it. The cover is made of light blue cardboard, woolly with age.

Etienne frowns. 'A file, it would seem, rather than a film.'

'Have a look.'

Etienne hesitantly takes it, opens it. On top of a stack of papers, bound into the file, is a set of rough pencil drawings. Etienne instantly knows: they are storyboards for a film scene. He flips through them. A boy lies in bed in the foreground, wrapped in blankets. A woman enters the room, bends over the hearth, pushes an apple into the flames. A close-up of the flames. There are arrows, dotted lines, notes in German. Etienne puts the drawings aside, starts rummaging through the rest of it. About eighty to a hundred pages of typescript. Occasionally there are more storyboards in between.

He goes back to the first page, on which is typed:

BERLINER CHRONIK
Director: Ariel Schnur
Production Journal – Irmgard Fleischer
1933

He returns to the pages. They are brittle, like winter leaves. He only understands a few things here and there – his high-school

German is rusty. He looks up at Axel. 'What *is* this?'

'You're working on this kind of thing, aren't you? Ghost films.' Axel widens his eyes, his tone ghostly. From the community garden, voices are rising up.

Etienne turns the pages. Although he can understand little of it, it is patently the records or diary of the production of a film entitled *Berliner Chronik*. There are lists of equipment. Names. Addresses and telephone numbers. His heart starts pounding. 'Where is this film?'

'Exactly.'

Etienne searches Axel's eyes. He wants to follow the optical nerves into the folds of the brain. '1933,' Etienne says distractedly. He keeps flicking the pages. Names with question marks draw his attention. Other names are circled, or ticked. 'These?'

Axel leans over, reads. 'Actors who are to audition. And technical people.' Axel presses his finger on a list. 'Potential cameramen.' He turns the page. 'Lighting people.' Below them, in the community garden, bongo drums are being played.

Etienne scans the pages in a frenzy, lingering arbitrarily on some of them. He asks Axel to translate fragments of text. There are minutes of production planning meetings, meetings with potential financiers. Above each set of minutes is written SECRET. There are timetables for filming, technical detail about cameras. Etienne takes out more loose storyboards as he thumbs through the pages. One shows a boy looking into the courtyard of a block of flats. Opposite him, the outline of a Christmas tree is visible in a window. Another board shows the same boy with a butterfly net, amid tall grass. Etienne keeps going through the file. Nearer the end, the pages look different – filled with long, dense paragraphs. Ultimately the dates disappear. At the very back, a bunch of blank pages have been bound into the file.

Etienne lowers the file onto his knees. 'Where on God's earth did you get this?'

Axel flicks back to the first page, points at *Irmgard Fleischer*. 'My grandmother. My mother was her only child.' Axel reaches over his shoulder, scratches vigorously. A vein is pulsating in his neck. From his armpit emanates the fragrance of leather and hot iron. 'Irmgard was a film production secretary. Or something like that. This file is all I have of her.' Axel takes out a storyboard, holds it up. 'The irony is that she would never have been able to see any of this herself.'

'Why not?'

'Because of her blindness.' In the community garden a man has started singing in a scratchy voice.

Etienne wonders, but doesn't ask, why a blind woman would be involved in film production. After a while, he says: 'Is she still alive, your grandmother?'

Axel has fallen silent; his eyes are cool. Etienne is concentrating on the file again, trying to make sense of the yellowed pages. A few more hollow-sounding voices are joining the drums in the community garden. After a few notes, the little choir falls into dissonance. The drumming stops; people start sniggering. Their giggling becomes louder, increasingly hysterical. As if they had inhaled laughing gas.

Etienne looks at Axel, thinking of how casually he announced that he had been wanting to hand over the file for a while. Why *hadn't* he? What else is being withheld, what else does Axel have up his sleeve? Then the file claims Etienne's attention again.

Tonight they are back in Bermondsey Street. While Axel is washing himself in the tin bath, Etienne thumbs though the file in the attic. He is struggling with the German, and remains dependent on Axel to decipher most of it. The file is suddenly making him curious about what else he might find up here. He pricks his ears: Axel's long body is rolling and splashing down in the kitchen. Etienne puts the file down on the floor, gets up and opens a crate. Materials: paintbrushes, cardboard, seeds, a bucket full of glass shards. He moves on to the next crate. He finds an A4 envelope containing some photographs. Children with tattoos - some of them babies. One child has a tattoo on his back of two children who are simultaneously tattooing each other's skins. Or are they drawing each other - giving birth to each other - with the needles? He squirms, puts the photos back.

He takes out a box, peeks inside. The remains, apparently, of a previous project. He unpacks it, and then another three boxes. He roughly sets it up: a little village of miniature houses, roofs ripped off, as if a wild storm has torn through the place. There are pigeons in the houses, going about their daily tasks like people: at the dinner table, in bed, sitting at a desk. But some calamity or other has struck the pigeon community; something has scorched away the roofs. Pigeon families' heads are turned skywards, beaks open, eyes and feathers burnt. Everything black and melted, under a layer of ash. Did Axel use a blowtorch?

Etienne is so absorbed by the spectacle that it takes a while before he realises the birds aren't stuffed. The stench enters his sinuses. Behind him the threshold creaks; he swivels around. Axel is standing in the doorway, dripping, towel around his waist.

'Put it away, fuck it!' he says. 'Can't you smell?' Etienne can: it is now a dense cloud in his nostrils. He looks back at the birds rotting away in their own houses. At the things they were doing when an unknown cataclysm struck – washing dishes, sleeping, reading a book. As if nothing could ever go wrong.

Axel smiles. 'I'm kidding. It *should* all rot. The installation is only starting to ripen now.' He lifts his nose, sniffing greedily. 'At last the fucking birds are starting to fall apart. *Now* it's smelling like something meaningful!' Something tells Etienne Axel had *wanted* him to stumble upon this, that more things are hidden away for him to find. There is a new shade of light in Axel's eyes as he approaches. A wolf's appetite.

Axel steps onto the blue file. He unravels the towel, grabs Etienne's head like a parched skull, forcing it towards his hips.

Chapter 10

A T NIGHT, ETIENNE works on deciphering parts of Irmgard's file. Sometimes Axel helps with unusual words or tricky sentences. Most of the time, though, he is too busy in the attic. Or just moody and reluctant. During the day Etienne searches catalogues and lists for a film entitled *Berliner Chronik*. At the film school, in film libraries, the BFI. Nothing. That the film, or at least parts of it, were indeed shot, becomes clear when he reviews the production schedule and Irmgard's notes more closely. It is the kind of lost film about which hardly anyone, except the few people who worked on it, would have known. And how many of *them* would have survived the war?

There are also a few letters bound into the file. Carbon copies of Ariel Schnur's correspondence in late 1932 and early 1933. Etienne casts his eye over these. The first letter, written in December 1932, is addressed to one Wilhelm Reich. Axel helps with the translation. He is fidgeting; it looks as if he would prefer to be somewhere else. Ariel refers to previous meetings with Reich. He expresses his admiration for a manuscript that Reich sent him, shortly to be published as *Massenpsychologie des Faschismus*. Ariel carefully broaches the possibility of making a documentary film about Reich.

Axel tires of the translation. Etienne goes to the Goldsmiths College library, where one of the Square's inhabitants works as a part-time librarian; she lets him in. He finds information about Reich. Austrian psychoanalyst, post-Freud. Sexologist and communist. To his relief he finds a copy of *Massenpsychologie* in English translation. The librarian lets him take out the book under her name. Back in Bermondsey Street, he goes up to the roof and thumbs through the book. The only sounds carried by the afternoon breeze are those of trains at London Bridge station and lazy autumn planes overhead. The roof hatch is open; below Etienne Axel is working in the attic. Etienne shifts closer to the hatch. 'Listen to this,' he says, even though he knows Axel doesn't like to be disturbed while he is working. 'This kicks ass. Let me read—'

'Please.' Axel's voice is tense. 'Just summarise . . .'

'OK. Reich is saying something like this: if you supress a child's sexuality, you make him frightened. Ashamed, scared of authority. "Well-adjusted." The rebellious instincts are thus paralysed—' Two trains thunder past each other above the Bermondsey Street tunnel, drowning him out. 'So, if you suppress sexual thoughts and curiosity in a child, you're bringing up someone who stays obedient. However fucking miserable he might be, and irrespective of how much you humiliate him. The family is a miniature state; once you are habituated to it, the *true* state has you in its claws forever . . .'

Axel's response is to emerge through the hatch and pull Etienne's shirt over his head. He is sweaty; he pushes Etienne onto the roof, kissing him. Axel smells of freshly sawn wood. The roof is rough against Etienne's back. They spill seed, then lie on their backs, the trails of planes dissipating above them.

'Wait here,' Etienne says. He lowers himself through the hatch, scoots down the ladder and stairs, grabs his blue file in the kitchen. On his way back up, he picks up Axel's well-worn German-English dictionary. Axel sighs when Etienne asks him to help translate the rest of Ariel's letters. Etienne's German is improving, but he still gets stuck. Axel looks up at the fresh lines being drawn across the sky, then peers askance at the pages Etienne wants to show him.

The file doesn't contain any response to Reich's letter. The pile of correspondence that follows is between Ariel Schnur and one Walter Benjamin. The correspondence stretches from late December 1932 to March 1933. They don't know each other; in the first letter Ariel introduces himself as an aspiring director. He expresses his admiration for Benjamin's essays, specifically complimenting him on a piece about Berlin that has just been published in a paper. *In these difficult times I am looking for my first film project.* He enquires whether Benjamin thinks that some of his work may fruitfully be used as a source for a film.

Benjamin writes back. Over the past year he has written several such fragments about Berlin. *Denkbilder,* he calls them. He wants to publish them as a book, but could also consider making them available as the basis for a film. *It would greatly please me, although I can hardly imagine how it could find a form in images alone.* He nevertheless includes copies of the pieces with his letter, he writes.

Ariel's next letter, in early March 1933, starts off with the menace looming over Berlin: the atmosphere since the inauguration of Adolf Hitler as Chancellor in January, the Reichstag fire, the arrest of communists. The brutality of Gleichschaltung. (Axel shrugs his shoulders – he doesn't know the term either.) *I have read all your* Denkbilder *about childhood in Berlin in one sitting; I am deeply moved and impressed by them. I will take up the challenge,* Ariel writes. *A film shall emerge from this material. I plead for your understanding that my ability – as a young director – to compensate you is limited.*

He refers to the challenge of trying to make a film *now, in these times*, to the *absurd light being cast onto all ordinary human activities*. To the *stench of unreason and violence in the Berlin air.*

You may use it without any advance payment, Benjamin writes back, *provided we can agree on a revenue share.* A wry joke? Etienne wonders. Though it is never expressed, by this time it is apparent that they are both Jews. They could surely not have been expecting that a film by a Jewish director would still be distributed – not to mention make a profit. Benjamin's only reference to the political conditions is the following: *Whether one will know the streets of Berlin, or the heavens above it, for much longer, is, needless to say, doubtful.* About filming: *I shall demand no involvement or control. All visual interpretation I shall leave in your hands.* As regards the title: *I plan to call the book* Berliner Kindheit um neunzehnhundert. *The title of the film I shall leave to you too. Should you wish to distinguish it from the book, consider* Parloir des Nichts.

'The consulting room of nothingness,' Axel translates, looking Etienne in the eye. It sounds to Etienne like another dark joke.

The Benjamin texts themselves are not in the file. Axel jumps up, stands on the edge of the roof. How small he looks against the City's glass towers. 'I have to go to the hospital. Kill a few children.' It is a standing joke. Axel rarely mentions his work at the hospital. If someone asks how he makes a living, he'll say: 'I'm a child murderer.' And then grin.

Axel disappears down the hatch. Etienne looks at him walking down Bermondsey Street. Without his hospital clothes. The sky is deep red and smelling of far-off fires. Etienne lowers himself through the hatch, locks it above him.

There isn't really a shift at the hospital tonight. Axel has other – secret – destinations somewhere in this city that always feels as if it is engulfed in flames.

Etienne skips some of his classes, goes to the Goldsmiths library and reads about Benjamin. Jewish philosopher from the early part of the century. He flees from Berlin to Paris in 1933, becomes trapped in Europe in the late '30s. In 1940 he dodges the Gestapo in Paris, tries to flee through Spain and Portugal to the US. The Spaniards cancel his visa at the border, forcing him to turn back. He takes his own life with an overdose of morphine rather than to be delivered into the hands of the Nazis.

Etienne borrows the English translation of Benjamin's Berlin texts from the library, under his librarian friend's name as usual. It *was* published. Only after Benjamin's death, though, and after he had tried in vain to find a publisher for years. It contains reworked versions of the original texts from the '30s.

Etienne lies reading under his skylight. He finds himself moved. Memories of childhood in a bourgeois Jewish Berlin household. Things, places, obscure associations. The labyrinth of a young mind and the retrospection of the older narrator shift across each other, and over the city. Like multiple exposures of film frames.

Late one evening, Etienne and Axel are sitting on rickety chairs in the Bermondsey Street kitchen. 'Listen to Benjamin,' Etienne says, and then translates: 'Memory . . . is the medium of past experience, just as the earth is the medium in which dead cities are buried. He who wants to get close to his own buried past must behave like a man who is digging . . .'

While Etienne is reading, he watches Axel from the corner

of his eye; the supple tree roots on his neck change shape whenever his head moves. Axel doesn't say anything, but Etienne can see he is pleased by how intrigued Etienne is by the file's secrets.

Axel takes the file from his hand, leads him to the attic, then further up the ladder to the roof. Axel traps him against the chimney, strips off Etienne's clothes, staying dressed himself. The bricks are cold against Etienne's buttocks. Axel's hands multiply across his body, as if a multitude of gods have joined him. As if Axel has as many fingers as the blue file has pages.

Etienne's limbs unfold in blind flashes. He is being flayed for the city: an insect behind a magnifying glass, pinned through the head, writhing. He is being exhibited for people on trains and behind office windows, for commuters on bridges, vagrants on station benches. He belongs to them now. And they can do with him whatever they will.

While delving deeper into the file, Etienne tries to imagine the film. He conjures up images using production notes, technical details and the incomplete set of storyboards. He fills in the gaps.

As he works through the Benjamin book and the file, he discovers how the Berlin texts fit in with the storyboards, which he has now stuck on the bedroom wall, their fragility notwithstanding. The image of the boy in the bed and the woman pushing an apple into the flames? From a piece called *Wintermorgen*, winter morning: the chambermaid coming in early, lantern in her hand, to stoke the stove in the hearth. The boy gets up, opens the stove, anticipating the apple's secret smell. He warms his hands against the apple's cheeks – hesitant to bite through the baked skin, afraid that the fugitive knowledge residing in the aroma might escape on its way to his tongue . . .

Etienne sounds Axel out again about the origin of the blue file. Axel just slips his hand into Etienne's shirt, smothers him with his tongue.

Etienne makes rough sketches of other scenes in the Benjamin book. Scenes that are also listed in the film plan but for which no storyboards exist. His sketches are rough and childish, too provisional even for storyboards.

In the back of the file there are a dozen or so blank pages. Etienne keeps returning to them, wondering about them. For long periods he stares intently at each page, as if ink would spontaneously darken from the fibres in the shape of letters, then merge into sentences.

Axel now often works evening or night shifts at the hospital. Or this is where he *says* he has been when he arrives in the Square at strange times, looking the worse for wear. Axel never talks about the hospital. Etienne sometimes senses distress or disquiet in Axel after one of his shifts. At first he asks him about it. All he gets in response are shrugs of the shoulders and 'Well, I only maimed *one* last night; nobody died', or 'Yes, a few were burnt and disfigured, brains were damaged, limbs amputated, guts spilled . . .' When Axel returns these days, they go on silent walks for hours. They don't talk about the file, or about Irmgard, Ariel or the film, even though questions are swirling inside Etienne.

They are out of synch with the city, Etienne thinks. They are becoming secret inhabitants, appearing when everyone else has disappeared, as if having fled an epidemic overnight. When the trains are rattling on their tracks, bright and empty, when

the City's thousands of windows are stripped of office heads,
they walk the streets that still hold the warmth of vanished
bodies.

Chapter 11

EARLY MORNING. ETIENNE is sitting by the well, hands clasped around his legs, chin on his knees. Axel joins him. It must have been a productive night in the attic - after an unsettling hospital shift yesterday, the restiveness now seems to have drained from his body. He puts an arm around Etienne's shoulders; they look down the well. Since Etienne found the decaying pigeons, his city joy has been waning. The blue file is consuming him, but it isn't lifting the weight from his chest.

'What's wrong?'

Etienne doesn't respond.

Axel nods distractedly. 'It's London. It happens: the city can start to—'

'There's no one else left,' Etienne blurts. 'Just me.' He listens to himself as if to a stranger. *Even where I'm not*, his thoughts continue, *my feet echo in the streets . . .*

Axel tangles his fingers in Etienne's hair, shakes him by the shoulder. 'We have to get you out of here. Come, I'll get some friends together. People who know how to let *go*, how to live off light and air . . .'

'Impossible. I have classes this morning. Why I attend them, God only knows, though. Nothing will come of it.'

'You've never been out of the city, have you? Except for Birmingham and Gateshead, that is. Which don't count.' Etienne shakes his head. Axel jumps up like a coiled spring.

'Forget the classes, forget the blue file. Shake off the weight. Let the light flow in.'

Etienne smiles. Axel too. It is already flowing.

Within half an hour Axel has gathered twelve or thirteen guys and girls from the squats. Pale and tender. Weightless and laughing, wearing T-shirts through which one can count vertebrae.

A cool mist rises in Etienne's chest when the train leaves London and starts accelerating. The landscape opens up. Someone knows someone whose uncle has a cottage in Suffolk; they are heading there for the weekend. After two hours they get off at a small station, walk half an hour further.

It is a bountiful afternoon. The cottage, with its heavy thatch roof, stands on its own beside a high pine tree and a shallow valley. They make a fire under the tree. They sit in a circle, put pills on each other's tongues, smoke joints, pass brandy around. Someone has brought a pet rabbit. The animal is passed along too, caressed, rubbed against cheeks. In the valley there are fields with wheat and bright yellow rapeseed. Some fields have been harvested; pollen and hay are floating on the air, making them sneeze. They look at each other through the flames. The air is becoming thinner; their heads are filling with light. All that remains is the crackling of the fire, and their sun-washed bodies.

A few jump up, start running. Then a few more, then the rest. Etienne jumps up too, even though he doesn't know why. Axel is ahead of him. They tear down the hill, through fields. Light-footed, like a herd of small animals. Everyone is laughing, the sun in their hair. Etienne is high, they are all high. Lighter than wheat, lighter than chaff. Their feet are no longer touching the ground. They strip off each garment while they run, throwing it into the wind. Now and then someone trips over, gets up and runs further, laughing. The pills make them faster. They run through hissing wheat, over yellow-white stalks. The sun is white; colour has bled from the landscape. Etienne closes his eyes; his feet are flying over the turf. He can't stop smiling.

He opens his eyes, looks in wonderment at a girl – thin as a deer, flame-red hair – who jumps on a row of straw bales and flies across it. Against her pallor the rust-coloured tuft of pubic hair is shocking. A lost autumn leaf. Axel and others also jump on the bales. They trip each other, roll off, climb up again.

They could run to the end of the earth. But the pills are running, rather than the legs; they have to stop after all. They fall down on a hillside, one by one, gasping. Etienne looks at Axel, at the red-haired girl sitting between his legs. Her elbows hook around his knees; her head rolls backwards against his chest. Etienne moves closer. The three of them take each other's hands, staring at the small cuts on each other's feet.

Around them, Etienne now notices, there are rock formations. From the Stone Age, or once rolled here by druids and witches. Their distribution seems arbitrary. Or in patterns only the gods can discern, like Axel's installations.

They get up, wander among the stones like sacrificial animals. They lean their heads against them, listening for smothered screams from inside. The sun is hovering on the horizon. They take more pills. After ten minutes, yet more. They walk in circles for a while, then sit down in a patch of heather. The girl curls up against Axel's chest; he folds his arms around her. The pills make her tremble; she is foaming a little around the mouth. Her body is bent at sad angles. Etienne's mouth is dry. He becomes aware of a rushing sound. He gets up, walks up the hill, beckons the others. Axel picks up the redhead like a newborn lamb, tries to make her stand on her own feet.

From the top of the hill one can see a rainbow and a spray of fine drops: a waterfall! The girl runs ahead, down the hill. By the time Etienne and Axel catch up with her, she is standing waist-deep in a dark pond. Her arms are like twigs, her little nipples pink and frightened. She has a hay rash and she is chafed over her back and thighs. Etienne suddenly wonders: didn't she have the rabbit with her earlier on? Has she hugged it to death and dropped it somewhere in the wheat? Etienne touches the straw and chaff in his hair. He wishes *he* now had a rabbit in his arms.

The redhead is standing under the waterfall. The bones of her shoulders hardly interrupt the water's violence. She washes off blood, stretches out her hands. Etienne wades towards her. He has never felt so much joy. The afternoon is ever more radiant.

The three of them sit down on a mossy bank, shivering. The others are no longer with them, Etienne realises. On which hill, or in which wheat field, they lost each other, he cannot tell. Axel has a handful of pills with him; he has somehow managed to hold on to it. Whenever they think they cannot get any higher, or the sun looks as if it is setting, the girl puts a pill on his and Axel's tongues. The mark of her finger is forever imprinted on his taste buds. In future, he will be able to recognise her forensically with his tongue. One day, when he encounters her in a dark city and her index finger serves him a magic tablet again, he will instantly decipher every groove.

The sun has frozen. The pills in their blood keep it just above the horizon. As long as they remain happy, as long as they keep touching each other, it won't set. The girl climbs a birch tree, the tuft of ginger between her legs shining like an oil lamp. They have lost all sense of direction, Etienne thinks. And their clothes are scattered across the landscape. It is getting cold. And they are flying high, so high . . .

The redhead descends from the branches, sits down between Etienne and Axel on the moss, stupefied. They are now allowing the moon to rise, letting the pale stars shine. They touch each other casually, feeling each other's burning skins. The pressure in Etienne's head is shifting and adjusting, as if quicksilver is swilling around in pockets of his brain. His happiness keeps growing. He and Axel lean in from both sides, resting against the redhead's shoulders. She smells of bark. Etienne wonders whether she has a name, or whether she is identified solely by her smell. She touches Etienne's face, her fingertips like ferns. They take turns: first Axel's tongue enters her mouth, then his own. How sweet is the crushing against her inner cheek! Etienne can taste traces of Axel in her honey-like saliva. He feels the pull of the earth; his head drops in her lap.

If he had to die here, today, after taking one too many pill, he would be content. Would be the brightest star in the firmament. Above him, Axel and the redhead's saliva is mixing slowly. His ear is resting against a little nest of pubic hair. He turns his lips downward, tastes the muddiness.

With his eyes closed, and his heart provisionally arrested, Etienne can still see them run: he, Axel and the redhead. Tearing endlessly across a landscape of moss and black rocks. Their feet bloody, her hair like a blowtorch in the wind.

They are back at the cottage beside the pine tree. It is around midnight. Etienne is not sure how they found their way back, but they have been walking for hours, descending from the pill heights. Probably ten or fifteen kilometres. The others have apparently been back for some time. When Etienne enters the cottage, they are sleeping: one on the bare floor, two on a sofa, a few on chairs. Three guys have curled up in front of the cold hearth. They fit into each other: wolf brothers from the same litter, bodies remembering the earliest entanglements. There are blankets everywhere. One girl has rolled a carpet around herself. Etienne looks back. Where Axel and the redhead are, he doesn't know. He is no longer sure whether they have indeed returned with him. Everything is starting to look uncertain. Etienne lights a new fire in the hearth. He nestles in between the three guys in front of the fireplace.

Slowly the day dissolves in sleep. He dreams in autumn colours: purple and orange and velvety green.

When Etienne wakes up, he is hungry. In front of him two eyes are glowing red. A wet snout sniffs his mouth, fur brushes against his cheek: the pet rabbit. He has no idea how long he has slept. It is still night, but light is shining through a parting in the curtains. A spaceship, he realises. They will all be transported up in a light beam. He gets up, walks out the front door. Not a gleaming flying saucer, it turns out, but a huge flame leaking into the sky. It is sucking up the air; it is nigh impossible to breathe. Etienne's feet are on the verge of lifting off the ground.

And there Axel is: standing under the tree, looking up at the bright violence. He is still naked, every rib casting a wary shadow. Has he been standing there all night? And where is the wisp of a red-haired girl? Etienne's memory is hazy. He looks down: he too is naked. The day has written the code of grazes and cuts on his body. Axel turns towards Etienne. They look at each other in the glow, trying to read each other's skins. Etienne approaches him.

They look penetratingly at each other. Axel's face is itself a flame when he speaks: 'We'll burn and burn, you and I. We're not ordinary; we're bodies in the deep cosmos. Blinding comets. Long after our death, the children of earth will see us. Like the ones sleeping in there. Through long, lonely evenings they will recognise us as a fiery pathway in the sky. They will know our names, follow our arc across the heavens. And we will take away their loneliness.'

'You,' Etienne says. 'You . . .' he says again. He doesn't get any further. He holds out his arms towards Axel, then touches his own lips. Then his own hair. He is surprised that he still has any sort of shape. The pills have taken away his speech, perhaps forever. It doesn't matter. They can cut out his tongue, sew up his lips with rough thread. He will communicate with Axel by way of tremors, electrical transmissions between their spines. *I'm burning with you, Axel*, is what he wants to say. *I'm soaring too*. Both of them look up at the tree again.

But now the flames loosen his tongue, like someone being filled by the Holy Spirit, someone bearing witness in a church full of the wretched. 'The tides have brought us here, Axel, phosphorous waves are washing us ashore, out into the burning night.' How undefended he is in this moment, Etienne thinks. These are not his own words. Like Axel's, they belong to the pills. For a long time they keep standing there, without touching each other, until the branches fall down around them and only the burnt-out tree remains, creaking and glowing. Etienne can no longer stay awake. Any moment now he will collapse in the dew. He sleepwalks inside, leaving Axel outside.

Etienne lies down with the others in front of the fireplace again. The last thing he sees before falling into darkness is the dim rectangle of the door. He listens to the tree cooling down, and the ticking embers. Ash is whirling in the hearth. Large flakes blow in from outside, descending onto the sleepers like snow. He is waiting for Axel to come and lie down with him, to come and tattoo him with soot.

Etienne is the last to wake up. Outside, the others are standing in silence around the black totem that remains of the pine tree. They are sombre, solemn. Branches are lying in a broken circle in front of their feet. Then he notices for the first time: the girl from yesterday, the one with the pubic hair like the sun at dusk – there are two of her. Identical twins. And everyone, including the two redheads, is looking down at a small corpse: the pet rabbit, pinned down under a burnt-out branch.

In the train on the way back, the wind is still in Etienne's ears, and his racing comrades' heels keep flickering in the corner of his eye. His head is bursting with sunshine and the open sky, wild thin bodies, mud on white skins, water streaming, seeds blowing in the late afternoon. If he had his way, he could live in those hills forever with Axel and the red-haired twins. One of them is sitting on the train seat opposite him; which one he doesn't know. She is fiddling with her kneecaps, as if trying to tune herself to a radio station.

Chapter 12

ETIENNE FEELS SCORCHED clean after their Suffolk excursion; he is ready for the blue file once more. Until now, he has been dipping into it arbitrarily, a dictionary by his elbow. Now he starts from the beginning. Axel sits next to him, carefully translating the portions of Irmgard's journal that Etienne points out, patiently answering questions.

The first entry is dated 4 March 1933. Ariel has just received consent from Benjamin to use his texts. Actors' auditions are hastily arranged, as well as meetings with cameramen, sound and lighting technicians and a make-up artist. There are minutes of meetings, notes on equipment and locations. Letters, schedules, plans, addresses. No script will be written, Irmgard notes on 7 March. They will be working directly from text to storyboard. Ariel is conceptualising. *And improvisation will be the order of the day.*

Filming starts in earnest on 12 April. Etienne reads the daily reports. Irmgard describes it all in painstaking detail, as if seeing everything herself: the position of tracks and dollies, as well as a tower for shoots from above. Etienne tries to monitor the progress with reference to the original film plan and list of scenes. But as the journal progresses, plans shift, and technical detail is increasingly interrupted by comments on political developments. On 2 June Irmgard writes: *Another plan of Goebbels announced. No further loans for film production except through the Filmkreditbank. Thank God Ariel's friends are financing him. And that our project is small and secret.*

There are still sentences with which Axel has to help Etienne. And references that Etienne doesn't understand. Irmgard talks about *the tyrants at the SPIO*. Etienne does some research – it is a reference to the Spitzenorganisation der Deutschen Filmindustrie: an organisation that controlled all the tools of film production. Only firms that were members were allowed to make films.

Etienne only drags himself away from the blue file when he has to go to the film school. He can hardly sit still in the classes, editing laboratory or camera workshops now. He marvels at his fellow students' competitiveness, their self-confidence. After their studies, they want to make commercial films, or BBC miniseries of classic novels, or underground projects in the spirit of Derek Jarman. Some want to imitate their favourite auteurs obsessively. Others want to shoot documentaries. In war zones or the Amazon. Films about the disappearing rainforests or the last Indians who have never met a Westerner. Or they want to take a handheld camera and live with tribes in Central Africa. Or make films about punks and junkies in West Berlin. For them, London is a dull place, a starting point. They dream of film festivals in Toronto or Goa, Cairo or Chicago. Or the glamour of Cannes or Venice. Etienne has little to say to them. And they don't talk to him in the cafeteria between classes.

His thoughts stay with Irmgard's journal. Even the film theory seminars, which he previously found so engaging, test his patience. He is now looking *through* things, like Frank the campanologist. And the smoky air of a 1930s film set is lingering in his nostrils.

On 10 May Irmgard writes about book burnings, the Säuberung: *You can smell the smoke drifting over from Opernplatz, the millions of letters floating upwards. I lift my nose, read the acrid cloud of words. Inhale it deeply, store the sentences in my lungs.*

A July entry reads: *Ariel has just read me this morning's paper. Goebbels' Reichsfilmkammer announced. The days of Jews in the film industry numbered. Is it lunacy to continue? I am afraid; Ariel and the team are fearless. Or so they pretend.* Early in August the providers of equipment, materials and filming locations start to withdraw. Also some financiers (*so-called friends*). The make-up artist and second cameraman are no longer affordable. The lighting technician has stopped turning up; others have to take over his tasks.

Letters, rather than names, are now used to identify people who are willing to help despite the risks. *The Bell & Howell cameras have both been taken back*, Irmgard writes on 24 July 1933.

Ariel first angry, then despondent. After a few unsuccessful phone calls – everyone wants to help, they insist, 'but the risks, the risks . . .' – X comes to our rescue. He lends us a brand new Bolex H-16. We have to switch to 16 mm for part III. Everything is scaled down and expedited. We are replanning, adapting. The portable Bolex, I tell Ariel, makes us agile. He lifts a cynical eyebrow, so I imagine. But I feel his hand around my shoulders, and put mine around his.

Etienne flicks the pages to September. They keep improvising – new equipment, new sources of financing. Acquaintances of Ariel at commercial studios make small personal loans. A, B and C are acquaintances of Ariel, similarly attached to (unspecified) studios, who undertake to help with editing. At night, in secret, in studio facilities, while Ariel and his team keep shooting new scenes by day.

The journal becomes increasingly chaotic. Etienne has difficulty following it. Things are deleted, rewritten in (Ariel's?) handwriting. The entire production schedule is being disrupted. On 28 September Irmgard writes that they are still working out how to have negatives printed. The laboratories are no longer allowed to help them. On the night of 2 October, an editing machine is smuggled out of one of the large SPIO commercial studios.

Ariel does a week's editing in one night. If only I could have helped him! I bring him coffee, sit next to him. Occasionally he takes my hand. Or I search for his.

No wonder the storyboards are so incomplete, Etienne thinks. Tonight he is sitting in the Bermondsey Street kitchen. It is becoming colder; coal is glowing in the iron stove. He sits back, looking through the windowpanes. The old glass distorts the City's buildings. He tries to imagine Irmgard: behind her typewriter, back straight, her little black eyes dogged and unseeing. Mousy brown hair, lips pursed.

Too vague, he thinks, too generic. And plucked from his imagination. Let him rather focus on technical information. He flicks back to the original specifications: Bell & Howell 35 mm cameras, model 2709, the Tri-Ergon system for sound synchronisation, the amplifier and loudspeakers, five standing lamps, two camera tripods, two dollies, the microphones . . . He works through lists, and amended lists. Gradually their equipment is being taken away. Etienne ignores Irmgard's personal commentary, which increases as the apparatus and facilities disappear. He rests his gaze on brand names, letters and numbers, as if that is where meaning is to be found.

In the back of the file, in a cardboard pocket, Etienne finds a folded sheet. He opens it. Large handwritten letters read: *Tonaufname! Grösste Ruhe! Eintritt verboten!* Sound recording! Absolute silence! No entry! Clearly, a notice that was used during filming. He puts it down; it closes automatically along the decades-old fold. He extends his right hand, makes a turning motion, as if feeding film with a hand crank into a shutter. He suddenly feels self-conscious, lowers his arm. He *shall* find it, this film. Or whatever may be left of it. *That* is what he will become: a film archaeologist. The ordering of images may escape him, but digging is something he can do. Blindly, fanatically.

They rarely go up to the roof in Bermondsey Street now; cold winds have started blowing. And Axel ceases his work in the attic, the new project half-finished. Usually, when he isn't working, he drapes a sheet over the installation-in-progress. Now the sheet never comes off any more. These days, Etienne does a minimum of work for his film-school courses. He handed in his film project two weeks ago, relieved to be rid of the camera. Today, for the first time, he feels like switching it on again. What a relief it would be to shoot something that doesn't have to fit into any project! Just a few free-floating frames. He goes up to the attic. In the changing light he takes lengthy shots of the sheet, draped over an assortment of unknown objects.

Late morning. It is raining. Axel and Etienne are sitting in the Square's café, where Etienne has previously worked as a volunteer. They are slurping steaming leek and potato soup.

It is the end of October. Even though he has only been here for about six months, it feels to Etienne as if he has never known any other life. As if he was born here among the squatters.

Axel is sitting at some distance from Etienne. Etienne surreptitiously breathes in Axel's scent. He knows how Axel smells after a shift in the hospital: of ointment and bandages, wounds and disinfectant. Sometimes he pretends he is going to work, but when he returns, he only smells of London, of the streets and the night.

'There's a place I've been wanting to show you,' Axel says. He avoids looking Etienne in the eye, blows on a spoonful of hot soup. When they were running wildly in the Suffolk hills, the sun shone behind his irises. Now only the dull light of menace is glowing around each pupil.

Etienne has grown wary of what others want to show him. Why does everyone he meets in this city want to foist their obsessions on him? As if he is a pane onto which to breathe their own vapour? He looks at Axel in the soup steam, wonders whether he is making *him* part of an installation as well.

The rain has stopped; it is cool and cloudy. At Denmark Hill station they get off the train and start walking. *Nunhead Cemetery*, Etienne reads above the cast-iron gates through which Axel enters after a while. He follows. The massive cemetery is overgrown and neglected; it has clearly been in disuse for a long time. Axel leaves the path, leads him into the bushes. The roots of fallen trees have ripped open graves, a hundred years or more after they were filled. Axel and he clamber over trunks, stepping on and over crumbling headstones. Axel walks fiercely ahead, his neck muscles tense. Etienne follows in silence, wishing he had brought his camera.

Through the foliage, a small group of black-clad men becomes visible. And music becomes audible, heavy post-punk rock. Axel increases his pace. They are walking in a row, the guys in black. Goths: the leader at the front, four others following like disciples.

Axel and Etienne stop opposite the goths, on the other side of a fallen tree trunk. The disciples are standing on either side of, and a step behind, their priest. On the sleeveless shirt of one is a faded picture of an angel with a dog's head.

Axel gestures with his head to the boom box that the goth leader is carrying on his shoulder. The speakers are vibrating. The music sounds like something emanating from the cadaver-sated tree roots. 'What's the song?'

'"Into the Abyss".' The goth has a strong accent. One of the others says something unintelligible. Russian? Etienne wonders. The disciple with the dog angel on his chest has the longest, thinnest arms Etienne has ever seen.

'So, who's the band?' Etienne asks. The goth-god looks at him as if he is surprised that he can speak.

'The name of the band,' Axel demands too.

'The Sex Gang Children.' The leader smiles defiantly at Axel. He sports a Mohican; his temples are clean-shaven. He is wearing a leather jacket, nothing underneath it: pale skin against leather. Etienne looks at the phalanx of hell soldiers, at their mascara eyes; it looks as if they haven't slept in a long time.

Axel and Etienne clamber over the trunk, walk past them. Etienne can't help looking back. The goths also climb over the trunk, disappear in the opposite direction.

'Russians?'

Axel shakes his head. 'Finns.' His hand is clasping Etienne's upper arm. The excitement in Axel's fingers has nothing to do with Etienne; his shoulder is simply available. He shakes off the hand.

'I like that music,' Etienne says. Not because it is true, but because he is trying to determine Axel's frequency.

'It's goth crap,' Axel says. 'Post-punk cemetery rock.' The music fades away behind them. Axel scrambles over roots, peers into open graves. Whenever Etienne gets close, Axel's skin resists him like a magnet's negative pole.

They walk in circles through the forest of graves – over grass that feeds off human remains, beneath lush cadaver foliage. The distance between them is growing with every loop. They walk past graves and fallen tree trunks that they have passed before. The intensity that has built up between them over the past weeks must find new escape routes, Etienne realises. And yet, the idea of the force field dissipating makes him anxious; he is frenziedly seeking a way to recharge the air between them.

Then he is back, the Finnish goth-Jesus. Right ahead of them, leaning against a tree. A black marble mausoleum would have been more suited, Etienne thinks. He no longer has the boom box with him. The disciples are nowhere to be seen. He is wearing a cross around his neck – filigree metal engraving. Etienne stares at it as the goth takes off his leather jacket and drops it on the grass. Etienne looks at Axel. To him, Etienne no longer exists. He looks back at the goth. Words are tattooed on his left arm – in Finnish? Below these are more tattoos: machines that look like medieval torture equipment.

'What does that say?' Etienne asks, pointing. His heart is fiercely keeping rhythm. The goth looks down lazily at his own arm.

He directs his answer to Axel, as if *he* had asked the question. 'The History of Fucking Machines. Name of my own band in Helsinki.' Etienne stands closer to see better. He wonders whether the complex machines depicted ever existed. They look like something that Axel could build into an installation.

The Finn leisurely takes a little plastic bag from his pocket, dispenses white powder onto his leather jacket, cuts it into three lines with a razorblade. He rolls a banknote, bends down, sniffs a line. Axel does the same, ignoring Etienne. The goth holds out his note towards Etienne. He shakes his head. Axel bends down again; the third line disappears.

Axel throws his head back and opens his mouth, as if sucking energy from the foliage. Then he bites the goth's shoulder, drawing blood. He pushes down his own pants, forces the goth's head to his hips. Etienne looks on; it is all happening fast. The Finn gets rid of his own tight black jeans. He smiles cruelly up at Etienne, reaches out and loosens his belt too. The Finn's hand is as transparent as fjord ice. He spits milky saliva onto Etienne's penis. On his right forearm, Etienne notices, a swastika is tattooed. Small and precisely drawn. Etienne starts, ejaculates. Axel reaches for the semen running down the goth's shoulder, licks it from his fingers like beestings. *Brutal calf* are the words entering Etienne's mind. Axel and the goth simultaneously stare at him. Did he say it out loud? Yes,

94

he realises, and in Afrikaans. *Brutale kalf.* The sounds are still hanging; the death foliage keeps holding the hard *r* in *brutale*, like a long note. The Nordic goth ejaculates too, spurred on by the incomprehensible words.

Etienne pulls up his trousers, starts walking away. He is trembling. He can hear a muffled exchange between Axel and the Finn behind him. Etienne is convinced he briefly saw a blue-black heart beating behind the Finn's ribs: a fist aiming to break through the sternum. He has been dragged into someone else's dark vision, Etienne thinks: a menacing addition to his Blake images.

Axel catches up with Etienne. His tread is now less furious, less certain than before. Neither of them utters a word. Etienne's throat is itching; his feet are growing heavier. There was poison in the Finn's spittle. It is seeping through his skin, starting to circulate.

On their way back to the station they stop in front of an empty Georgian house. Axel takes Etienne by the arm; he pulls away. The pointing is crumbling, the wooden window frames are as dry as bone. They press their faces against panes, hands shading their eyes: bare walls and wooden floors, all in washed-out grey. Axel stands back, looks up. He is assessing it for studio space, Etienne knows, plotting the trajectory of the sun relative to the upper floors' windows.

Axel tries to take Etienne's hand. Etienne slackens his fingers; Axel lets go. They walk around the house. There is an unusual silence in this house, Etienne thinks: the inverse of the sounds of birth and death. And then there they are in the back garden: the goths, their lower bodies bisected by waist-length grass. Everybody stops in their tracks. Like two sets of purchasers at a show house, Etienne thinks, on the verge of making competing offers. Only the estate agent is missing.

Etienne turns on his heels, walks back to the street. It is getting colder; he turns up his collar. When he is close to the train station, he looks back. Axel is on his heels, the goths on his. 'They are following us,' Etienne says. Axel shrugs. 'Perhaps,' Etienne continues, 'you should move into that house with them. With the Finnish Jesus and his entourage. A perfect little family.'

'Fuck you,' Axel says. There is the rumbling of thunder; they look up. The sky is aubergine-coloured.

They get off at London Bridge station, walk to Bermondsey Street in silence. The goths weren't on the same train. Even so, Etienne keeps looking back. He is dragging his feet, slowing down as they approach the house.

Chapter 13

THE AFTERNOON LIGHT has green and purple tints. The well is breathing poison, which is rising and forming a dome over the city. The City's buildings are gleaming coldly. On the roof in Bermondsey Street, Axel is looking bewildered. They are sitting close to the edge, pedestrians passing below. Axel rests his head in Etienne's lap. He pushes Axel away, gets up and kicks a dead bird in an arc into the street.

Etienne starts pacing back and forth. His chest is feeling pinched; there are pins and needles in his fingers – the toxic Finnish saliva, no doubt. Somewhere beneath Axel and himself, tectonic plates have shifted. Etienne wants to shout out words that smell of sulphur, recriminations that would further disrupt the landscape between them.

Axel takes Etienne by the shoulders, forces him to a halt. He looks Etienne in the eye. He is trying to measure the seismic activity in my chest, Etienne thinks. He turns away. *I am going now*, he wants to say. *And I'm not coming back*.

Just as he opens his mouth, there is a ruckus in the street. A dog running at frenetic speed. Just ahead of him, a city fox – one of those that live under hedges – is tearing down the street. The dog has an awkward run: half-cripple, nose on the ground. He storms straight into a lamp post, before finding the scent again and charging off. The distance between dog and fox increases. They disappear around a corner.

'Foxes,' Axel says. 'So quiet and slight, always on the margins of one's consciousness. Until, that is, they start wailing in the mating season . . .' Copulating foxes: *that* explains the howling he sometimes hears in the community garden at night, Etienne realises.

'Sometimes they become stuck,' says Axel. 'During mating. Then they keep standing like that for hours, their backsides attached, trying to pull apart. They become frantic, nails digging in – conjoined twins who must tear apart, even if it kills them.' Etienne looks at a train rumbling over the viaduct into London Bridge station.

I'm leaving now, he wants to say. Axel is too quick: 'But then, at times, they just stand there, as if nothing's amiss. A meek double-headed animal. But they always ultimately escape each other.'

A commotion behind the house. They move to the other side of the roof. In the alleyway behind the backyard, the fox has become trapped. The dog jumps at the fox, but he miscalculates, hits a wall. His skull smacks against the bricks; he drops to the ground. The fox slips away.

I'm going, Etienne finally wants to say. What emerges is: 'What's wrong? Why does the dog hurt itself so badly?'

'He hangs around here. Indiscriminately chases foxes and rats. Completely fucking deaf and blind. Have a look at his eyes when he comes around again. And his scores of old injuries. Broke a leg once, then lay down in the tunnel for weeks on end. Crawled into the electrical substation, among the live cables. I sent some of the guys to splint the leg. To feed him, take him water. Until the leg healed, albeit crookedly. Then he crawled out, started all over again . . .' Etienne looks at the dog, still motionless. There is blood on his jaw. The fox has long since found a safe hollow somewhere. Etienne regrets not having his camera. It could have made a closing scene for his film – perhaps he can still add a scene.

Axel turns towards Etienne. 'Stay over,' he says. 'Stay with me tonight.' There is dread in his voice.

'You knew they were going to be there, didn't you? In the cemetery. The Finn with his disciples.' The depth of rage in Etienne's own voice startles him. He ignores the remorse in Axel's eyes. 'You knew he'd be there. You went there to meet him.' Axel doesn't reply. 'And, while we're at it, why don't you tell me where you go at night when you're not at the hospital?'

Axel remains mute. 'I have to go now,' Etienne says and lowers himself through the hatch. From the studio he looks up at the rectangle of light. He walks down the stairs, out the front door. Axel doesn't call him back. Is he standing on the roof, his toes curling around the edge? Etienne doesn't look back when he walks down Bermondsey Street. To this house he will never return.

Etienne stops at the Tavern, downs a few beers. Before he knows it, he is in a street near the Square. It is almost dark. He looks at his watch: he has lost two hours. Did he encounter Jimmy Somerville again? Did they slip their tongues into each other's cheeks? The Finnish poison is warping time, he thinks. He conjures up a picture of the narrow-torsoed goth. Like an animal with fatal bacteria in its mouth. Etienne's clothes smell of smoke and stale beer. He is seeing himself through a lens, angled at a Dutch tilt. He is feeling nauseous, bruised. Under his clothes, black-green blots are forming, of that he is certain. Necrosis. Or sepsis. He lifts up his shirt under a street light. The skin underneath the trail of hair descending from his navel looks pink and healthy.

He carefully walks further, doubting the ground underneath his feet. In the Square he first sees the back of No. 52, across the community garden. There is light in his bedroom window. How strange: he left in the daylight hours; no lights were left on. He walks around, goes up the stairs. Patrick's door is open. He shrugs. 'Sorry, mate, I couldn't prevent it. I'm not the owner – no one is. So it goes . . .' Etienne frowns, ascends the next flight of stairs.

Music is sounding from his room: The Sex Gang Children. Outside the door, on the small landing, his drums have been dropped in a pile. And his clothes.

Etienne opens the door. Inside are the Finns. All five of them.

'What the fuck?'

The chieftain, the Nordic goth-Jesus, walks right up to Etienne. He places a soft palm against Etienne's cheek. 'We're living here now,' he says. 'Time for you to go elsewhere.'

'What do you mean?' He slaps the hand away. 'It's *my* place. *My* stuff.' He gestures towards the drums and clothes on the landing. (Certainly not all his clothes. Where are the rest?) The bedding has apparently been appropriated. So too the television, videocassette recorder and records.

The Finn smiles patronisingly. Etienne wants to crush his gaunt face. 'Your place?' He shakes his head. 'You sound like someone from a different world, friend.'

The accent hurts Etienne's ears. The mumbled vowels, the slippery consonants. And he is not this man's friend. He wants to enter, but the thin arm is blocking his way. 'Go and talk to your friend,' the Finnish Jesus says. 'The one whose seed I drank today, whose saliva I can still taste. Ask him. He gave me this address; he let us have the place.'

'Let you *have* it? Do you think Axel is the master of housing in this city? Or in your weird fucking sub-world? In never-never land, where everyone wears black?' The Finn's irises are phosphorescent green. His friends are gathering around him. What an absurd little gang, Etienne thinks. Like the youngsters in the film *Children of the Damned*. Unstoppable, as chilly as the North Pole. Eyes glassy, bones as brittle as ice.

'Property,' the Finn says and slowly shakes his head. 'The root of all evil. Of all injustice and oppression. There is room for you at your friend's. Don't leave those who are lost out in the cold, let the children come to—'

Etienne laughs scornfully. 'Don't even bother with the pseudo-Biblical nonsense. Really. Where I come from, I got more of that crap than I could digest in a lifetime. And even that was more convincing, the church-picnic nonsense of my youth.' All of this he says in Afrikaans. He has made his calculations: he will, for now, have to back off. 'I'll be back,' he says in English. 'I'll be back.' He lets some steam out of his voice: 'Just give me the letters. Please. My mother's letters. Two piles under the bed.' The Fin wavers for a moment, then brings him the envelopes. Etienne points at the storyboards on the walls. "That too." The Fin's eyes glow; he turns around and rips off the pictures. One gets a long tear. He presses them against Etienne's chest.

Etienne takes them, retreats. The Fin closes the door. The music has fallen silent. Etienne slips the storyboards under his shirt, where they are safe against his stomach. He looks down the stairs. Patrick's marijuana clouds are drifting up; he is peering out into the corridor. When Etienne calls his name, he slams his door.

He goes to No. 42, knocks. Glenda opens the door. He tells her what has happened. She shrugs. 'That's how it goes.' She looks impatient. He can smell something on the stove. Green peppers and onions, cloves and basil. A vegetarian stew? He is waiting for her to invite him in, give him an apron so that he may help her cook. He wants her to ask him to stay for dinner, offer him a sofa for the night. And, tomorrow morning over breakfast, to ask him to move in. Etienne looks over Glenda's shoulder, towards the afternoon glow in the rooms behind her. Hilde asks a question from inside. 'It's no one,' Glenda says over her shoulder. 'Just the guy who used to live in No. 52.' She turns back to Etienne. 'I have to go.' She starts closing the door.

'A bag,' he says through the crack. 'Please. For my clothes. Just a supermarket bag.'

'We don't keep plastic bags.'

He wedges his foot in the door. He wants to enter, wants to sit down in the warm light. Wants to hear Hilde's stories over a steaming plate of food. Or the stories she ought to be telling. About hunting lodges, bison heads and reindeer horns mounted on walls, valleys shrouded in fog, snowy peaks in the winter sun, musty rooms, oil lamps glimmering behind heavy curtains, mouldering brocade, tables with silver service. Later, over coffee, Glenda would have to tell the story of the Square again. Of the early days, when they had to tame it, carve domesticity from the rubble. Stories about resistance and protest, love and familiarity. About the oases of inner thighs and cheeks. About the vegetables grown in stolen gardens and the music they have heard over the years . . .

She looks down at his foot in the door, lets go. 'Wait here.'

She disappears, brings back a dirty cotton bag. He removes his foot; she closes the door. He hovers around, looking at the ivy snaking up walls. He walks around aimlessly, peering into windows, lingering in the shadows. The Square has become lusher since his arrival.

He returns to No. 52. Outside his room, he bundles as many pieces of clothing as he can into the bag. He feels the brittle paper of the storyboards under his shirt, only now realises that he has left the blue file behind at Axel's place in Bermondsey Street. He feels relieved that it is there. There is music behind the closed door. He knocks on Patrick's door. He is on his bed, half-vanished in smoke. 'Can I store my drums with you for a while?' He nods, looks on while Etienne carries his stuff into the room. There are a few new scratch marks on the drums, Etienne notices.

He stands outside Vauxhall station with his bag of clothes, next to the Elephant & Castle pub. Inside the pub, as on every other evening, a drag show is in progress. Gloria Gaynor and Madonna songs are being played behind black windows.

This is how it is when one doesn't have a home, he thinks. He is hardly the first person to experience it. He is feeling calm and clear. Like someone who has been fasting for weeks. He wants to ascribe it to the Finnish goth poison, but he has to admit, at last, that he hasn't really been poisoned. His limbs are still working; his facial muscles aren't paralysed. It feels as if the entire city is made of glass, perfectly transparent. He keeps standing there for a long time, looking at buses lit up like aquariums.

It starts raining. He seeks shelter in the station. Two petite figures halt in front of him. He blinks. Indeed, it is the red-haired twins with whom he once ran naked across the Suffolk hills. How long ago that feels! Their hair has been extinguished; it is now hanging in wet strings from identical woolly hats. They look at him with surly – accusing? – faces. They turn around simultaneously, disappear into the station.

He walks back to the Square. He heads for the fire in No. 37. No one else is there; he lies down on the sofa, under the London night sky, looking at the rain and drifting clouds. The fire sizzles and smokes. Water seeps into the sofa. A few noisy drinkers arrive, come and stand near Etienne. He goes to the room with the community television. The door is locked – the first locked door he has ever encountered in the Square.

He walks out into the rain, crawls under a hedge in the community garden, curls up around the bag of clothes. The storyboards rustle and crumple against his stomach. He reckons it might be warmer in the electrical substation in the Bermondsey Street tunnel. Perhaps he should go and join the blind dog there. Just before he falls asleep, a skittish fox sniffs his head.

He washes his face at a leaking fire hydrant. When he looks up, the goth leader is standing on the flat roof outside his old room. He is stark naked and white as paper. Hairless, androgynous. He is slowly rubbing cream into his thighs, looking down impassively at Etienne.

Etienne heads to the station, takes the Underground to Kilburn. In Kilburn High Street he stops at a shop window. Old-fashioned trinkets: sherry glasses, pillboxes, napkin rings. He will never have a house where a patina accretes on such things. Even his drums can rot away; he won't care. Perhaps he thinks, he should start collecting useless things: locks for which there are no longer keys, old tresses of hair in satin boxes without discernible owners, the cufflinks of strangers' dead grandfathers . . .

His reflection shifts over a silver male grooming set. It reminds him of a Christmas from his childhood. He had bought his father a set containing a shaving brush, aftershave and cologne. It had cost more than his pocket money, but the scent had convinced him, and his mother had contributed some money. The wrapping was messy, even though he had done his best, and had started over twice. His father frowned when he opened it, and looked over his glasses, like a diagnosing physician. 'Real men,' his father said, 'do not rub perfume all over themselves.' He kept shaking his head. 'This is not a gift one man gives to another.'

Later, Etienne tore the model planes that he and his father had once built together from the fishing lines hanging from his bedroom ceiling. He looked at the oozing mess of glue where he had attached wings, and at the perfectly smooth joints where his father had glued bombs and rockets. He first broke off the wings, then crushed all of them under his heel and kicked the pieces under his bed. When he lay under the sheets, he thought: I am not even a man. Not yet.

The next morning the maid had to crawl under the bed to retrieve the plastic shards. His mother threw them on the compost heap, where his father wouldn't find them. In the kitchen, she took Etienne by the elbow and whispered: 'Last night, before we went to bed, he opened the cologne and smelled it. A few times.'

He pulled away. 'I don't care.'

He walks on, stops in front of Miss Jackson's door. This time she receives him in the lounge. She is wearing tights and leg warmers (just back from aerobics?). And a synthetic camisole, one strap slipping from her shoulder. She folds her legs under her on the sofa. It is just after nine in the morning. She is sipping from a glass of wine, doesn't offer Etienne anything.

Etienne drops his bag of clothes on the floor, sits down. She lights a cigarette, picks tobacco fragments from her tongue. She studies the bits on a fingertip, her mouth turned down.

Etienne looks at his cold fingers. 'I wanted to ask: has a room by any chance opened up here yet?' He looks her in the eye. She is lazily blowing smoke sideways, looking half-bored, half-amused. His jaws tense up. 'I don't mind sharing a room.' Her eyes are blurring in the smoke. 'Even with yourself.' Whether she is considering or ignoring the request is briefly unclear. Then she shakes her head almost invisibly.

He gets up and walks out the front door. His cheeks are burning. When he is some distance down the street, he hears someone behind him. 'Etienne, wait!' He stops. Brent. His pushy mentor in matters of the conscience. 'Wait,' Brent says again when he reaches Etienne, even though Etienne is already waiting. Brent is panting, stooped over with his hand on his knees. Too unfit to run even one block. 'Let me buy you a cup of tea,' he says. Etienne allows himself to be dragged along by the arm. They go to the greasy spoon where they went before. The place smells of cooking oil and disinfectant. For the first time since the previous day, Etienne starts warming up.

The moment Brent starts talking, Etienne regrets coming along. The same old story. About the Struggle, the injustices, the freedom that is just around the corner for South Africa. Brent's head angles forward like a tortoise's. 'Do you have any idea of the suffering of black South Africans? Of the kind of lives they lead in townships, on farms, in factories and mines? The worthlessness of black bodies? Does it perturb you at *all*? How can you simply detach yourself? As if it has nothing to do with you?'

'You want to add *as if you have no conscience.*' Etienne looks down at his muddy T-shirt. This is the worst he has ever had to suffer: a single cold night without a bed. Of real struggle and suffering he understands nothing. This he knows well.

Brent is now looking at the mud stains as well. 'Yes,' he says, 'as if you have no conscience. How can you simply expel that country from your system, like shit? You're making an historical error, Etienne. One day you'll be denounced as a traitor. As one of the enemy. History will leave you behind.' It is the first time that Brent has addressed him by his name. He feels unexpectedly moved. And then annoyed *because* he is feeling moved.

He looks Brent in the eye, searching his own thoughts. 'South Africa washes over me like a cold river on a strange continent.' He slurps milky tea through numb lips. 'I'm a stranger to that country. That place and her brutality have nothing to do with me. To give it up, to disown it – that is also something. It is also "no".' He sips more tea, sits back. 'That's the best I can do for you, Brent.'

'My need for an explanation is not the point. That's not what this is about.' Accusation has drained from his voice. For the first time they are sitting opposite each other as true fellow countrymen. Brent unfolds his arms. 'You can stay with me for a while.' He looks down at Etienne's shirt again. 'Until you find somewhere else to sleep.' A lair, Etienne thinks, like an animal in the veld.

Brent sits back, wringing his hands. 'You have to understand that my attempts to recruit you are all about *your* conscience, the welfare of *your* soul.'

Enough, Etienne thinks. He pushes his chair back, picks up his bag of clothes. 'I'm perfectly fine, thanks. And I have a refuge.'

It is raining again. When Etienne descends into the Tube station, he thinks of the word 'refuge', of the load it carries. He compares it to the weight of the bag of clothes in his right hand. He is feeling light on his feet. And giddy in the head.

'How dare you? Who are you? What do you want from me?' Etienne shouts when Axel opens the door in Bermondsey Street. He is rain-soaked, and angrier than he could have predicted. The bag of clothes is shaking in his hand.

Axel smiles like a blind dog. 'Welcome,' he says. 'Welcome to my lair.' He stands aside.

Where else, Etienne thinks, would there be a bed for him in this city of cold surfaces? He crosses the threshold. Axel leads him upstairs. Only in the dim interior does he realise that he left his Blake book behind in the Square. It now belongs to the Finnish goths. Insofar as anything belongs to anyone.

Chapter 14

THE GERMAN IN Irmgard's journal is now decoding itself right in front of his eyes. The sentences simply open up. He hardly needs Axel's help any more.

They move from location to location, Irmgard writes in October. They are moving deeper and deeper underground. From the small sound film studio where they started, to empty industrial sites, then to flats belonging to members of the film team. They hardly ever shoot twice in the same place. One evening they film in a former pornographic studio. The next day in a Nachtlokal where, until a year or so before, women used to box naked in front of audiences. Everywhere they black out the windows. *Thank God for the portable Bolex camera! Irmgard writes. To be carrying around those Bell & Howell coffins now would have been a nightmare!* Outside scenes are the most dangerous, she writes on 19 October. For these they have to slink through the icy streets in the morning hours, *cloths draped over our equipment like crape. Always just a step away from being arrested.*

In mid-November there are secret negotiations with contacts at commercial studios to print the first two – hastily edited – reels and make copies. In the meantime the filming is steaming ahead. Unexpectedly a former cabaret theatre is made available.

For an entire week's filming! Ariel has been here before. The impresario back then was one Lowinsky. Only the

*most talentless individuals would participate in his cabaret
– the Kabarett der Namenlosen. Ariel recounts: singing
housewives, hypnotists who would fail to bring volunteers
out of their trances, schizophrenic dilettantes . . . Only the
most pathetic candidates would be encouraged. Lowinsky
would heckle his drunk audiences. 'Jüdischer Narr!' they
would snarl back. The place has been standing empty since
the Nazis closed it. The sound of sneering and cackling
still swirls in the corners . . .*

At dusk Irmgard and Ariel go for wary strolls in the Tiergarten.

*I feel Ariel's heat next to me. And cold currents from
elsewhere. The air is polluted: one can smell wolves . . .*

They dare to go and see a film at the Titania-Palast cinema
in Steglitz-Zehlendorf. For a change, it's not showing a propaganda film.

*My feet are wobbling on the cobblestones outside the
cinema. Ariel's grip bruises my arm. We enter. I feel the
chair's velvet against my neck, Ariel's breath beside me.*

*Ariel describes the ceiling: brightly lit ridges in rhyth-
mic arches. 'Like ribs,' he says. 'If the theatre were a chest,
we are where the heart should be.' He puts his hand on
mine; the film starts. He describes everything in my ear:
each camera angle, each frame.*

A voice from behind: 'Shut up, Jew!' Ariel freezes; so do I.

*'Raus!' a voice says. Out! Another voice, louder: 'Raus!'
A heckling choir, now.*

We get up; I cling to the back of Ariel's shirt. People

hiss when we push past them. I feel an insect against my cheek. It drips down: spittle.

'Chont!' someone shouts at me. From a different direction: 'Kontroll-Girl!' Ariel steers me. Only when we are outside in the street do his fingers start trembling; he disentangles them from mine.

After a long search in the Goldsmiths library, Etienne establishes that the Yiddish word *Chont* refers to a low-class Jewish prostitute. *Kontroll-Girls* were government-regulated prostitutes, also known as Bone-Crackers or Railway-Girls.

Etienne wakes up around midnight. Axel isn't next to him. Abducted by the ghost boys, is his first sleepy thought. He gets up, heads upstairs to the studio. Axel no longer tolerates the crowds who used to drift through this place; the house is empty. Amid the detritus of the previous installation – drawing pins and fragments of photographs – the new project is awaiting completion underneath a sheet. Etienne ascends the ladder, exits through the open hatch.

Axel looks around with a start from where he is sitting on the roof's edge in the chilly night air. Etienne squats some distance away, as if approaching a wild animal. After a while, Axel comes closer, rests his head on Etienne's lap. Etienne places a hand on Axel's shaved temple, stubble like a scorched savannah under his palm. He feels something warm and damp on his upper leg. It confuses him; tears are not what he wants from Axel. 'Let's go for a walk,' Etienne says.

They put on extra pullovers, go out. They cross London Bridge. Etienne looks furtively at Axel against the glimmering water, trying to imagine scenes from Axel's childhood. A boy with a school satchel on a train, next to his mother. She leans over to him, whispers in his ear. The child's shoulders droop, the weight of her sentences pushing him down into the seat. Or behind his father's back on a city bicycle. The lines of rubber tyres cross in fresh snow. The father is silent, cap pulled down over his eyes. The child is looking down, letting the tip of his shoe whirr against the spokes.

This is the first time Etienne has ever been in the City. They walk past blind buildings enveloped in glass sheaths reflecting stone churches. Past porticoes of limestone. Except for security guards pacing in overlit glass lobbies, all is still. They linger in a narrow street. The weighty concrete of the Barbican towers above them. Next to them are the remains of the city's Roman walls.

Axel's sinews are taut; electricity is sparking down them. His body is hunching, as if in pain. Etienne feels Axel's pulse, then his temperature. Etienne looks away. He forgives Axel for that afternoon in Nunhead. And anything and everything else. They can cross the river again. He will crawl into bed behind Axel. Black rain will fall on the roof. Their pores will open; their skins will exchange messages through the night.

Etienne places classified advertisements in community papers – an appeal for information about *Berliner Chronik*. He lists the names of the film production team. Bösel the cameraman, Schwarz the lighting technician. Smaller papers place his advertisement for free. To the larger papers, who charge a fee, he sends a shorter version. He traverses the city, posts notices in art cinemas. And on community noticeboards. The Square's, as well as in Camberwell, Southwark, Kilburn, Chelsea, Notting Hill and Islington.

The more he struggles with technical subjects, the harder he tries to find *Berliner Chronik*'s trail. His fellow students in the lost continental films seminar just shake their heads when he reports on his project. 'My search efforts may look amateurish,' he says, 'but it's only a starting point.' It isn't even *that*, his sceptical fellow students' expressions suggest.

The lecturer smiles condescendingly. 'Don't spend too much time on this. Look how little success the British Film Institute has had in uncovering lost films. And that despite their funds and reach . . .'

'There are so many documentaries demanding to be made,' a feminist student explodes. 'So many urgent issues. For God's sake, do something useful!'

Etienne is unfazed. He writes to the London family registry, as well as the Genealogical and Biographical Society in New York. Most Jewish escapees from Europe would have ended up in these cities. He lists actors and production team members, requesting information about descendants. And, if possible, extracts from immigration records of the '30s or early '40s in which these names appear. He also writes to the archives in West Berlin.

Axel wakes Etienne up early. He is heading to the hospital for a double shift.

'I need your help.'

'In the hospital?' Etienne is only half-awake. His lips are numb, his eyes scratchy. A garbage truck is making a racket in Bermondsey Street.

'With my project.' His finger points to the attic. 'I need to get it going again.' Axel takes Etienne's hand, presses it against his own chest. The agile torso of a fox. 'Meet me at eleven tonight at St Thomas. We'll be harvesting material.'

Etienne crosses Westminster Bridge on his way from the Tube station. Below him the currents pass violently and without a sound. Axel is awaiting him at the hospital reception. He takes him into a dressing room, gives him hospital garb to wear. 'Is this allowed?' Axel doesn't respond. He takes Etienne into the paediatric section. A senior nurse observes them from behind a counter.

They walk down the corridor. It is after bedtime; there is dim night lighting in the wards. Machines peep and flicker. Axel indicates that Etienne should put on his protective mask. He first breathes in deeply, as if the mask will smother him. They walk past a closed door: *Intensive Care*. Outside a second door – *Burns Unit* – they stop. Axel takes something from his pocket. The light is low; Etienne brings his face closer.

'Pigeon feathers? What's that for?'

'Shh.' Axel peers down the corridor. 'You'll see.'

There are a dozen beds in each ward, six on each side. 'Wait,' Axel says at the door. He enters on his own, moves from bed to bed. He studies the patients and – so it seems in the gloom – rummages through patient files. Sterile silence governs here, like in a vacuum or outer space. There are only the sucking noises of Axel's rubber soles on the vinyl floor.

He returns to Etienne. 'Tonight we're collecting hair samples.'

'Hair?'

'Cut just enough off each head so that it's not visible. I've marked them: just harvest from each patient on whose feet I've left a feather.'

Etienne frowns. Axel gives him a sealable plastic bag and scissors. The blades' surgical steel is cool against his palm.

Axel walks down one wall, Etienne down the other. On Etienne's side there are four feathers. He is jumpy. The little sleeping figures' breathing is shallow. They are swathed in bandages. He observes Axel, carefully snipping off locks. He does the same, keeping the sharp points away from the thin skin, the smell of disinfectant in his nostrils. The patients have been rubbed from head to toe with ointment. Where the skin isn't bandaged, it is shining like roast lamb.

When they are done, Axel collects the feathers. Outside, in the bright corridor, he studies the plastic bags, shakes his head. 'I need more.'

Axel holds a finger to his lips. They go into the intensive care section. More peeping and flickering. Axel scans through files again, leaves feathers on seven beds. The harvesting continues. While Etienne is cutting hair off the last little patient, the door opens. He drops the strand on the sheet, grabs it in a reflex movement, folds it in his palm.

It is the senior nurse. She looks at them in silence, closes the door again. He slips the lock of hair into his pocket.

In the corridor Axel takes Etienne by the wrist, presses his finger against Etienne's lips. He folds Etienne's hand tightly around the scissors, points the blades to yet another door. It is too dark to see the sign on it. Etienne's eyebrows curve into a question. 'Just you this time,' Axel whispers. It is a blind mission, Etienne realises, like those on which Axel used to send his Bermondsey Street assistants. *I'm neither your disciple, nor your assistant*, Etienne wants to say. Axel gently pushes him forward.

With his hand on the door handle, he looks around. He

is curious, and he does want to please Axel. Axel retreats, disappears in the gloom. Etienne goes in. There are rows of lit glass cases on either side. And, in each, a premature baby not much larger than a man's palm. Half-formed, unprotected. Skin that would tear if touched. He recoils. He wants to flee, but something is compelling him. He holds his breath, reaches with the scissors into the warmth of one of the incubators. His hands are trembling; the blades are longer than the child itself. There are downy hairs on the head, a fuzz growing around the shoulders. He closes his eyes, snips. Snips again. When he opens his eyes, there is nothing. The down is too fine.

He looks around, finds a pair of nail scissors on a steel tray. He reaches in again, cuts, closer to the skin this time. A few strands of blonde hair fall onto the sheet, next to the little misshapen ear. He picks them up. They look like the sea silk that Etienne once read about in the *Children's Encyclopaedia*, the golden filaments with which mussels attach themselves to rocks. Then he is out in the corridor.

They walk through the hospital. The hospital gown is cool and loose, too large for Etienne. Now that he has the hair samples, he feels free, almost naked; the cotton sleeves sweep and whistle. He observes actual nurses in the corridors, then looks down at himself, the imposter. It isn't in fact an ordinary nurse's outfit, he realises. Perhaps a theatre gown. Or a surgeon's operating garb. He imagines the gown under ultraviolet light, showing the traces of years of procedures: stain upon stain, soaked into the deepest fibres. The fluids of operations and amputations, of transplants and tumour removals.

Axel pulls him into a dim space. A tea room. There is the hum of electricity. Scattered tables and chairs, all stackable or foldable. The lights are off. Beyond wide glass panels he sees the river and the brightly lit parliament building. Light is reflecting off the water, creating patterns on the walls and ceiling. They stand opposite each other, water and light playing on their faces. Etienne solemnly hands over his sealed bag of hair.

He wants to ask Axel what he is planning to do with it. Wants to ask what the meaning of the ritual was, and why he had to come along. Those would be the wrong questions. Where Axel's art is concerned, you are better off playing the obedient apprentice. What he does ask is: 'You select those who are going to die, don't you?'

'One can never be sure who will survive . . .'

The glass and the river and Axel's eyes are shimmering. Beyond this, there are only shadows. Etienne feels sentiment surging, and tears. 'Promise me you'll stay with me,' Etienne says without wanting to, 'when I'm no longer a child. Until I'm old, and tired, and bent double. Until pearls grow over my eyes.' He says it in Afrikaans. The hospital's machines are droning. The river is flowing silently. Etienne thinks of London, of this city of stone. Of the thousands of lovers' promises it has had to absorb without ever being warmed up by even a single degree Celsius.

Axel feels Etienne's collarbone, rests his finger in the indentation beneath his throat. With his own finger Etienne feels Axel's pulse (as regular as a watch). 'You know I can't follow what you're saying,' Axel says. Etienne takes the lock of hair from his pocket, opens Axel's hand, lets go of it.

Chapter 15

AXEL IS WORKING with his hair samples in the attic. Etienne is reading the last pages of Irmgard's diary – that is, the typed text preceding the blank pages at the back. There are no further references to the filming or production process. Nothing about editing or post-production work. Have they abandoned it all?

The entries become chaotic. Typos appear. Dates disappear, then paragraphs. Only dense text remains. Capitals and punctuation – even full stops – ultimately fall away. Irmgard is typing in a frenzy. A stream of thought. They apparently rarely venture outside any more. She refers to candles, oil lamps, light through cracks – all the things she cannot see. *i just wan togo wandering one more time on unter den linden ariel say s if icould see what he sees i'd know ho crazy it is to brave thta lair*

She writes about a secret Brecht performance where the SS showed up. A play for the education of workers. Ariel was there. The SS casually walked in during the performance and sat down in the audience. People fled from their chairs; the SS let them go. The players froze in their tracks, were arrested on the stage. The director too. The small theatre's Jewish owner was dragged away; a cabaret singer was hit in the face with a rifle butt.

Irmgard describes how she and Axel sit through long evenings holding hands, making plans to leave Germany. Then the text just breaks off. In the middle of a sentence. She is writing about menstruation: *i wait for the flow ifeel the tension buildin up the pain in my abdomen thesore joints m y back everything is so tender and ontop of that the w orld is so*

Late November. The semester is almost over. Today Etienne has to listen to his film – *Waking up in Axel's World* – being assessed. If he himself has no confidence in it, how could the experts? It is a cobbling together of fragments, and the arrangement doesn't feel right. He has since thought better of every sequence, has imagined alternative shots and scenes, conceived of cleverer concepts. In his mind he is constantly re-editing.

They are sitting in a small auditorium: Etienne's lecturers for camerawork and cinematography, editing, scriptwriting and directing. And the film theorist. They have already written their report, but have to watch the film with the candidate too. Etienne loads the reel onto the projector. While scenes in the Bermondsey Street house are flickering across the screen, he looks from one to the other. The cinematographer is playing with his beard; the images are reflecting in the editor's glasses. The faces betray little. Etienne looks at the screen, where the lens is zooming in on Axel's back. He is in the tin bath in the kitchen, cigarette in his hand. The oak tree is out of focus. The supple branches ripple along with the sinews.

When the film ends, the theorist gets up to switch on the light. He is moving swiftly and nervously, his fringe falling over one eye, shirt buttoned to the top. Like a veritable New Romantic, an odd style for someone in early middle age. Only the humming of equipment is audible, the vibrations of electrical currents in the walls.

The cinematographer's tone is pedantic, pontificating.

'After Tarkovsky's death, his production manager told an interviewer how, one morning in the '70s, when they were working on *Stalker*, they had to film a scene in a field of grass. The previous evening Tarkovsky had studied the landscape from every conceivable angle. When they started shooting, he jumped up, waving his arms. "Cut, cut."' The cinematographer makes silly waving movements; the theorist frowns. 'Overnight a few wild flowers had started blooming. The assistants had to move sideways through the grass, crablike, so as not to disrupt anything, and pick every last flower. Only then could the shoot continue . . .'

The lesson isn't obvious to Etienne. 'Yes,' the editor says, 'and after all that the material was destroyed in a Soviet library that didn't know how to develop the American Kodak film. Tarkovsky had to start from scratch. He ultimately used five thousand metres of film.' He gestures towards the cinematographer. 'What we're trying to say is: our students have to develop a fine eye. Attention to detail, skill. Perseverance, even obsession. There *is* such a thing as raw talent . . .' A fan starts hissing in the projector. The theorist jumps up, switches the machine off. The editor continues. 'And, yes, there are Americans like Warhol or Bruce LaBruce – or their predecessor Kenneth Anger – who elevate amateurishness to art, but that kind of work has its own context. Our students *have* to apply acquired technique.'

It is the scriptwriter's turn. He is wearing a tweed jacket and black-framed spectacles. 'There is nothing wrong with an instinct for spectacle, but narrative is a better starting place. Or at least show us some patterns. Let me be blunt: you're hardly demonstrating a feeling for story. And the spectacle is hardly something to write home about. Your material is promising, but the parts of your film keep hovering separately. The whole ultimately amounts to less than the sum of the—'

'We've prepared a report with more complete commentary,' the theorist says. He glances quickly at his colleagues, holds out the document towards Etienne. 'Alas, it's not a pass. Back to the camera for you, and to the editing laboratory.'

On his way home on the Underground, Etienne reads the report. First the summary at the end:

> *Although there are therefore interesting choices of material, and a few frames deliver strong images, the student has not absorbed enough basic techniques in the lectures and workshops. The successful images feel like flukes, and do not save the project. The will to acquire technique, and consistently apply same, is a prerequisite. Even taking into account that this is a first attempt, the student is not adequately demonstrating this will.*

An earlier paragraph catches his eye:

> *The student might want to consider the Lumière brothers/ Méliès dichotomy. The focus on truth versus the fantastical, shooting on the scene or in the studio, the documentation of events versus the telling of an engaging story, the camera as witness of true events or the truth-maker of fantasy, truth on the surface as opposed to embedded truth. The student has to place himself in this framework, find his place.*

Axel is awaiting Etienne when he arrives home, report in hand. Axel's eyebrows twist into question marks. He rubs his own knuckles, his fingers intertwining. Etienne just shakes his head. He is surprised to feel emotion welling up. This city is constantly keeping him close to tears these days. He turns away quickly.

'I have something for you,' Axel says. He heads upstairs, pulling Etienne along.

The sheet is still there, with something unknown underneath it. The shape is now regular, though, a rectangle – an item has been removed and is leaning uncovered against a wall. The afternoon light is falling upon it: a painting on a huge canvas. In hyperbolic Blake style, a figure in a radiating robe. A shortened perspective, the angle sharp from below; the viewer is looking into scorching white light. The face in the painting is Etienne's. Chin lifted, the expression haughty. From the skull magnificent ram's horns emerge; they are rubbing against the skies, emitting sparks.

'I didn't know you painted,' is all Etienne says. Many things occur to him while he is looking at his strange likeness. He swallows a sob. I *will stay with you*, he wants to say, among other things, *until you are old, and tired, and bent double. Until pearls grow over your eyes.*

In the film-school library, Etienne takes out a book to read about the production history of *Stalker*. About the precision to which his editing instructor had referred, and the obsession. He reads about how the team filmed in Estonia over long periods, and under difficult circumstances. In old factories, near chemical plants. In a poisoned landscape. Several members of the production team later died of lung cancer, including Tarkovsky himself. Etienne sits reading on the studio floor, underneath the painting of himself as a horned Satan-God. He rests his face against the oil paint. It is still damp, and fragrant.

Axel smells vaguely of death when he comes home. He smiles, touches the paint stain on Etienne's cheek with the back of his hand.

Etienne receives a swift response to his query to the archives in West Berlin. A German bureaucrat points out that many family registers in Germany, particularly those of Jews, were destroyed during the war, or scattered thereafter. Many of those that were preserved ended up in East Germany. This kind of search, where so few facts are known – in essence a name and a year during which the relevant individuals lived in Berlin – is rarely successful.

He hears nothing from the London family registry, but a few days later there is a letter from the New York Genealogical and Biographical Society. *Your information is too limited, and therefore does not enable us to respond in a meaningful way,* writes a blunter American. *Clearly you are searching for a needle in all the haystacks of the world. You need a fine comb rather than a pitchfork. And a thousand years.*

For weeks he has been following up responses to his classified advertisements in community papers. Attention seekers, it turns out every time. Hoaxers, tricksters, swindlers. Individuals who are greedy or bored or disturbed. They try to lead him astray. One woman writes a long letter describing how her grandmother had supposedly acted in such a film, how she herself had watched the film over and over as a child in a terraced house in East London. They arrange to meet for coffee in Holborn; she doesn't turn up. She confesses in a further letter that she does not in fact know anything about the film and had simply wanted to meet Etienne. She watched him waiting in the coffee shop, she writes. She hopes he can forgive her. She is now more sure than ever that divine intervention has brought them together. Over the course of twelve pages she declares her undying love. (The paper is drenched with perfume.) Then there is a man who alleges in a letter that he possesses a full print of *Berliner Chronik*. In fact, he had acted in the film himself! He suggests setting up a treasure hunt for Etienne, with clues hidden all over London and the long-lost film as the prize at the end. Etienne looks at the recent photograph of himself that the man has included. At the earliest, he was born two decades after 1933 . . .

One night he dreams that he is suffering a strange kind of blindness. All he can still see is *Berliner Chronik*, projected in an endless loop on the inside of his lids. These are the only images that he will ever see again, he realises with dream logic, until, one day, they flicker and die with him.

Afternoon, mid-week. Axel is at the hospital. Etienne goes upstairs to the studio. Against his better judgement, he plucks at a corner of the sheet. It crumples at his feet. In front of him is a large glass case. Inside: a cityscape in miniature. The execution here is more detailed, the scale more ambitious, than in the earlier installation using pigeons. There are streets, buildings, train tracks, buses and cars. And human figures this time, instead of birds: tightly woven from hair, like voodoo dolls. Dozens of them – that night in the hospital certainly wasn't Axel's first harvest. The roofs of buildings are, once again, scorched open, as if torched with a flamethrower. Over everything lies a thick layer of ash.

Chapter 16

EARLY DECEMBER. BUILDINGS look brittle, frozen. Streets and pavements sound hollow underfoot. The windows in Bermondsey Street are closed; now the morning fog slips around, rather than through, the house. The gluttonous Dover is being fed with coal; heat rises up to the attic. They arrange the rooms with furniture they collect in the streets. One day Axel comes home with newly purchased bed linen. 'You're becoming domesticated,' Etienne says.

Axel grins. 'Don't be so sure.' But a few days later he brings home a television and videocassette player that he bought second-hand somewhere. At night, they also light wood fires in the fireplaces. They cook together. Soups and stews. Axel prepares heavy southern German dishes. Their thin bodies are growing stronger. On dark evenings they linger in boiling water in the tin bath, washing each other thoroughly.

Etienne is letting his hair grow; it is now touching his shoulders. Axel's is shaved against his scalp every few days. In the evenings Etienne lays his head on Axel's chest, or vice versa. They listen to music, or foxes in the streets. They watch films on video. Or they dress warmly and walk through the city streets for hours. Etienne inhales the cold air deeply, looking at the ice crystals forming in Axel's hair, smiling. Axel doesn't smile, just reaches for Etienne's knuckles every now and then.

When Etienne wakes up, ladybirds are clustering at the window.

In South Africa he had imagined London as a frozen winter landscape. To his surprise, his first few months here felt like eternal summer. An unusual season, everyone told him, we don't usually have such summers in this city. In the meantime there has been a short autumn; now winter has properly arrived. Dull days, low clouds. In his mind, London and long summer days have nevertheless become synonymous, afternoons in which one can unwind in generous light.

This morning, out of the blue, it is warm again, as if summer wants to send a last message. Morning sun is pouring through the window. Axel is still snoring. A few ladybirds crawl through the crack between the window and frame, fly around clumsily, crawl in circles on the sheet. More follow, confused by the seasons, still drunk with summer lust. Perhaps the earth has slipped on its axis, and true north has shifted infinitesimally. Unmeasurable by a compass, but enough to disrupt animal radar: shortly bats will start crashing mid-air, migrating birds will turn around mid-flight and head back north, or kill themselves against wires and masts.

Gradually the bugs start finding their way. They ignore Etienne, aim towards Axel. He is emitting pollen aromas. Or insect pheromone. 'I know only too well,' Etienne says to the little swarm, 'how the signals of that skin can throw you off, how it can meddle with the seasons.' They land on Axel's back, in his hair. Crawl into his sweaty armpits. He stops snoring, shakes his shoulders. The swarm is becoming denser. He sneezes, sits up. Rubs his fingers in his ears, blows bugs from his nose. Spits insects from his mouth, dusts off his shoulder blades.

'Fucking horny ladybirds!' Axel mumbles, stumbling to the bathroom. There is the sound of a thick stream of urine against porcelain. And of brushing and slapping. Are they flying into his hairy groin? Sliding down the gulley between his back muscles? Etienne smiles: he and the ladybirds share a secret.

Axel falls back down on the bed, still sullen and indifferent with sleep. 'Flying terrorists!' he says, looking askance at Etienne. Then Axel yawns. 'By the way, I forgot to mention – yesterday, when you were at film school, someone delivered an envelope for you.'

'Who? Who'd even know I'm here?'

Axel lifts a forearm, shades his eyes against the sun. 'How should I know? Probably one of your stalkers, those loonies responding to your ads. When I got home, it was lying on the threshold. Like a foundling in a basket. It's in the kitchen.'

Etienne scoots down the stairs, finds the letter by the stove. His name is typed on the envelope. The note inside is assembled from individual letters cut from newspaper headings. Ominous, like a threat found on a car windshield by a victim in an American horror film. *VISIT THIS ADRES TODAY AND YOULL FIND SOMETHING THAT INTREST YOU.* An address in SE16 follows. No sender name. He turns the envelope over. Blank. Something falls out, slips under the stove. He bends down, claws it out: a flat key. A bright red ribbon is tied to it.

Upstairs he finds Axel, still in bed, still naked and surly. He shows him the anonymous note, and the key. Axel takes the key, strokes the ribbon. He turns it over once or twice, gives it back, shrugs his shoulders.

'Well, I guess I should go and find out what it's about. And, yes, it's probably some wacko again . . . Coming with me?'

Axel shakes his head. 'Heading to the hospital.'

Etienne hasn't been in Rotherhithe before. On either side of the road, corrugated-iron sheets stretch for several kilometres, forming a narrow, straight corridor parallel to the Thames. He is on a bicycle that someone once left by the well in Bermondsey Street. His lungs are burning. There is no one ahead of him, no one behind him.

He stops, drops the bicycle, peeks through a crack in the corrugated iron. An expanse of barren soil. Etienne has heard other squatters talk about this. Blocks and blocks of social housing have been razed to the ground, ploughed into the soil to make room for private developments. It is Saturday; bulldozers and lorries are standing idle. Cloudlets of dust whirl above the disrupted earth.

He rides on. An abstract trip: a line dividing the road, bicycle wheels singing, grey sky overhead. Except for the flickering ridges of the iron sheets, nothing indicates movement. Everything has fallen away – as if you are coming from nowhere and heading nowhere.

Towards the end, the corrugated-iron plates open up into a circle, surrounding a lonely 1930s block of council flats – the only building still surviving. When he puts down the bicycle, a few frozen ladybirds fall from his clothes. The morning's stolen summer hours are over.

He looks at the address on his ominous note again, feels the key in his pocket and enters the building. On a board there are notices of protest action against the demolition of the building, as well as announcements of meetings. Someone who changes locks for free has posted an advertisement. A yellowed banner reads: *Join the barricade, keep Thatcher's demolition men out!*

As he ascends the stairs, rotting warehouses on the north bank become visible. To the south there is a network of ghost streets where surrounding buildings once stood.

He rings the bell. A young Caribbean man opens the door, his hair woven into neat patterns. Etienne wants to say something, but the man turns and disappears. Etienne enters. It smells of medicine and bodies inside. For a while he stands dithering in a dining room. Figures are moving deeper in; there is whispering.

Etienne walks hesitantly down the corridor, encounters a group of people around a bed. The curtains are drawn. He peers through the bodies. The man under blankets in their midst looks dead. And yet his nose is shielding short, shallow breaths like a falcon's beak.

Etienne leans over to a beautiful black woman in her thirties. 'Who is it?' he whispers.

'How could you not know?' She looks suspicious, as if he could be a Thatcher spy. 'Who are *you*?' The head of the man under the blankets turns a degree or two in their direction.

Etienne takes the anonymous message from his pocket, unfurls it. 'What does *this* mean?'

She takes it, reads. She frowns, whispers loudly: 'How should I know?'

'Who is it?' Etienne asks again, his eyes gesturing to the man on the bed.

She rolls her eyes. 'It is Bernhard, of course. Bernhard Sauer, who led the resistance against the eviction. If you're not a resident or family, what are you doing here?' The others apparently only hear the word 'family'. They open up a tunnel, pushing Etienne gently to the front. The woman follows, her lips against Etienne's ear. She is hardly trying to whisper any longer. 'Why are you here? There is nothing to scavenge here. *Go!* We're all here to show our respect.' She looks around, announcing in a louder voice: 'He's not family, he's an intruder!'

Heads turn towards Etienne. He avoids the gazes. He is now in front, right beside the bag of fluid that is dripping into the man's hand, which is blackened with bruises. The bedside lamp is so bright, it seems as if light is emanating from the patient. The sick man's head turns towards Etienne. He tries opening his eyes; his mouth is gaping. 'Shimmering days,' he manages to utter. 'And nights as black as wine.' Or that is what Etienne hears.

Etienne starts retreating. For a brief moment he was family; now hostility is spreading like a virus. He can feel it in the skins brushing against him. Are the grieving inclined to violence? The bodies are working him from the circle, closing in a cordon around the bed. He hesitates at the bedroom door. Through the bodies he can see the old man's lips moving, as if tasting something for the last time. Someone is massaging his temples; another places a palm upon his chest. 'A bruising of shadows . . .' are Sauer's last words, or the last words Etienne thinks he hears before slipping out.

In the dining room he stops in his tracks. A prominent silver lock is fastened to the handle of a sideboard, a red ribbon tied to it. Etienne takes the key from his pocket: the ribbon is identical. His breathing quickens. He looks back down the corridor, then approaches and puts the key in the lock. It turns; the locks opens. In front of him, when the door opens, it is there, and unmistakable: a steel film case. His heart starts hammering. He looks over his shoulder, back to where loud sobs are now sounding. He grabs the case, rushes outside. He runs down the stairs, gets on the bicycle.

Between the corrugated-iron plates, he pedals as fast as he can. He doesn't encounter anyone before he is back in London's ordinary streets. The steel container under his arm is cool against his ribs. Thatcher's barren fields lie behind him.

Etienne heads straight to the hospital, where Axel is. But when he reaches the abandoned Bankside power station, he can wait no longer. He drops the bicycle, opens the case, pulls out a section of the film and holds it against the light.

At the hospital he storms into the reception and insists that Axel be called. The receptionist stares at the weathered round steel case as if it might be infected with flesh-eating bacteria.

'You have to *come*,' he says to Axel. 'Home. *Now*. I have your grandmother's film. *How* I don't know, but I *have* it. Part of it, at least. One reel . . .'

Axel looks laconic in his stained uniform. 'To do with that crank letter of yesterday, I presume. And you reckon it's the real thing?'

Etienne gets his breath back. 'I looked. On the way here. After just a few frames I knew . . .'

'And how did you imagine we were going to project it?' In his excitement it has escaped Etienne that they don't have a projector. He looks down sheepishly at the reel. Axel smiles, continues: 'Not really my grandmother's film, by the way – she wouldn't even have been able to see it. I have to complete my shift first. And find us a projector . . .' Axel is leaning against the reception counter. 'Tell me, before I go, did you find it or did you have to steal it?'

Etienne suddenly feels as ashamed as he had last felt in South Africa. Stolen, yes. From a dying man.

Later that night Etienne tells Axel about the narrow escape he had with the strange little crowd around the dying Sauer's bed, about the key ribbon that matched the lock's. Axel frowns, looks concerned when he tells him about the grievers. 'I wonder whether your anonymous source had really intended that you should encounter *that* bunch . . .'

The next day Etienne borrows a projector from the film school. He and Axel set it up in the Bermondsey Street back-yard, aim it at a white wall. The light fans out over the well like a megaphone. Steam rises through the bright beam.

Will it be the masterpiece he has hoped for? A revolutionary work, given the technological limitations of the time, one that would have recast the history of film? Will it be worth his hungry flights of fancy?

These are the wrong questions, Etienne realises. *Any* questions are redundant. He can only empty his thoughts while watching. And be hypnotised slowly.

The quality of the print isn't good; the film has decayed. The screen flickers, sometimes turns black, then flashes white before the image returns. There is an underlying droning sound on the warped soundtrack, a dissonance that one feels on one's skin rather than in the inner ear.

The film starts with an aerial shot of Berlin. Irmgard's diary says nothing of a plane or aerial shots, and they wouldn't have been able to afford those anyway; it must be material from elsewhere. Probably, Etienne thinks, from a newsreel.

Then feathery clouds appear. Berlin becomes hazy, then disappears behind the clouds. The droning isn't that of an aeroplane engine. It is a soundtrack of avant-garde music.

Violins and cellos, sometimes a hoarse trumpet. A mystery, Etienne thinks. He doesn't remember Irmgard's diary saying anything about music . . .

Each sequence is preceded by a title frame. The first is *Wintermorgen* (Winter Morning): a shadowy room, a maid entering to light the fire and push an apple into the stove. Close-up: a young boy's nose wrinkling under the blanket. In the next sequence, entitled *Das Telefon* (The Telephone), the camera moves through a dark Berlin flat (how smoothly the dolly glides, as if on ice). The viewer starts when a phone starts ringing tremulously in an ultra close-up. *Schmetterlingsjagd* (Butterfly Hunt) works with lengthy shots in tall grass: the perspective of a child running with a butterfly net.

There are double exposures, frames shifting over each other, scenes bleeding into one another. Often, slow motion. 'Where,' Etienne asks rhetorically, 'were they hoping to ever find an audience for such dreamy material? In a time of silly slapstick and stylised melodrama? And in 1930s Germany . . . ?'

Etienne stands up, enters the projector's flood of long-lost light with his eyes closed. Axel joins him, folding his arms around Etienne. A few stray snowflakes drift down and settle on their foreheads.

Chapter 17

ETIENNE KNOWS HE should be depositing the reel of *Berliner Chronik* somewhere safe. It should be preserved in archival conditions. At the BFI, for instance. But he cannot bring himself to do it. He considers returning to the flat in the barren lands of Rotherhithe – who knows, perhaps the rest of the film is there too. He doesn't dare, thief that he is. And Bernhard Sauer – whoever he may be – must have died shortly after his departure, or even before he left. By this time, the flat must have been vacated; perhaps the entire building has been demolished. Also, his fervour for finding the rest of the film has subsided somewhat; he is breathing more easily.

Axel rarely works at the hospital any more. Most of the time he is busy in the attic. Etienne finds the shuffling and knocking noises overhead calming. He still attends his film-school classes, but his confidence is low. His smaller practical projects are all failures. And over the next two semesters he will have to make two more films. He is expecting a high mark for his lost continental films seminar. But how he will pass the year overall, he doesn't know.

A telegram arrives for Axel. He reads it, then goes out to make a telephone call from a public phone. When he returns, he is pale and distracted. His lips are thin, his neck muscles tense.

'I'm on my way,' is all he says. He hardly looks at Etienne.

'What do you mean? Where to?' Axel shrugs off the questions. Etienne swallows. 'When? Can I come?'

'There are things I have to do alone.' Axel is distant; the closeness of the last few weeks suddenly seems inconceivable.

It takes Etienne a long time to fall asleep that night. In the early hours Axel presses himself against Etienne's back, wakes him up. Etienne knows the ghost boys are listening from behind the wallpaper, their breath breezing coolly through the room. He pulls the blanket up to his chin. 'It's my mother . . .' Axel says and swallows. 'I'll tell you more later. But you do have to come with me.'

Etienne's head is still thick with sleep. 'What's going on, Axel?'

'Come with me. Just come with me.' Etienne hasn't heard such urgency in Axel's voice before.

'My situation, Axel . . . I can't just . . .' His mouth tastes of city rain. 'Explain to me what's going on, then I can—'

Axel turns on his back. 'I thought you wanted to come. You said so. Just last night . . .'

'And I *do*. But you're keeping me in the dark. What's happened? Where would we be going? For how long?' He waits in vain for an answer from Axel, then continues: 'I can't just abscond overnight. Surely you know that. My scholarship, film school, my asylum . . .' Axel doesn't answer, moves away. Etienne dozes off again. In Etienne's dream, or perhaps just before he falls asleep, Axel says: *Forget about everything here. Let go of it all. Come with me.* He keeps repeating it. *Come with me.*

Early the next morning, Axel visits a travel agent. Etienne isn't allowed to join him. When Axel returns, he starts packing a suitcase. He is preoccupied and ignores Etienne, who is lingering and loitering. Etienne looks surreptitiously at the plane ticket lying next to the mattress. As he suspected: Berlin. And, he notices, a return flight has been booked to London in a week's time. He breathes more easily, relaxes his shoulders. He goes down to the kitchen, makes a note of Axel's flight details and warms his hands in front of the stove.

That night, before Axel's early-morning departure, it is Etienne who wakes Axel in the small hours. 'Why am I not allowed to know anything? What's happened to your mother?' Axel doesn't respond. 'I'll be here. In London. I'll be waiting for you.' Axel turns away.

When they part company at Heathrow, Etienne curses the tears that he cannot stop. There are things he wants to say to Axel. Melodramatic, exaggerated things. Like: *You are a blade in my side, an indispensable pain. You are my downfall and my lifebuoy, everything that is unbearable and immeasurable.* But his lips remain shut.

Axel doesn't look Etienne in the eyes. He bends his head as if searching for heat in Etienne's neck. Then he turns around and exits through the security doors without saying goodbye. Etienne follows his shape through ribbed glass; then he is gone.

Back home, Etienne sits cross-legged on the attic floor. He looks up at the painting at a Dutch tilt. His wild alter ego towers towards the heavens; the sparks exploding from his horns are as bright as a welding flame. He is wearing sunglasses. His lips are fuller than in reality. Why would Axel paint him in this way? As a sensual god (or devil or goat) towering above the earth, seeking friction in the weather systems up high?

He gets up, wanders through the empty house. He finds his mother's letters, which he had rescued from the Finns' bony claws, in one of the rooms. He does not doubt that two streams of letters are still arriving dutifully at No. 52 in the Square. What might the Finns be doing with them? Throwing them in the lit hearth for a few moments' heat? Using them for scrap paper, writing goth songs about blood and excrement on the back?

He takes the letters up to the attic, sits down under the painting again. In the self-censored pile, only the first envelope has ever been opened. Earlier Etienne had read a few of the more intimate letters. He is ready for the rest. He opens one, reads how hurt his mother is feeling about his unrelenting tone, about how coolly he is renouncing his mother country. Does he have access to a phone? she wants to know. She will call. Or he can make a collect call. *Any time. I will stay at home over the next month, waiting by the phone.* In her next letter she writes that she will be visiting Etienne. His father initially agreed to finance the trip, but has since refused. She will borrow money from her sister. Disappointment, in the next letter, because Etienne isn't responding. She will nevertheless buy a plane ticket. She asks that he send her a photograph. *I want to recognise my child when I see him again.* Gradually her tone becomes less needy; as time passes, she starts carrying her yearning more lightly. Or underplaying it. Even the handwriting is steadier. She speculates about what he does, what his days might be like. She suspects he is busy with his music. And he has probably met a British girl by now, one with porcelain skin? Is he studying? Little of what is happening in Pretoria would probably interest him. She nevertheless writes about the death of Selina, their maid of the past twenty years. How she hadn't realised that she would be so moved, how she had wanted to attend the burial, but Etienne's father had barred her from doing so – it isn't safe in the township. She went there in secret, the only white woman. She stayed at the grave until all the funeral-goers had left. She left a chiffon scarf on the pile of soil. Why she did this, she doesn't quite know. *It felt to me as if I were standing next to your grave, Etienne.*

Then the false letters. The tone is bright, everything is hunky-dory. She vaguely enquires about his well-being, shares sunny news: one of his former school friends who has won a trophy from the Afrikaans Trade Institute, the outcome of high school rugby matches. She sends cuttings from *Beeld* or *Citizen* of cute news stories. About baby elephants, for instance, who had been injured in a veld fire and were now being cared for by young (white) volunteers. News about his father's working life, his grandmother's ailments.

He ties up the letters with a ribbon again. He can smell something chemical. Is it emanating from the well, or the sewage pipes? Is it the vinegar factory a few blocks away? He notices one of Axel's little plastic bags on the floor. He picks it up, turns it around, shakes it. A few remaining hairs fall in his hand. A bitter harvest: the hair of a child who is probably dead by now.

His thoughts float back in the direction of *Berliner Chronik*. Shreds of Benjamin's texts keep churning in his thoughts. And some of the matching film sequences he now knows too, frame by frame. He has borrowed a film-school projector again. He resolves never to return it. Each night he watches the first reel. He ought to be more careful; the film might disintegrate in his hands, or melt away in the projector's gears.

Irmgard's diary refers to urgent post-production work on

the first two reels, before filming was completed. Judging by the number of scenes – all roughly of equal length – on the first reel, and taking into account Irmgard's original list of scenes, the film should fill three reels. Somewhere another two reels are awaiting Etienne. In an archive cellar or sideboard. In an attic. In a trunk underneath a bed, in a dank storeroom or dark garage. In a cupboard smelling of the cologne of someone who has been long dead.

He closes his hand in a fist, pockets the hair.

Etienne no longer stokes the Dover. The rooms are icy, the attic the coldest of them all. What has stayed with him from his mother's letters is her request to send a photo of himself. He rummages around in the frozen attic chests, finds one of Axel's post-mortem photos: a recently deceased Victorian boy, his head resting on his mother's lap (is his ear still warm?). He puts it in an envelope, just that, writes the address of the house in which he grew up and posts it. His first letter in months (if you can call it a letter). And probably the last.

Two hours before Axel's flight is scheduled to land, Etienne is waiting at the airport. The week has passed slowly. Except for a few fellow students and his film-school instructors, Etienne hasn't had contact with a soul.

Jet-lagged passengers walk into the arrivals hall. Etienne is playing with his knuckles, feeling his collarbones. He thinks of how Axel would always seek out the weakest points of his body: the tender skin of his lids, the thin bone over his temples, the cartilage of his throat, the testicles. The places in between pleasure and pain. Often he would blow on Etienne's eyeballs, knock his knee until it jumped, press a thumb on Etienne's sinuses, or on the funny bone, or the little triangular bone below the sternum. 'This bit of bone,' Axel would say, 'can be converted into an arrow point with *one* thump. Driven straight into the heart.'

The arriving passengers have thinned to a trickle. Axel's luggage must have been the last to emerge, Etienne thinks. Another twenty minutes pass. Etienne keeps an eye on people's baggage; there haven't been Lufthansa labels for a while. He is reluctant to abandon his post, but goes to the airline desk to make an enquiry. They refuse to provide information about a passenger. He waits for another hour, eyes fixed on the entrance doors. He cannot understand how they could have missed each other. Is Axel waiting for him in Bermondsey Street?

He takes the Tube back to the city. He unlocks the front door at Bermondsey Street, calls out. He walks up the stairs, looks into every room. He ends up in the freezing attic. Winter sun is pouring in through the wide windows. Train wheels screech against tracks. Then all is quiet again.

It is slowly dawning upon Etienne that he doesn't have a single piece of useful information about Axel. He doesn't know why he went to Berlin, has no address or telephone number. Is his surname Fleischer, like his grandmother Irmgard's? Etienne doesn't know the name of a single other family member. Not one of his London acolytes, the ones who used to swirl around him, would know more than Etienne. The brochures for his exhibitions used only his first name. Axel might as well be one of those names in Etienne's list of *Berliner Chronik*'s production team members, pinned on some forgotten noticeboard. A name lost in the Berlin mist. Etienne frantically searches rooms, goes through all of Axel's pockets. He doesn't find a single personal document, not one bill showing Axel's name. Not one letter or envelope or form. How does someone exist like this? Is 'Axel' even his real name?

The hospital would have a record of him. But Etienne knows they won't help him. In his mind's eye he sees a stern nurse in uniform, asking intrusive questions, and himself standing in front of her like a mute schoolboy.

How is it possible that you could have discovered every centimetre of someone's body, every sinew and every freckle, the labyrinth of each ear, could know the fumes of soot and iron he gives off when he is hungry or aroused, but know nothing about him? Not a single fact that would equip you to go and search for him in a strange city.

Etienne waits for a day. Maybe Axel has missed his flight. Perhaps he has decided to stay on longer with friends or family. All that briefly brings Etienne relief is to go up to the attic and have a look at the little figures made from children's hair. He tries to imagine what might have been going on in Axel's thoughts. It is as if he had to fend off something with his weaving. As if he could save the children in this way, could make them fire-resistant.

The little figures are all he has of Axel now. That and the rotting pigeons. And a handful of remaining photographs of dead children pretending to be alive. Well, the painting too. He is less and less convinced by the latter, though. It doesn't seem to fit; it is a false note.

Another day passes. A week. There is no sign of Axel, no news. Three weeks. Then six. He hardly registers Christmas and New Year.

A needle in all the world's haystacks. That is Axel, now. And he, Etienne, too. They have both disappeared.

II.
DEEP ARCHIVE

(Berlin, October 1987–May 1988)

Chapter 18

DESPITE THE ADVANCED German lessons he has taken over the past two months in London, Etienne is still not fluent. He can read, but in his stuttering practice conversations, he garbles prepositions and inflections.

He lands at Tegel airport in West Berlin. From there he takes a bus and overground train – the S-Bahn – to the Friedrichstrasse border crossing. There is no control on the western side. His limited German makes him sound brusque when addressing the East German passport official, who then calls a colleague. They observe Etienne with neutral gazes. He has a refugee travel document rather than a passport; on the cover it says *Travel Document/Titre de Voyage*. His asylum enables him to travel as if he is a Brit. The official thumbs through it, looks in his register. Etienne's name is on a list, it turns out; they have been expecting him.

A border guard unlocks a series of doors. Etienne follows him through the corridors. Somewhere behind them, West German visitors are queuing beyond barriers, slowly snaking into the station. He and his guard follow a secret route. Etienne keeps an eye on his travel document. The guard is holding it in front of his chest, elbow pushed out. As if in a salute.

A woman is waiting behind the last door. She is wearing a light brown skirt and jacket, and flipping through the pages of a women's magazine called *Sybille*. Her glasses point upwards on each side, a 1960s design. Next to her stands another guard. Etienne's travel document is returned to him. Both guards disappear into the station.

'Ich bin Frau Finkel. Sie sind Herr Nieuwenhuis?' I'm Frau Finkel. You are Mr Nieuwenhuis? They start walking. 'Welcome. I'm from the film school's administration department.' Outside they get into a muck-coloured Trabant. She takes a thin file from under her seat. 'For you.' While she is struggling to get the little car started, he opens it. In the front is a city map. *Stadtplan: Berlin Hauptstadt der DDR.* There is a stylised representation of city landmarks on the cover. On the back, so a note indicates, there should be a Zeichenerklärung, a key to the map. But when he turns it around, there is nothing. A printing error? There is a separate map of the transport system. And brochures of the film school. He closes the file. For now he would rather observe the new world outside. They are travelling down a wide boulevard, past grandiose old buildings. 'Unter den Linden,' his hostess says. 'You'll discover it doesn't look like this everywhere. Here everything is polished to a high gloss.'

They drive past a low, copper-coloured glass building. 'Der Palast der Republik,' she says. 'The seat of our government.' He tries to gauge her tone when she says 'our government', but it isn't betraying anything. The building vaguely reminds Etienne of the State Theatre in Pretoria. Above and beyond the government building, the silver ball of the Fernsehturm – the television tower – is visible.

Frau Finkel takes him to the Volkspolizei's headquarters, where his name is entered into another register and he is issued with a student residency permit. They stamp his travel document, affix something like a postage stamp next to it. She takes him to another government office, where he obtains a visa that permits him to travel freely into and out of East Berlin – a rare privilege.

She has to hurry back to the film school in Potsdam. She hands him an envelope with a handful of Ostmark. She points out the address of his lodgings in the file, and the route to get there. She drops him at the underground station – Alexanderplatz U-Bahn – and departs without saying goodbye. He stands on the sidewalk, looking up at the Fernsehturm that is gleaming like a lamp in the afternoon sun.

He doesn't have coins for the U-Bahn ticket machine. Hardly anyone uses it, he notices, and there is no control point. He boards the train without a ticket, travels through stations with names like Rosa-Luxemburg-Platz and Dimitroffstrasse. In the rocking coach he studies the train map, testing the shape of station names between his lips. He chooses favourites based on the sounds: Storkowerstrasse, Rummelsburg, Leninallee, Nöldnerplatz. He will be sure, before long, to pass through all the stations with the most beautiful combinations of consonants.

He alights at Schönhauser Allee station, turns left in Stargarder Strasse. Map in one hand, trunk in the other. It is as if photographs of everyone else who has walked here with a suitcase before are being projected onto him – each photo a transparent membrane. The street is almost empty. Only one or two figures are moving at a distance in the autumn haze. The buildings are worn, the way they looked right after the war, and have decayed further since. This is what he expected: disconsolate streets with disconsolate buildings. He stops at No. 72. The building's plasterwork is a patchwork of gravel; the façade is scarred with decades-old gunfire. Balcony railings are lined with steel plates.

Most bells don't have names on them. His landlady's – Frau

Drechsler's – does. He rings. Nothing. After a while, again. A figure appears behind the glass doors, opens up. A young man, about his own age. Tall and thin, pointed face. Surrounded by an aura of silence.

'Nils.' His voice is hushed.

'Etienne.' Nils doesn't take the hand Etienne extends, doesn't look him in the eyes.

Nils has descended several flights of stairs from Frau Drechsler's flat; her button to remotely open the building's front door is broken, he explains. 'You have to sign in first with the building caretaker,' Nils says. He gently knocks on the door of a ground floor flat.

The door opens slightly. 'Ja?'

'Wir brauchen den Hausbuch, bitte. Frau Drechsler nimmt heute einen neuen Untermieter ein.' We need the house book, please. Frau Drechsler is taking in another tenant today.

The man opens the door wide, observes Etienne over plastic-framed spectacles. He is in his sixties, his cheeks hanging over his jaws like a bloodhound's. His voice is sharp, whistle-like: 'Und für wie lange bleibt er?' And for how long will he be staying?

Nils shrugs his shoulders. 'Für einen Jahr, ungefähr. Er ist Student—' For about a year. He is a student—

'Nóch ein Student!' Another student! The man snorts. 'Es wird ein Höhle, dieses Haus, von Unruhestifter und Bummler!' This building is becoming a filthy den for trouble-makers and bums!

Etienne catches the drift of Nils's ensuing explanation. If it is *Nils* to whom the man is referring . . . well, he is not in fact a student. Nils's tone is patient, weary. As if this kind of defence is routine. And all the students in the GDR, he continues, are, after all, model citizens of the socialist state. He gestures towards Etienne. *He*, for instance, is an anti-fascist who had escaped South Africa and ended up in Britain. And who has now come to the GDR to be educated. (Is there a sardonic undertone in Nils's soft voice?)

Saggy Cheeks remains sceptical, keeps watching Etienne while he signs the register. He takes the book, studies the entry as if Etienne might have provided a false name. He is offended by the Afrikaans nomenclature. 'So, du bist nicht Deutscher?' So, you're not a German? Etienne remains silent.

Nils's voice has a deep, natural calm: 'Als ich sagte, er ist ein Austauschstudent von Grossbritannien.' As I said, he is an exchange student from Great Britain.

The man demands Etienne's passport. He shows his refugee travel document. He tries explaining in German, then switches over to English. Saggy Cheeks interrupts him. 'South Africa,' he reads – slowly, in a heavy accent, clearly proud of his English. Then, suspicious again: 'Südafrika.' He keeps thumbing through the pages, studies the East German stamps. 'Nicht Grossbritannien, aber Südafrika!' he shouts at Nils. His cheeks tremble. How does one harbour such rage without it damaging your body? Etienne wonders. Saggy Cheeks makes a note next to Etienne's name in the register, then apparently decides that this is a matter for a different forum. He holds out the travel document, haughty like a border guard.

Nils gestures with his head towards the document when Etienne puts it in his pocket. 'Be sure always to carry that with you.' Etienne follows him upstairs with his suitcase. The stairs are covered with reddish-brown linoleum; the walls are peeling. On the ceilings there are traces of old frescoes. Different kinds of tex-tured glass on the stair landings warp the view of the courtyard.

'Nothing personal, by the way, the house book. Anyone staying for more than three nights must sign it.' Nils climbs the stairs with unusual concentration, eyes fixed on his feet. He stops so suddenly that Etienne crashes into him from behind. Nils bends over double to compensate for his height – and the higher stair he is standing on – and then speaks softly into Etienne's ear: 'The Stasi has free access to each book . . .' Nils continues walking up the stairs in a careful march. Etienne is surprised by the frankness. He follows, looking at Nils's long legs.

Frau Drechsler is waiting for them on the fifth-floor landing. Her hair is tied up in a librarian's bun and she has the blunt face of a factory worker. She is wearing an olive-green dress with a 1940s cut. Her face has premature signs of age – she can't be much older than fifty, Etienne reckons. The eyes are small and round; nothing else is moving in her flat face. Etienne stands panting next to his trunk. She looks him up and down, then enters the flat. Etienne follows, Nils behind him. Frau Drechsler points out Etienne's room. Deep inside the flat, across from a bathroom. The flat is in the Vorderhaus; the room is spacious and looks out on the street. There is a small desk, even a basin against the wall. 'Nicht zu benutzen,' she says, pointing at the basin.

'Broken,' Nils says in English, as if Etienne doesn't understand any German. 'Don't use it.'

'And,' Frau Drechsler wiggles an index finger in Etienne's direction, 'you're not allowed to put up anything on the walls. No nails, no self-adhesive tape. And no electrical appliances in the room. About the other rules – meals, the curfew, telephone and hot water – *he* can inform you.' She points at Nils.

Nils does not inform Etienne about any rules; he doesn't

enquire. Frau Drechsler provides two meals, it turns out. When she is dishing up the pale-boiled food, her face is like an empty page. Etienne is thankful Nils is at the dining table too. Frau Drechsler's silences carry the heavy weight of suspicion and warning.

Etienne wanders through Prenzlauer Berg. The few pedestrians on the streets avoid each other's gazes. He is apparently the only one walking without a fixed destination. At Schönefeld Allee station there is a supermarket. *Lebensmittel*, it says in green letters on the front. Whatever there is on the mostly empty shelves, one buys. Gherkins from the Spreewald. Apples, potatoes. White cabbage, red cabbage. Sausages. Sometimes a Hungarian salami. Across from Stargarder Strasse 72 there is a bakery. Early in the morning the rye bread steams when you break it. Etienne enters a clothes shop. Everything is synthetic and – this he can see even without trying anything on – badly cut.

A week after his arrival he has to report to the HFF – die Hochschule für Film und Fernsehen – in Potsdam. The commute is long; one has to travel in an arc around the southern part of West Berlin. He takes the S-Bahn south, changes to a provincial train. From Potsdam station he takes a tram to the film school.

The HFF is accommodated in several old buildings. Once they must have been proud Prussian villas; now they sport dusty linoleum floors and mustard-coloured picture rails, walls painted in dove grey and brown.

He has an appointment with the school's director. His office is spacious and looks out onto a garden. The wallpaper has yellow patterns from the '70s. 'Herr Nieuwenhuis.

Willkommen!' The director switches to passable English. 'We are excited to have you in our midst. Your instructors at the London Film School speak of you with great regard.' His tone is oddly grandiloquent. Etienne thinks of his low profile in London: the failure of his first film project, and of the subsequent two. The exchange programme was an opportunity to get rid of him. It is entirely credible that they might have sung his praises to Herr Direktor.

Etienne doesn't skip a beat, starts explaining how he has long been yearning to study at a film school of the calibre of the HFF – 'Konrad Wolf,' he corrects himself. Wolf, after whom this proud institution has recently been renamed, even though no one actually uses the new name, was (so his information file explained) an East German director, and had once been a heroic soldier in the Red Army. Etienne solemnly tilts his head. 'The ideological and aesthetic values of this institution will certainly find favour with me, Herr Direktor.' Two heads nodding, two frowning foreheads feigning sincerity: a little dance on either side of a wide desk. Etienne thinks of Mister van Rooyen, his erstwhile history teacher with his muscly buttocks, and of his father. He can adapt quickly. He doubts whether much will be expected of him here at the HFF. The fact that he is here – the implied ideological camaraderie – is, he suspects, already more than enough.

The director pushes a button on a plastic intercom, summons Frau Finkel. She doesn't return Etienne's smile. She takes him on a tour of the buildings and lecture halls. He is introduced to lecturers in musty offices, and a few fellow students. Then he attends a film history lecture – an introductory overview of what they will be studying this semester. The way the lecturer ignores most Western film movements and directors astonishes him. Clearly, social realism is the only approach deserving of their attention.

When the class ends, Frau Finkel arrives to fetch him. She accompanies him to a seminar on scriptwriting for documentary films. The lecturer's focus is objectivity, a 'scientifically factual' approach; the techniques he sets out are, however, those of propaganda. A video film by an alumnus is shown. It is about Experimentalbau – experimental building methods and housing. It starts with a report on the recent demolition of an old gas plant in Dimitroffstrasse (not far from Etienne's lodgings, he realises when Stargarder Strasse is briefly visible in a wide shot) and its replacement by blocks of concrete flats. A super-modern planetarium has also just been erected on the same site. The film becomes a rising paean to the East German housing authorities and their indefatigable dedication to progress.

Etienne looks around him, at the demure students. They are listening in silence, not asking anything, nodding their heads. He thinks of the grouchiness, anxiety and anarchy of his fellow students in London, of their challenging questions and objections. Their entitlement, their self-confidence. Their vulnerability. Their messy hair, their punky outfits.

It feels as if he is back in South Africa. All the self-soothing and self-congratulating. All the forbidden thoughts hiding deep inside skulls.

Chapter 19

IT SURPRISES ETIENNE that one so rarely sees or hears children in this city. And it feels as if the heavy air hasn't been stirred by wings in a long time: have the birds already migrated south for the winter, or headed off in a final exodus?

On his walks Etienne is greeted by blind windows, rotting Trabants and courtyards filled with rubble. The East German government has long wanted to implode Prenzlauer Berg's crumbling buildings, Nils tells him. They want to bury them with the rest of the century's rubble and erect new structures. Want to make everything new and grey. To restore old buildings is expensive. And it reminds one of other times, the *wrong* times.

Months have passed since he last saw Axel. He is starting to forget the texture of his skin. But the new city is fuelling his sense of loss. One morning, on the way to film school, he is walking underneath Schönhauser Allee's tracks when the rumbling of a train conjures up Axel's face. He retreats, presses himself against an iron pillar. He forgets where the pillar stops and he begins: steel, noise, flesh. Axel's body enters his own, pressing the breath from his chest. When the rumbling subsides, Etienne has a painful erection. His legs won't obey him, won't ascend the stairs to the station. For the first time he wonders: is Axel dead? For the rest of the day, something keeps moving like worms between his ribs.

Contrary to Frau Drechsler's instructions, Etienne uses the basin in his room. Perhaps water is seeping all the way to Saggy Cheeks' flat, clumping the Hausbuch's pages together, making the ink smudge. Perhaps the damp will rot the beams, causing the building to collapse. And will it trickle yet further, into subterranean archives, washing pages clean of their secrets?

The *Berliner Chronik* storyboards, including the rough sketches he has made himself, are stuck onto the wall with adhesive tape. To hell with Drechsler's rules. The first reel of the film stays under his bed. Sometimes he recalls frames from it, but then realises they are images that he has conjured up himself in the apocryphal storyboards.

He secretly keeps a kettle in his room. In the two weeks since his arrival, he has tried a few times to start a conversation with Nils, has offered him some of the pure coffee he brought with him on the recommendation from one of his London lecturers – the film theorist – who previously visited the GDR. He was there in the '70s, during the coffee crisis. Coffee hasn't in fact been as expensive or as rare for a long time. Even so, Frau Drechsler only keeps cheap chicory coffee. Tonight Etienne is standing outside Nils's door again, across from his own, with two steaming mugs. Nils lets him in, hesitatingly takes one. He takes cigarettes from his pocket, HB Filter, offers Etienne one. They light up; Nils opens the window to the courtyard. The autumn air is cool against Etienne's forehead; the smoke burns his throat. 'East Berlin is a place from which people want to escape . . . *You've* come here voluntarily. Why?' Nils's facial muscles tense up as he speaks. Each syllable is uttered with difficulty.

Etienne shrugs his shoulders, looks at the tree in the court-yard. 'It's better than where I'm originally from. *Anywhere* is.'

He asks Nils questions. About his plans, what he does for a living. There is a long silence before he responds. A muscle starts twitching in his neck. 'Last year I was refused admission to Humboldt University. And the year before that.'

'Why?'

He looks down at his cigarette. 'Does one ever know? . . . My parents, probably . . .' Nils leans against the window ledge. A first he is careful; then it starts flowing. He has always wanted to study Japanese. Now he is trying to teach himself from the few books one can find in public libraries. But he has no one with whom to converse in the language.

Nils stops talking, approaches the bedroom door, listens. He comes back, switches on his cassette player at low volume. Etienne looks at the handwritten list of songs on the cassette case. British New Romantic bands. Spandau Ballet, Adam and the Ants, Duran Duran. The recordings are woolly, recorded from the radio. Outside the classroom, Etienne has gradually realised, his fellow students are not quite such exemplary citizens. They were the ones who showed him where to find Western music on the radio. The frequencies of RIAS I and SFB, the West Berlin stations, are not calibrated on East German radios, but easy to find just left of DDR1 and Stimme der DDR – the voice of the GDR – with their local kitsch. Very little Western music can be heard officially. There are still quotas in nightclubs to play GDR music, Nils tells him. Music from selected Western bands is released in small quantities, but such music is easier to find on holiday in Czechoslovakia or Yugoslavia. Nowadays Etienne records music from the radio too. Since he left the pre-recorded cassettes that he brought from London in the sun one afternoon, they have been producing warped sounds. He resolves to bring back some proper recordings for Nils when he goes to West Berlin.

Etienne carefully enquires about Nils's parents. Nils sighs, goes and listens at the door, comes back, turns up the music. His parents, he tells Etienne, made themselves unpopular in the '70s. They were friends of Wolf Biermann—

'Biermann?'

'Before my time. Singer, poet. Marxist idealist . . . Back then he had a falling-out with the government. Wanted to change things from within the Party . . . They deported him to the West. My parents stayed behind, and . . .' He approaches the door for a third time, opening it slightly. The radio can be heard in the kitchen - good news about the GDR, bad news about Western countries. Nils shuts the door again. 'They were made to regret it forever. Later they became active in the Lutheran church, in the peace circles . . .'

'So, now you're being punished?'

'Who knows?' Nils says flatly. Etienne flicks his cigarette though the window. Nils extinguishes his own, closes the window.

There is a long silence. Etienne asks Nils about the minor mysteries of his daily routine: is it necessary to purchase U-Bahn tickets? Is there a proper variety of groceries some-where, or do you always have to scour several supermarkets? Nils gives tips. Also, of his own accord, about how to recognise social types in East Germany by their shoes.

They sit down on the single bed. It creaks and squeaks. Nils looks at Etienne, smiles shyly for the first time. Etienne grips his shirt. Nils lifts his arms like a reluctant child having to change before bedtime; Etienne pulls it over his head. Nils is gaunt, and at least two metres tall. The skin is taut over the sinews; he doesn't have an ounce of fat. Etienne starts counting the vertebrae with his fingers. Nils warily rests his head on Etienne's shoulder, kisses him behind the ear.

In the centre of the flat is the Berliner Zimmer: a spacious, gloomy room. Close to the front door is the kitchen, Frau Drechsler's bedroom and a bathroom. Diagonally across from the Berliner Zimmer is a short corridor with Etienne's and Nils's bedrooms and a second bathroom. Frau Drechsler clearly finds silence intolerable. When there isn't radio chatter in the kitchen, a black-and-white television is droning in the Berliner Zimmer. The only time when there is silence – and then Etienne wishes there *were* noise – is when they sit down to dinner like an uneasy family. In this forced silence Frau Drechsler apparently finds perverse pleasure. Like a paterfamilias insisting that the children eat in silence before family prayers.

Tonight, after dinner, Etienne and Frau Drechsler are sitting in brown armchairs like a married couple. They are watching a documentary television programme that is applauding the uncompromising modernity of the state's building projects. (The same director as the film he saw about the demolition of the Dimitroffstrasse gas plant?) It is Drechsler's version of family prayers. She sits there nodding, as if someone is reading from the Bible.

There is a master plan for the city, one realises quickly, and a master narrative for the past and future. It is a simple story; it doesn't take long to master it. You see a few documentary films, hear a political speech or two, and then you can recite the mantras. You close your eyes, visualise a crowd in a stadium. And there you have it. Your tongue no longer belongs to you. You have been successfully initiated into the chorus.

Etienne is a free walker. Unlike in London, where he had pushy guides, he explores Berlin on his own. City adventurers aren't welcome in these parts. In a city where the rhythm of your feet should indicate a clear destination, his exploration is too random. How long, he wonders, before shadowy figures in brown coats start following him on his aimless meanders? Before they stretch open his jaws with an iron clamp and force the right words from him? Before, like the other figures on the streets, he purses his lips and pushes forward, straight into the wind?

To doubt is to betray. To be curious is to disrupt.

On a cloudy afternoon he walks down Karl-Liebknecht Strasse. It is muggy, too warm for autumn. He enters a shop that sells nothing but fur hats with ear flaps (the joys of central planning!). Soviet hats, made of the hides of Russian rabbits. Etienne is the only customer. The shop assistant (he looks like a Mongolian) pulls a hat over Etienne's head. It squeezes his head; the roots of his hair start itching and sweating.

There is no mirror; he observes himself in the window. Behind his own reflection, a tram passes. A toddler steps into the shop, wraps his arms around Etienne's legs. He gets a shock when he looks down at him: his eyes are filled with mature, knowing horror. The mother follows the child inside, pulls the child away. He keeps clinging, looking accusingly up at Etienne. At last he lets go; mother and child disappear in the street. The Mongolian is unperturbed, puts a bigger hat on Etienne's head. Etienne enquires about the price. It is unaffordable. He shakes his head, leaves the shop.

He walks in the direction of the Brandenburger Tor, up to where he is barred by the inner wall. Behind it is the death strip with its watchtowers, then the Wall itself. He walks back to Alexanderplatz, where a gathering of the Freie Deutsche Jugend is in progress. He looks at the young men with their uniforms and flags, at their calves and shoulder muscles. Like young Voortrekkers in South Africa. Like cadets with their sturdy legs, their sweaty buttocks and armpits. Etienne looks up at the television tower's gleaming blue sphere in the sunshine. It is time, he thinks, for a trip to West Berlin.

He has been here for a month. He first wanted to acclimatise to the drabness of East Berlin's streets, to the fumes of Trabants and Ladas, had to settle into life at the film school, but now he has to start his search. He must find Axel, and he shall. In that walled half-city beyond the death strip nobody could, surely, disappear without a trace.

On the U-Bahn to Friedrichstrasse station Etienne observes a tattooed girl. No East Berliners have tattoos. Is tattooing officially proscribed? Regarded, at least, as antisocial behaviour? She has to be a day visitor from West Berlin, or perhaps from Prague or Budapest. The arm tattoo is a dandelion; the downy seeds are blowing away, up her arm, neck and cheek. There are a few lost seeds on the shaven temple. Behind her, through the train window, the Fernsehturm is visible, towering like a thermometer.

Etienne warily enters Friedrichstrasse station. When he came through here the first time, he got a glimpse of the extensive network of corridors and platforms. East and West Germany – and the overground and underground train systems of each – together in one complex. Like a termite nest in which the tunnels cannot cross. He walks into the departure hall – 'Die Tränenpalast' in common parlance, according to Nils. The palace of tears. Where families or friends who are separated by the Wall say goodbye to each other after day visits.

Etienne shows his refugee travel document at an initial control point. The official frowns, but he is waved past. There is consternation at the currency exchange counter when it turns out he isn't allowed to take East German marks with him. And they aren't exchangeable for West German marks either. He will be returning tonight, he explains; he needs his Ostmark. A guard approaches; Etienne lowers his voice. The cash isn't being confiscated, the sullen clerk explains; he will be able to withdraw it again upon his return.

In one of a row of cubicles, each containing a passport official, his travel document is stamped. He has crossed over; he is in the West. He walks through a long corridor, then over the S-Bahn platform. Down a flight of stairs, through a tunnel to the U-Bahn. A maze. He looks up at the ceiling – if his calculations are correct, he is more or less below Friedrichstrasse. Above his head East German feet are walking in the street. Up there you are in one country, down here – a metre or two below them – you are in another.

Chapter 20

IN THE EAST something akin to dust settles in your thoughts: the more he scanned his West Berlin tourist guide last night, the less any concrete plans took shape. Where does one start such a search? Hospitals? Some government office? Or will a team of spry German blokes from a police station help him scour the city for Axel?

He arbitrarily boards a West German U-Bahn train. He doesn't know a soul here. His German is inadequate. He has hardly any money – he has just exchanged most of his remaining pounds on the western side of Friedrichstrasse station for a modest sum of West German marks.

He isn't far from Prenzlauer Berg. But in a different world. Faster, filled with colour. And it has a different *smell*. He suddenly feels fiercely loyal towards East Berlin. He is missing the toxic fumes, the bitter smoke of autumn fires stoked with low-grade coal from Leipzig. He is missing Nils. (Not quite yet Frau Drechsler.) He observes his fellow passengers; everybody looks so shut off and self-satisfied. He wonders whether they can smell he is from the East. The punk across from him looks no different from his counterparts in East Berlin. Plus tattoos, that is. Etienne smiles; the punk bares his teeth. Beelzebub's face is tattooed across his Adam's apple.

A few nights ago, Nils took Etienne to an impromptu Ost-rock concert on a bomb site in Schliemannstrasse. Such gatherings are illegal. A frenetic refrain has been stuck in

Etienne's mind ever since: Arbeit, Brot und Wohnung für alle! Over and over the singer shouted these words, sounding increasingly raw and hoarse. The cord of the microphone ran amid feet, among weeds, past a car wreck, over a wall. One could imagine it winding further, through cellars and tunnels, under barbed wire and landmines, to a power socket in the West. Ost-punks danced and smashed beer bottles on the ground. The electric cable was getting trampled; the amplifier cut out. The voice kept shouting and the drummer kept thumping until his drums broke. Everybody danced, joining in the shouting. Etienne left, fearing that the Volkspolizei would arrive. For all he knows, that raw screaming is still continuing.

Etienne opens his West Berlin U-Bahn map. Now he knows where to go. A café that Axel once mentioned in London as one of his hang-outs when he lived in Berlin: Anderes Ufer. The other shore. Where better to start his search? He has one photograph. It is in his pocket; his hand is resting on the little square of the Polaroid right now. Taken by a squatter at Axel's exhibition of dead Victorian boys. Axel's face is turned sideways, out of focus. There is a crowd in the background. He has a rare smile on his face.

At Mehringdamm Etienne changes trains; at Kleistpark station he gets off. He finds the small café, sits down, orders a beer. When the waiter brings it, he shows him the photo.

'Someone you know? Or have seen around?'

The waiter, thin with a blond fringe and oily skin, takes it and studies it. 'Yes,' he says nonchalantly. 'Everyone knows who this is. Axel.' Etienne's blood starts fizzing, his temples pulsating. The first person in this entire city to whom he shows the photo. And he recognises him!

He sits up, places a hand on the waiter's arm. 'Where is he? Has he been here recently?'

The waiter shakes his head, hands back the photo. His arms are too long for his body. 'He's living in London now. But I remember him from the old days. Many people know him in the night spots. Especially the gay places. He came back to Berlin a few times for visits. Sometimes hung out here—'

'But he's back here. He's returned. And then disappeared. Surely he'd be visiting the old places again . . . ?'

'The old places . . .' the man repeats slowly, then shakes his head. 'He's not here. People would've known.'

'Who would've known? Tell me more about his life here, about his friends. Please. I'm looking for him.' Etienne's hand grips the waiter's wrist. 'He is my . . .'

'Your what?' He extracts his wrist, places a slender hand next to Etienne's elbow on the table. There is something elastic about the man. And Etienne's anxiety is awakening something in him: his camel's eyes are changing into those of a predator.

Etienne shakes his head. 'I *have* to find him.' He is trying to sound composed, but his urgency is impossible to hide.

The waiter raises his hand in camp defence. 'I don't know much about him, dear. He's a wild one, that much I can tell you. Hasn't been in this place in about two or three years. Will let you know if he shows his face.' He tucks his fringe behind his ear. 'Try some other places. Tom's Bar, for instance. Or the clubs.' He winks. 'There are other places, of course, of which few people know . . .'

'Which places?' But the waiter is done with Etienne; he is looking at the bar counter, where orders are being prepared. 'Wait, I'll give you an address. In case you hear – or remember – something.' Etienne writes down his Prenzlauer Berg address on a napkin. The man takes it like a feather with his fingers. He looks uncomprehendingly at the East Berlin address, then down at Etienne's shoes. He pushes out his chin and walks away. Etienne is sure the man knows more than he is letting on. His urge is to follow him to the kitchen and bombard him with questions. To press his pale narrow hand against a hot stove.

Etienne stays, orders more beer. And then another. A different waiter is serving him now. He keeps showing the photo to people coming and going at tables around him. Everyone shakes their heads. No one recognises Axel. The dour-faced responses discourage Etienne. Just as he is getting up, and paying his bill, three men about his own age sit down at the table next to him.

He leans over for the last time. 'Entschuldigung,' he says. 'Do any of you know him?' He holds out the photograph.

Three pairs of eyes sparkle; muscles stir. One of them takes the photo, puts it down on their table. They study it with intense concentration, heads together. They look up simultaneously. 'No,' the first one says. The other two shake their heads. 'Never seen him.' Etienne gets up to leave, reaches for the photo.

'I'm Matthias,' the first one says.

'Christof.'

'Frederick.'

'I'm Etienne.'

They shake his hand in turn.

'We're in a band,' Frederick says. He presses the photo into Etienne's palm. His own hand is large and wide, out of proportion to his muscled, compact body. Just like in London, Etienne thinks – *everybody* is in some sort of band. He knows the scenario well by now: almost without exception, seriousness and enthusiasm far exceed talent. He sits down again, looks sceptically at the three of them.

'It's my first time here. I've just arrived in West Berlin,' Etienne says when they keep looking at him in silence. All three of them have dark, thick hair. Matthias's eyebrows meet in the middle, Christof is lean, with a scar on his neck. Frederick is a head-length shorter, his eyes sky blue.

'It's an institution,' Matthias says, 'this place. The first gay bar in the city. It came to Berlin at the same time as good music, the gay—'

Christof sits forward, cuts Matthias off. 'Yes, when Bowie and Iggy Pop came here in the late '70s, the city was a desert – for music, gay stuff, all of it. A really drab place—'

'How do you know? Weren't you too young back then?'

'My father told me . . .' Christof looks sheepish. Etienne regrets interrupting him.

Frederick jumps in: 'As Christof says, in the '70s the real music was in Cologne and Düsseldorf. In Berlin it was all Kraut-rock and ambient electronics. Then Bowie arrived in '76. And everything changed. In '77 we got PVC, the first Berlin punk band, and not long after that SO36, our punk club, opened. And then Anderes Ufer . . .'

Frederick orders four beers. Etienne looks from one to the other. They could have been three television comedians. But they are deadly serious while bubbling over with arbitrary and unsolicited information. He likes them.

Matthias again, now: 'Our fathers were all in bands. Didn't have much success. Still doing local gigs, though.' He points to the other two. 'We all grew up here in Kreuzberg. Our fathers were in the same bands at times. But their music . . . All Krautstuff . . .'

Frederick pulls a face. Christof slaps a faux-embarrassed palm over his eyes. 'Yes, Berlin was a dreary place before Bowie came, I tell you. Decaying old buildings, and even worse, those drab blocks that appeared overnight in the '50s and '60s—'

Frederick sits up, his shoulders taut and dense with muscle. He cuts in again: 'After Bowie a whole bunch of good bands came on the scene: Salomé's Geile Tiere, for instance. And Malaria!, an all-female band—'

'And Einstürzende Neubauten, of course,' Matthias says. 'No one had wanted to sing in German. Then they started singing nothing *but* German.' He swigs beer, wipes the foam from his mouth. 'So do we. Only German.'

Frederick: 'Yes, Berlin is now a kick-ass place. Where everything happens. You'll like it.'

They sit there in a row. Silent now, waiting.

'I was in a band too,' Etienne says tentatively. 'In South Africa.' Why he finds it easier to mention South Africa here in the two halves of Berlin, he doesn't know. 'American Rock. MOR stuff. There we thought it was revolutionary, subversive. The most radical music people there could imagine was Bob Dylan or Leonard Cohen. Or Tom Waits.'

The three faces in front of him simultaneously turn sour.

'Pretentious hetero dreck,' Frederick says and shakes his head. The other two nod.

They are like three early-morning birds on a branch, their hands and faces as agile as quicksilver.

'I would guess you're a guitarist,' Christof pipes up. His neck scar moves along with the muscles.

'Or a vocalist,' Matthias adds.

Frederick isn't far behind. 'No. Definitely percussion.'

Etienne nods in Frederick's direction.

They look excitedly at each other. 'I don't believe it,' Matthias says. 'How fucking long have we been searching for a decent drummer!'

'Our new band doesn't have a name yet – for a while we were all in different bands. But things are on the verge of happening,' Christof says.

Frederick looks right through Etienne with his bright blue eyes. 'On the verge, yes.' Frederick quickly glances at the other two, turns his gaze back to Etienne. 'How about auditioning with us?'

Etienne takes a slow mouthful of beer. 'What? Now?' This kind of ritual he knows from his London days too. All the bands are constantly searching: for vocalists, guitarists, drummers, audiences . . . Everybody is always joining a band, or leaving one. Growing closer to, or apart from, their fellow musicians. Developing their style, finding their sound. Trying to track down a soul who can feel their vibrations, or getting rid of someone who is slipping out of synch.

Matthias nods. 'Why not?'

'Yes,' Christof says. 'We have a sound studio in Kreuzberg.'

'*Sort of* a studio,' Matthias says.

'Well, I can't, I'm afraid. My drums are still in London . . .' He had never picked up his drums at Patrick's in the Square. When Etienne left for Germany, Patrick undertook solemnly to look after them. Whether the drum kit – and Patrick himself – is still there in the Square is an open question. 'And I live in the East.' Etienne quickly adds: 'But because I'm an exchange student, I can come and go as I wish.'

Frederick shakes his head, eyes closed. His index fingers and thumbs are moving as if drumming. 'We have everything you need. And we don't care where you live.'

Matthias calls the waiter, pays for the beers, which they haven't finished. Etienne stands around for a few moments, wondering whether they are taking the piss. Are they planning to rob him? Surely only swindlers can make you feel comfortable so quickly. Then he gets into a taxi with them, all four of them in the back like sardines. They head to Kreuzberg.

Etienne misses his drums. He didn't want to keep them in the Bermondsey Street house. After Axel left, the house was claimed by his erstwhile disciples. And the elements. Anyone felt free to come and party or stay there, whether for a night or weeks on end. At some point, the back door disappeared, some window frames were removed. The worst of winter was over, but spring was cold too. Towards the end, the tin bath in the kitchen had gone, so too the banister. People would smoke and listen to music in the attic; beer bottles were flung from the roof. One evening, when Etienne was sitting up there among strangers, a girl asked him: 'Who are you? Where do you live?' He didn't have an answer.

As he looks at the West Berlin streets through the taxi window, he remembers how impatient he was for the last few months of his London studies to be over. He found out from COSAWR that he would be able to get asylum status in Germany too; he could, it turns out, have accompanied Axel. Even so, he had only his scholarship money to support himself. And *that* was dependent on his studies. He was trapped in London. There was a deep grief about Axel in his bones. The streets of London felt more desolate than ever . . .

The taxi drops them in a street with a row of bars. *Oranienstrasse*, he reads on a sign. They enter a courtyard through a rusty gate. Unlike in East Berlin, where there isn't so much as a paint mark on any building, the graffiti has built up on these walls in dense layers. There are also corroded pipes, through which gas or steam must have been pumped once. Piles of rubble in the corners, grass pushing up through the paving.

They walk through a tiled corridor, past yet another courtyard, to an abandoned factory space with glass panels in the roof. In the middle there is a collection of instruments, both traditional and improvised. Pipes, an oil drum. Iron rods that look like sections of a train track. Parts of a lorry or locomotive engine. An anvil sits in a container filled with old motor oil. They take their places, the quasi-triplets. Etienne looks on. Matthias is the vocalist, Christof the guitarist, Frederick on the synthesiser. When they start playing, the main influence is instantly apparent: Einstürzende Neubauten. Etienne knows the band; his neighbour in the Square who used to weld iron sculptures was a fan.

Etienne is touched by their utter seriousness, the absolute intensity. Imitative nevertheless, he thinks, without the brutal charisma or the concentrated menace of the original. They stop, look enquiringly at Etienne. 'We're a bit stiff,' Frederick says. 'Things will warm up.' Etienne approaches, his footsteps hollow against the bare walls, and sits down at the drums. He taps with his stick on a drum, then lets go. He is out of practice, and the drums are not the same quality as his own. He tests the pipes and rods. The oil drum, an engine block.

The others join in. They look at each other. They improvise, they jam. Then all four of them cease playing at virtually the same moment. Etienne rests a hand on the cymbals, dampening the resonance. The sound lingers, then fades into the concrete, like a dying factory siren.

The three of them look needily at Etienne. In this light

Frederick's eyes are more grey than blue. 'What do you think?' he asks. 'Would you like to make us a foursome?'

'Shall we start a shockwave?' Christof asks.

'Turn it all around? Make everything new?'

It is as if they have just auditioned for *him*. As if *they* are being tested. He is moved by these three men. Boys, really, with their hungry eyes, their bodies tensed in anticipation. Like receptive triplets, the same clear current flowing through all three of them. It feels as if they are his lovers. Or his brothers. He doesn't believe in their music. Or not yet. But he believes in them. Why they are pulling him into their midst – with such suddenness and surrender – he has no idea.

'Yes,' Etienne says. 'Everything new, all from scratch. Let's start with the name. We'll call ourselves Stunde Null. We'll make music together, music that no one has ever heard before.' Like wild children, he thinks. Like gods. Like guides in the dark.

They squirm with delight, the three dark-haired men. Frederick wipes his fringe from his face, embraces Etienne without warning. The other two hug him too. Etienne stiffens slightly; the intimacy is so unexpected. And yet so unforced. For the first time since his arrival in Germany, he feels cherished. In this dripping factory where something like bombs or helmets or boots was once manufactured. Where his new friends' shuffling feet are echoing, where the rustling of their clothes against his own sounds louder than the music of moments ago.

Chapter 21

FROM THE WESTERN side, Etienne takes a different route back through Friedrichstrasse – through more corridors, past more guards. He is thinking of his new band, of his conversation with them about Axel. After the audition, they made him sit down among the instruments. They wanted to know about the Polaroid photo, about the man looking out beyond the frame, laughing. He started telling them, gaining pace as he progressed: of his and Axel's first meeting, their time together in London, the disappearance. Too much, he knew. Too fast and too easy. His growing wariness had been causing him to bottle things up. Like a true East Berliner, he had instinctively started withholding, had stopped trusting anyone with information. There in the factory, two courtyards deep from Oranienstrasse, in the face of their intensity and the echo-like silence, he opened up. It was as if he were telling a story about strangers to strangers.

When he had said all there was to say, he suddenly thought of his mother's letters. He had brought them to Berlin. He had promised he would notify Patrick of his German address; Patrick would then forward correspondence and ship his drums. A month has passed, yet he hasn't contacted Patrick. His mother doesn't know he is here. Apart from Frau Drechsler, Nils and the personnel of the two film schools – and whoever monitors 72 Stargarder Strasse's Hausbuch – no one knows where he is. He is travelling towards oblivion, becoming a swift pencil sketch, a silver shadow. Patrick is his only contact in London, and his only link with his mother. Patrick, who could himself at any moment float into the ether, drift away like marijuana smoke.

Here in Friedrichstrasse's underground labyrinth, Etienne suddenly feels light and free. And lost.

After the three West Germans had heard the story of the disappeared Axel, in an ever denser cloud of cigarette smoke, they were full of ideas. If was as if the search was their own biggest problem. Frederick promised to ask around in Tom's Bar and other places in Motzstrasse and Kreuzberg. In SO36 and also straight clubs like Park and Jungle. In cafés like Slumberland and Die Rote Harfe. The bandmates wanted to take the little Polaroid photo, but Etienne couldn't part with it. They would pin notices on community noticeboards. And place a classified advertisement in a paper. *Bild* would be too expensive – rather the *Berliner Morgenpost*. Frederick did the writing, while Etienne dictated: 'Missing: Axel . . .' He stopped, remembering that he didn't know Axel's surname. 'Axel from London. Etienne is urgently looking for you in Berlin. Last contact 12 December 1986 . . .' Etienne wanted to leave money for the ad. They refused.

In the East German passport official's little booth, there is the usual confusion about his travel document. He puts the bag of items he bought on his way to the station down by his feet without speaking. With the *titre de voyage* open in front of him, the guard gets instructions on the telephone. There has to be a hidden camera somewhere: it is clear the person on the phone can also see the document.

After a customs official has carefully sifted through Etienne's shopping, he withdraws his Ostmark at the currency counter. At last he makes it across the platforms, past the barriers and counters and control points, through the tunnels and cubicles and corridors with their pale green tiles. When he counts his money outside on Georgenstrasse, Goethe and Engels are staring up from the twenty- and fifty-mark notes, past him, towards the East Berlin sky. He has to orientate himself after the maze of the station. He opens his nostrils, lets the fumes of Trabants and Wartburgs in. He listens to the trams, looks up at the sky – murkier on this side, the colour of congealed fat. Maybe, he thinks, he prefers things so dreary: here in the East graffiti is written on your guts, and you wear invisible tattoos.

The iron sounds of Stunde Null's noise are lingering in his ears. They will be able to make something of it. He will have his drums shipped to West Berlin, even if it costs half his month's scholarship money. He could store it in his new friends' little factory.

It is ironic, Etienne thinks on the U-Bahn to Prenzlauer Berg, that his lack of talent has brought him to the other side of the Iron Curtain. His two later film projects in London didn't show much improvement. In one of them, his focus was on Bonnington Square. It was winter; there were no longer parties and music in the open air. The streets were empty, the trees bare. In No. 52, Patrick was lying in a haze of smoke that had apparently robbed him of his speech. Etienne hovered on the stairs, listening out for the Finns. He took a close-up of his closed bedroom door. There were new squatters everywhere who didn't know him.

Some of the old inhabitants had forgotten him, or so they pretended. Nobody was, in any event, in the mood to perform for Etienne's lens. He went back to the café, where the volunteer cooks were irritated by the camera in the cramped kitchen. The drinkers in No. 37 were annoyed too. Hilde and Glenda, each with a glass of red wine in her hand, turned their backs. Others pushed away the camera.

Without a Trace, Etienne called this film. It ends with a shot of the frozen community garden, Frank's bells audible in the background.

For the third project, he took Miss Jackson's cubs in Kilburn as his subject. Young South Africans, as pale as subterranean plants. They weren't in the mood for Etienne's camera either. Etienne kept returning, lingering in the rooms of a few who had half-heartedly started talking on camera. He tried to gain their confidence, probing them about their escape from South Africa, and their lives in London. He wanted to avoid a political angle insofar as possible, wanted to get under the milky skins. Some unfolded their arms, stretched out their legs on the single beds, started talking more freely. Generally, they didn't say much; the soundtrack consisted mostly of Etienne's unanswered questions. He didn't film faces. The lens would instead pan over worn rugs, or posters of films and art exhibitions. Over bookshelves: sociology and anthropology, Gordimer novels, a biography of Che Guevara. And bodies: toes stirring, pale sunlight on a rough knee. One morning he arrived to find Miss Jackson blocking the front door. In a thin kaftan, despite the cold. Her expression was vague, her arms folded. She shook her head. He had to manage with the material he had. It was his shortest film, entitled *Refusal*.

His instructors shook their heads over the cobbled-together results, the films about failed attempts to make films. They were increasingly reticent in their comments. At the assessment meeting for *Refusal*, only one had something to say: 'Your theme is unclear. There is a strangeness of atmosphere, but there is hardly a story to follow, and we get to know little about the people in your film.' The formal report entailed a single sentence: *The candidate has not succeeded in organising his material in an engaging manner.* They had given up.

The good mark for his seminar project could not carry him. He wrote it in diary form – an echo of Irmgard's production journal. His 'diary' consisted of a chronology of his search, as well as copies of correspondence, notices and newspaper advertisements. And his own storyboards for imagined scenes in *Berliner Chronik*. The day that Etienne had gone to Rotherhithe was described, although the presence of the dying Bernhard Sauer and the finding of the film reel were left out. According to the 'diary', Etienne had arrived there in Thatcher's barren field to find nobody at home; the anonymous note was just another false clue, the visit another cul-de-sac. The diary ended with Etienne pedalling home empty-handed.

His seminar lecturer showed Etienne's so-called diary to the scriptwriting instructor. The latter called Etienne to his office, suggested that he might want to focus on scriptwriting. 'If you were to sharpen your plotting – tighten the tension, dramatise events more vividly – something might come of it. Write another ending. Let your character find the film.' But Etienne was happy with the open ending. The only two people who would ever know about the real ending – and the evening of projector light, ghost images and silver snow in a Bermondsey Street backyard – were he and Axel.

When it became clear, just before Christmas, that Axel wasn't coming back, Etienne wanted to go and search for him in Berlin. There was no way he could afford it. He had to calm down, wait for an opportunity. In early January, information about the student exchange programme was made available. The possibilities were New York, Vancouver, Stockholm, Barcelona, even Mexico City. And the HFF in East Berlin. Berlin was the only place where Etienne wanted to be, *had* to be. Axel was there, and, he hoped, the remainder of *Berliner Chronik*. West Berlin wasn't on the list. He chose the HFF, hoping no one else would. The London Film School was surely keen to get rid of him. In light of his anti-apartheid aura, and the political intervention around his admission, it would have been hard for them to force him out. In March he heard that he was on his way to East Germany's only film school. And that his scholarship money would be increased. He was stranded in London until the new academic year, but a new city was beckoning.

Etienne gets off at Schönhauser Allee, turns left in Stargarder Strasse as usual. Chilly fog is floating around his ankles.

When he enters the flat on the fifth floor of No. 72, Frau Drechsler is sitting in the Berliner Zimmer. The radio is on. The voice of Erich Honecker, the East German leader, is droning. Etienne's earlier, tentative feeling of arriving home, when he had exited Friedrichstrasse on the eastern side, instantly evaporates as Drechsler's beady eyes meet his gaze.

He has brought back gifts from West Berlin. A bottle of French Chablis and Swiss chocolate for Frau Drechsler. Cassettes for Nils: Bronski Beat, Depeche Mode, Roxy Music. These he had hidden on his person. Chocolate imports are rationed; the customs official had weighed it. Frau Drechsler frowns at the wine, as if she is planning to throw it away. The next day he hears her humming and smacking her lips; he catches a glimpse of her with a glass brimful of Chablis in her hand. A welcome change, he is sure, from her nasty Rotkäppchen Sekt. And better than she would find at Exquisit – the Ost-Delikatessen in Kastanienallee – even if she could afford it. She is tuned into Stimme der DDR, propelled by East German Schlager music. She isn't dancing. Or not quite. Her oscillations between the Berliner Zimmer and the kitchen aren't entirely independent of the swerving melodies. Etienne looks at her swollen feet in slippers.

Etienne has greater freedom at the HFF than in London. The fact that he left South Africa in protest, and is vaguely focused on anti-fascist films, is enough. He is not expected to do any practical work. Not that the standard of student work here intimidates him; it consists of sycophantic documentaries toeing the party line or, in the case of narrative films, sentimental social realism that defies any sense of reality.

He has been attending classes for almost six weeks, and now he has to select a research topic. 'Trümmerfilme are what I wish to study,' he announces to Herr Direktor. He is sitting in the director's office, on an orange chair. He wants to do a comprehensive investigation, he explains, into this genre that was so popular in the 1940s. Stories of people trying to survive in the rubble of destroyed German cities while being confronted by moral and ethical questions. He initially wanted to profess that he would be working on 'mountain films' from the 1930s – films featuring heroic adventures in the Alps, with hardly any dialogue. The uncomfortable associations with filmmakers who were later co-opted by the National Socialists would, he subsequently decided, make this genre a suspect choice. Leni Riefenstahl, Hitler's favourite film propagandist, had, after all, once enthusiastically performed in such a film.

'That is a dignified and promising subject,' the director says. 'The semi-documentary nature of several Trümmerfilme offers a firm base for the kind of work we encourage here at Konrad Wolf. Insofar as both production and theoretical study are concerned.'

Etienne listens to his robotic cadences, like a child reciting portions of the Bible. He was right not to mention anything about his true subject, *Berliner Chronik*. His first meeting with the director served as a warning as to what could be said. Although Benjamin was once nominally a communist, his position is far too complicated, his class background too decadently Jewish-bourgeois, to fit in with this man's – or his masters' – schemes. Etienne looks into the director's watery eyes, at his ill-fitting jacket. Yellowish and rough-textured, like curtain cloth. He suddenly feels sorry for him. How does his internal life align with what he is reciting? Which thwarted creative ambitions are simmering inside his skull?

Or could it be that he does his work with conviction? It is difficult to read men here. They remind him of South African men: closed and fierce, with a secret yearning for violence.

Herr Direktor keeps nodding. Here is Etienne's chance: Trümmerfilme as smokescreen, the freedom to quietly do what he wants. Veiled projects are nothing new to him. Nor the uttering of compliant sentences that belie the rhythm of the heart.

Chapter 22

ETIENNE EXITS NO. 72, turns left in Stargarder Strasse. Is Frau Drechsler watching him from the bay window? He doesn't look back, crosses Pappelallee. Then Lychener Strasse and Dunckerstrasse, registering the cobbles through his soles. Stained sheets hang in the windows of some former shops; others have been covered up with wooden planks. On stone façades are weathered letters from the previous century. The modernisation of some shopfronts during the GDR era has exposed Jewish traders' names. *Rawitz Kristall und Glas. Kronthal Silberwaren.* Apart from the bakery opposite No. 72, there is only one functioning shop in the street: a Fleischerei. Lumps of shockingly red meat are exhibited in the window.

He crosses to the middle of Prenzlauer Allee; a grey-green tram rattles past, centimetres from his toes. Opposite him is a building with a domed roof. He immediately recognises it: the new planetarium. It looks like a stranded jellyfish, twin brother of the Fernsehturm's dome floating in the distance when he looks down Prenzlauer Allee.

When he was a child, he remembers, his father took him to the Johannesburg planetarium. There was an official narrator: a disembodied voice unlocking the secrets of the cosmos in a soothing voice and SABC English. Other sons and their fathers lay back, drinking in the secrets with shiny eyes. Etienne's father wasn't giving the heavenly narrator a chance. He was elucidating what was happening on the ceiling himself – in an increasingly thundering voice, and an apparent attempt to drown out not only the heavenly voice but the rumblings of the universe itself. Etienne put his hands over his ears, screwed his eyes shut. He dreamt up counter-sounds in his own voice: cacophony to battle the cacophony. His father grabbed him by the arm, took him outside.

Zeiss-Grossplanetarium, it says next to the entrance. Etienne enters, buys a ticket from a woman with a drab face and dull hair. Another man enters behind him, he sees from the corner of his eye.

Etienne sits down in the dark; the chair smoothly tilts back. The glittering universe drifts by above him, but it feels as if *he* is moving. A disembodied voice starts narrating. Heavenly bodies and constellations glow more brightly when the voice refers to them. Etienne's eyes don't follow the illuminations; he is more interested in the darker stars on the edges and the burnt-out planets. The narrator intones comforting cosmic truths, his very tone suggesting infinity. Etienne can hear a grey-faced bureaucrat somewhere behind it.

The other man sits down a few chairs along. They are the only ones in the auditorium. Overhead, explosions and solar systems shift past in a sluggish current, the waters of a sorrowful heavenly river taking leave of tiny human figures in velvet chairs. Stars slip over the edge and disappear. The chairs are ergonomically ill-designed; within minutes Etienne's neck is aching. It is stuffy too. His scalp is itchy, sweat is soaking into the velvet. He can't look away from the drama overhead. The river – an equatorial night river – is now beneath him; he is on his back in a boat. Oarless, heading towards the fast-approaching rush of a waterfall . . .

The man is looking at Etienne rather than the ceiling.

Etienne's eyes have become used to the dark. He returns the man's gaze, annoyed. Was there a subtle hand signal? He ignores him, lies back again.

Underneath the light of the synthetic East German stars he suddenly misses Axel, in his bones. They were only together for a few months. And yet Axel has caused his bone plates to shift tectonically. His body is functioning differently from before. Chunks of bone have split off, attached somewhere else. He is now more scar tissue than healthy flesh. If he were to be cut in half and dipped in formaldehyde, he would be a peculiar specimen. The only other halved body that would look like that is Axel's . . .

The man gets up, sits down right next to him. Etienne turns his head. It is the most beautiful man he has ever seen. Shiny eyes, stubbled chin. He is staring at Etienne. In the radiance of Jupiter and Mars, Etienne can see an erection in the man's trousers. He thinks of Axel, of their blasphemous nights in London's vinegary air. He sighs, though it sounds like a sob. He rolls his head sideward to meet the man's lips. The cosmic-bureaucratic god speaks soothingly of explosions on the sun. It is getting warmer and warmer. The sun's flames are roaring, shooting across the firmament. (Will the velvet chairs catch fire?) Then he sees it, through half-open eyes in the orange light: the man's shoes. Etienne pulls back, snarls. He jumps up, shuffles past the chairs. He stumbles, hurries up the aisle, into the lobby and then frenziedly out into the pale afternoon light.

He scurries around the back of the planetarium, turns into the park. 'Idiot,' Etienne addresses himself. 'You stupid bloody idiot!' What had Nils told him? Look at the *shoes*. Shiny Western shoes mean someone is either a visitor from West

Berlin or Stasi. Why would a visitor from West Berlin come to this planetarium? And no ordinary East German would so nonchalantly take risks. He looks over his shoulder at the back of the planetarium, walks into a copse of trees. He won't be tricked again so easily. There is nothing as intimate between men as being strangers; this he learnt in London. In this half of this city, he will have to learn, intimacy doesn't exist, and especially not between those who are closest to each other.

A document that allows Etienne access to the GDR film archives has been issued. Herr Direktor calls him to his office, hands it over personally. It is co-signed by some government official. Why, Etienne wonders, does Herr Direktor show so much interest in him? There are other exchange students here – from Yugoslavia, Romania, Bulgaria. One from Mozambique. Does he give as much attention to them? The director opens a map, draws a red circle around the Staatliches Filmarchiv. He summons Frau Finkel, hands her the map.

'Frau Finkel, won't you show the student the route, please?' Etienne follows her to her small office. She draws a dotted line to a destination on the edge of Potsdam, hands the map to him with an inscrutable smile. Etienne looks at her hair, stacked in a beehive. He half expects her to perform a little dance: the jive or jitterbug, the Lindy hop. She keeps standing there uncomfortably, blinking her eyes. Her smile becomes a grimace.

Every morning, Etienne commutes an hour to the film school. Today he takes a bus even further. He waits in front of the villa where Herr Direktor has his office. It is a cold, foggy day: his first taste of winter here. On the bus he follows Frau Finkel's red dots with his finger.

From the bus stop where he gets off, he has to walk a hundred metres or so further to the Staatliches Filmarchiv in Kohlhasenbrücker Strasse, a cul-de-sac. On the right is a low asbestos building, beyond which a young forest stretches. Soon, winter will be stripping the leaves, but, for now, light is still filtering through the foliage. Trails of fog are seeping through the sprigs; tiny drops are forming on his cheeks.

The front door is locked. He rings a hoarse bell. A woman opens the door, lets him into a reception area. She turns the lock again, walks to her counter. 'Can I help you?'

'I am Etienne Nieuwenhuis.' He extends his hand; she just looks at it. He clears his throat, unfolds the permission document on the counter.

She puts on her glasses, reads, takes them off. 'I am Frau Fuchs.' She walks out from behind the counter, to the opposite side of the space. Etienne follows. She opens a door to a tiny room. She switches on a desk lamp; it emits a small circle of cold light. 'This is how it works: you may sit here . . .' She switches on a light box in front of him. 'A microfiche reader. We only use the newest technology here.' She bends forward, feeds a microfilm into the machine, turns a knob. Categories and lists roll across the screen. He looks furtively at her lower lip, from which her neck runs down chinlessly. She has bulging eyes, as dim as a fish's. Her hair is spiked and peroxided.

'This is how the system works.' She starts reciting an explanation. They have material from the pre-war Reichsarchiv, as well as everything produced in East Germany under the aegis of DEFA, the government film studio. 'And everything from other countries that embrace the socialist system. There are categories and subcategories for newsreels, documentaries, feature films, short films and television programmes . . .'

She drones on in a robotic voice, gives repetitive and contradictory descriptions of the obscure numbering system. The
Reichsarchiv items, she explains, go back to 1934. 'What was
left after the war was taken to Russia for safekeeping. This
material was later brought back. But a lot of things had gone
up in flames. Dissolved into the heavens.' Her hand opens, as
if letting go of a balloon. 'Poof! Smoke and ash. And in 1945
the Americans had looted crates full of Reichsarchiv material.
Whatever might've happened to *that*, no one knows . . . but the
post-war material, administered by the GDR, in *this* archive,'
her finger points at her own chest, as if her body houses shelves
full of film, 'is complete, and scientifically catalogued.'

The little room is chilly; Etienne pulls his arms closer into
his sides. A far-off siren sounds. 'But most of what I've told
you, you may as well forget. What *you* are looking for, those
heart-rending rubble films from the 1940s, you will find here.'
She taps on the screen with a blunt finger, on the category
DEFA Fiktionfilme seit 1946. 'That's what you'll get access to.'

Etienne feels drained by the long-winded explanations.
Why the information about categories and collections to which
he won't be granted access? He takes a deep breath, tries a
shortcut. 'Do you by any chance have lists of lost films? Film
fragments, stills? Or promotional posters? Production notes,
storyboards . . . ?'

She turns her head, observes him. 'What use would you
have for those things?'

'One never knows,' he says smoothly. 'Perhaps there are
Trümmerfilme of which only fragments remain.'

She shakes her head slowly. Her wet lower lip moves
peristaltically, like a naked slug. 'I don't think so.' Her voice
sharpens. 'That history is well-documented. It would be best if

you keep to the confines of your permission.' She hesitates, the protruding eyes opening wide. 'There are,' she says, 'catalogue categories apart from the ones you are seeing now, but you don't have access to those collections.'

'And which categories would those be?'

She shakes her head resolutely. 'Your permission level does not permit disclosure of the categories themselves.' She places a form in front of him. 'If you find something that interests you . . .' She thinks for a moment. 'That you *need*, complete this form. In triplicate. We have a projection room. Frau Keller, my colleague, will review and consider your requests. You have to give us twenty-four hours' notice. Not a minute less.' Each request probably has to be approved elsewhere, Etienne reckons. By bureaucrats in dim cubicles, behind bunker concrete. Or in overlit offices with plastic phones and synthetic carpets.

He tries again. 'I would also be keen to get access to films that were classified as degenerate art by the fascists. And censorship certificates from that time.'

She pouts her lower lip above the negative incline of the chin. 'As I said, material outside your field is not accessible. This archive is for specialist research.'

She looks at him in silence, exits and closes the door. It has a layer of sponge for soundproofing, like in a cell or institute for the mentally ill. What sounds has it had to dampen? If you pressed your ear against the sponge, would it release the absorbed information?

He turns the knob. The microfilm catalogue starts moving. His face is reflected in the screen; lists of film names scroll over his forehead and cheeks.

Chapter 23

IN THE WEEKS that Etienne has been here, he has spent far less time in West Berlin than he had originally planned. He has, indeed, only been there once. He has been occupied by his life in the East: long days at the film school or archive, and long nights with Nils at parties in bombed-out buildings, where they drink beer in the cold eastern winds. After that night on Nils's single bed they have not undressed each other again. For Etienne it was a moment of hesitation and forlornness. He has not had the urge to repeat it.

Axel will not let Etienne go, keeps whispering at him. Etienne cannot make out the messages, but it is *his* voice: behind the noise of trams, or in the windy wake of underground trains. The vapour of his breath hangs in the quiet streets. Etienne *sees* him: in profile behind windows, loitering in the city haze. He fears that winter will cause Axel's mutterings to freeze, will bury his footsteps under snow.

It is especially in the gaps, cracks and breaches that Axel keeps appearing. One evening at dusk Etienne is on the bridge above Warschauer Strasse S-Bahn station. Rubber wheels are hissing on the tar. A red moon is rising over a river of gleaming tracks. Halfway down the stairs to the station a little light lures Etienne closer. In a bridge pillar, a shrine has been carved out: Mary with Jesus in her arms. A battery is protruding from Jesus's back; light is shining from his heart. When a train thunders by in a shower of sparks, he sees it: Baby Jesus has

Axel's face. In the radioactive glow of the moon and the infant's neon heart, Etienne suddenly feels ill. He drops to his knees. 'You're an island of fire, Axel. I'm trying to hear what you're saying, I want to answer you.' People are scurrying past. He wonders whether his words emerged in English, German or Afrikaans.

One evening Etienne accompanies Nils to an exhibition of the work of arts students at Humboldt University. It is in a dilapidated old brewery in Mitte that still smells of fermentation. One work immediately draws Etienne's attention: the skeleton of a minotaur. Body of a bull, head of a human. Axel would have liked this, he thinks. He studies it close up. Has it been built up painstakingly? Or carefully carved out – rib by rib, vertebra by vertebra?

'The skeleton of a bull, in part. With plaster of Paris components added to it.' Etienne's ear instantly places the accent of the voice behind him. He turns around. The man is smiling broadly in the electrical light. 'Mthuthuzele. You can call me Mthu.'

'Etienne.' They shake hands. Etienne points at the minotaur vertebrae where they curve up to the human neck. 'I can see it now, yes. The colour and texture changing subtly.' Etienne concentrates on his self-taught British cadences, closely observing Mthu. 'Are you the artist?'

'No,' Mthu laughs. 'A friend of mine.' He gestures vaguely at a group of students. 'I'm also studying at Humboldt, but in a different field.'

'A different field?'

The sharp light above them translates Mthu's smile into a grin. It is the first time Etienne has ever met a black South

African who is not a manual labourer. Here in East Berlin, pondering the skeleton of a minotaur. His cheeks are burning with shame.

'Usually, of course, it's the other way round,' Mthu says. Etienne looks at him questioningly. He points at the skeleton. 'The *body* of a human and the *head* of a bull.' He smiles. 'But enough of skeletons. Shall we go and grab a beer?'

Etienne hesitates, then gestures over Mthu's shoulder to Nils, who is engaged in conversation, that he is heading out. Nils looks at Mthu, then back at Etienne.

The Kneipe that they go to is a sombre place; the only other patron is a silent old man. The fluorescent light above their table emits cold blue light. How sickly his pale skin looks in such light, Etienne thinks.

'So, what's your field of study?' Etienne asks when their beers arrive.

Mthu takes a swig. 'First tell me – what do *you* do?'

'Studying anti-fascist film in Potsdam.' His tone lies somewhere between satire and self-justification.

Mthu is silent for a while, his mouth pulled askew in the unnatural lighting. Etienne can't gauge his expression. 'I'm being trained in counter-insurgency and revolutionary strategy at Humboldt. With others from South Africa, Mozambique, Angola . . .' The cool light catches the white of Mthu's eyes. 'You're from South Africa too, aren't you?'

Etienne looks away, says nothing. Pins and needles in his cheeks again.

Mthu sits forward. 'There is work to do, you know. We organise things from here. The liberation in South Africa is coming, but we need hands. And minds. They are equipping us here, giving us money.' Mthu is silent for a while. 'Join us,' he says. 'You have connections that could be useful to us.' He flashes a blue smile. 'Very useful.'

Etienne feels the blood cooling in the back of his neck. What does this man know about him, about his ties? When Etienne says nothing, Mthu continues: 'Surely you understand: here you are either *in* or you are *out*.' Mthu calmly swigs beer. 'This is your chance, my friend. Opt in.'

Etienne lifts his beer, takes a mouthful. It is all so sudden, so direct. His heart is beating fast. Mthu bends down, takes something from his backpack under the table. Etienne's hand clenches around the cold bottle.

It is a cassette that Mthu produces; he puts it down in front of Etienne. He doesn't touch it. 'What is this? What's on it?'

Mthu laughs. 'Don't worry. It's not explosive intelligence. Or plans for treason. It's music, comrade. Music for the revolution. I think you'll like it.' He takes something else out, puts it down on the table: a bright red Sony Walkman.

Etienne looks down. Not at the cassette or device, but at Mthu's long, well-shaped fingers. He lifts his hand, strokes with the tip of his finger along a bulging vein on Mthu's forearm. Mthu pulls back swiftly, shifting his chair back. He looks down at his arm in astonishment, as if a cockroach has crawled across it. Then he looks at Etienne. The corners of his mouth turn down. He gets up, leaves money next to his beer and walks out.

Etienne looks at the banknote on the table. Depicted on it is a woman sitting behind the control panel of a nuclear station.

Whatever had possessed him?

Later that night, he and Nils are in Etienne's room. 'I have to tell you,' Nils says. 'One afternoon last week I heard something in your bedroom. When I peered in, old Drechsler was there—' A tram rattles past in Pappelallee, crossing Stargarder Strasse. 'There she stood, looking at the pictures on your wall—'

'The storyboards?'

Nils nods. 'She studied each of them, taking notes. Possibly took photos too.'

Etienne nods seriously, but he feels like laughing. Of what conceivable use could those drawings be to anyone? He looks at Nils, at his sharp nose and delicate hands, the meditative intensity of his eyes. How accessible he suddenly seems!

'You once asked me why I'm here, Nils. Well, I'm looking for a film. Or rather for my beloved.' The word *beloved* hovers strangely on his tongue. He assesses the aftertaste. All he can discern are the autumnal coal fires of Berlin, the air that mixes so acridly with memories of love. One gets used to the pungency; after a while you have to think about the air in order to taste it. Etienne continues, tells Nils more than he had intended to: how he left South Africa, his summer in London, how he met Axel. Etienne looks at the washbasin while talking. Nils is listening patiently, Etienne sees from the corner of his eye, head bowed. He talks about *Berliner Chronik*. About Axel's disappearance, his encounter with Matthias, Christof and Frederick, with whom he is going to play gay industrial rock. 'But Axel . . .' He shakes his head. 'I don't even know where to start the search. How can someone just vanish like that?'

There is a long silence. 'Perhaps,' Nils says, rocking slightly, 'you shouldn't tell me so much. Remember where you are.' It is too dark to make out Nils's face. The next train shudders past in Pappelallee, resonating in Etienne's jaw. He feels a cold draught against his neck muscles, which have been contracting in a painful spasm since his afternoon in the planetarium.

After Nils has gone to bed, Etienne studies the cassette that Mthu gave him. Nothing is written on the plastic case. He takes out the cassette. Written on it with felt-tipped pen, in childlike letters, is the word KOOS. He takes out the paper lining of the case, unfolds it. Written on this is *SING JY VAN BOMME?* Are you singing of bombs? Written with the same felt-tipped pen.

He picks up the red Walkman, wondering whether the earphones might explode against his temples. He puts it on, screws his eyes shut, presses Play. His skull doesn't shatter. It is a song in Afrikaans, but unlike anything he has heard before. Punky and dissonant, pissed off, anarchical. The lyrics are: 'We shall sing for the sleeping ones who dream of violence and blood. We must sing for the harmless ones who make bombs BOOM! BOOM! BOOM!' KOOS must be the name of the band, then? And 'SING JY VAN BOMME?' the track's title? He plays it again. This time it sounds like avant-garde jazz, with an industrial weft. There is nothing else on the cassette.

He takes off the earphones, listens to the silence. Where would Mthu have tracked this down? Etienne thinks of the guards on their towers in the death strip, changing shifts in the dark, the glowing ends of their cigarettes briefly engaged in a dance. He suddenly wonders whether a sliver of space might have been available to him in South Africa after all, whether his solo exile really was the only way out. Then he thinks about Mthu's recruitment effort. How carefully he and his fellow counter-insurgency students must have targeted Etienne with this rare piece of Afrikaans punk, all the way from South Africa. He takes the cassette out of the Walkman, slips it back into the case, puts it under his bed.

Etienne's pockets are filled with bits of paper. A note with Matthias, Christof and Frederick's phone number, an address of their shared flat in Kreuzberg. Another with names from Irmgard's diary. Bösel the cameraman, Stahl the sound engineer and Schwarz the lighting specialist. Irmgard's diary provides no more than functional nuggets of information about their tasks and skills. Whether they were Jews is unclear. Did they rise into the skies as ash decades ago, either from concentration camps or in Allied firestorms? This search remains an impossible task.

Etienne can't provide anyone with a phone number: Frau Drechsler's grey plastic telephone, exhibited in the Berliner Zimmer, is not available for receiving calls. 'I had to wait four years to get a phone connection,' she says. 'And now I don't want to be bothered constantly by lodgers' calls.' She allows calls to be *made* at a fee, provided the duration is less than ten minutes. When Nils phones his parents in Dresden, she times his conversation with a stopwatch.

She is always at home, old Drechsler. Nobody visits and she doesn't call anyone. On Etienne's way in or out, he has to pass her in the gloomy Berliner Zimmer. She is guarding her phone. And the radio. And the food in the pantry. And her washing machine. Doing one's laundry attracts a fee for each washing cycle. He and Nils consequently stuff the washing machine as full as possible. This does not escape her attention. These days she weighs the bundles, charging by the kilogram. Soon she will probably start issuing invoices for toilet visits. Even under

Frau Drechsler's roof, the values of Marx and Engels have to yield to entrepreneurial cunning.

Etienne seeks out Frau Drechsler where she is sitting in front of the black-and-white television. He greets her with a nod. She gazes at him impassively.

'May I use the phone directory, Frau Drechsler?'

'What for?'

'To look up the number for Frau Finkel, the film school secretary,' he lies. She hands him the directory, reaches for her stopwatch. He takes the directory back to his bedroom. She starts getting up from her chair, trying to formulate an objection. He closes his door. Why should he thumb through it under her supervision?

Anton Bösel. The name of the cameraman. According to Irmgard's production journal, there are initially two cameramen. Later, when finances become tight and the atmosphere increasingly menacing, just Bösel remains. Etienne keeps scanning the directory pages. What luck – there are only seven Bösels in all of East Berlin! Three have A as one of their initials. He looks up Schwarz and Stahl. Hundreds of each. He cleanly tears out the page with the Bösels, scrunches it up and sticks it into his pocket.

Back in the Berliner Zimmer he hands over the directory. He smiles serenely, walks out the front door. He will yet come to regret provoking Frau Drechsler in this manner, of that he is sure. He heads to a Telefonzelle on Schönhauser Allee. He takes coins from his pocket, and the crumpled page. He arbitrarily selects an *A Bösel*. With the coins in his palm, he changes his mind. He will not overcome suspicion and resistance in a telephone conversation. He stands a far better chance by arriving on someone's doorstep. Three addresses, three destinations.

He takes the U-Bahn. The first address is in Mitte, a block of flats near the Hackesche Höfe on the deserted western edge of East Berlin. He knocks on the door; there is no response. At the second address, in Friedrichshain, an old woman opens the door slightly. She shakes her head when he starts telling the story of the Benjamin film. There is incomprehension in her eyes. Then naked suspicion, fear. She interrupts him: 'I don't know anybody who is involved in movies or TV or anything like that. I come from Dresden,' she adds, as if that explains everything. As if evading an official interrogator. She shuts the door.

He takes the U-Bahn again, gets off at Magdalenenstrasse station. From Frankfurter Allee he turns into a side street, the crumpled phone-book page in his hand. He stops in front of a Plattenbau block. The flats look like modules stacked on top of each other by a crane. A woman answers the intercom. There is a long silence after he has rattled off the story of the film and his search for it. For a moment he thinks the intercom has been disconnected. Then she mentions the name of a hotel bar on Frankfurter Allee. 'Meet me there.' The little speaker crackles, cuts out.

He is sceptical, but walks back, finds the hotel. It is in a modern building, communist architecture. The bar's interior, a faux-Bavarian space, is out of step with the exterior: fireplace, dark wood, idyllic pictures of reindeer and snow. He waits. For almost forty minutes. Just he and a bored waiter. It is stuffy in there. The winter sun is shining through the window. The air smells of old carpets and dry wood; the windows can't open. He looks at his watch. He should have known: she just wanted to get rid of him. Just as he gets up to leave, she walks in. Middle-aged, a pale-green dress, brown hair in a bob. She looks around, sits down opposite him.

'Can I order you something to drink?'

She doesn't want anything. He orders a bottle of Hungarian Riesling for himself. Bugger his student budget, he thinks. He is celebrating prematurely and recklessly: perhaps today there will be a breakthrough.

Now that they are sitting opposite each other, she isn't saying anything. He repeats the story that he recounted over the intercom. He is becoming well-practised at this. She looks through the window at the wide, deserted street. 'Where do you come from?' she wants to know.

'Finland,' he says without hesitation. 'I'm an exchange student at the Hochschule für Film und Fernsehen in Potsdam.' He can feel her tension. He tells her where he is living, lies about how good the film school supposedly is, and about how fascinating he is finding East Berlin. She suddenly sits forward, takes his glass of Riesling, empties it in one draught. She interrupts him bluntly. She explains, without taking a breath, as if in one long sentence, that she has an uncle who was in the film industry in the 1930s, who, insofar as she knows, was a cameraman, that she doesn't know where he lives, but that she has her uncle's daughter's address. And, although she doesn't have contact with her cousin either, *she* probably has contact with her father.

She gets up agitatedly. Etienne too. 'Your cousin's address? Please, it's important.' She looks intently at him, as if she cannot believe that she has allowed herself to be drawn into this. He takes a pen from his pocket, holds it out towards her together with a napkin. The waiter looks on cynically. She hesitates, then writes something on the napkin. She walks out of the bar without looking at Etienne again.

He has no idea why she was willing to talk to him. He looks

at her crossing Frankfurter Allee, with little steps, head bowed. He wonders whether she is so lonely that she would exchange information for a few minutes' engagement, irrespective of the risk. The first rule here is to distrust strangers. The second rule is to distrust those you know. Information is dangerous, however trivial it might seem. And traitors come in many guises.

But if she is hungry for company, why would she rush out? Was he a disappointment? Did the waiter look like an informant? Perhaps, he thinks, she is slightly nuts. She would hardly be the first. Thus one learns: next time he will rather try to extract information before imparting too much.

Etienne sits down again, beckons the waiter for more of the Riesling. This isn't the first time he has noticed East German waiters' habit of withholding wine. They pour a little, then immerse the bottle in a bucket of lukewarm water some distance away. They wait until you beg for it, then come and pour another dash, take it away again. A kind of stand-off: there stands the waiter, guarding the bottle. And here he sits, craving the crisp flavours of Hungarian vineyards.

At last the waiter approaches to pour him half a glass. Does Frau Bösel with the green dress have a sinister agenda? Etienne wonders, as the wine washes against his palate. He doesn't have the vaguest idea, he realises, of how anything here actually works.

The next afternoon Etienne walks to the planetarium again. He buys a ticket, stretches out in one of the reclining chairs. He is vigilant, keeping an eye on the sparse audience of men. Then he concentrates on the ceiling. It is the only place, this theatre of catastrophe, where Etienne can tolerate his own tears. It is here – with heavenly bodies crashing and exploding above him – that Axel comes to him. The bureaucrat's voice unravels the secrets of the universe: dark matter, black holes, brown dwarfs, wormholes. Axel is sucked in and spat out by a wormhole, devoured by colossal forces. Just a cloudlet of molecules remains. Only Etienne's yearning can patch him together again: a new Axel appears, shining brightly in the splintered light of stars.

He must urgently return to West Berlin. A post-mortem image of Axel in the stars is not enough. He must go and search in the real world, in the streets. And he has to return to the triplets with their industrial instruments. He has been walking around with their address and telephone number on a scrap of paper in his pocket for over a month now. It has been through the washing machine already, battered by Frau Drechsler's cheap industrial washing powder, but he can still decipher it. The three West Berliners were so generous, receiving him into their midst so unconditionally. The beginning of something was flickering: a movement, a revolution, a band to surpass all others. Despite his promises, he hasn't contacted them again. The unreliability of phone connections to West Berlin is no excuse.

Etienne notices movement: men shifting towards each other, fidgeting, fussing. And there you have it: he has discovered the local pick-up joint! Was the man with the Stasi shoes indeed just looking for a kiss? For a mouth like a tunnel in the dark? What Etienne is seeking out is the velvety darkness. The fiery tracks of meteors. Forces that give human form to the energy of desire. The groaning and sucking in the back rows bring his séance to a swift end.

Chapter 24

IT IS ETIENNE'S second visit to West Berlin, and his fourth time in Friedrichstrasse station's oppressive labyrinth. It is easier to navigate the corridors and platforms and counters this time round. He is nevertheless aware of his heartbeat when he enters the passport official's little cubicle. It is long and narrow, clad in fake wood. The entry door closes automatically behind him; there is a stuffy intimacy between him and the expressionless man in his dull brown uniform. When the ritual of the phone call regarding his travel document is over, an invisible button is pressed. There is a buzzing sound; the second door opens with a loud clack.

He is feeling less strange in the West this time, doesn't immediately miss East Berlin's sour air. When he closes his eyes, he can see the shape of the West Berlin U- and S-Bahn on the back of his lids.

He called Frederick last night – Frau Drechsler at the ready with her stopwatch – and arranged for them to meet again. Frederick was simultaneously happy and dejected. 'I thought we were never going to hear from you again.'

'Sorry. Life here in the East isn't always simple. But I'm coming! Tomorrow.'

They arranged to meet at the old Oranienstrasse factory, but when Etienne exits Kottbusser Tor U-Bahn station, Frederick waves at him from across the street, fringe hanging over his eyes. He gives Etienne a long hug, with greater force than one would expect from his size. He is more muscular than Etienne remembers, and on the verge of developing a belly.

In the factory space, the other two are lying on an old sofa, smoking. They jump up to welcome Etienne back, without any trace of annoyance about his long absence. What has he done to deserve such seamless inclusion in their ranks? Such warmth and unconditionality?

They make him sit down, inform him that the classified advertisement in *Berliner Morgenpost* has not yielded any clues. Nor their notes on noticeboards or enquiries in bars, cafés and clubs. They try to convince Etienne again to lend them the photo to show around. 'No,' Etienne says, 'that I cannot let go of.' Christof tells him that they prodded the blond waiter at Anderes Ufer again. He doesn't know anything else, Frederick says and wipes his long fringe from his eyes. A few people in Tom's Bar still remember Axel, but no one has encountered him over the last two years.

Matthias's dense eyebrows twist asymmetrically. He clears his throat, empties a glass of water in long swigs. His Adam's apple beats like a heart as he swallows. 'Are you sure he *is* here?' he enquires cautiously, putting down the glass.

Christof adds: 'He might've said he was coming to Berlin, but *did* he . . . ?'

'Who knows?' Frederick sighs before Etienne can respond. As if the loss is his own, and the mystery impenetrable. He holds out the advertisement that he has torn from the paper. Etienne takes it between two fingertips, like a piece of skin.

Etienne wants to place the advertisement a second time. 'And a new one. About *Berliner Chronik*.' They nod.

Etienne then dictates the same kind of request for information as in his previous notices in London community papers.

Matthias gets up, stretches his tall body. 'We *will* find Axel and the film, but let's first make some music now.'

Etienne, Christof and Frederick take place at their instruments, Matthias in front of the microphone. They start haltingly. Then they catch each other's eyes, probing the noise. Etienne waits, holding his drumsticks at shoulder height until his arms ache. The sticks sweep down, bashing a steel pipe. Over and over again. The other three grin determinedly. They react; momentum is building.

The mutual glances become increasingly tense; the violence is growing. He underestimated them before, Etienne thinks. Their noise now seems to swallow the city: the trains, the black night sky, the bullet holes. The death strip with its landmines, barbed wire and mutilated cemeteries. The dead factories and hostile lakes, the steaming bodies of men like ploughed winter soil. It is as if the four of them are tied up with dirty ropes. The more wildly they try to wriggle loose, the blacker and denser the sound becomes.

When they are done, and the energy in the air discharges, they light cigarettes. There are dents in the steel pipes next to Etienne. 'The reason,' Matthias says distractedly, pulling on his cigarette, 'why, at any given moment, you can tear an inferno from your guts in this city, is that you're constantly aware of being in a fucking cage. Whichever direction you start walking, you'll always ultimately come up against a wall.'

The scar on Christof's neck has swollen into an angry red welt. He keeps scratching it ferociously, interrupting Matthias:

'And also because everyone knows: as soon as world politics fuck up, we'll be the first to ascend to the heavens in a cloud of fire.'

Frederick draws smoke deep into his lungs, lifts his T-shirt and rubs his swarthy stomach. 'When you turn towards the wind, you can already smell the ash,' he says.

Etienne looks at his friends with fresh eyes. The four of them are going to make a kind of music that no one has ever heard. They walk out into the courtyard – in file, as Stunde Null – and look up at the square of sky above them. Etienne feels so emptied of desire that he loses all interest in his cigarette. The others' cigarettes also burn down to the filter, forgotten. One by one the butts fall from their fingers.

When they say goodbye at the U-Bahn station, they make Etienne promise that he won't stay away so long again. In return, they promise to keep searching for Axel until they find him. Frederick decides at the last moment to accompany him to Friedrichstrasse. Before Etienne enters the border station, Frederick takes his hand. Over the summer months, on the shore of some Berlin lake, the sun has darkened Frederick's wrists. Small black hairs sprout from his knuckles. He is breathing right by Etienne's ear, as if blowing into a horse's velvety nostrils.

The first film that Etienne requests from the Filmarchiv is *Die Mörder sind unter uns*, a 1946 production. He'd found a summary of it in a film textbook. A Jewish woman returns from the concentration camp to find a traumatised military surgeon living in her flat. She lets him stay on. One day, the surgeon encounters his former captain, who mowed down civilians in cold blood during the war. The captain is now manufacturing steel pots from old war helmets. The surgeon wants to kill him. His Jewish friend convinces him to hand the brute over to the authorities instead, after which she and the surgeon start a new life together.

Once more, Etienne is the only visitor to the archive. He is sitting in the projection room – next to the catalogue room, and not much bigger. He ordered the film from Frau Keller the day before, as required, in her little office in the corridor leading to the storerooms. He offered her the forms through an opening in the wall. 'Just leave it there,' Frau Keller said with a lisp, her face in the shadows.

Frau Fuchs has set up the projector and cautioned Etienne not to interfere with it. While the film is whirring through the projector's gears, Etienne pushes aside a little black nylon curtain. Outside, the trees are dripping. A distance away there is another building, identical to this one. Beyond that, a dark tower.

Before, Etienne had pictured this archive as a formidable old building rather than asbestos structures in a young forest – a musty stone colossus, he'd imagined, with subterranean storeys and stacks of films on endless shelves. He would recognise the vinegary smell with his eyes closed: silver nitrate eating away at steel cases, films working their way towards the light . . . But however dull this archive might be, he would like to search the storerooms himself, without the mediation of Fraue Fuchs and Keller and their forms in triplicate. Alas, access is strictly limited to staff.

He looks at his watch. Just after one. The film is still running. He gets up, opens the door a little. Frau Fuchs isn't behind her desk. He walks quietly across the reception area's linoleum and into the corridor, peers through the hatch into

Frau Keller's office: an empty chair. Both of them are apparently on their lunch break.

He stands still, listens: just his own breath. He looks back at the reception area. There is no movement anywhere. He walks further down the corridor, tests the first door. It is open; fluorescent lights click on automatically inside. He quietly pulls the door shut behind him, opens his nostrils wide. A narrow room with banks of shelves along one wall, tight against each other. Each shelf has a crank. He turns one. The shelves to his right glide away without a sound, opening up a little corridor between them. And there they are: weathered steel containers in neat piles. Dozens of them.

Etienne feels a cool draught on the back of his neck. He swivels around, his scalp tightening. The door is open. Frau Fuchs is standing there, hands on her hips. She slowly shakes her head, her fish eyes bulging. 'You're not allowed in here, Herr Nieuwenhuis. Surely you know that.'

He lets go of the crank; the shelf glides a few centimetres back on the track. He blinks his eyes against the sharp light. Her bottom lip pushes forward, wet and shiny. 'And your permission can be withdrawn. That, I am sure, you know too.' The peroxided spikes of her hair are as stiff as thorns. Her voice rises by an octave: 'What is it you are *really* looking for? What do you think we won't be able to find for you?'

He doesn't respond, just walks sheepishly past her to the reception area and into the projection room. She follows him, stops in the doorway. 'I suppose you are done with that?' She points at the projector, the turning reels. On the screen the surgeon is on the verge of killing the heartless captain. Just before the Jewish woman can intervene, Frau Fuchs switches off the projector. For a few moments it is pitch dark. Then she flicks on the light.

Outside the train window, Schrebergärten are flitting past – little slivers of garden on the outskirts of the city where Berliners grow vegetables or sit on garden chairs in the summer. Even though the film storeroom in Potsdam was far removed from the mouldy Berlin cellars of Etienne's imagination, the smell of vinegar rose unmistakeably when the shelves slid open like gates. The smell of promise, of discovery. In the very moment that Frau Fuchs discovered Etienne, something else caught his eye: rows of files, on a low shelf, of the GDR censors. What he is looking for is similar material from the Third Reich. But would there be much of it? The control of the means of production, and the pre-emptive judging of film projects, would have made censors' cuts during the Nazi era all but superfluous. Surviving degenerate art from the Reichsarchiv would be of greater value, or at least lists of films from the 1930s that were banned or burnt.

The catalogue to which Etienne has access is of no use. There are catalogues and catalogues, Frau Fuchs has indicated – always more categories and subcategories, more shelves. Materials out of reach. In the twilight or pitch dark. Rooms beyond rooms. Further doors, with more complex locks. At Etienne's level, one isn't even allowed to know what is being kept secret: ghost categories keep hovering just beyond one's vision. He doesn't have the right letterhead, the right stamp, the right forms.

He sits back in the train seat. Somewhere amid all the thousands of reels – those that melted in firestorms, were unspooled in the war rubble or have remained preserved in the most unlikely places – must be the *one* film that is haunting him. It is in this archive that he stands the best chance of finding *Berliner Chronik*'s lost reels, or catching the scent of their tracks. It is better than looking up surnames in a telephone directory. If he had free access, he would surely be able to comb through the asbestos building on Kohlhasenbrücker Strasse in a few days. That he has to be at the mercy of such petty obstructions! Having been caught red-handed in the storeroom will make his search trickier, may even have brought an end to it. Information is flowing behind the scenes, that much he knows. Notes are made, and phone calls. Reports are written, privileges revoked. At some point he may well find out that a display of anti-fascist sentiment can only take one so far.

Etienne visits Frau Bösel's cousin. Her flat is in Alt-Hohenschönhausen. She is surly on the intercom. When he mentions Frau Bösel's name, the speaker cuts out. He presses the button again. Nothing. A green-grey van drives past, a delivery vehicle with the name of a butcher on the sides. (Are carcasses swinging behind the panels?) Ringing the intercom with increasing urgency, he thinks of the city's blind spots. Buildings – even entire street blocks – that don't appear on maps.

Nils had told him of the Stasi head offices on Ruschestrasse, near the hotel bar where he and Frau Bösel met. Light-footed and fortified by Hungarian wine, he walked to the massive complex afterwards. He stood in front of the buildings, unfolded his city map. Nothing. A blank space. The contrast between the weight of the buildings in front of him and their absence on the map made his skin crawl. He folded his map, walked briskly away.

He presses the intercom one last time. He should give up,

but he is tired of everything being so impenetrable, of all the suspicion and mistrust. Of secrets behind hostile façades. He will wait right here. For days, if that is what it takes. At some point she will have to leave the building. He sits down on the threshold step. After a while he has to get up to let a young man exit. Shortly afterwards, for an old lady. He is on the verge of leaving when the door opens for a third time. A middle-aged woman with loose grey-streaked hair and a bag for buying groceries.

'Are you Herr Anton Bösel's daughter?' She is startled, heads off down the street. He follows. 'You are, aren't you?' She picks up the pace; he too. Her panic is now tangible. Good, he thinks. In the land of the Stasi one takes one's cue from the Stasi.

He catches up with her, blocks her way. She is wheezing. 'What do you want from me? And from my father?'

'Ah, so he *is* your father!' She leans against a wall, looking for help over his shoulder. He softens his tone: 'Just information. I'm looking for a film. I'm not Stasi. I'm from the West.' She looks down at his shoes. His voice rises again: 'The address! Now!' Amid tears she blurts it out. He stands aside, lets her pass. She pulls in her shoulders, folds an arm across her soft organs.

Etienne doesn't bother with practical film-school projects. The anti-fascist from South Africa is, after all, occupied with his important project about Trümmerfilme. Until now, he has been attending lectures, but he doubts whether anyone would care if he didn't. One afternoon he skips class, takes an early train back. Berlin rain is pouring straight down, returning the factory smoke to earth. He is drenched and soiled with soot when he unlocks the flat. From the Berliner Zimmer he notices a shadow in the corridor by his bedroom. He approaches: Frau Drechsler, on her knees in the bathroom. The laundry basket has been turned over. She is sifting through clothes, turning Etienne's trouser pockets inside out. By her feet there are little stacks of receipts and notes. She unfolds each new piece of paper. Rain is drumming against the panes. He steps forward. Frau Drechsler freezes, her eyes on his shoes. She falls backwards against the edge of the bath, starts rattling like a machine gun: 'Coins in pockets break washing machines . . . I'm just making sure . . .'

She stands up briskly. Again, he realises that she is younger than she looks. Her face, as round as a cheese, has a reddish-yellow glow. Her anger makes her look as if she has been exposed to radiation. 'You should be grateful that there *are* facilities here! Not everyone in the GDR has washing machines or telephones, I'll have you know!'

Suddenly Etienne starts wondering: how *does* she afford these luxuries? Surely not from his and Nils's modest boarding fees? He picks up the bundle of clothes, carries it to his room. A futile gesture – it will only have to go back to the laundry basket. He drops it on the floor, sits down on his bed. The tram rattles past in Pappelallee. From now on, Frau Drechsler will surely hate him.

Then it occurs to him: what does Nils do to earn an income? How does he pay *his* rent?

Chapter 25

OVER THE LAST week, Etienne has been dining alone with Frau Drechsler. Nils's bedroom door is now always shut. He hardly speaks to Etienne any more, doesn't call anyone. Etienne hears his cassette player late at night. Traditional Japanese music, alternating with British synthesiser bands. Someone will have to drag him out of his stupor, Etienne thinks. Whether Nils has friends, he doesn't know – he has never met one.

He knocks on Nils's door; the music is turned up. He opens the door, enters. Nils is sitting cross-legged on the bed, staring at the sheets. Etienne turns down the volume. 'Nobody knows I'm here,' Nils says without looking up. His skin is dry, his eyes grey. 'Nothing is moving outside. Not in the courtyards, nor the streets. Not in the air above, nor the tunnels beneath us.' Etienne pricks up his ears: nothing but the rustling of leaves being chased along the streets by the wind.

Nils is rocking slightly. It looks as if his shoulder bones might tear through the T-shirt. Etienne has noticed how Nils avoids eye contact when their paths cross at the bathroom door, each with a towel around his waist. Etienne would stand there in the lingering steam of Nils's shower, dropping his towel in front of the mirror, wondering whether Nils would like to intertwine his thin body with Etienne's again. Etienne remembers their hands in each other's groins. There wasn't much heat between their skins; it hardly broke the ice.

He looks at the blue half-moons under Nils's eyes. He touches Nils's elbow. 'Come and attend a few film-school classes with me. I can't imagine the lecturers would object.'

Nils smiles wryly, shakes his head. 'This isn't England. You can't just turn up. You have to be registered, authorised, approved. Be declared desirable.'

'Walk around in Potsdam, then, while I'm in class. Just get out. Get some fresh air.'

The next morning they board the train together. When they get off at Potsdam station, Etienne says: 'Let's see if they allow you in my class. I'm the anti-fascist from the South, I have room to manoeuvre.'

Nils shakes his head. 'There is something else I want to do.'

'As you wish.'

Nils walks down the street. Etienne takes a tram to the film school.

When Etienne's classes are over, they meet back at the station. Nils's cheeks are red, his head pulled into his shoulders. He has clearly been out in the cold for much of the day. His eyes are shining. 'I want to show you something,' he says. They take a bus, get off after about twenty minutes. Nils veers onto a narrow pedestrian track, between two villas. Etienne follows, looking at the Prussian woodwork on the buildings. The track is wet and slippery. In front of them is one of the lakes that surround – and in places slice through – Potsdam. The villas' gardens stretch down to the shore. The track ends in stone steps that disappear into the lake, as if leading to streets and villas under the water.

Nils wavers on the top step, as if contemplating descending into the chilly watery city. Then he turns left along the shore, towards moored pedal boats shaped like swans. Etienne turns up his coat collar, follows. They stop next to the swans, chained together in pairs. Each has two seats and two sets of pedals. And fibreglass necks like the bowsprits of gondolas. Small wavelets make the hulls collide and the chains rattle. 'Come,' Nils says. He gets into one of the two boats at the back. The circles under his eyes have vanished. He beckons. Etienne hesitates, looking back at the villas' blind windows. 'Those belong to senior Party members,' Nils says in a low voice. 'They're given weekend homes.'

Etienne looks at Nils. 'Surely we can't just *take* a boat?'

Nils starts unstringing the chain. 'I've been going around in one of these for much of the afternoon. It's fine, really.'

'Where's the border? Doesn't it cut across the lake? I don't want to drown with a bullet in my spine.' Or, Etienne thinks, with my arms around a swan's neck and a hole through my heart. Or with a head wound and bloody hands trailing through the water.

'The border is far enough. Do you think they'd take the risk of people drifting over to the West on plastic swans?'

Etienne pulls his coat tighter around himself. In the middle of the lake there is an island with a forest of bare trees. The branches are so dense that one can't see beyond the outer trees. He bends forward, knocks on the fibreglass.

'Did you know,' Nils asks, 'that swans choose partners for life? And often males pair up with males.' He strokes the plastic neck in front of him abstractedly.

Etienne gets in the boat; Nils smiles a little. The fresh air and movement are clearly doing him good. They start pedalling, first backwards until the chain slips off, then out on the open water. Neither of them says anything; only their feet are moving. The wind picks up as they glide further out. Etienne looks over his shoulder at the villas' frozen gardens. He is convinced a dozen eyes are trained on them, perhaps also the crosses of telescopes. His feet are becoming heavier, his neck starting to sweat under his coat. Except for the swan's chest breaking the swell with soft lapping sounds, all is quiet.

'I don't think you're supposed to go out this far,' Etienne says and stops pedalling. 'Perhaps we should turn around.' Nils's hair is sweaty; the veins on his hands stand out in ridges. He is pedalling as hard as he can. 'Nils!'

He keeps going. The water isn't as flat as it looked from the shore. Etienne is now experiencing pure dread: fear of the wide-open space, terror of the depths. Ahead of them, the island's shore is approaching. Etienne starts pedalling again, as if for his life. The swan's neck is arching proudly, anxiously. They get stuck in the shallows; there are tree roots on the bottom. They get out, tug at the swan. It is heavier than one would expect. They drag it across the roots, losing their footing, onto a little beach.

They enter the thicket of trees – a seam of protection against the water and the dark forms that might rise from it. Etienne involuntarily touches his own head, then looks at Nils's, as if to confirm they haven't been shot in the skull. They stop, take off their wet shoes, hang them by the laces around their necks.

The shoes keep the rhythm against their chests as they walk. Etienne's bare feet are freezing and getting muddy, but the wet shoes are likely to be worse. Nils gestures towards the outlines of a colossal building that is now becoming visible among the trees. 'That's what I wanted to show you.'

They stop some distance away from the façade: a grey wall

among silver trees. The scale of it astonishes Etienne. 'What is – or *was* – this?' His voice sounds small.

'An old hospital.'

'Why so isolated? A hospital for what?'

'No idea. Infectious diseases, perhaps?' Plants are trailing and twining everywhere; silence is emanating from the walls. A few tall trunks have fallen and are leaning against the building. Further away, saplings are growing in what used to be a garden.

'How do you know of this place?'

'I discovered it as a child once, while we were holidaying on the other side of the lake. There used to be a few wooden huts and a little beach there. I wanted to come here today and see whether I had made it all up.'

Etienne's feet are getting even colder. This isn't the kind of place, he thinks, that the authorities would want one to visit. Too far from signals and radio waves, from surveillance equipment. The East German government prefers its citizens in the city. In streets with names and houses with numbers. In public housing, preferably, for which the authorities have floor plans. They don't like places where one disappears off the radar, like in Schrebergärten on the edge of the city, or summer houses outside it. Not to speak of a ruin in the shadows, surrounded by so much silent water.

The double doors under the portico are hanging askew. Nils and Etienne enter. Columns of light slant through the tall windows – like those of a wrecked ship – above the central stairway. A tree has fallen and burst through the windows. It is leaning on the stairs' balustrade, as if in a deep sleep.

Halfway up the stairs, the tree trunk blocks their way. Nils looks Etienne in the eye. The urgency that Etienne can sense in Nils makes him queasy. 'I have to tell you something,'

Nils says. Etienne squats, passes underneath the trunk, comes up on the other side. 'Frau Drechsler is making enquiries about you. She wants to know things.' Nils strokes the trunk between them. 'And she's still spying. She takes photos of the pictures on your walls. Looks at your documents, your books and notes. Lifts up your mattress . . .' Etienne rests his palm on the cool bark. The temperature of someone in a coma, he thinks. 'She isn't just nosy,' Nils continues. 'She's reporting to someone.'

Etienne stretches his neck muscles, which are on the verge of cramping. He is listening more closely to Nils's overeager tone than to his words. Nils also crawls under the trunk. They climb the rest of the stairs in silence. They walk down a dim corridor, looking into derelict wards. Iron beds are chaotically dispersed, as if some heavy-footed animal has stomped through the place.

They enter one of the wards: crumbling plaster and rusty beds, old drip racks like hatstands. Blankets that fall apart when touched. 'You're not telling me anything new,' Etienne says. 'I have caught old Drechsler going through my pockets. By the way, the "pictures" on my walls are in fact "storyboards".' Nils's shoulders droop. Etienne instantly regrets his dismissal; the revelations were what Nils had to offer.

It takes a while before Nils speaks again, his voice now sounding distant. 'I must've been eleven or twelve when my brother and I swam out here. The place had just been closed.' Etienne looks around in the gloom. Leaves have stacked up in the corners; he can smell the compost underneath. 'It was summer. There was still a garden around the building then. Medicine in the cupboards, blood-drenched swabs, needles strewn everywhere . . . As if a deadly epidemic had struck the place overnight.'

They enter another ward. There is animal dung on the plank floors. No names of lovers on the walls, no gang symbols. No sign whatsoever of any recent human presence. 'So, what has become of your brother?'

'Gone. Disappeared.'

'Gone?'

Nils opens and closes his hands, as if looking for something to hold on to.

'Two years ago. On his twenty-third birthday.'

'Where? How?'

'Will we ever know? Dead, probably. Perhaps in prison.'

Etienne looks at him enquiringly. Does one ever get full disclosure from East Germans? 'How, Nils? *How?*'

Nils sighs, starts recounting. Two years before his disappearance, his brother became fed up with life in the GDR. The sins of their parents – their activities in peace circles, their association with the resistance figure Wolf Biermann, who by that time had been expelled to the West – had been following him everywhere. He couldn't go to university. The only work he could find was in a radar factory in the north, near the Baltic Sea. His girlfriend in Berlin, who had started her own underground band and had been singing protest lyrics increasingly openly, simply disappeared one day. 'She was taken' is how Nils expresses it. (It sounds to Etienne like an abduction by aliens in an American film.) Shortly afterwards his brother lost his job. Then he too disappeared without a trace.

After months without any news, Nils's mother revealed that his brother had been planning to escape to the West. For Nils's own sake, he had not been informed. His brother had built a tiny submarine in his cellar – from a chimney pipe, the engine of a scooter and the fan of a Trabant cooler. A water pony, he called it. It would have dragged him deep into the Baltic Sea, to the Danish coast, with him breathing through a snorkel. On his birthday he packed his components in a suitcase and travelled to the coast, where he was to don his extra-thick wetsuit and brave the waters . . .

When Nils starts opening the steel drawers of the bed pedestals one by one, as if he could find an ending for his brother's story *there*, Etienne leaves him alone. He walks down the corridor, into a smaller ward. Birds fly up, exit through broken panes. Etienne walks up to the window. He closes his eyes, listening to the wind. He wonders whether he can believe Nils's story. He tries to imagine the voyage, under the surface of a leaden sea. But strange voices interrupt his thoughts. Like a radio on which the stations are playing simultaneously, or telephone lines crossing: . . . *hibernation in the palace of diseases . . . coma on a rusty bed . . . under a blanket of leaves . . . narcosis of the morning mists . . .*

The rustling wind behind him interrupts the strange, insistent voices. Etienne turns around. Not the wind, but Nils. He is naked. He drops his little bundle of clothes by his feet, approaches. He presses himself against Etienne, his dry lips touching Etienne's. Nils clasps him in his arms: the cool grip of a skeleton. Nils's mouth seals off his own. Nils's breath is a dark fire sucking the life out of him.

There is a loud tearing noise outside: a falling tree. It hits the forest floor, sending a tremor through the ruin. Nils freezes. Etienne prises himself loose from the embrace, retreats, sits down hard on the bed. His buttocks sink through the rotten bedding, onto the iron. Dust and fibres rise in a black cloud; he starts coughing. Nils dresses, quickly and silently.

Etienne touches his chest. Has Nils left scorch marks on his skin? The shadow of a skeleton?

He gets his breath back. 'I already have someone, Nils. A phantom, perhaps, but even so.' *To steal my breath*, he wants to add, *or Axel's from me, won't work*. But Nils has gone.

Etienne gets up. His body aches; his feet are numb with cold. He walks down the corridor, down the stairs, crawls through under the trunk. The front door frames the trees outside. Nils is walking away. Etienne follows. Through the branches, the sky is even paler than before.

They struggle to get the swan in the water. The neck jerks stubbornly and arrogantly when they drag it out across the roots. They put on their wet shoes, pedal to the sound of gentle splashing. Neither of them says anything. Nils is looking out across the lake. Etienne is looking down into the water. Images from a period film that he saw in his London days return to him. It is set on a Venetian island that is used as a quarantine area. Carriers of the plague are spewed from boats, then huddle together fearfully on the quays. Fires burn high on the shore; seamen are hurling shoes and clothes into the greedy flames. Heaps of dead bodies are thrown into holes. Cadavers sizzle and crackle, exhaling black smoke . . .

As they approach the shore, Etienne stops pedalling. Next to the moored swans, a man with dark glasses is waiting. Nils also stops. Etienne is remembering something he only half-remembered earlier on: it's *black* swans, in particular, that often pair off in male couples. Etienne suddenly wonders whether a deadly disease is clinging to him, with the fibres of decaying hospital blankets. Something medieval. The man on the shore walks on. Etienne immerses a hand in the lake water. Is Nils's brother still zooming along on his underwater pony? he wonders. On his way to the North Pole, the snorkel's tip just a speck in the fog?

As if Nils has read his mind, he says: 'I don't know whether I should hope that they caught him or that he is still floating somewhere.' He swallows. 'I think he is sleeping on the bottom, my brother, beneath all that water. The Baltic Sea barely contains any salt.' Light, wild waves, Etienne thinks. Slaves of the wind. 'Boats capsize easily. Bodies sink quickly.'

Nils's tears arrive. *Those*, Etienne thinks, are heavy with salt. He starts pedalling again; the little boat glides forward. In his mind's eye he is observing an underwater scene. The current around the swan's water wheel whirls downwards. Bones, densely compressed and water-smoothed, are stirred up from the sludge – the bones of deceased patients dumped into the lake when the hospital was closed. They tumble upwards, grouping together in skeletons: a chaotic revolution of the dead.

Chapter 26

ETIENNE WRITES A letter to Patrick in Bonnington Square. He enquires about Patrick's well-being, elaborates superficially about his life in Berlin, asks for his drum kit to be sent. He provides the address of his three friends in West Berlin for delivery. Etienne will arrange with his new bandmates to send Patrick money through a West Berlin bank and then reimburse them.

He walks out onto Stargarder Strasse to post the letter. When he has inserted the letter into the yellow postbox's mouth, he suddenly cannot stand the idea of returning to Frau Drechsler's buzzing radio. He walks on, past the Bäckerei with its fresh bread smells. Trade names hardly exist here: a shop is simply Laden, a butcher's shop Fleischerei and, indeed, a bakery Bäckerei. Even the pale neon signs spelling out the names look the same. Probably all from the same factory.

He crosses Prenzlauer Allee, buys a planetarium ticket. Someone approaches, stands in the queue behind him: a man with a reddish-blond beard and a woollen pullover. Etienne sits down more or less in the middle of the theatre, tilts his chair back. He closes his eyes, hoping that the second reel of *Berliner Chronik* will magically be projected against the ceiling. Or that Axel's face will appear in the Milky Way. Not the one in the fading Polaroid, but Axel as he looks now. When he opens his eyes, Axel's face shatters into synthetic East German stars. Etienne looks around. The other man is nowhere to be seen.

Then he feels breath against his ear; his scalp crawls. For a fraction of a second he thinks it is Frau Drechsler, having followed him here – blowing a curse in his ear with her proletarian breath. He jerks the chair upright, looks back: the man in the pullover. He shrinks back, as if expecting Etienne to assault him. 'Sorry,' the man whispers. 'I didn't mean to startle you.'

Etienne waits until his heartbeat has settled. 'What do you want?' he asks out loud.

The man sits up straight, looking Etienne insolently in the eye. His lips are encircled by deep beard. 'You.'

For a while neither says anything. The man gets up, waits in the aisle. Etienne looks at his shoes in the radiance of the Milky Way: dull brown, East German. Etienne gets up too, follows the man to the exit. Just before exiting into the foyer, Etienne notices a third figure in the dark auditorium. Something about his posture seems familiar in the gloom, but Etienne can't immediately place him.

The man's pullover is olive green, Etienne notices when they exit into the blinding afternoon. His father, he remembers, used to have a similar pullover. His mother had knitted it when they were young and in love. While he and the man walk down Prenzlauer Allee without speaking, Etienne remembers a photo taken on Hermanus beach when he was a baby. His mother is looking up, laughing, arms stretched upwards. She has just thrown Etienne into the air, is standing by to catch him. His father is looking on, arms folded. He is looking at her rather than at Etienne, suspended against the blue sky. His father is wearing bathing trunks, and the green pullover. Is the framed photo still exhibited in his parents' bedroom? he wonders.

Amid the noise of a tram on Prenzlauer Allee, Etienne and the man look properly at each other for the first time. The veins in Etienne's neck are pulsating. They turn right, walk to Helmholtzplatz. The man unlocks a door; they walk up one floor to his flat. The man makes small talk, asks whether Etienne ever goes to the disco on Buschallee. A gay nightclub, the man explains. It is state-run, he quickly adds. Etienne goes to a window overlooking the small square. Alcoholics are sitting on benches. Reflected in the glass, Etienne can see the man undressing behind him. He is very pale and muscular, with a fleece of reddish-blond chest hair. He approaches, presses himself against Etienne's back. His upper body and groin squeak against Etienne's leather jacket. The beard is soft in his neck, the lips as cold as snow against his ear. Etienne looks up at the ornate ceilings. Adrenalin is coursing through his arteries like light. He could grab the man by his beard and force him onto the floor, could flay and tear and slaughter him.

Suddenly it strikes him: the other figure in the planetarium was Mthu, the South African counter-intelligence student. His blood heats up like that of prey. He is being watched. And this man is surely his pursuer's deputy. He disentangles himself from the man's grip. He walks out the room and out the front door, down the stairs and across Helmholtzplatz, past the alcoholics on their benches, up Dunckerstrasse. He doesn't look back at the figure behind the first-floor window. He wonders whether he has put on his green pullover again. Then he stops thinking about him.

Herr Bösel, Ariel Schnur's purported cameraman, lives in a concrete block right by Alexanderplatz, a massive GDR-era building. The man sounds cheerful, even chaotic, over the 1970s intercom. Etienne has barely started explaining the purpose of his visit when the speaker vibrates: 'Come in! Come in!' The lift only has a button for every other floor, Bösel being on one of the in-between floors. Etienne gets off on the floor above his. He tries to go down one level, but different sets of stairs similarly only serve particular floors. The place reminds him of the brutalist buildings that Aodhan showed him in London. Or of Aodhan's fantasy cities: bridges, walkways and squares floating in the air. Buildings in which people are born and die without ever setting foot on the earth.

After several sets of stairs up and down, and walking the length of various corridors, Etienne is at his wits' end. He is in a vertical labyrinth. He imagines the diagram being drawn by his movements through the building. He is no longer even sure which floor he is on. The apparently arbitrary numbers on the doors of flats don't help. Herr Bösel's flat remains just out of reach, as if sealed off from the rest of the building. He takes a lift back down to the ground level. One lift, he now realises, only serves the floors with even numbers, another one those with uneven numbers. When, at last, he walks down the right corridor, an old, bewildered man is awaiting him.

'Herr Bösel, I presume?' The man's plastic spectacle frames have been repaired with masking tape; one lens is cracked. Etienne involuntarily thinks of Eisenstein's *Battleship Potemkin*, of the iconic close-up of the wounded old woman: her broken pince-nez, her bloody face twisted in a scream.

'What took you so long?' Herr Bösel says. 'Come in! I have tea!'

Etienne follows Herr Bösel into the little kitchen, where he fusses with cups and a kettle. His hair is thin but voluminous, like candyfloss. The mouth has collapsed inwards; it looks as if he has forgotten his dentures. He wheezes when he talks. Etienne starts explaining: the film, Ariel, Irmgard. 'Your daughter has given me your address . . .'

'Yes, yes, I know everything, I know what you're looking for!' He drops a cup; it shatters.

'You *know?*' Etienne is baffled.

Bösel ignores the shards of porcelain by his feet. 'Yes, yes, I worked with such a director in the 1930s! We were trying to do something. Something new, yes. And I have the film, or part of it.' Hope expands like light in Etienne's chest. But something seems odd. Could the search really have been so easy, the route so short? A telephone directory and a few enquiries?

Herr Bösel walks into the living room; Etienne follows. 'No, no,' he says over his shoulder, vehemently waving Etienne away. 'I will go and fetch it. Just me!' He disappears through a door. Etienne is caught off guard by the manic energy. On a little table, next to a plant with sharp-tipped green-and-yellow leaves, is a framed photo of a younger Bösel with a woman. Etienne bends forward to read the writing in the corner of the picture: *Norna, Dez.* 1976. He returns to the kitchen, picks up the pieces. Except for the cup, everything in the kitchen is made of plastic.

Herr Bösel returns. Under his arm he is carrying a worn film case. A little vein starts throbbing in Etienne's temple. 'Is it . . . ? Do you really have Schnur's—?'

'Yes, yes!' the man says. 'Of course!' Etienne looks at the metal container. His urge is to grab it, to shake it next to his ear. To *listen* rather than to look.

'I've been searching for so long . . .' Etienne warily extends a hand, as if to a growling dog. 'I'm astonished that it would materialise just like—'

'Take it. It's yours!'

It is too light in Etienne's hands: empty. The spark of hope dims. He holds it in front of his chest like a shield. He speaks slowly now, as if addressing a child. 'I don't think there is anything in here.'

'Oh! Sorry, I'm sorry!' Bösel grabs the container, disappears again. Etienne waits, deeply sceptical. When Bösel reappears after a minute, he hands over an even more tatty case, sealed with masking tape. This time, the weight is about right.

'Thanks,' Etienne says cautiously. If this man is who he says he is, Etienne will have a thousand questions. He is itching to open the steel box, to look at a few frames. Patience, he thinks, patience. He can always come back. 'Thanks, Herr Bösel. I will borrow this then.'

'Keep it!' the older man shouts after Etienne when he walks back to the lift.

When he exits on Alexanderplatz, Etienne can no longer contain himself. He enters the melange of people by the fountains. In the vapour of mingling breaths, he peels off the masking tape. At first the lid sticks. He manages to prise it open, unspools a strip of the film, holds it up against the fountain. He shifts it through his fingers, frame by frame. Images of a young woman, picking fruit in an orchard. He realises at once it is not what he is looking for.

He looks at the people around him, stiff with cold. Today he wishes he had a rabbit-fur hat. The shop he once visited is just around the corner. He will go and just *touch* one of those hats. He walks to Karl-Liebknecht-Strasse. The Mongolian shop assistant looks at the film reel under Etienne's arm, fits a hat over his head. Etienne closes his eyes, touches the pelt covering his ears. He feels like one of a snug litter. He nods at the Mongolian. The hat costs him more than half of his month's grant money.

Back in his room in Stargarder Strasse he studies the frames more closely. He saw such films when he was studying in London. One of his fellow students – the feminist filmmaker – did a project about them: French pornographic shorts from the 1930s. In this one, an innocent-looking girl is skipping through an orchard, picking cherries. She is lifting the hem of her skirt with one hand, dropping the berries in it. She is not wearing any knickers: between her legs there is the flickering of coal-black pubic hair.

By now, Etienne has virtuously sat through all the Trümmer-filme in the archive: unconvincing sets of cities lying in ruin, artificial daylight shining on the faces of long-dead actors. Etienne's secret project – to search the archive freely on his own – has stalled. Frau Fuchs has been reigning with an eagle eye from her counter since she caught him in the storeroom. He is biding his time.

As he arrives in Kohlhasenbrückerstrasse this morning, he stops in his tracks. Opposite the archive, a baby-blue Trabant stands idling in the drizzle – the only vehicle in the cul-de-sac, steam coiling from its exhaust. Etienne looks straight ahead as he passes the car.

Inside the archive, the exhaust fumes are still in Etienne's nostrils when he shakes the drops from his sleeves. As usual, there is no one but himself and Fraue Fuchs and Keller. He has never encountered another archive user. The place feels like a film set. Or a set of rooms lined with one-way mirrors: a vivarium with Etienne as insect.

Frau Keller silently accepts his forms in her gloomy little

office. His most recent request is for *Anders als die Andern*, a Weimar film from 1919 that he discovered while at film school in London. A story about a violin teacher who falls in love with his pupil. The first true gay film. All copies were probably burnt by the Nazis in 1933. But who knows what might have ended up on these shelves, and via which detours? His request form omits a catalogue number; the film is not listed in the categories to which he has access. If the true catalogue is the universe, then the little corner illuminated by his microfiche is but one solar system. There must be larger microfiches elsewhere, with brighter lights. Further categories, more lists, grander storerooms. Perhaps an entire additional building – with cellars and attics, shelves stretching into infinity. This banal little building is surely just a faint reflection of the true archive, with its corridors, ladders and steel containers stacked to the ceiling. With its rooms full of hundreds of kilometres of unspooled film, being wound back onto reels by blind children, year in, year out, their fingers weak and raw from the chemicals, their lungs destroyed by the vinegary fumes. (Did they become blind in these rooms? Or are they given the task *because* they are blind?) And perhaps, even, there are giant subterranean theatres where one can lie back while every film you have ever desired to see is projected onto the ceilings . . .

Surely it won't yield anything, his presumptuous request for *Anders als die Anderen*. It is a shot into the empty universe, but what is there to lose by grasping at dark matter?

Frau Fuchs comes and innocently threads a film through the projector. She is well-practised at it, and usually dexterous. Today, however, her scaly hands are struggling. She clicks her tongue, repeatedly pulls the film out and starts over again. Is she taunting him?

Etienne notices raw patches on Frau Fuchs's neck: eczema. And her hair seems to be thinning; the bleached spikes are now flat against her scalp. Her eyes are bloodshot behind the glasses. She is breathing heavily. It looks as if she has been exposed to radiation and is experiencing a gradual decline.

When the film finally starts, it is in Russian. He encountered this kind of Soviet film in his London film-history classes. So-called 'production films'. This one is about a soldier in the Red Army who returns to his home town and imbues the revolutionary ideals of the cement-factory workers and his comrades with new life. There aren't even subtitles; only the title is written in German on the container: *Der Zement*. Frau Fuchs is clearly hell-bent on embedding socialist principles into Etienne's education.

Etienne sits through the barren film. He keeps his face neutral when Frau Fuchs arrives to change reels. In between he grinds his teeth, yawns, stares at the ceiling.

When the last reel ends and the loose end of the film keeps flapping, Frau Fuchs arrives to wind the reel back.

'Frau Fuchs, I think there might have been some kind of error.'

'How so, Herr Nieuwenhuis?'

'This is not the film that I requested.'

'But that is inconceivable. Frau Keller is extremely precise. She knows the catalogue like the palm of her hand.'

'I think if you compare my request form with the title of this film, you will appreciate the mistake.'

She is quiet for a while, then brings the steel box closer to her eyes, shakes her head. 'Alas, I'm not wearing my glasses.' She scratches her scabby neck. 'If you wish to submit a formal complaint, you may request the applicable form, Herr Nieuwenhuis. Then we shall investigate.'

They stand opposite each other in the dark. Her face is a blurry mirror.

Chapter 27

IT IS AFTER two in the morning. Etienne is turning the pages of Irmgard's blue file for the umpteenth time. He thinks he can hear a far-off tram, but they don't run this late. A ghost tram, perhaps: echoes of the day's noises still travelling through the streets, rebounding from façade to façade. He stares at the sheaf of empty pages in the back. Unused paper. He hasn't paid much attention to them before. Tonight it is as if the bare sheets are saturated with secrets, like human skin, as if they could become legible at any moment. He keeps looking. And waiting. For the secret fibres to darken, for something to take shape. He brings the paper to his face, holding it at an angle next to the desk lamp. There *is* something. He turns the lamp, bringing the paper right up against his eye. His lashes brush against it like insects' feet.

And there it is! He can't believe he hasn't noticed it before: invisible letters, inklessly imprinted onto the paper. *This* is what must have happened, he instantly understands: the typing ribbon broke without Irmgard realising, and she just kept on typing. He tries in vain to read the indentations against the light. On a hunch, he rummages around in the drawer, finds a pencil and starts lightly colouring the page, the lead flat against the paper. Then it happens: the indentations become legible, lost letters lifted from the past. One after the other the words emerge from the blank page.

He first colours all the sheets, then returns to the beginning.

He reads wildly, breathlessly. He takes in entire paragraphs in a single glance, like a starved prisoner chancing upon a banquet. The entries are even more chaotic than before, and error-ridden. The film's production programme no longer features anywhere. The topics are haphazard; Irmgard is mainly describing her daily experiences in the increasingly threatening city. One fragment catches his eye:

> one is so scared when you relise what is hapenning on the streets of berlin where will it all end this btutality Ventured out this morningt almost caught upin the voilence. I come aroudn a corner, hear the shouting it s the Sturmabteilung young communists being arested. Were they still courageous enough to appear in publci were they dragged fomr theuir hdiing places I prss myusefll against a wall, make mysel small right in the mdidle of it all! Rouh uniform brushing against mhy arm the breath being hit out of someone s lungs, a baton a head crakcing againdtst the pavement . . .

He turns the page. The last entries vaguely mention Ariel's – and some of the production team's – plans to leave Germany. Irmgard contemplates how she might be able to safeguard the film material (she doesn't say how many reels or copies there are) from destruction.

Pehraps, she writes, we should divideit betwee n the team mmebers. Smaler risk of l oss?

Ariel: what doess his future hold? Ours? Amidst all the teerror, Irmgard writes on the last page, a child is rowing inside of me. Ariels. And the film

The darkened grooves change into a monochrome haze of

lead, which washes up on white space like a wave on a beach.

A child *rowing* inside her? Then he realises: it should be *growing*. He sits back, holds his breath. Axel once mentioned that his mother was Irmgard's only child. If Ariel Schnur impregnated her, it follows that he was Axel's grandfather. Dark figures are taking shape in the fog.

Etienne breathes out, returns to the first grey page, reading more slowly now. There isn't much new information. When his fever around the discovery of the invisible text – and of the family connection between Axel and Ariel – subsides, he realises he is still stuck. He reverts to the old doubts. Was the film ever completed? This is still not clear – the recovered text was itself apparently interrupted by some event. And, even if it was completed, did the other two reels survive?

And Axel? Does he want to be found? Or see Etienne again? Does Axel even *remember* him? And, the question his mind has been sheering away from: is Axel still alive?

There is a knock on the bedroom door. He sits up with a start, looks at his watch. It is past three. He opens: Nils.

'I saw the light under your door.' Nils looks at the washbasin. 'Do you want to make us some of your Western coffee?' It is the first time Nils has spoken to him since their voyage on a swan to the island hospital a week ago.

Etienne puts his last two spoonfuls of pure London coffee in the percolator. Nils is pacing between the bed and the basin. Etienne pours two cups. 'Let's take a walk,' Nils says unexpectedly. His coffee is left untouched on the basin's edge. Etienne puts down his own steaming mug.

They walk out on Stargarder Strasse, turn left. Nils stays a few steps ahead. For a few moments he wonders whether Nils is going to take him into the planetarium, whether he has a secret key. Just the two of them: on their backs under the relentless river of the Milky Way, floating in the soothing sea of commentary. But Nils aims past the planetarium, into the park behind it. Etienne thinks of the massive structures of the old gasworks that used to stand here.

In these early hours there isn't a soul in the park. Etienne wants to enquire where they are heading. He catches a glimpse of Nils's tense face in the gloom, keeps quiet. They stop in front of a huge monument. It is lit by cold spotlights: a bronze bust, fist aloft, rising to ten times the height of a man. 'And this colossus?' Etienne's voice echoes against the bronze.

'Ernst Thälmann. Leader of the communist party in Weimar Berlin. Shot in Buchenwald shortly before the end of the war.' Nils looks gaunt against the massive monument.

'What is it that you want to tell me, Nils? Why do you bring me here at four in the morning?'

Nils comes and stands in front of Etienne, takes him by the shoulders. 'I've been admitted to Humboldt University.' Etienne can only see the outlines of his face. 'Japanese studies.'

'But that's wonderful!' Etienne puts his hands on Nils's shoulders too. They look at each other, their arms doubled. Nils drops his head; shadows collect in the contours of his face. Etienne thinks of a swan boat, of lake water and the comatose trunk of a fallen tree. Something is amiss. 'So suddenly, Nils? What made them yield?'

Nils drops his arms by his sides. 'Nothing comes without a price in this country.' He shrugs off Etienne's arms. Etienne is trying to make out Nils's expression. 'It is time for you to leave East Berlin, Etienne. You have choices. You don't know how lucky you are.'

A cavern opens up in Etienne's innards. 'What do you mean?'

Nils looks utterly depleted; his silhouette is that of a parched angel. Some distance behind him, in one of the few streets in Prenzlauer Berg with street lights, a vehicle drives past, its engine inaudible. It is one of those green-grey vans with the name of a butcher on the sides. The street lights are far apart. It moves slowly through the bright patches, appearing and disappearing.

Nils turns around without answering, briskly walks away towards the planetarium.

Frau Finkel comes and takes Etienne out of his class, interrupting the lecturer. The director wants to see him. Her eyes are serious behind the rock-and-roll glasses. Is Etienne imagining it, or is Frau Finkel's hair getting progressively higher?

The director is wearing his dirty-yellow jacket. Outside, the sky is murky. The soil is frozen, wind is gnawing at exposed skin, icicles hanging from the roof.

'I am keen to know how your project is progressing, Herr Nieuwenhuis. Are you, for instance, getting proper cooperation from the archive personnel?' The director is swivelling in his chair. Before Etienne can answer, he adds: 'And of equal importance: are *you* giving *your* cooperation in the light of our mission here?' The director's eyes are dull but piercing; his fingertips are pressed together.

Etienne doesn't respond. He wishes his chair could swivel too.

'Be sure,' the director continues, 'to keep to the parameters of your research. The archive has prescribed procedures. All of us have to comply with them.'

Etienne wants to get up and leave, but he can see the director isn't finished yet. In the meantime Etienne's thoughts wander to Bösel: the manic old man with his idiotic smile. Was he really Schnur's cameraman? Does he have a copy of the film somewhere up there in his concrete cube, or is he just dotty? Did Etienne find him by accident, or is he maliciously being led astray? Is someone playing a game of which Etienne doesn't know the rules?

'Why don't you hand in a first draft of your research work?' the director says. 'You have, after all, been working on it for more than a month.'

'I'm only in the early stages—'

'Bring whatever you have. We are interested.'

Etienne smiles and nods. He won't be bringing anything.

The next day he goes back to Herr Bösel. He holds out little hope, but he has no other leads.

This time he takes the right lift. When he arrives, Herr Bösel is already making tea. Etienne holds out the reel. 'This is the wrong film, Herr Bösel.'

Bösel apologises humbly and effusively. 'Wait. Now I know where it is!' He scurries away to his mysterious little archive. Etienne switches off the kettle when it starts boiling over.

Bösel reappears after ten minutes, out of breath, sweat beading on his forehead. The place is overheated; Etienne's armpits are itching. Herr Bösel has a film case in his hand. 'Here! I've found the right reel!' Etienne imagines a dusty old archive connected via a secret passage to Herr Bösel's flat. He sees Bösel going up and down dozens of stairways, scurrying through passages, descending into the earth in a private lift, hurrying through hidden annexes and an endless series of rooms. Moving ladders on tracks, climbing to the highest shelves, blowing dust from steel cases . . .

Etienne takes the holder. There is something in it. Herr Bösel bids him goodbye outside. When he looks back from the lift, the old man is waving, grinning and fanatical, his hair forming a halo around his head.

Etienne walks to a narrow alleyway before pulling out a strip of film and holding it against the narrow ribbon of sky above him. He moves the frames through his fingers. Another piece of antique pornography. Probably French again. A man with a handlebar moustache, a woman with a nineteenth-century frock. Layers and layers of clothes, the impatient French gentleman burying his head under the flounces of her dress. Etienne can imagine the copulation that is to follow: flickering, at comic speed. The film is so brittle that it splits and crumbles between his fingers.

Etienne dreams of a blue file. A report of some kind. He is sitting in front of an empty desk in an empty office. Someone has instructed him to review the content carefully and correct it where necessary. When he opens the file, it is written in Japanese. He cannot read a word of it, flicks the pages to the end before realising it is in fact the beginning. He returns to the front – to the actual end, that is. At the bottom it is signed by the author, whose name is the only word written in the Western alphabet: *Nils*.

Chapter 28

FRAU KELLER IS behind the reception counter today. Frau Fuchs is ill, she explains. She looks fresh, with a ponytail and nylon blouse. For the first time, Etienne sees her face in the light. She has a surgically repaired harelip. She no longer mumbles, and her lisp is less prominent now. She is swift in her responses, even talkative. It is as if Frau Fuchs's absence is profoundly invigorating her.

She sets up the projector in the viewing room as if nothing is amiss. When Etienne filled in the form in triplicate yesterday, he dared to request *Berliner Chronik*. He is waiting to see what will end up on the projector.

A 1970s film, it turns out, about communal farming in Hungary. Women with headscarves, ploughing, and feeding slaughter animals. A three-hour torture session. Promptly every forty-five minutes Frau Keller arrives to swap the reels.

Etienne wakes with a start. It takes a few moments to remember where he is: the projection room. It is just after ten. On the screen the Hungarians are now harvesting, and milking cows. Etienne's hair is sticking to his sweaty neck. He opens the padded door slightly. Frau Keller isn't behind the counter. She must be having her morning tea somewhere. He tiptoes out, through the reception area and down the corridor. He tries the door of the storeroom where he was previously caught in the act by Frau Fuchs. Locked. He goes further, tests more doors.

The third one is unlocked; lights flicker on inside. It is large, with double the shelf space of the room he has been in before. The shelves are densely stacked with reels carrying the DEFA symbol: post-war East German films. He exits, closes the door.

He tries another room. Locked. So too the next one. The door beyond that is open. The shelves are packed with films from other Eastern bloc countries. *Czechoslovakia, Romania, Bulgaria*, the labels on the sides read.

The next room's door also swings open. For a moment he wonders whether it is a trap, these selectively unlocked doors. His eyes find it immediately: on one shelf, next to a long catalogue number: *Entartete Kunst (Dritte Reich)*. He bites his lower lip, slips into the room. He turns the shelf's crank with both hands. It slides open without a hint of friction. He reaches for a random reel, freezes when he hears a sound. A film sequence plays out in his mind's eye: a medium shot of himself here between the shelves, from behind. A close-up of an anonymous hand turning the crank. His body being crushed between the shelves, the sound of ribs cracking and snapping . . .

He takes the reel, peeks out the door. Nothing. Just the rectangle of light from the reception area at the end of the corridor. Yet he has lost his courage. He closes the door softly, returns to the reception. Across the street, he notices through the window, is the same baby-blue Trabant as before: fumes steaming from the exhaust, windows fogged up. He must be clearly visible from outside, Etienne thinks. Here under the fluorescent lights, with a film reel in his hand.

He enters the projection room, pulls the door shut. His brain is expanding against his skull; his palms are slippery against the steel of the film container. He quickly swaps reels on the projector, his fingers unsteady. He drops the reel of the Hungarian film on the floor; the steel rim bends. He tries in vain to bend it back. He puts on the new reel, starts the machine. It is a film from the late '20s about the spectrum of drugs obtainable in Berlin – from the cocaine, morphine and opium sold on street corners to the extracts, magic potions and tonics for heightened libido in specialist shops. Radium creams make penises glow; a tincture of yohimbe bark from West Africa makes them grow . . . Etienne tilts his head, pricks his ears. Nothing penetrates the soundproof door. He returns to the film. It is a kind of guide for consumers. A volatile breakfast elixir is demonstrated: a mixture of chloroform and ether. A woman with a long string of pearls twirls a white rose in the solution, then bites off the frozen petals . . .

It is a short film, barely fifteen minutes. He rewinds it, puts the bent Hungarian film reel back on the projector. He puts the drug film on the chair, peers out the door. Frau Keller should have been back by now. Through the reception area's window he can see a man leaning against the Trabant. The engine has been shut off; the rain has stopped. The man is wearing a raincoat and a homburg. He touches his hat, suddenly starts walking to the archive's front door. Etienne's heart starts pounding. He crouches, stays below the level of the windows. He scurries to the reception counter, still hunched. Behind the counter he tries the handle of a door. It is open: a toilet. Inside he waits for a few moments, listening. Then he climbs onto the toilet, wriggles through the window, lands soundlessly on the mud outside.

He starts running in a random direction. The carpet of leaves is pneumatic underneath his feet. He comes upon a footpath, follows it around the back of the second asbestos building and the dark tower, which is slippery with moss. He touches it as he passes, as if the texture would reveal what is inside. He runs a few hundred metres into the trees, then squats and pants.

When he catches his breath, he starts walking back. Before he gets to the tower and the archive buildings, he turns onto another path. He walks in a wide arc around Kohlhasenbrücker Strasse, to the next street. He hears the Trabant's engine through the trees before he sees it. He has lost his way; in his state of disorientation he has been walking *back* to the archive. Dammit! He turns on his heel, starts running towards his bus stop.

When he is fifty metres away from the stop, the bus arrives. He runs and waves, but it departs without him. Fuck! He slips around the back of the bus shelter, presses himself against it. The next bus is only due to arrive in fifteen minutes. A woman is watching Etienne through the window of a flat. He can see her picking up a telephone, making a call. He can hear the cars passing. Almost all of them Trabants, the engine noise unmistakable. He holds his breath. Every minute feels like fifteen. Then the next bus is there. When the doors open with a sigh, he slips around the shelter and into the bus. He sits down, turns up his collar, looks away from the window.

When he enters, Frau Drechsler looks intently at Etienne from the sofa. He stares at the whining radio on the sideboard. It is slowly driving him insane. He doubts whether he can stay here one more day.

He shuts his bedroom door, strips off his clothes. He is simultaneously warm and cold, like someone with a fever. He sits on the bed for a while, the synthetic bedspread slippery against his palm. He pulls it over his sweaty body, kicks it off again. He thinks of the bent film reel and the Weimar film that he left there in the projection room, of the open toilet window, of his tracks all over. What was he fleeing from? An idling car, an empty reception area, an unattended counter, a man with a hat. Is he losing his mind?

Every now and then, he looks through the window at the street. The temperature falls; the radiator clicks and creaks. He holds his hands against it. Outside, it starts snowing. The snow is late this year, Frau Drechsler has been saying over the past weeks. Over and over again. He goes to his door, listens. Where is Nils? Usually he is at home this time of day. Etienne opens his door a little. Frau Drechsler's radio is off now, perhaps for the first time since he moved in here. There is just a dim glow from the Berliner Zimmer. He takes out the reel of *Berliner Chronik* from under his bed, strokes the steel box. He hasn't watched it since leaving London. He will try to find a projector somewhere. He puts the reel in his rucksack. He dresses, puts on his fur hat, takes the rucksack, exits his room. Frau Drechsler is still sitting on the sofa. The reading lamp is on, but she isn't reading. There is an unusual smell. On a side table there are two wooden figurines. Räuchermännchen, smoke unfurling from their glowing mouths. Traditional over the festive season, Nils explained when they recently saw such figurines in a shop window, even though Christmas celebrations have been secularised. 'I'll be back for dinner at the usual time,' he says. He has never explained his movements to old Drechsler before. She doesn't respond.

It is freezing outside. He tightens his scarf, hooks his thumbs into his rucksack's straps. He walks towards the planetarium.

Inside it would be warm, but he goes past, through the park, all the way to the Ernst Thälmann monument. He looks up at the surly bronze as if consulting an oracle, snowflakes falling in his eyes. He thinks of the demolished gasworks again. Who will miss them, write an elegy for them? He heads back, turns down Prenzlauer Allee and walks with a long detour to Kastanienallee.

He enters a beer garden. There is a wooden building teeming with merry drinkers. The garden itself is deserted. Etienne wipes snow from a table with his sleeve, sits down on it. He looks at the mute jollity behind the Kneipe's expansive windows: men with Santa Claus hats dancing to inaudible Schlager. Etienne shuts his eyes, places his hand on his chest like a stethoscope. He thinks of the Transvaal sunshine on your cheeks when you look up, of the heat radiated by slate paving in his parents' garden. He is missing Axel, wishes he could rub his cheeks against his. And he sees his mother's face, even though he doesn't want to.

The cold seeps into his bones, the rabbit fur over his ears notwithstanding; his teeth are clattering. He thinks of the child who once grabbed him by the legs in the fur-hat shop. When he opens his eyes, he notices, amid the merriness in the Kneipe, a motionless figure looking out of the window. Etienne gets up, walks towards the building. The figure still doesn't move. He walks right up to the glass. It is Mthu. Etienne looks him in the eye. Mthu doesn't flinch. For a few seconds they remain like that, as if there is iron between them, instead of glass.

Etienne turns away, walks out on Kastanienallee and further up on Schönhauser Allee. He is stiff with cold. When he turns into Stargarder Strasse, he slows his pace, then stops. Some distance ahead of him, opposite No. 72, in front of the Bäckerei, an idling Trabant is parked. Two men in coats are standing on the pavement. One is pulling on a cigarette, exhaling smoke and steam. Etienne looks up. In the bay window of the flat, Frau Drechsler's profile is clearly visible. She lifts her hand, points towards Etienne. The Trabant-men's heads simultaneously swivel towards him. Etienne turns in his tracks, starts walking back rapidly. He pulls his head into his coat collar, his eyes fixed on the snow-covered pavement. When he looks up, Mthu is heading towards him, hardly forty metres away. They both stop, look at each other. Etienne makes a swift turn left, down Greifenhagener Strasse, but quickly stops in his tracks. There, ahead of him, is Nils, coolly leaning against a shopfront. And, in an identical position across the street, is Etienne's father. He blinks his eyes. No, not his father, but the man from the planetarium with his green pullover and his ginger beard. Etienne turns around, starts jogging. He crosses Stargarder, casting quick glances in both directions. To his right, the two men are getting into the Trabant, switching it on. To his left, Mthu is running towards him with long strides, his coat flaring behind him. Etienne is now running as fast as he can, further up Greifenhagener Strasse, without looking back, to the back entrance of the S-Bahn station. He rushes down the stairs. There is a train on the tracks. The doors are closing; the alarm is already ringing. He forces the door open with his shoulder. He slips in; the rucksack is caught in the door. He leans forward, tugging in vain, then lets the rucksack slip off his shoulders. It falls onto the tracks outside; the train departs. He is sure he can hear the wheels crunch over the film reel. The other passengers look vacantly at him.

He tries to get his breath back. Beneath his coat, his shirt is drenched with sweat. The train gains speed. Through the windows he looks at buildings cut in half when the track was built, intimate courtyards exposed to the violence of trains.

He changes over to the U-Bahn at Friedrichstrasse. He looks searchingly at everyone he passes, ready to flee at any moment. He keeps one hand on the travel document in his pocket. What luck that he always carries it with him! He feels through his other pockets: twenty Ostmark and a handful of West German coins.

In the Tränenpalast, Etienne is made to hand over his Ostmark, ostensibly to withdraw them again later. He enters the border guard's cubicle. The door closes behind him; he keeps his eyes on the locked exit. The guard picks up his phone, dials. Etienne can hear the engaged tone. He puts down the receiver, lifts it and dials again. Still engaged. He says something under his breath, looks at Etienne, thumbs through the *titre de voyage* a second time. He stamps it; the exit door unlocks.

Downstairs in the West German tunnel, Etienne's legs give way. He crouches, leans a cheek against the tiled wall. A metre or two above his head, East Germans are walking through the snow in Friedrichstrasse, in a country where Etienne will never set foot again. He listens out for the creaking of plastic soles on fresh powder. He takes off his hat, presses the fur against his chest.

Something has caught up with him, entered him. Something like epilepsy. Or history. His body is quivering, as if he is being struck by lightning on a vast city square. He is a reluctant conductor. The volts must find an outlet; his body cannot contain them. The electrical energy will make him tear across the streets in a smear of white light; he will burn a fiery road through the city. The terror of his involuntary copulations will leave behind broken bodies: bite marks, bloody abrasions, convulsing sinews, drugged tongues . . .

When he regains consciousness, it feels as if his arteries have bled out.

Chapter 29

HE ARRIVES AT his three friends' home on Chamissoplatz with only a few Pfennig in his pocket and the sweaty clothes on his body. At least he managed to get away with his coat and hat. His body feels irradiated. He pushes at his teeth (are they becoming loose?), tugs at his hair.

He is trembling; his body is aglow. He closes his eyes, tries to speak. The words won't fall into place. A large, cool hand rests on his forehead. He opens his eyes: Matthias. And, behind him, Christof and Frederick. Matthias looks stern and concerned, his single-line brow in a kink above his eyes. He silences Etienne when he tries to speak. The three disappear. Deeper inside the flat a bath is run. From where Etienne is lying, he can see steam swirling into the corridor, as if from the exhaust of an idling Trabant. He lets go of this image, lets go of *all* thought.

Matthias leads Etienne down the corridor. The three of them undress him, put him in the bath. Frederick strips off his own clothes too, slips in behind Etienne, starts lathering him up. First he washes Etienne's back, then sticks his hands under Etienne's arms, scrubs his chest with the sponge. Foam spatters and drifts. Matthias and Christof stand frowning in the steam. Etienne sighs deeply, lets his body slacken, leans backwards in Frederick's arms.

'You'll be staying here with us. Sharing a bedroom with

Frederick.' Matthias is speaking. Etienne has slept a few hours; it is evening. Or night. The curtain is open; it is not as dark outside as in East Berlin. Inside it is warm, and the light is soft and generous.

Christof is standing over Etienne. 'We must show you something.' He helps Etienne to sit up and then get up. Etienne walks unsteadily down the corridor. Outside the door of a small room, Christof makes a showy gesture that is incongruous with his serious, harried body. 'Arrived the day before yesterday . . .'

Etienne inhales deeply. Inside the room is his drum kit. He approaches it warily, inspects it. He gently touches the cymbals, as if they are fragile body parts. He knocks on the drums with a knuckle, touches the pedals. Everything looks fine. He could rely on him after all, on Patrick with his dreadlocks and undiscriminating wishes for peace. Patrick who doesn't believe in private property.

Over the next two days, a sense of bliss descends upon Etienne. His friends cook for him, care for him as if he is a lost child who has crawled to the West through tunnels and pipes, under the death strip.

On the third day he says: 'Thank you. I'm fine. I can eat – and bath – without help now.' He smiles. Frederick smiles back, his teeth large and healthy; he acquiesces, although the bright blue vigilance in his eyes remains undiminished.

When Etienne enquires about news regarding Axel, they at first respond vaguely. Ultimately Christof admits that their search has not yielded any clues. 'I don't know what else one could do,' he says. His head is bowed, his index finger drawing tight patterns on the kitchen table.

'Perhaps,' Matthias says, 'you should reconcile yourself to the possibility that you won't ever . . .'

Etienne gets up, walks out.

On the fourth morning Frederick brings Etienne a package, wrapped in brown paper. The undisguised anticipation on the triplets' faces is too much for Etienne. He turns his back on them, goes to the bedroom, pulls the door shut. He sits on his bed, tears open the package.

The letter on the top is from Patrick. The handwriting is scarcely legible – spidery, with hoops and lines shooting away from tiny letters.

Hey bruther!

Howre u man! Heres your drums! Alls cool in London man! Hope Berlin is treating u well bruther! I hear that Citys cookin man!

Oh your muther came here man. She wus lookin for u. Bout 2 months ago. She looked lost seemd pretty upset that u wusn here. Offered her my room for sleepin in man but she wusn too sure-looking, sayin she wanted to sleep in the house you wus sleepin in, just once, but will find a hotel. Told her u wus in Berlin but you havn told me no address yet. She came back 2 days later before goin back to Africa that wus only 1 day before i got your letter man. She didn say much man she left without sayin anythin. She has lots of pain in her heart man. That lady. Your muther. She lookin for u.

Also letters been arrivin for u. Everyweek man. From her. Aksed her if she want it back. She said keep it for u. Sendin u those too man.

Peace bruther

Patrick

Etienne takes a deep breath, looks out into the snow-covered courtyard. Poor Patrick – he has no idea how inconceivable it is that Etienne's mother would spend even a single night in the squat. Etienne tries to imagine her in Patrick's nest of a room. Her shapeless body, lost on the threadbare futon into which marijuana smoke and reggae rhythms have seeped. Among Bob Marley posters and a collection of pipes. Having to share a bathroom with the Finnish goths. Like a polar animal in the tropics.

The other letters are neatly tied with a ribbon. His mother's correspondence that has been arriving weekly, while he was living in Bermondsey Street, and afterwards in East Berlin.

He hesitates, then opens the envelopes one by one. There are no longer parallel streams of letters. Only the more intimate letters, in her own voice. The second voice – supposedly modulated for his father – has fallen silent.

She steadfastly keeps sending news, undeterred by Etienne's silence. The tiniest particulars of daily life in South Africa. His cousin's graduation ceremony. Drought, bad harvests, how difficult things are for the farmers. He can hear how a male voice would read this news on the SABC's Afrikaans radio service. *Her* voice, when she writes about these things, is momentarily lost: she is using words imposed on her by other voices. There is more: she writes about a female friend whose daughter has a rare blood disease, about the neighbour's son – an engineering student, as Etienne once was – who is constantly fixing and kick-starting his motorbike. When she addresses Etienne directly, the undertone is sorrowful. She no longer confronts him with questions. She sketches scenarios, hypotheses – a barely disguised invitation for Etienne to replace them with the truth. She imagines Etienne's life alongside a

248

British girl. With porcelain skin and fine features, the bridge of her nose lightly freckled. And perhaps he has managed to finish his engineering studies. Maybe he is playing the piano again. *Or your drums in a pop band.*

Only three letters are left. They date from November, when he was in East Berlin.

I didn't want to burden you with this before, but your father has been ill. For months now. Cancer of the vocal cords. He hasn't been able to speak over the last few weeks. Etienne lowers the letter; his eyes are struggling to focus. He reads on haltingly. *I didn't want to tell you this prematurely. You wouldn't, after all, have been able to travel here, even if you wanted to.*

The next letter gives sparse detail about the progress of the illness. She writes: *He is refusing further treatment. He is asking for you, Etienne, or his lips are forming the letters of your name. Constantly. I have asked whether he wants to include a letter for you, but he refuses pen and paper.* Etienne opens the last envelope. She must have written it shortly before her visit to London. His father is dead. *I don't expect you to reply. (It feels as if I'm sending letters into a void.) And I know you won't be able to attend the funeral, but I think you would want to know.*

For days Etienne doesn't get out of bed. He wishes his friends would leave him alone, but they take turns to check up on him. Like three angels arriving to stir the waters. They come and sit with him, one at a time, trying to lift his mood with weak jokes. They bring him food that he never touches.

He sleeps for hours on end, dreaming of cheerless, interchangeable South African landscapes: monotonous mountains, grasslands, bleached beaches. Highways and suburbs, tarred parking lots and petrol stations.

Frederick comes into the room, makes Etienne sit up against his will.

'You *have to* come and listen to something.' Etienne shakes his head, grabs hold of the sheets. Frederick drags him out of bed, forces him into the bath. Frederick washes him, dresses him warmly.

The four of them walk to the Oranienstrasse studio. Etienne is dragging his feet like an obstinate child. 'A new song,' Matthias says when he unlocks the factory doors and presses a sheet of music in Etienne's hands. Written at the top is *Sonnenfinsternis*. Solar eclipse. Matthias takes his place in front of the microphone; the other two sit down, start playing falteringly. It is good, Etienne knows even after the first few chords; it works. The muscle fibres in his arms tighten. His drum kit is there; they must have brought it from the flat. He approaches, sits down behind his own drums for the first time since leaving South Africa. He takes the sticks, puts them down, takes off his shirt. He shivers, picks up the sticks again.

He lets loose the violence inside him. Thousands of volts. It connects their four bodies, makes their blood rush. They are testing each other. Then their attention shrinks back; nothing but each one's own instrument exists any longer. They move down, underground, to where the rats live. To deeper places then, abandoned even by the rats. Then up into the city skies, where statues live on columns or parapets, their eyes empty, as if pecked out by crows with iron beaks.

They keep holding it *right there*, a menacing mix of sounds. Pure noise. It has taken a while to find this exact spot. Matthias's overstretched voice in hoarse falsetto, Christof convulsing over his guitar, Frederick with both elbows on the synthesiser. And there they keep it. *Keep* it. It is the raw sound, Etienne thinks, of his own blood.

Then they stop abruptly, almost simultaneously. The silence is so stupefying, Etienne has to gasp for air.

'Fuck,' Frederick says, and takes a step back, stunned, his fringe over his eyes.

Christof and Matthias sit down on the floor, wiping their shiny foreheads. The sweat dripping through Etienne's lashes makes his eyes burn. Slowly his skin starts feeling the cold again.

That night Etienne tells Frederick about everything that happened in East Berlin: about his landlady, the film archive, Fraue Fuchs and Keller. About his friendship with Nils. About Mthu and the men in Trabants, how he had to flee. He doesn't leave out anything.

Frederick listens in silence, then says: 'The exiles who arrive here from the East have stories about the dirty tricks. They always get someone to gain your confidence, usually skin against skin. And, after you've been betrayed, they torment you: lock you up alone, keep you awake, bombard you with questions. Then they match you with a sympathetic cellmate. Someone with a similar story, a good listener. An actor, it later turns out. Whose job it was to extract the real story . . .'

Etienne thinks of the stubborn neck of a plastic swan, of Nils's vertebrae like prayer beads.

Chapter 30

CHRISTMAS 1987. MATTHIAS, Christof and Frederick. And Etienne.

On Chamissoplatz the snow is half a metre thick. Frederick cooks a ham. They drink beer. There is no Christmas tree, no Räuchermännchen. Etienne tosses his mother's letters into the fire. His thoughts are now entirely here, focused on the glowing skins next to his own. Only on Christmas Eve did he catch himself thinking of the photo from his childhood, the one on Hermanus beach. Of the washed-out colours, the sand beneath his mother's bare feet. Of his father's distracted expression, his green pullover. Of his toddler self, suspended in the air, out of his mother's reach. As if taking off, rather than falling back to earth.

In the quiet days between Christmas and New Year, when it feels as if the earth has frozen on its axis, they talk endlessly. Mostly about music, sometimes about films or sex. They spend days and nights in the Rote Harfe, their favourite café. They drink beer, sit in front of the fire until it burns to ash.

Midnight, 27 December. Short films by Kreuzberg film-makers are projected against the Rote Harfe's walls - an endless loop of images. Frederick is talking about bands. Over Frederick's shoulder, Etienne is watching the film. The camera - and viewer - is in the driver's seat of a West Berlin car. It pulls away, accelerating directly towards the Wall. Each time, *just* before impact, the image cuts out. Then it starts again – the view through the windscreen, the acceleration, the approaching concrete. Over and over.

Etienne forces his attention back to Frederick. He thinks of Frederick as a boy, but when he talks about music, he is suddenly a man. His verdicts are merciless. Bands are either brilliant or opportunistic copycats. Etienne knows barely half the bands he mentions. Names like Fehlfarben, Die Krupps, Throbbing Gristle, Cabaret Voltaire, Leather Nun, Attrition. The 'hardest and best' only surface in late-night conversations, when a lot of beer has been imbibed: Sprung aus den Wolken, Laibach, SPK.

Matthias interrupts Frederick. The original industrial music, he explains, as if Etienne needs to be educated, was played for factory workers while they were making implements of war. Foxtrots, Viennese waltzes and Brahms through tinny megaphones. Etienne is half-listening. Behind Matthias a second film is playing on the wall: short fragments of Nina Hagen tearing her clothes at concerts, on one stage after the other.

Etienne can see Christof can't wait to add his own insights. The sinews in his neck are clenched. But he is waiting for Matthias, who is telling Etienne about Last Few Days, 'the most important band in history', to finish.

'British band. Almost impossible to follow. Only perform at the most unexpected times in the most unexpected places. Don't distribute recordings. Sometimes send a few tapes to a few shops, only to ensure that they almost immediately disappear from the shelves again.' On the wall behind Christof images of burning cars and riots are projected onto a beating drum hammer. 'I managed to see them once. In the Electric

Cinema in London. At four in the morning. They never advertise – you have to find out from other fans. Afterwards I begged one of the band members for an address. The next day I wrote them a letter, asking everything I'd ever wanted to know about their music. Six months later I received a response. Just one page: a picture of a church bell.'

Frederick gets going again, rattling off bands, speaking ever faster: Nurse with Wound, Nocturnal Emissions, Pornotanz, Deutsch Amerikanische Freundschaft. After each name the verdict follows. He makes short shrift: revolutionary or banal, absolute genius or utter shit.

Christof sits back; he has given up any hope of getting a turn. Matthias waits until Frederick has vented fully. 'Stunde Null can learn a lesson from Deutsch Amerikanische Freundschaft.' He speaks slowly, with emphasis. 'To be circumspect with the fascist stuff. DAF once arrived to play at a festival in the UK. And encountered thousands of amped-up skinheads waiting for them in a cloud of sweat and adrenalin.' He turns to Etienne. 'Do you know DAF?' Etienne shakes his head. 'Gay, lefties. One of their songs is "Der Mussolini". But people hear what they *want* to hear, filter the riffs through their own hate. It's naive to expect an ironic ear, or a sense of parody. Skinheads don't do nuance.'

'What about Eintstürzende?' They look at Etienne in silence. He should have known: Einstürzende Neubauten is untouchable; their music trumps anything anyone could ever dare to say about it.

When they get back home, Matthias shows Etienne his cherished single cassette of Last Few Days. The title is *So The Last Shall Be The First And First Last For Many Be Called But Few Chosen.*

Apart from the endless conversations in cafés and bars, they also write songs. The four of them together. At the kitchen table, while someone is cooking. In the steamy bathroom, while someone is taking a bath. On the parquet floor of the living room. In the icy morning air on the building's roof. The music is emerging, songs being spewed out as if from a geyser. For hours on end they sit in front of their instruments in the Oranienstrasse factory, breathing vapour through their scarfs. Songs get titles like 'The Language of Men and Machines', 'God's Idiots', 'Ritual Bombs', 'Infinite Violence'. They let the currents flow, the ideas from four heads into a single reservoir. It comes to them with ever-increasing speed. Lyrics such as 'learn the language of engines, of exploding organs', 'fear doesn't protect you against what you fear'. Or 'in order to discover the unknown, you have to gain pleasure from pain'. Overblown, yes, Etienne thinks. But it works with their sound.

Early morning. They are walking back from the Rote Harfe to Chamissoplatz. As they cross streets and walk around corners, phrases and ideas come up, are exchanged. 'Before the beginning and after the end everything is as pure as hate' is one of the lines that occurs to Etienne while they walk past huge graffiti letters. RENOVIEREN NICHT ABREISSEN! the letters say. Not that different from Prenzlauer Berg, he thinks. Here too the authorities want the squatters out. Old buildings have to make room for new ones, for cubes with square windows.

At home in Chamissoplatz, Frederick goes rummaging in an old crate, anxious to show Etienne something. A rare memento, it turns out: a pamphlet for a 1975 gig of the band

Monte Cazazza. It reads: *Sex-religious show; giant statue of Jesus got chainsawed and gang raped into oblivion.* 'How's that for promotion?' Frederick says and grins.

Etienne is feeling increasingly at home in the West. He tries to avoid the parts of the S-Bahn that pass underneath East Berlin. Something plunges in his chest when the West Berlin train crawls through ghost stations, past twilight platforms where East German guards stand ready with machine guns. He remembers the traces of such stations above ground in the East: bricked-up doorways, or steps leading down from the street only to end abruptly against a raw wall. He cannot match all these stations with their blocked entrances on the surface – in East Berlin the station names have been removed, and, in some cases, the structures at street level have been demolished. The names of some streets or places have also been changed and no longer match the names on the 1930s wall tiles down here. There are some tracks that blindly end in a wall. If the shunter were to make a mistake – a single rail switch clicking in the wrong direction – then the passengers would be crushed against the bricks, or burst through to another world.

Etienne tries to make out the guards' expressions in the dark. Does he expect that it will be Axel who returns his gaze? The faces remain invisible. Ghost faces. There are too many such things in his world, Etienne thinks: ghost films, ghost stations, ghost guards, a ghost lover. And his ghost country of origin. He looks down at his fingers; they too are becoming half-transparent. Only his three West German friends are still of flesh and blood.

An invisible hand twists his intestines when the train starts accelerating again.

They figure out their sound labyrinths in a communal mania. They already have a dozen or so songs. But the frenzy takes its toll. Sometimes Etienne needs to escape the pressure-cooker atmosphere of the flat. Then he spends hours on his own in Zensor in Belziger Strasse – surely, he thinks, the best record shop in the world. He smells the vinyl and weathered cardboard of the covers, gets lost among the shelves. He lifts oil-black records from their sleeves and studies the grooves. Sometimes he works his way alphabetically through bands or titles; sometimes he listens only to records that he doesn't know. The earphones tranquillise him. He escapes his body, washes up on a shore called Nowhere.

Late in January, Stunde Null starts playing at underground parties in Kreuzberg. In Oranienstrasse and places around Kottbusser Tor. All the new songs. The first time they play 'Sonnenfinsternis', the air in the Lokal crackles. The noise crashes into the listeners' skulls; within moments, revolt is in the air.

Over the next few weeks they play a gig virtually every night. Since arriving in West Berlin, Etienne has been growing his hair again, and his beard. He looks like a Californian hippy of a decade or two ago. He never wears a shirt when he is behind his drums. Sometimes he wears his Russian fur hat, rips it off when he starts sweating through it. Matthias, Christof and Frederick have shaved their hair against the scalp and now wear black shirts buttoned all the way to the top. Before long, Stunde Null has become one of the most popular bands in Kreuzberg. The walls of small Lokale fling the sound back at them: a dull, cruel wave, a blast of scorching air against Etienne's bare chest.

It is a blunt scream, their music. Without beginning or end. Birth and death in the same breath. A new heaven and a new hell.

A crumbling old factory on the Spree River. Dark Prussian architecture. Their biggest gig to date, almost a thousand people. Behind the stage there is a huge sun – a stage light wrapped in layers of amber cellophane. As the evening progresses, a dark moon gradually moves in from the side. When it shifts across the sun, they at last sing 'Sonnenfinsternis'. It is what everyone has been waiting for, and the first few notes send the audience into a frenzy. Etienne closes his eyes. In the most intense moments, all distances dwindle to zero – between him and Berlin, between his body and others', between here and elsewhere. It is then that he gets closest to exorcising Axel, to pulling Axel's shiny blade from his side. To letting his father's face dissolve into the noise, and his mother's. To dimming the sun of his continent of origin. In these moments he sometimes also sees a vision: of an angel dragging its wings backwards through a city, and the rubble that remains – shattered gargoyles, the marble limbs of statues, the shards of fountains.

Etienne dreams of his mother. He finds her in a burnt-out car under a desolate bridge. She has been kept hostage for a long time. He is startled by her appearance. She is just skin and bone, like a prisoner. Her skin is like wax. 'Didn't they feed you, Mother?' he wants to know. 'No,' she says, 'I'm no longer familiar with food.' Her voice is calm, neutral, but he can sense her sorrow in his bones. And he knows it is his fault that her eyes have sunk so deep into their sockets. He lifts her like a child from the car seat, carries her through an empty street. She is too weak to hold on to him. Her head bobs against his chest.

The next morning there are two letters again, forwarded by Patrick from Bonnington Square. The handwriting is his mother's. The first letter contains a single sheet on which his mother has copied a poem:

William Blake

Hy het veronrus in die late
nagte deur Londen se strate
rondgedwaal; en is vereensaam van die mens
teruggedryf tot by die grens
waar hy gesels met blom en dier en gees;
maar weet dat God in iedereen moet wees
met eienskappe ingeperk
teenstrydiglik in tand en vlerk,
in wurm en die roos, die lam, die tier;
dat Hy die hartstog is, maar ook die vuur
wat alles lok tot daardie gulde gang
waarna die moeë sonneblom verlang.

He is unsettled: she clearly remembers how he used to isolate himself in his room with the Blake book. He reads the poem again. Where did she get it? Who wrote it? Is it meant to catch him unawares, to soften him? The Afrikaans feels strange on his tongue. The poem has power, but it also irritates him, especially its religious slant. She has miscalculated; he is done with Blake, has been for some time. He flings it aside.

He opens the second envelope. Her handwriting is

becoming unsteady, wandering across the lines. *One drives past a park*, she writes. *A woman with a child is standing on a lawn. It could be any woman, any child. We are interchangeable, she and I. So too her child with mine. It could be any park, any city.* That is all. She does not address him. She does not sign her name at the end.

Stunde Null is starting to make money from their gigs; Etienne's friends no longer need to cover his living costs. They are getting an increasing number of enquiries from elsewhere, and Christof is making plans for a concert tour outside Berlin. To Bremen, and smaller cities near the Baltic Sea.

During the first weeks after Etienne's arrival in West Berlin, he was penniless. His grant instalments are probably still being paid into his East Berlin account, but he no longer has access to it. Perhaps the GDR authorities have been confiscating the money. He doesn't dare contact the film school in London about the payments. What if they want to recoup everything from him?

Now, with his portion of the earnings from their performances, he can also pay for a next round of newspaper advertisements. One about Axel, another about *Berliner Chronik*. Not just in the *Berliner Morgenpost* this time, but also in *Bild*. He arranges for the advertisements to appear repeatedly in February and March, every second week. His nights he spends searching in bars and clubs, armed with his fading Polaroid. He shows it to people, or sits around for hours scouring a sea of faces. The days he spends going from hospital to hospital. Sometimes sympathetic male nurses give him access to patient registers. He also tries to find out whether Axel is claiming unemployment insurance in Berlin. This is confidential information, but an acquaintance of his three friends works in a government office. This does not yield anything either; the fact that Axel's surname is unknown renders the search impossible. To tentatively hook 'Fleischer' or 'Schnur' to his first name makes no difference. Etienne visits a police station, but they will only assist once someone has been formally reported missing, and if he was last seen in Berlin. They don't get involved in lovers' disputes, a policewoman with a wide jaw explains spitefully in the Berlinische dialect.

He doesn't visit morgues, nor does he request death registers. Not yet.

Chapter 31

ETIENNE IS SITTING on his own at Anderes Ufer one afternoon. The blond waiter swiftly looks from side to side when he brings Etienne's beer, bends over conspiratorially. 'Are you still looking for him?' Etienne regularly encounters the waiter on his search expeditions in bars and clubs. The man often observes him; Etienne has at times wondered whether he is following him.

'Presumably you mean Axel. And, yes, I'm still searching.'

'Perhaps you're looking in the wrong places.' He stands up straight, lets a dramatic silence ensue.

Etienne looks at him sceptically. 'I think,' he says coolly, 'I've been pretty much everywhere. What's the name of the place you have in mind?'

The waiter's fringe falls over his eyes; he laughs sharply. 'Not everywhere, I'll have you know. And such places don't have names. You have to *know* people . . .'

'And now you're going to inform me that you are one of the people one has to know.'

He nods. 'You won't believe who you encounter there. All the cockroaches slipping from the cracks, ghosts returning from the other side . . . This is your one chance.'

Etienne isn't immune to the hope. 'Where?' he says. 'And when?'

He meets his blond guide at Bülowstrasse U-Bahn station. At two in the morning. Etienne didn't expect he would show, but he is standing there, waiting. Or not quite *he*: his transformation is so complete, Etienne hardly recognises him. He is wearing laced boots and a military harness of sorts, a kind of straitjacket. Nails are woven into his sleeves. He looks taller and tougher than Etienne remembers. His voice is an octave lower, his movements more brusque. Only the long fringe is the same.

They walk to Pallasstrasse. Underneath a '70s block of flats is a large concrete structure. Etienne imagines how it would make Aodhan tremble.

'A war bunker?'

His companion nods. 'Built in the '40s by women and child slaves. Three metres thick. Indestructible. The flats had to be built on top of it.' Even the rhythms of his speech are different from before. Is this his true self? Is his camp waiter persona a guise that he casts off at night like a cloak?

A gate is opened electronically – a camera has registered their arrival. They wait for a while in front of a solid steel door, which is then opened just wide enough to let them in.

The music is deafening. Echoes clashing with echoes. The history of the last few hours' noise is still darting and reflecting through the rooms, mixing with music from loudspeakers. It is impossible to say which noises are old and which new, whether you're listening to sounds belonging to this moment or from an hour ago.

The concrete space, with a low ceiling, is packed with men. Apart from the bodies – some shirtless, most of them naked – there is just raw concrete. And stroboscopes flickering at high frequency. Etienne follows the blond fringe up a flight of stairs. The next level is identical. The same music, the same flashing. The music is industrial, iron upon iron, the violence of machines. In a corner a woman is sitting in front of a console with rows of buttons, like someone in control of a power plant. She sports an impeccable black bob. And, he notices when he approaches, a moustache. She looks at the bunker full of men as if they hail from the past, as if she no longer knows any of them.

Here and there the blond man talks to someone. Someone gives him a little bag of pills. Everything is revealed in stroboscopic moments – independent frames refusing to merge into scenes. The man puts a pill on Etienne's tongue. His finger tastes of insect poison.

They go up to the next floor. The same. Bodies in grey flashes, the music even louder. The higher they go, the warmer and stuffier it gets. Etienne touches the damp wall. The blond disappears among people. Around Etienne bodies are moving epileptically, writhing sweatily. No one is talking; no one is making eye contact. Two men are pissing against the concrete; the stream is running between Etienne's feet, under his shoes. There are no toilets here, no taps or windows. Just pills and bodies and concrete. For the first time, Etienne thinks, he understands his erstwhile lover Aodhan. *Here* he would be fully at home.

He blinks his eyes, shakes his head. The pill is kicking in. Everything sharpens. He can now hear the tiniest sounds above the music: sweat being parsed through pores, lashes brushing up against each other, cement dust whirling up from soles.

He walks up a third flight of stairs. Once again, identical. The same music, the same flickering light. Men are copulating in groups like machines.

Someone approaches Etienne, shouts in his ear: 'It's not for humans, this place!'

Etienne looks around. What are they then? Automatons?

The man leans over again. 'I mean, the Nazis built the bunker for weapons and supplies. There's no ventilation. No oxygen supply. Can you feel it?' Etienne looks at the two men next to his interlocutor. Square, strong bodies. Their mouths lock, muscular tongues find each other. It is not a kiss, Etienne realises, but a battle: they are sucking the air from each other's lungs. He can now feel how heavy his own breath has become.

Light is blooming in Etienne's forehead. A bouquet of blinding blossoms. He tries to shake the light out of his skull. *Yes*, he wants to say, *I can feel it*. But his tongue is too heavy.

'The people who organise these parties,' the man shouts, 'told me that the bunker can sustain about a hundred and fifty people for twenty-four hours. Then everyone suffocates in a huge pile!' A shortage of air, Etienne realises, *that* is why everyone is so roused, wanting to devour each other.

He leans over, tears his tongue loose from the floor of his mouth: 'But there are far more than a hundred and fifty guys here!'

The man shrugs, shouts in Etienne's ear. They roughly calculate how many people are coming, he says, calculate the hours. Everyone has to be out by six in the morning. 'But, fuck it, nobody here is a scientist. You yourself have to decide whether you want to risk asphyxiation!' Etienne can feel his lungs burning. The flashing inside his head is synchronised with the flickering in the room. The thoughts being illuminated by the flashing light won't fall into any pattern. After each party, the man continues, they open up the few small vents and let new air circulate for a month.

The man takes him by the arm, pulls him up the last set of stairs. Up here there are fewer people. The music is even louder. Everyone is copulating; there is a smell of fresh blood in the air. The man takes him to the furthest wall. Before them is a roster of blocks, like drawers in the wall. Each with a steel handle, numbered from one to eighty-four. 'Look,' the man shouts, and only now does Etienne notice he is naked. 'An escape route!'

'Escape? How?'

'Each block is three metres long. You pull them out one by one!' He yanks one of the handles. Nothing happens. He smiles, shrugs his shoulders.

For the first time, Etienne looks properly at his informant. He gets a fright, steps back: it is *Axel's* face! How can it be that he only recognises him now? And how can it be it that Axel doesn't recognise *him*? How can they just stand here and converse so coolly? Etienne tries to calm himself, but then he puts his arms around Axel, pressing the air from him.

Axel is caught unawares; then he relaxes, opens up his body. He slips a hand into Etienne's pants. Someone else presses against Etienne from behind. He is astonished to see that that too is Axel. Or his twin brother. Then there is another body. Axel, yet again. Etienne opens his eyes wide, defying the flickering. Everyone is Axel: a hall filled with upside-down oak trees, a hurricane in an ancient forest. He looks straight into the stroboscope. Let them become blind together, he and all the Axels. Now he too steps out of his clothes, slick with sweat. He and the Axels are all wearing only boots.

He urgently needs oxygen, tries to find it in the throats around him. His tongue recognises all of the throats. One Axel-mouth isn't enough. He empties one set of lungs after the other. The bodies are as hard as concrete. Etienne isn't yielding an inch himself.

He can sense he is on the verge of losing consciousness. He stumbles towards the escape door, reaching for the handle of block No. 84.

When Etienne surfaces, he is lying on a slippery, warm cement floor. The blond waiter is bent over him, hair covering his face. There is silence, and electrical light. The party is over. 'You found him, didn't you?'

Etienne just nods. His jaws are made of iron; his vocal cords have been destroyed.

The sharpness has returned to the man's voice. 'I told you so, didn't I?' He holds out a hand towards Etienne. 'We should go, there is no air left in here.'

The next time Etienne goes to Anderes Ufer, the waiter with the long fringe is nowhere to be seen. He never encounters him again. Neither at the café, nor anywhere else.

Chapter 32

'SOMEONE HAS RESPONDED to one of the most recent ads,' Christof says when Etienne wakes up late afternoon after his night in the bunker. Christof's mouth moves in a nervous twitch while he scratches a rash in the crook of his arm.

'I screened the calls last time,' Frederick says. 'You won't believe what a bunch of loonies and swindlers call up. One was supposedly the director of *Berliner Chronik*. First wanted a thousand marks before—'

Matthias shakes his head. 'Well, let's focus on this guy. He knows specifically that the film was made in 1933. The ad just says "in the early '30s". That's something. He's willing to meet. He hasn't thus far mentioned anything about payment.'

None of them asks Etienne about his movements the night before, but he can sense they are itching to know. 'What is there to lose?' is all he says. Frederick fusses, looks around restlessly.

The flat is in Neukölln. On the U-Bahn on the way there, Etienne feels weary. It is becoming a pattern: he fumbles around in the dark, there is an unexpected lead, hope is ignited, there is a glimpse of a breakthrough. And then? A false trail. Disappointment. Nothing.

A needle in all the world's haystacks indeed. It is the end of March. He left London almost six months ago. He is still no closer to either Axel or the rest of the film. Soon he will have to apply for a refugee visa in West Germany. His British asylum doesn't allow him to just settle here. If he isn't careful, he will be deported and his entire search will be at an end.

Etienne gets off at Hermannstrasse station. The nondescript block of flats he is approaching dates from the '50s or '60s. Etienne takes the narrow lift, knocks on the front door. A man in his early forties opens, turns around and walks back into the flat without a word. Etienne hesitates, then follows. The flat smells of cauliflower, old smoke and something unidentifiable. Detergent? Drugs? Etienne imagines a little laboratory: a simmering pot, steam that could make you lose consciousness. 'Volker,' he says when Etienne asks his name a second time.

There is just a tired sofa, a chair and a table. On the carpet are stacks of paper, as well as scattered cigarettes, matches, badges. Volker sits down on the sofa. He is tall, wearing a vest. His muscles were once well-toned, Etienne can see; now the skin is starting to loosen. Etienne isn't invited to sit down. 'So,' Etienne says. 'You know why I'm here. I understand you have information.' Outside the window a children's play area is visible in the snow. It doesn't look as if a child has ever played there.

'It will cost you,' Volker says. His arm is resting on the back of the sofa. The hairs in his armpit cling together. There is a tattoo on his neck: the face of a dog baring its teeth. His arms are inked too.

'And what is it that you reckon I should pay you for?' A waste of time, Etienne thinks. He should go.

Volker is not to be discouraged. 'The movie.'

'I see. Well, perhaps you should show it to me first? Before we talk about money?'

Volker lights a cigarette. He puts one arm behind his head, inhales the smoke, doesn't say anything else. The chemical smell is becoming stronger. Is something mixed in with his tobacco?

'I'm going now,' Etienne says. 'I don't have time for games.' Just another dead end, he thinks. Another chancer and swindler. He has run out of patience.

'Suit yourself.' Volker smiles. A dog smile, teeth showing. Through an open door Etienne can see into the bedroom. Knee-length Doc Martens boots stand against a white wall. Polished to such a high gloss that they look varnished. A photo on top of a stack of paper draws Etienne's attention. It shows a younger Volker, among a group of men: shaven heads, suspenders, boots. They are shouting. Screaming, in fact. Veins stand out on their temples, neck muscles taut.

He looks back at Volker. Somewhere under his clothes, where the police of the new Germany cannot see them, there must be one or two swastikas on his skin. And various knife scars.

'Three thousand marks,' Volker says. On his arms are tattoos of barbed wire and medieval symbols. And phrases in Gothic script. His shaved hair is a messy in-between length – clearly it hasn't seen a blade recently.

'Two hundred,' Etienne says. 'Provided it's what I need.'

Volker sits with his legs spread wide. 'Do you want to know how I got it?'

'I'm sure you're going to tell me.'

'My woman's – well, now my dead woman's – mother worked on the movie.'

For a few moments, Etienne is silent. He tries to keep his voice steady. 'And what would her name be?'

'Irmgard,' the man says. 'Irmgard Fleischer.'

Etienne sits down on a chair. 'Let me see it,' he says after a while. He doesn't care that his voice is cracking. 'I will pay you what you want. Please. Just let me see it.'

The man takes his time extinguishing his cigarette in a saucer, gets up. He pulls out a film case from beneath the stack of paper, puts it down on the table. When Etienne reaches for it, Volker hits hard on the lid with his open hand. 'Remember, mate. Just *look*.'

Etienne nods. He opens it, pulls out the end of the film, studies a few frames. He takes out the whole reel, threads a longer piece of the film through his fingers. He knows instantly: it is *Berliner Chronik*. The second reel.

Etienne looks Volker straight in the eyes. He wishes he could avoid such a pleading expression. 'Axel,' is all that Etienne says at first. His voice falters. 'You,' he tries again, 'are Axel's father.'

Naked anger spreads over Volker's face. Then something else. Fear? Revulsion? Then nothing. Volker shakes his head, clears his throat. 'Who is Axel?'

When Etienne is on his way down, the lift briefly comes to a halt between storeys. When it shudders and then moves further, he suddenly manages to link a memory to the odour in the flat: the flea collar of his parents' German Shepherd in South Africa. How smells tend to evade one! Faces are easy to recall. But memory's archive has no shelf dedicated to smell.

He told Volker he would come back for the reel. And would bring a thousand marks with him. 'You can't go there on your own again,' Frederick says when Etienne recounts what happened. 'I can't believe we sent you on your own to such a crazy fucker.' Then, calmer: 'How in God's name do you know he was Axel's father?'

'Irmgard, Axel told me, had just one child. And Axel himself is an only child. So it follows that this man is his father.'

'Not necessarily.' Frederick's eyes turn from blue to grey. 'OK, he's her lover, calls her "my woman". But what if she had lots of lovers, of which he's only one?'

'Why would she give him the film if he's just another lover? And, I'm telling you, I saw it in his eyes. The moment when I mentioned Axel. But he won't talk, or give me the reel, if I don't pay. And it will take months of gigs to get the money together . . .' If he could find out Volker's surname in the meantime, Etienne thinks, that might help. It is probably Axel's also.

A wintry wind is blowing. Etienne is back in Neukölln today. Frederick is accompanying him; he and Matthias and Christof have managed to gather several thousand marks in a few days. Etienne didn't want to accept, but they insisted. If it only concerned the film, he would not have taken the money, but this is about Axel. And only money will get Volker to talk.

Frederick was adamant about coming along, and now wants to enter the building with Etienne. 'No,' he says. 'I have to put him at ease, get him to talk.' Frederick grudgingly agrees to wait outside.

Volker is as defiant in his attitude as before. 'Why don't you just admit you're Axel's father?' is Etienne's opening gambit. *That* Volker wasn't expecting. His head jerks back. Something shiny catches Etienne's eye. A badge lying on the table, small and polished. Twin flashes of lightning: an *S* and another *S*. It would have been pinned to a uniform, once. Just as Etienne thought: Volker is one of those cliché bullies. Someone who stirs shit with his neo-Nazi friends. He is washed up now; his high point must have been in the 1960s and '70s. Etienne can picture Volker and his henchmen. Sitting around drinking beer in empty lots, the steel points of their boots polished with spit, arms lifting in drunken salutes while comrades go and piss in the cold with semi-erections in the steam. Nights of kicking and punching immigrants, until they go home, slick with blood, to unload wildly inside their girlfriends. (Is that how Axel was conceived?) Etienne steps forward, his chest touching Volker's. He doesn't know where he is gathering the anger and courage from. 'Tell me *now! Everything* about Axel! What has happened to him? Where is he?'

Volker brutally pushes Etienne back. 'Don't you come and tell me what to do in my own home! That cunt-head is no longer my child. I know nothing about him. Don't want to either.' Etienne notices a scar on Volker's arm. A recent one, a reddish-purple ridge.

Etienne retreats. 'Just tell me *something*. Please. I've been searching for more than a year . . .'

'Where's the money?' Volker's expression changes with Etienne's tone of voice. He is in control again.

'I have it.'

'Show.'

Etienne takes the notes out of his pocket, thumbs them. Volker reaches for the film reel next to the SS badge. 'I know nothing about that little fucker. A year or so ago he was here once. I don't have the vaguest fuckin' idea where he is now. Do you think he keeps me informed? He hates me, just like you.' Volker exposes his dog teeth, holds out the film reel. 'There it is. Give me the money.'

Etienne puts the cash and a scrap of paper with the telephone number in Chamissoplatz written on it down on the table. He takes the reel. Volker counts the money twice. 'Now fuck off,' he says.

They sit in a row in the Oranienstrasse factory's courtyard, Etienne's three friends. Wrapped in blankets, mugs of coffee in their hands, their breaths steaming. Like children at a bonfire concert. It is cold, but spring is in the air. March was windless. Snow started melting, dripping from roofs. April blossoms are blooming in sheltered courtyards.

Etienne has insisted on setting up the projector. They have borrowed it from a little Kreuzberg cellar cinema that shows vintage films. He threads the film through. The reels start turning. Christof and Frederick make room; Etienne sits down between them. Frederick takes his hand, pressing it tightly.

In a sequence entitled *Ein Gespenst* – a ghost – there are lengthy shots in a bedroom: gowns hanging behind a velvet curtain, textiles stirring in abstract night movements. In *Die Speisekammer* – the pantry – a close-up shot shows a hand pilfering currants from a cupboard. Etienne sits up. Behind some frames he can vaguely make out a second image. A huge angel, its wings spread out. Or so he imagines. Are two images shifting across each other – a technique of double exposure that was also used in the first reel? Or is the angel just a chemical stain on degraded film?

Etienne tries to figure out how the images, or the dim shadow of an angel behind them, manage to bring such consolation. Frederick's hand stirs clumsily in Etienne's lap.

The cold returns; blossoms freeze. Two weeks after Etienne visited Volker, Volker calls him. His tune has changed. He has information about Axel, but he wants another thousand marks. The other three come up with the money in three days. Etienne doesn't want to accept it at first. Then he gives in, undertakes to sell his drums to pay them back. 'Don't be ridiculous,' Matthias says. Christof waves away Etienne's offer with a gesture of his hand. Frederick vigorously shakes his head.

Frederick goes with him, once again waits, under protest, down in the street. Volker is looking self-satisfied. Since Etienne's last visit, his hair has been shaved to the scalp. The flat is smelling worse, of mothballs and hydrochloric acid, a chemical stew. Volker is shirtless, wearing tight jeans and old boots without laces (the shiny new ones are still exhibited in the bedroom). He is sitting on the sofa, smoking, legs spread wide. Etienne gawks at the tattoos on his chest. Signs and codes, over and across each other, as if each tattooist had imagined he was starting on clean skin. As if an entire army had wanted to write out its anger on one man. A chaos of meanings, or the complete absence thereof.

Etienne puts down the money on the table, keeps his hand on it. 'Where is he? Where is Axel?'

Volker is looking at something far behind Etienne. His pupils are large. He picks a sheet of paper from the floor, writes something on it. Slowly he folds it into a paper plane, launches it towards Etienne. It glides as if on a hot current. Etienne catches it, unfolds it: an address in Hannover.

'That's where you'll find that little mother's cunt. I only saw him once, as I've told you. When he arrived in Berlin.'

'Why Hannover?'

'Go ask him yourself.'

'I'm asking *you*.'

Volker's face screws up venomously. 'Your little bed bunny was locked up for a year, mate, in the fuckin' clink, where he belongs! Now he's living in Hannover, with his other bed bunnies. Slammer friends.'

'Jail? I don't believe you. Why?'

Silence.

'And I want to know about Axel's mother, and about Irmgard. About Axel's childhood days spent with you. Why can't he talk about it? What did you do to him? I'm staying right here until I've heard everything!'

Volker gets up. There are still traces of youthful leanness. Underneath the tattoos the chest muscles attach to the sternum like fingers. 'You'll hear fuck all else from me! Go and search for him yourself, go and listen to the kind of shit he tells people. Get lost! Out!'

Volker's cigarette falls on the dirty carpet. He aims wildly at Etienne. Etienne retreats, walking backwards to the front door. Volker stops, slaps his hand over the little pile of bank notes on the table.

When Volker turns away, Etienne sees it. There, at the base of his spine, is the source of his power: a neat tattoo of a swastika. Not too large, not too small. Just right.

Christof has been planning Stunde Null's concert tour for the last month. Their first performance is in Bremen. It will coincide with a solar eclipse that will be visible there in two weeks' time, in early May. Now they will add a visit to Hannover along the way.

At first, Etienne urgently wanted to take a train to

276

Hannover. 'How can I wait?' he asked Frederick. 'If I only get there in two weeks' time, he may well have left again.' Volker had not provided a telephone number; there was no way to contact Axel beforehand.

'I know you've been searching for a long time, Etienne. I know it's urgent. But he's not going to just disappear again overnight. You can't take the trip through East Germany on your own. What kind of notes do you think there are next to your name for the border guards? Just two weeks, Etienne, then we'll all go together.'

Etienne can't afford a plane ticket. Overland, through two East German border posts, is the only route. He can't embark on such a trip without the other three. He wouldn't want to disappear into a twilight world, like Nils's brother on his endless voyage across the Baltic Sea. And he knows these three won't allow him to be torn away from them.

Chapter 33

MATTHIAS PAINTS *Stunde Null* on the side of their grey 1964 Volkswagen Kombi. In black Gothic letters. His brow twists; the little gutter running from his nose to his upper lip tightens in a strict line. Christof and Frederick look on sceptically. They veto his work, paint over it. Christof starts from scratch, this time with red paint. It drips down the steel. Matthias shakes his head. 'Looks like someone has shattered a rabbit's skull against the bodywork.'

The three of them look at Etienne for a final verdict. 'No,' he says. 'Nothing should be written on it.' Frederick paints over it all. Then they spray paint the entire vehicle black, also the back windows. Like a craft designed to avoid radar detection.

Matthias is driving, with Christof sitting next to him. The back seats have been taken out. Etienne and Frederick are lying on cushions on the steel floor. In the very back the instruments and sound equipment are stacked. To get onto the Transitstrecke – the strip of highway that runs from West Berlin through East Germany – they cross at Kontrollpunkt Dreilinden. Matthias's face is sullen when they stop. The skin on Christof's neck tightens; he sucks in his cheeks. Frederick takes Etienne's hand. The East German guard sticks his head through the window, looks at Etienne and Frederick in their nest of cushions. The passports and *titre de voyage* are taken away. The guards return empty-handed, insist that they all

278

get out. Etienne's heart starts racing. The guard searches the front part of the cabin, then orders them to unload the instruments and equipment. When they start unknotting the ropes, the guard changes his mind. They have to get back into the Volkswagen. The guard disappears.

They wait for ten minutes. Then another ten. Vehicles on either side of them are let through. Fog starts wafting from the trees next to the highway, wraps around the border post's buildings. Then the guard approaches, carrying the passports. Etienne's travel document isn't with them. The guard looks silently at Etienne, hand on his gun. They wait. The guard's gaze does not shift. A minute passes. Then another guard emerges from the fog, hands Etienne his travel document through the window.

When they are through, they laugh with relief. A joint is lit and shared. Before long they are relaxed, floating. What a *home* this is, Etienne thinks, this cosy nest of friends. His brothers, comrades, protectors, co-conspirators, fellow noise-makers. How safe one feels in this ship, this lit tank speeding across the strange flat earth.

It is cold. It should have been almost summer by now, but spring has waned again. Etienne lies back against the pile of cushions. He can hear his cymbals vibrating and resonating in the back. With his skilful hands Christof has connected an old domestic heater to the car's electrical system. He is their technician, always setting up the sound equipment at gigs. The little heater is rattling against the car's metal body. The elements are glowing brightly. Matthias has been selecting the music thus far, but now it is Christof's turn. He inserts his cassette into the car radio, then lies down in the back next to Etienne and Frederick. Christof's favourite post-punk bands are playing: Gang of Four, The Fall, Can, Bauhaus, The Birthday Party. Matthias turns up the volume. The three of them are singing out loud; Etienne only knows a few snatches of the lyrics.

They stop at a petrol station to refill. Matthias waits for The Birthday Party's 'Release the Bats' to finish before taking the key out of the ignition. The joint smoke lingering in the hollows of Etienne's skull is making him dizzy. He looks up at a tower next to the parking area. 'Stop staring like that,' Christof says through his teeth. 'That's probably where the Stasi is stationed.' They are hidden everywhere along this route, Frederick explains in a hushed voice. To ensure that East and West Germans don't engage with each other, and that nobody gets into the boot of a West German vehicle. Or is folded double in a suitcase, or hidden in secret compartments beneath false bottoms.

Etienne seeks shelter in the men's toilets from the all-seeing eyes. The steel urinal is rusting and peeling in the shades of a faded baroque painting. His urine spatters against the veils of chalk and moss. He closes his eyes. From the cavities of his head, Axel addresses him. Etienne can't hear what he is saying, just senses the droning of his half-formed words. The tone is dangerous. Then it is drowned out by his father's voice, or the voice he had before his illness. That too fades, becomes only breath.

Frederick's breath, Etienne realises when he opens his eyes. Frederick is standing next to him; he places a hand on Etienne's shoulder. Frederick's stream of urine starts murmuring reassuringly next to his own against the steel. Etienne sighs; his head tilts backwards. Comrades in fragrant piss steam, the lukewarm fluid spattering against their hands. Frederick's fingers clench around the back of Etienne's neck, tousling his hair.

Then it occurs to Etienne: a trap must surely be set for him. In an hour and a half they will be crossing the border to West Germany at Helmstedt. *That* is why he was allowed to cross at the first control point, he now realises: to coax him into East German territory. As soon as he gets to the second border, they will have him . . .

Axel's voice emanates from the bone of his skull, ominously: *Have you considered that your three 'friends' may be collaborating with the East Germans? Think of how suddenly you met, of how smoothly and easily it has all progressed. How deep into your mind do you think they have managed to penetrate . . . ?* Etienne shakes his head until Axel falls silent. *Not as deep as you*, he answers in his own skull voice. He and Frederick look at each other while zipping up. Frederick's eyes are watery, mournful.

Back in the Kombi, Etienne airs his suspicion that the guards may be waiting for him at the border. Matthias frowns. Christof presses his lips together like a scar. 'Surely not,' Frederick says.

They drive on, the atmosphere now dampened. The radio stays off. The road is slipping by underneath them with a monotonous hiss.

'Let's tell each other stories,' Frederick says. 'The stories of our first loves.' The tension eases somewhat. He nods in Matthias's direction. 'You start.'

Matthias inhales deeply, looks in the rear mirror. 'It was my last school holiday. Christmas time. I was touring France, hitch-hiking at night. Was mostly picked up by lorries.' At first he wanted to see as many places as possible, he goes on, but after a while he started enjoying the lorry rides as such. Nights spent in dark lorry cabins were better than hanging around in tourist spots with backpackers who would drink until they fell over. 'Paris? Didn't do anything for me. Lourdes? Aix-en-Provence? Left me cold.'

Matthias sinks deeper into his story. He travelled arbitrarily. North to south, east to west. Back and forth. Most of the lorry drivers *talked*. For hours on end. He too. The invisible nocturnal landscapes gave him the freedom to say things he hadn't been able to say before. 'At first I struggled to stay awake, but soon my patterns fell in with those of the drivers, my days and nights switched.' He visited much of France, almost every corner, but saw none of it. Just blue tar and dotted lines in headlights. Road signs flitting past. The ghosts of trees on the side of the road.

'Get to the story now,' Frederick says, his face lit by the heater's glow.

One evening, Matthias continues, Adil from Morocco picked him up. And then he didn't get off again. They drove back and forth between Paris and Marseilles, night after night. Adil had to spend weekends with his wife and child in Marseilles, but during the week they covered thousands of kilometres together. In the daytime they would sleep in a lorry park next to a highway. In the back of Adil's cabin, in his cramped little bed. In each other's arms, the tyres of lorries whining on the tar outside.

It was consoling, the endless driving. Without heading anywhere, without arriving. Adil transported wine. Tons of it. Between Paris and Marseilles they had to pick up cargo in various wine regions. They never saw the scenic parts of cities or towns. They would always drive around the edges, through the outskirts. At dusk or in the dark. Whenever they stopped, it would be at industrial sites or warehouses.

'You're digressing again,' Frederick says. 'Get to the love part!'

'One night, when we stopped at a warehouse in the Rhône, there was a commotion. Temperatures had suddenly fallen unseasonably. The black frost was on its way – the harvest was under threat.'

Etienne's head rolls against Frederick's; he pulls up his legs against the cold.

The owners of the wine estates were desperately looking for hands. The men had to stoke huge fires in the vineyards to fend off the frost. 'We had to run back and forth with armfuls of dry vine cuttings. Later we poured petrol onto the flames. Just before sunrise, I turned away from the fire with an empty petrol can in my hands. Adil was standing there. Shirtless and out of breath, at the edge of the glow. In that moment I fell in love with him.'

Etienne is startled when Frederick shouts, 'There you have it!' in his ear. He has clearly immersed himself in the story. 'And what became of him?' Frederick asks. 'Of Adil?'

'He immediately realised that everything had changed. In the morning hours, when the harvest had been saved, we went to sleep in a barn. Just there on the cement floor, in a pile, men from all over. All of us high on petrol fumes. We were covered in soot, there was smoke in our lungs.

'Adil and I opened up each other's bodies, tasted the soot on each other. Right there between the others—' Matthias brakes so hard that the three in the back shift forward. 'Fuck,' he says, 'an animal crossing the road.'

'What kind of animal?' Etienne wants to know. He

gets halfway up in a crouched position, looks through the windscreen, searching in vain for a shadow between the tree trunks.

Matthias shrugs his shoulders. 'God knows! Things here probably mutate. Radioactive deer, bush pigs glowing in the dark, wolves with iron claws . . .' He changes gears, accelerates again. 'Anyway. The next morning, when I woke up, Adil was gone. And his lorry. I never saw him again.'

Etienne looks at Christof. He is vaguely starting to suspect that the other two know this story: a well-practised exercise.

'Now you,' Frederick says, putting his hand on the chest of Christof, who is lying next to him, half-propped up against the pillows.

'OK,' Christof says. 'It's not as good as Matthias's story. It was in Vancouver. Midwinter. I was eighteen. My first time away from Berlin alone. I didn't know a soul in Canada, stayed in a youth hostel. On the first night, I leave the hostel to check out the night life. It is cold, below zero. I randomly follow a bunch of guys into a club. One of them draws my eye. After a while I realise he's not in fact part of the group – he sits around on his own, doesn't take off his coat. Less than half an hour later he leaves again. I follow him.'

'Yes, yes, and where to?' Frederick is like a rude aunt. Etienne smiles in the dark.

'First the man walks through the streets, then into a deserted park on a peninsula. My heart is racing, but I keep following him.'

Through the Kombi's windscreen Etienne can see signs above the road: warnings indicating that stopping is prohibited. *Achtung!* It reminds him of signs by the Spree River in West Berlin. Dozens of East Berliners have drowned there, or have been shot, while attempting to swim to West Berlin. *Achtung!* Etienne keeps hearing it in his mind like a refrain. Perhaps a song could be made of it.

Christof continues. The man kept going deeper into the park, then turned off the path into a copse of trees. Christof kept following. The sea glistened through the foliage; he could see the man bending down, picking up something and putting it into a bag. Underneath Christof's feet something cracked like glass. Ahead of him, the man stopped, turned around and listened to him approaching, helplessly making loud crunching sounds.

'You know what you're stepping on, don't you?'

Christof's lips were half-frozen. 'Ice? Broken bottles?'

He shook his head, held out something towards Etienne. 'Frozen frogs. They bury themselves underneath the leaves. Their hearts stop beating, the blood freezes, all the organs arrest. This is how they survive the winter.'

The man held up a frog, took a leg between two fingers, snapped it off in a single movement, like the stem of a champagne glass.

Achtung! flashes past the Kombi's windscreen. From where Etienne is lying, he can see only the black sky and, now and then, the dimly lit warnings. He thinks of the speck of a head in the Spree, of water spattering where guards' bullets hit the surface like pebbles, until the head slips away.

They walked back together, Christof continues. The man kept picking up frogs, which were clinking gently in his backpack. He took Christof to his house. In his backyard there was a wooden lean-to with heated glass cages and dozens of amphibians. He was a zoological researcher at a university, he explained. He emptied out his backpack in a bucket.

Inside the house, he put one of the frogs down in front of the fireplace. He lit the fire. Before long, the heart started fluttering underneath the thin skin. Minutes later, the frog started hopping about. While the zoologist's fingertips started feeling Christof's temples, he explained how frogs can also go into a summer sleep when it becomes hot and dry. How the mud then hardens around them, how the skin dries out and forms a cocoon. Months later, when the rains come, they crawl out of the crust, as if being reborn.

The frog professor's palms were as soft as an amphibian abdomen. His body was cool and dry, his stomach like dough. The croaking in the backyard kept Christof awake all night. Before dawn he crept out without looking at the glass cases again. That night he returned to Germany.

Matthias shakes his head. 'What a sudden ending. Where's the love? It sounds to me like a narrow escape rather than—'

'Creepy, yes,' Frederick says and smiles contentedly. '*So fucking creepy.*'

It is Frederick's turn. He was visiting his cousins on a farm in Friesland, he starts telling, where his mother is from. And (surprise, surprise) he too was eighteen. It was nearly Christmas. The cold was so bitter on that flat piece of land that one's bones became brittle. He shared a room with his two cousins with their large, cautious hands. One was a little older than he, the other a little younger. There wasn't any central heating. Fires burnt in hearths through the night; the sheets smelled of smoke.

One night his uncle woke them up. 'The newborn lambs are dying,' he said.

'I'm from Berlin. What do I know about dying lambs?' Frederick mumbled from under the blanket. His uncle hustled them out of there. He threw woolly hats and blankets after them, stayed indoors himself.

The blankets, it turned out, weren't for them but for the lambs. The neighbours' sons had been commandeered too and strolled sleepily towards them. There wasn't a shed or barn. The boys had to make a fire.

'Lambs, schlambs!' Christof's head hinges on his long, scarred neck. 'Where does love enter the picture?'

Etienne is now almost certain: they already know the stories. Their pleasure in the retelling is obvious. The interruptions and commentary, the pseudo-frustrations, are all part of the ritual. The lambs had to be caught, Frederick continues. It wasn't difficult; they were sluggish due to the cold. The boys wrapped the animals in the blankets, rubbed them, blew warm breath in their noses. The large fire was stoked with peat. Before peat is lit, Frederick says, it smells like seaweed, hay, moss, tree sap. His nostrils widen as he describes the smell; when it burns, the smoke has the aroma of tar and autumn leaves, of bitter tea. They sat with the struggling, bleating lambs in their arms, clumsy as if holding babies. Their faces were lowered towards the lambs' noses, self-conscious and bemused by the gentleness that was suddenly expected from them.

The ground on which they were standing was peat too. It was dry enough to catch fire right underneath their feet. And then the peaty fumes erupted in flames too. In the blink of an eye they were standing in a firestorm. The heat was unbearable – one's primary urge was to run naked into the icy night. Lambs screamed and wriggled. Frederick's older cousin grabbed a kettle that had been on the fire, poured the water into the flames. It was useless. The entire world was on fire. 'My younger cousin and I dropped the lambs, and wrapped the blankets around ourselves. We tried running through the flames, but flinched and retreated. Then we looked at each other, took each other's hands and just went. When we emerged from the flames, we saw my uncle running towards us.'

Frederick's head rolls against Etienne's. It feels as if the story is being transferred directly to him at the point where their scalps touch.

'My cousin was trapped in the circle of flames. Neighbours came running with buckets of water, tried putting out the flames with hessian bags. My older cousin, when he finally appeared, was badly burnt. He stood there naked and shivering, crying like a child. He wouldn't – *couldn't* – let go of the scorched lamb in his arms. They had melted into each other, their heads equally black. The ambulance men had to come and peel the dead animal away from him.

'When dawn came, we went home, my younger cousin and I, dead tired. We crawled in bed, got out of our clothes under the blankets, consoling and stroking each other. There was a shared memory – not only his or only mine – of writhing lambs. Everything smelled of wool, our skins were oily with lanolin. We cried, sought comfort in each other's bodies. He was warm and smooth, my cousin, his tongue sweet . . .'

Etienne looks back at the vibrating jumble of their instruments and equipment. It is as if it is on the verge of blaring out a dark piece of metal rock: a wild orchestra without players.

'The neighbours' two boys didn't make it. The firemen found them hours later, when the last flames had been extinguished. The next morning we got up and watched them remove the bodies. My cousin and I had not yet washed – his soot was in my hair; mine was smeared over his chest. The two boys' bodies were shrunken like dead spiders. They must have clung to each other as they died. The firemen couldn't prise them apart, had to put them on a single stretcher. The firemen kept looking down at their own hands, black with human ash.

'My cousin and I then took a shower, silently washing the crusts of semen and ash from each other's bodies.'

There is silence after Frederick's story.

Chapter 34

EXHAUST FUMES RISE through the gaps in the Kombi's floor. And the smell of hot rubber. Are any of these stories true, Etienne wonders, these stories of fire and ice? Where in the northern hemisphere, for instance, are lambs born in December? And who harvests grapes in winter?

The three of them concentrate their attention on Etienne. He is thinking of the animal that ran across the road a while ago. Did the Kombi graze it? Will the border guards waiting for him at Helmstedt find a bloody tuft of fur clinging to the chrome bumper? Will they touch it with forensic circumspection before leading Etienne away by the arm, making him disappear forever, so that he and Axel will never see each other again?

He banishes these thoughts, hesitantly tells them the story of Axel again. He repeats what they have already heard, fills in the gaps, changes a few details. He describes the meeting in the substation. He tells of himself and Axel lying under the green-and-purple London sky, looking at Blake drawings. Tells how they observe a possessed blind dog chasing a fox. He elaborates on the exhibition in the attic studio, on the photographs of dead Victorian boys.

'But when was the exact moment? When did you fall in love with him?' Frederick's eyes are emitting silvery-blue light. His voice is shiny and cool.

Etienne thinks of how he and Axel would pounce on each

other like animals, carve each other up in a fog of sweat and spit. He wonders whether he loves Axel. And, if so, when it started. Are his visions of Axel symptoms of love? Or the sharp pain when he thinks of him? The underwater voice that emerges from his sinuses? Etienne's story, or his ability to tell it, can't compare to the others'. He isn't even gripped by it. He shrugs his shoulders in the dark. 'I don't know.'

Cool, familiar sparks are flickering among the four of them. Frederick pulls Etienne across his chunky upper legs, so that he is now half-sitting, half-lying on Frederick's lap. Frederick starts stripping off Etienne's clothes. Christof smiles a white smile in the dark, takes off Etienne's shoes and socks. The heater and the instruments rattle. It is as if the Kombi is on the verge of shaking apart. The cabin has now heated up. Etienne relaxes his muscles; sweat is running down his sides. Matthias glances back. He changes gear, starts whistling an unfamiliar tune. Frederick's and Christof's clothes also come off in the tangle of cushions and legs. Christof rolls Etienne onto his stomach, lets his palms glide across Etienne's back and buttocks. Frederick lowers his chest until it touches Etienne's shoulder blades. Etienne's cheek is pressed against the steel; the vibration rises from the East German tar into his skull.

Etienne surrenders: to the signs with their warnings, to the trees and the clearings next to the road where meetings between East and West Germans may be unfolding in the dark, to the mutated animals testing the tar with their hooves. The ropes that tie the instruments together are loosening, the muted noises of a ghost orchestra sounding. All these impressions merge with Christof and Frederick's bodies, with their insistent hands and their generous emissions. In this moment, at least, Etienne belongs to no one but them.

Later, Etienne thinks of the three friends' stories. They date from the same time. Their last high-school holiday, apparently the only time the three had ever been apart from each other since childhood. It would seem that each of them tried out the world on his own, but then returned to the others. And has never looked back since. They are, after all, *each other's* first – and only – loves.

And now he is being invited in, after months of courtship, via this elaborate ritual. He isn't just here to play the drums. He is the missing piece of the puzzle.

The border guard opens the side door, aims his torch into the Kombi. They are like bushbabies shrinking back from the light. The beam settles on the heater. The guard barks at them to get out, takes away the passports and *titre de voyage*. They stand sleepily on the road. Two other guards order them to open the back doors and unload the instruments. It takes them several minutes to untie the ropes. They sit sheepishly on the kerb while the guards search everything, ignoring the conventional instruments, focusing instead on the pipes, machine parts, fragments of car wrecks. Dissonant noises sound as they move items about. The guards are composing something, Etienne thinks: the first notes of a border requiem.

Etienne waits for them to come and arrest him. The other three cluster ever tighter around him.

The guard returns with their documents. 'Etienne Nieuwenhuis?' Frederick tries to hold Etienne back, but he steps forward. The guard smiles. It is the first time Etienne has ever seen an East German guard show emotion. He first hands back the three West German passports. Then he turns to Etienne and, with an exaggerated gesture, hands over his travel document.

They pass through the West German border post in minutes. For a while no one says a word. Matthias turns on the radio. A West German station. The song is '99 Luftballons' by Nena. Matthias immediately switches it off again. Frederick folds his arms around Etienne, looks through the window. Or what would have been the window, had it not been spray painted black. Matthias looks at them in the rear-view mirror above the windscreen. Christof puts his slim hand on Etienne's shoulder. It feels like the grip of an old man.

They arrive in Hannover after eleven at night. Christof is navigating using an outdated map. On his lap is also the page with Axel's address, which still shows Volker's paper-aeroplane folds. They get lost. Everyone is simultaneously trying to give Matthias directions, including Etienne. He sounds just like them now. Another bird on the branch. They stop in front of a dark warehouse. Etienne suddenly wonders whether he was given a false address. Have they come all this way just to be tricked by Volker? He looks up at the building. On the top floor, he can see dim light. *Achtung!* he hears the refrain inside him. *Achtung!*

He might have been expecting surprise or astonishment, even consternation. Shock, perhaps. Joy, anger or shame. But what he is completely unprepared for is Axel's utter indifference. His dead eyes.

It isn't that Axel doesn't recognise him. 'It is you,' Axel says when he opens the door. His voice is as flat in tone as his face is without expression. Sharp light from inside illuminates Axel's and Etienne's faces. Behind Etienne, his three friends are standing at the ready, like bodyguards. They found their way up here through the labyrinth of corridors with Etienne.

'I've been looking for you,' is all that Etienne says. He swallows. 'For so long.' Axel's hair, previously shaven close to the scalp, has grown to almost shoulder length. His face has become thinner. Here they are, standing in the light, the two of them. It is almost midnight, is Etienne's only thought. Behind Axel, two men appear from the gloom. An uncomfortable symmetry: Etienne and Axel standing opposite each other like delegates of the figures behind them. As if to settle some dispute, prevent an imminent war.

In these rooms that Axel and his two companions inhabit, no food is to be found.

Christof clears his throat, asks in an overly polite tone whether any shops might be open this time of night. Axel shrugs his shoulders. Matthias and Christof go out, return with bread and salami and beer. They sit on mattresses, eating in silence. Etienne notices Frederick surreptitiously observing Axel. Matthias and Christof keep an eye on the other two men. Nobody has been introduced, nobody says a word. Etienne can see in the two nameless men's eyes that they are on something. Every now and then they, as well as Axel, disappear into another room. What they are swallowing or sniffing, Etienne doesn't know, but he is sure that, but for that, they wouldn't be this docile. One of Axel's mates has a tattoo on each wrist: *IM KNAST*, it reads on one. *FREI FREI FREI* on the other.

Axel may be acting as if Etienne's arrival is of no consequence, but Etienne picks up contradictory signs: eyes turning away too quickly, fingers hovering for a moment, as if reaching towards Etienne. Axel turns his back on Etienne. The oak branches are only just visible through his grubby long-sleeved vest.

There aren't mattresses for everyone. Etienne will be sleeping up here with Axel and the other two; Matthias, Christof and Frederick will have to spend the night in the back of the Kombi. The three of them are uncomfortable leaving Etienne alone with Axel and the other two characters. Axel has in the meantime, at Frederick's insistence, introduced the latter; they are called Horst and Ulrich.

'Everything will be OK,' Etienne whispers to Frederick. 'I'll see you in the morning.'

Frederick purses his lips, lets his fringe hang over his eyes. He whispers loudly. 'Come on. Please. Leave this bunch. They're bad news. Let's just drive straight through to Bremen. Right now.'

'I'll come with you in the morning. They won't do me any harm.' He gestures towards Axel, Horst and Ulrich. What exactly, Etienne suddenly wonders, is it that they *won't* be doing to him?

For the first time Etienne and Axel are on their own. An iron floor lamp is standing next to the mattress, the kind used by factory workers for sorting or soldering. It casts a narrow band of light, hardly illuminating anything.

'Shave it off,' Axel says.

'What?'

'My hair. Shave it off. Like when we knew each other.'

Don't we know each other any more?

Axel kneels, his back facing the dark, only his head visible in the strip of light. He hands Etienne an electrical hair clipper, takes off his shirt. Blood hisses in Etienne's temples at the thought of Axel's tender white scalp.

His skin erupts in goosebumps when he switches on the clipper. Buzzing blades connect with skin, tufts of hair tumble into darkness. He dusts the hair from Axel's shoulders and back. Under his palm are strange new skin textures. Axel winces, as if Etienne is hurting him. Etienne continues shaving, but tries to turn Axel's back towards the light without his noticing.

Suddenly the light goes off. The clipper slips under Etienne's hand, stops. He can hear Ulrich or Horst swearing in another room.

'Jesusfuckingchrist,' Axel says. 'The power again. This thing's probably short-circuiting, this torture machine of yours.' *But you want me to torture you.* For a few seconds they don't move. Ulrich or Horst stumbles around audibly in another room. There is the click of a switch; the light flickers on. Simultaneously the clipper starts vibrating in Etienne's hand. Startled, he drops it. It rattles and spins on the floor.

Axel gets up, stomps his foot on it. A single trail of blood is running down his temple, and further down, into the dark. Etienne looks at Axel's nicked scalp from close up. There are shaven strips and spots in his hair. He looks like a cancer patient. Etienne quickly lets his hand slide over Axel's dark back. There are rough patches of skin, like misshapen fruit hanging in the oak branches. Are they scars?

Axel quickly pulls away, retreating to the deeper shadows. Just half of his face is visible.

Etienne swallows. 'What is that on your back?'

'I was in jail,' Axel says brusquely.

Etienne's throat is pulsating. 'I know,' he says. Axel frowns at him. 'But what happened to your back?'

'How do you know about me being in jail? And, while we're at it, how the fuck did you find me?'

Etienne swallows. 'Tell me about the scars.' Axel looks as if he is going to physically attack Etienne. His head is bonier than when they knew each other before, and the half-shaven skull makes him look feral.

Axel looks away. 'Shave off the rest. Finish what you started. You probably want to shock me to death, finish me off . . .' Etienne can hardly see him where he is standing in the dark. 'Or, no. Just leave it as is.' He moves a little closer to the light, tousles his patchy hair. It looks as if rats have gnawed at his head. 'I like it like this.'

For a while they stand in silence. Then Axel lies down on the dark mattress. Etienne lies down behind him, his lips touching the scars. Axel stiffens. Etienne can feel Axel's heart racing against his cheek. He pulls a blanket over them. The marks feel like burns, like skin that has melted and hardened. Axel is like a wound coil, barely tolerating the intimacy. Etienne keeps rubbing his face against the rough fruit, falls asleep in that position.

He dreams of border guards scorching him with lit torches. He wakes up sweaty. It is pitch dark. He takes Axel's pulse. 'Are you asleep?' Axel just sticks a sleepy thumb in Etienne's mouth. Etienne probes the scars on Axel's back with the tip of his tongue, one by one. Every groove and welt. Axel makes little noises under his breath.

They study each other's bodies as if each of them is en- countering a new species. Axel's hands become dumb again, slacken. He pulls the blanket up to his chin. He is asleep again, or perhaps he was never awake. Etienne hovers over Axel's face, tastes the lids. The eyeballs are jerking and jumping under the skin, as if he is having a fit. Who knows what Axel may be sniffing and swallowing with Horst and Ulrich all day long. Etienne sits upright, watching Axel, waiting. A glimmer of morning light is filtering through. Sweat is glistening on Axel's forehead.

Axel's eyes open. 'They branded me.' Etienne flinches, moves away a little. Axel looks up at the ceiling, continues. There were factions in prison, he says. Gangs of neo-Nazis. He became a kind of mascot, a trophy. Each faction wanted to demonstrate that they owned him. Each side branded him with glowing iron rods. Over and over again. 'Now I'm forever theirs.' Axel lowers his head onto Etienne's chest, then rolls away again after a few seconds. 'They always came at night. I had needles. I tattooed myself in the dark. Over and over. Trying to keep myself awake.' He reaches for the scars on his back. 'I reckoned, if I could colour my entire body, every centimetre, I just might become invisible.'

The morning sun catches Axel's lashes. His eyes close, his breathing deepens. Etienne doesn't sleep again. After a while Axel is awake again. He kicks off the blanket. Etienne's heart starts beating heavily. On Axel's arms and chest, there are words and lines and shapes. Criss-cross, over each other. Like angry schoolboy exercises on a piece of slate. And on his sides, on his legs. They look like charcoal marks rather than tattoo ink. Etienne touches them; Axel doesn't stop him. There is no texture; it is all below the skin. Here and there Etienne can make out words in the chaos: *Fieber, Junge, Sehnsucht*. Like the crooked writing of someone who is half-literate. There is also a target, a rough black rose and a spear with poison (or blood?) dripping from its tip.

Axel as living parchment. It looks as if his entire body is legible. But nothing makes sense. Words have been scratched out and rewritten, then deleted again. Etienne recently saw something similar – on Volker's chest. This is worse.

Etienne has questions for Axel. For instance: did he in fact brand *himself*, his story about the supposed neo-Nazis notwithstanding? This isn't the time for asking, though. They look at each other in silence, exchanging undecipherable codes in the current of their gazes. There are loose strands of hair on the pillow. And, on Axel's head, wild tufts alongside raw strips of white scalp.

Etienne wants to add something. Wants to write on Axel until the pen breaks through the skin, slips into a vein and infects his blood with all the alphabets of the world.

'Under no circumstances,' Frederick says when Etienne proposes that they take Axel with them to Bremen, to the gig. They are standing on the pavement outside the warehouse. There is a new stiffness between Etienne and his three friends. Since Etienne came down early that morning, after his night upstairs with Axel, they have hardly looked him in the eye. Christof's gaze remains fixed on the Kombi's wheels; there is a scabby rash on his arm. Matthias's eyebrows are twisted; he is looking down the street. Frederick surreptitiously tries to sniff Etienne's shoulders, as if he wants to smell Axel on him.

'Non-negotiable,' Etienne says. 'Otherwise I'm staying behind. We can't just leave him here with Ulrich and Horst. Who knows what will happen once their drugs run out? When the two somnambulists wake up? *They* are probably the ones who mutilated Axel.'

Etienne thinks of a moment from last night, when Axel started pulling at his skin, as if wanting to flay himself. As if his body were a book whose offensive pages should be torn out. Only after a while could he make out what Axel kept muttering like a mantra: 'Set me on fire. Let me burn . . .'

Frederick retreats. He avoids Etienne's eyes, and his touch.

Chapter 35

THE HOUR OR so to Bremen passes in silence. Matthias is driving again. The Kombi is too full. Axel is sleeping next to the mountain of shuddering instruments. Before their departure, Matthias and Christof tightened the ropes. As they drive, the ropes slacken again and the pile of iron and electronics comes to life. The Autobahn's tar is whispering below them. Here in West Germany, the black Kombi with its black windows feels out of place. The perfect highways and the orderly cities and towns are hardly the ideal habitat for Berliners. In Hannover they drove past the prison with its silver rolls of barbed wire, where Axel had spent a year. Even that looked new and neat: the high gates, the anonymous buildings, the concrete surfaces. All impeccable. From the outside, in any event.

Near Bremen they turn onto a secondary road, then onto a narrow single lane. Christof is giving directions. They stop at the edge of a field, slide open the Kombi's door. The day is unseasonably warm. Only now that Etienne can feel the heat on his skin does it erupt in goose pimples in memory of last night's chill. The mineral scent of tomatoes starting to ripen rises from the field.

'Shit,' Christof says. He puts on his sunglasses, looks out over the expanse of tomato plants. 'This is where we're supposed to be playing tomorrow evening. But look at all the fucking tomatoes!' He tugs at the scar in his neck, as if to dig out something from underneath it. He gestures: '*There* will be the stage. And *here*, right in front of us, the fans will be hanging out. What possessed the bloody owners? Why did they plant tomatoes for all of Germany? They know the place is booked for tomorrow. The photos showed only a bare piece of land. And a little snow.'

Behind them Axel stumbles out of the Kombi. He is wobbly; strings of hair hang in his eyes. He will have to finish shaving his head, Etienne thinks. Axel puts on dark glasses.

'Cool,' he says. He clambers onto the Kombi's roof, surveys the world with his legs planted wide apart. 'Tomatoes for Africa.'

'For Europe,' Christof mumbles. 'For Europe.'

Etienne imagines a crowd where the tomato plants now stand in such lush and silent profusion. At seven o'clock tomorrow morning, workmen will arrive to erect the stage, Christof explains, walking around and touching the leaves. At four the gig will start. Just after five will be the eclipse. Christof is aimless, anxious. He is addressing the tomatoes, rather than Etienne and the others.

At the entrance everyone is given cheap plastic sunglasses – protection against the sun's anticipated ring of fire. The tomatoes cause chaos. And joy. The early arrivers giggle when the hairy leaves rustle against their jeans. Plants are crushed underfoot, people start throwing tomatoes at each other, pips and juice splattering.

The opening band is called Namenlos. They play their first song; Stunde Null is waiting behind the stage. Mindless copycats, Etienne thinks. Echolalic music.

There is a single prop in the middle of the stage: a huge grey-green sound recorder. A mute piece of equipment from some government office or other, built – so it seems – to withstand a nuclear war. Christof – 'our technical boffin', as Frederick refers to him – tracked it down somewhere in Berlin and had it delivered.

They look at each other. Then the three gazes settle on Etienne. He isn't sure what he should read into them. A plea? A threat? How does it happen that the three of them always simultaneously make the same demands? And that – this he is only realising now – a collective chill can emanate from them as suddenly as collective warmth?

Namenlos ends their session, leaves the stage. Smoke is pumped out of machines, enfolds the instruments. The four of them jump light-footedly onto the stage, one by one. Screams rise from the crowd. While they saunter to their positions, the huge sound recorder's two reels start turning, magnetic tape tautened between them. Loud, declamatory male voices can be heard: speeches by East and West German politicians interrupting each other, talking over each other until it becomes sheer cacophony. No single voice can any longer be distinguished from the others. Etienne enters with an extended drum roll, foot on the drum hammer's pedal. Sparks fly when he rubs steel files over each other. Frederick emerges from the smoke behind the synthesiser: an ominous note is growing, a siren straight from hell.

They play. *Play*. As none of the echo-bands can. They recycle noise from the void. It merges with the sounds of cars on highways, tractor engines and power plants' furnaces. New noise ensues, killing old noise. And then it starts all over again. They have to let go of everything – extinguish everything

– that preceded the noise. There is no longer any history, nor any future. No bodies and no consciousness. Everything is sound.

The surging crowd grinds the tomatoes to a pulp. Stunde Null play 'God's Idiots'. They play 'The Language of Men and Machines'. There is a moment of silence; the eclipse begins. The four of them look at each other, then start playing 'Sonnenfinsternis'. The moon punches a hole right through the sun. Below them everybody is going into a frenzy. A black cloud shifts over the whole of Germany, making everyone deaf.

The evening air lays a lulling hand on Etienne's forehead. But it isn't evening; it is afternoon. They are playing to drain the sun of its warmth. At the height of the eclipse they keep an impossibly long and cold note. Vibration from the blood. Then they let go. They chase the moon off, bring back the light.

Etienne sees only one face in the twilight crowd: Axel's. Around him, people are rising and falling, as if under a vast sheet. Axel isn't wearing any glasses, is looking at Etienne with naked eyes. Etienne plays his drums for the tree resin dripping from Axel's back, for the childlike scribblings on his skin. For how small he looks underneath the German sky.

Around Axel, dozens of people have stripped their clothes off. Ready to follow the music's commands, to march straight into the flames.

It takes a while before Etienne realises he is the only one still hitting his drums. The other three are watching him in silence. Somewhere they have lost each other. They know he is now playing for Axel only.

The crowd has been wounded, Etienne thinks as he touches his painful erection. They are covered in blood and slimy scraps of flesh. Like a scene of mass surgery – an open-air operation room, patients who start wandering when the anaesthetic fails. But what is actually clinging to them, he realises, is tomato pulp.

His three friends' eyes have become cold. They no longer know him. Etienne looks out over the heads, finds Axel's face.

The lyrics of the last two lines of 'Sonnenfinsternis' linger on: 'Everybody knows this is Nowhere / Follow the fire and it will guide you home.'

III.
LABORATORY

(Elsewhere, April–October 1990)

Chapter 36

YESTERDAY MORNING, WHEN Etienne looked out from the descending plane to the washed-out horizons, smoke and blonde grass, he could already sense the dry autumn silence. In the northern hemisphere, South African landscapes had started resembling, in his mind, pictures from a children's Bible, or the mountain peaks and lakes in European paintings. Of such intimate light there proved to be no trace in the Highveld skies.

Now, in Natal, where they are travelling, the light is different. After an earlier thunder shower, steam is rising from the tar. The hills are glistening beneath a double rainbow. Etienne's mother joined him and Axel after they landed at Jan Smuts airport; in the afternoon the three of them took a flight to Durban. Today they have been driving from the coast to Pietermaritzburg, and from there southwards. Etienne is behind the wheel. They are approaching a village called Ixopo. Axel is alert in the passenger seat; little hairs on his upper cheeks catch the sun. In the rear-view mirror, Etienne can see his mother in the back: hunched up, motionless.

The letter with the news of her illness reached him in Berlin via Patrick in Bonnington Square. Weeks after it had been sent. He borrowed money from several friends and booked flights for himself and Axel to Johannesburg. His mother's neighbour, Frans Vermeulen, had apparently written the letter; his mother had dictated. Vermeulen also brought her to the airport to meet them. Etienne remembers the man from his childhood: a senior civil servant, now retired. Robust and ruddy, with heavy lids. Etienne was surprised by his meekness at the airport, as if Mandela's recent release from prison had robbed his body of its power. And Etienne could see how Vermeulen found him disorienting: the fact that he spoke Afrikaans, but was so obviously out of place – so lean and pale and stark. Vermeulen stared at Etienne's black clothes, perhaps smelling something on him: the air of Berlin's U-Bahn tunnels, or the stale silt of ancient river beds below the city. Vermeulen also gaped at the oak roots on Axel's neck, and the rough ink marks on his arms. Etienne, too, shrank back when he looked at Axel there in the southern light. As if for the first time. His body had suddenly acquired a new kind of power.

Etienne's mother's lips were chapped and pale. He could see right through her irises. Her hair had turned white. She was stiffening, changing into stone. Before each act, and each sentence, she momentarily lingered or froze. The control centre was now located somewhere outside of her. She was listening to a voice whispering messages in her ear.

She only had eyes for Etienne. She watched his every movement – putting down the suitcase, brushing a hand over his shaved head – with astonishment. While Frans was leading her to the departure hall for domestic flights, Etienne and Axel in tow with the luggage, she kept looking back. In the letter that Etienne had written her from Berlin, his first in about four years, he had told her he was bringing Axel along. Whether she received it, or could still comprehend it at the time, he doesn't know. There was no reaction when he introduced Axel to her. She regarded him as if he was a porter, turned back to Etienne.

She lifted her hand: 'Give me your cream cheese. Let me bury it.'

Etienne frowned, involuntarily turned to Vermeulen.

Vermeulen whispered behind his palm, too loudly: 'The illness makes her jumble words. She means: "Give me your luggage. Let me carry it."' Her outstretched arm kept reaching towards him. Etienne instantly resented Vermeulen in his role as interpreter.

Some distance beyond Umzimkulu, Etienne turns east, towards the distant coast. Axel's eyes are closed. His mother looks as if nothing could ever trouble her again.

At Jan Smuts airport, Etienne almost bumped into two policemen. He stopped in his tracks, his father's voice in his ears: *If I had known what you were planning, I would have handed you over to the military police myself.* The policemen weren't the moustachioed, heavy-buttocked men one might have expected. Boys, rather, young and unsure. The German Shepherd that one of them had on a lead completely overshadowed its owner. He could smell Etienne's adrenalin, jumped at him. The sinews in the young man's arm tensed when he yanked the animal back. Etienne looked the policeman – police *boy* – straight in the eye.

His mother is drifting in and out of sleep, Etienne notices in the mirror. Next to him, Axel's jaw has gone slack. He stops for fuel. He might as well have been travelling alone.

She wanted to see Etienne one last time, his mother (or rather Vermeulen) had written in the letter. And she wanted him to travel with her to Natal: a nostalgia trip. At the airport, Vermeulen tried explaining which places she had intended visiting. Earlier, before the brain cancer had started terrorising her sentences, she had apparently made him promise to ensure that the trip happened.

The three of them – Etienne, his mother and Axel – spent the day before in Durban. Planning, crouched over city maps in a stuffy hotel room. He tried to jolt his mother's memory, to make her recall street and place names. He mentioned schools in Pietermaritzburg, where she had spent her high-school days. She momentarily perked up when she heard her alma mater's name. He started listing neighbourhoods in the hope that they could scale down to the address where she had lived in her youth. She interrupted him, started verbalising her own kind of map. Keyless, with landmarks of smells and tastes: 'Down the hill you walk, until you smell jasmine dog and bananas. Left, then, to the river's bitter algae and mackerel . . .' Or: 'Right at the heavenly shrub, straight ahead until the sea air stings you and you can taste salty moss. Turn under the pepper hedge, where sweet chlorine tickles noses . . .' Routes that she once walked to school, or to sports fields or a bus stop? To a shop or park, or a friend's house? While she was stringing together unfathomable scents and flavours, she pointed out positions on the map. That was where they would be searching.

Their chronology is inverted: they keep travelling further into her past. This morning it was her Pietermaritzburg youth. The places where Etienne had made crosses on the map, and where in situ his mother perked up in apparent recollection: an austere face-brick home (had it replaced her childhood home?), an empty pavement (had there once been a school bus stop there?), a golf course (built over her old school hockey field?).

Whether the places themselves had changed, or whether the illness had eroded her sense of direction, nothing looked as it should have. Landmarks had disappeared. The smells his mother had described the day before didn't match the landscape. As if to compensate, smells from Etienne's own schooldays unexpectedly mingled in his nostrils: slow afternoons smelling of grass and sandwiches and teenage sweat.

This afternoon they are heading for the domain of her childhood. Or what might be left of it. Most of the land around here is covered by government plantations. Etienne struggled to find a place for them to spend the night. They are travelling in a tiny rented Japanese car, on a narrow track. Somewhere they have missed a turn-off. Etienne opens his window, makes a U-turn. The body scrapes against a tree trunk. Branches protrude through the window into the cabin; bits of bark sift onto the seats. The smell of pine displaces the smell of plastic. Etienne hangs his head out the window, searching in the mist. Water drops roll down his cheeks. Then, at last, he spots it: a vague sidetrack across a carpet of pine needles.

The car emerges from the fog; the plantations give way to indigenous forest. A dimly lit industrial building appears in a clearing and, next to it, a row of chalets. They stop, get out. There is a fungal smell in the air. Muscular roots appear and disappear from the soil like the humps of sea monsters. Etienne wipes pine needles from the bonnet.

A woman wearing Wellington boots emerges from the industrial structure. There is a little mongrel dog at her heels.

'A mushroom factory,' she answers Etienne's question. 'We only harvest and package what we pick in the forest.' They are the only guests. She takes them to one of the chalets. Even inside one can smell the mushrooms.

The woman keeps standing uncomfortably in the door. 'Is

there somewhere we could buy food?' Etienne asks. 'We were hoping for a restaurant or shop . . . ?'

She shakes her head. 'Wait, I'll make a plan.' She disappears, comes back with a basket. She lifts the corner of a cloth, shows them the mushrooms, each as big as a man's hand. 'There is cooking oil in the cupboard.'

She disappears behind the factory, the little dog like a shadow behind her. Etienne rinses the forest soil from the fresh mushrooms under the kitchen tap.

'Here are little helpers,' his mother says, holding out the matches. 'To light the cassanova.' She points at the gas stove. Etienne lights the stove, cuts the mushrooms in slices, fries them in a pan. She sits down at the kitchen table. Axel lays the table, sits down opposite her. The two of them look at each other in silence.

Etienne serves the fleshy slices with glasses of water. His mother looks uncomprehendingly at her knife and fork. Axel leans over, cuts her slices into smaller pieces.

'A little reindeer,' she demands. Etienne thinks of animals in the forest. She is impatient now: 'To eat the anemones!' Etienne thinks of the sea; his frown deepens. Axel gets up, fetches a teaspoon from the drawer. She takes it, smiles at Axel, then scowls at Etienne.

They test the rubbery mushroom flesh on their tongues. The flavour is delicate, intoxicating. They have second helpings. Then more. It is like inhaling compost fumes. Their shoulders become drowsy, as if someone has draped blankets around them. To fend off a trance, Etienne gets up and boils water.

All he can find in the cupboards is tea. Even that tastes of mushrooms. Like a forest that has been dried, ground up and soaked.

Axel builds a fire in the hearth. The wet wood steams and crackles. Etienne feels his mother's icy hands. He leaves her behind in the glow to go and prepare her room. He switches on a little heater and the reading light, folds back a corner of the sheet. A movement outside catches his eye. He shudders, pulls the curtain to close it. It falls noiselessly off the pelmet. For a few moments he stands helplessly with the curtain in his hands, listening to Axel unzipping a suitcase next door. He puts the curtain down on the floor, inserts a hand between his mother's sheets, sweeps back and forth for insects.

Earlier, at the airport, and also in the car, Etienne noticed that his mother was keeping a tissue tightly scrunched up in her hand. It is now lying on the bedside table. When he touches it, he realises it is firmer than tissue. He unfolds it. The creases have almost wiped out the image, but Etienne recognises it at once. The photo he had once sent his mother from London: a dead Victorian boy with his head on *his* mother's lap.

He hears his mother mumble in the living room. He goes to her, the photo still in his hand. She is standing in front of the fire; she is holding a glowing log in her bare hands. The flames are licking towards her eyes, as if her gaze is serving as fuel.

'No!' Etienne takes two long strides to her, knocks the log onto the rug, which he then rolls around it. The photo has fallen on the floor. He picks it up, throws it into the fire.

She turns to him. 'You have broken me.'

He grabs her by the wrist, pulls her behind him to the kitchen, holds her hands under cold water. He opens the fridge's freezer compartment. Her face contorts. Blisters are already forming on her palms and fingers. Etienne presses her hands against ice. He can see the wounds are serious. Axel comes running into the kitchen. 'What's happened?'

Etienne just shakes his head. 'Hold her hands against the cold.' He leaves them in the glow of the open fridge, runs outside. The factory doors are closed. The mineral smell is overwhelming, as if there are crates of mushrooms in his head. He has no idea how to find their hostess. He can't even recall her name. Rebecca? Andrea? Did she ever introduce herself? He stands next to the factory and calls: 'Rebecca!' His voice is deflected by the corrugated-iron walls, dulled by the trees. The name is absorbed by the foliage. He calls again. In the dim light from the factory he notices a footpath, starts walking along it. It leads around the back of the building.

The little mongrel dog approaches, and behind him their hostess. She is wearing tracksuit pants and a dressing gown, flashlight in her hand. She is rubbing her sleepy eyes. 'What are you shouting for? Rebecca is the dog's name. I'm Andrea.'

'Help. Please.'

Andrea has brought antiseptic ointment, which she is applying like a layer of fat. Etienne's mother is pulling away; Axel has to hold her down like an animal on a veterinarian's examination table. She looks at him accusingly; he is gently whispering to her in his heavy accent. Etienne is standing to the side, can't hear what he is saying. Andrea has taken a sheet off Etienne and Axel's bed and torn it into shreds, which Axel is winding tightly around each injured hand. The little mongrel dog keeps interposing itself, as if he wants to gnaw on the raw palms. Only when the dog starts licking Etienne's own fingers does he realise he too got burnt when he slapped the log out of his mother's hands. He puts his hand in his pocket. Andrea takes Etienne aside. 'You have to go to a hospital in Pietermaritz-burg,' she says. 'The wounds are deep; the next step is infection.

I've seen it. Our factory workers sometimes burn their hands in the mushroom drying ovens.'

When Andrea has left, they sit on the sofa in front of the fire, Etienne's mother in the middle. She looks at Etienne, then at Axel. She leans her head against Axel's shoulder. 'Do you know how much I missed you?' she says to Axel, puts her wounded hands in his lap. 'All those years you spent out there in Siberia, in the tundras. I placed you in Jesus's hands, left it all to him. Thought He would wrap you in His arms. What else could a mother do? He left you behind in the snow, walked away from you. And from me. Yes, Jesus's fields of ice have robbed me. There is nothing left. Even the smallest little feet have been scorched by the cold . . .' She holds up her hands, looks at them in amazement. 'Here was an accident,' she says croakily. 'Shattered candles!'

Etienne's heart is thumping. Her outburst takes his own words away. It is the most she has said since his arrival in South Africa. Axel lowers his head, rests his cheek against hers.

Etienne gets up, walks past the log's scorch mark on the rug, goes outside. He hears a generator thudding somewhere. His mother's new sentences sound different. The encounter with the flames has clarified her language on the surface, but has scorched away meaning. Does she have more control over her words than she is pretending to? Is she taunting him, testing him?

Etienne tries to close his and Axel's curtains; but they are stuck. When they lie down, Axel turns away. He coils up in the fetal position, knees almost touching his chest. Is he blaming Etienne for his mother's twisted formulations, for the blisters on her hands? Etienne loosely folds a hand over

Axel's buttocks. Dim light from the factory falls in through the window, across the sheetless bed.

He thinks of his mother's words: 'braken me'. He tries to match it with other words, searches for companion words – ones that remotely rhyme with or mirror it. Counterparts. Broken me? Hated me? Taken (something from) me?

Forsaken. That is the word at which he halts while the shadows of bats outside the window flit across their bed and arms. They resemble light more than shadows, these darting shapes. He can feel them glimmering on his skin.

He tiptoes out into the corridor, listens at his mother's open door. In between slow breaths she makes little noises, like an injured puppy. Here too patterns are darting across the walls and bed. Bats are crackling under the overhangs outside. They are bringing tidings, which are spreading like a virus.

Chapter 37

'LEAVE ME ALONE,' she says. 'Let me knot my hemlock.'
She is sitting at the kitchen table with a cup of tea.
Andrea has brought rusks for breakfast. Slowly, Etienne thinks,
he is starting to learn the codes of her short circuits. She means
to say, 'Let me dip my rusk.'

'Please, Mother. You need a doctor *today*. We can come back
tomorrow. I promise.'

She purses her lips, vehemently shakes her head. 'We have
to go and find the fort. It is the last gates.' She means the home
of her childhood. And that it is her last chance.

This is why they have travelled to this outpost, to search for
the little settlement where she spent her primary-school days.
During *his* childhood days, Etienne had to listen endlessly
to stories about this idyllic place. Inkungu. The name had
a mythical aura. She would respectfully whisper each Zulu
syllable. Her descriptions were lush: a cottage of corrugated
iron, surrounded by indigenous forest; Italian prisoners of war
working as loggers and walking past the house in the afternoons, singing Verdi arias; deer grazing in the garden, rabbits
hopping among the ferns . . .

She wants to find the remnants of that four-roomed cottage.
And the road on which the singing Italians used to march home.
These were the wishes that were channelled by her mouthpiece
Frans Vermeulen. How accurately the man managed to convey
her needs is unclear. He hadn't had the presence of mind to

ask her the right questions before it was too late. On Etienne's detailed regional map there is no 'Inkungu' to be found – whether a village, station, farm, river, road or mountain. Now he has to navigate the slippery spaces emerging in between his mother's memories, Vermeulen's interpretation of them and a landscape that has changed over decades.

They depart after breakfast. Andrea introduces Etienne to a government forest ranger, who has agreed to be their guide. There is a sector of the plantation called the Inkungu Forest, he says. If anything remains of the settlement, it must be there.

As they drive through the neat, hushed pine forest in a dou-ble-cab pickup, Etienne looks furtively at Axel. The year in Hannover had stripped him of his fervour, left him half-dazed. Over the last few months he has been expanding around the waist. There is now a fleshiness beneath his chin. The air here is doing something to him, though, slowly restoring his power.

Etienne and Axel lead a quiet life in Berlin. They live in a spacious albeit musty flat in Charlottenburg, for which they pay a nominal rent. Etienne has had asylum status in Germany for the past two years. Sometimes he stands in as a drummer for bands, which earns him some money. Axel gets an un-employment grant. He no longer makes art. There is little left between them other than shared recollections: of cities, of themselves in those cities. Something melancholy lingers when they kiss coolly before Etienne switches off the light at night. Berlin's night breath is tepid against their skins.

Etienne and the three West Berliners' paths diverged after the eclipse concert near Bremen. Etienne and Axel took a train back to Berlin. The other three travelled northeast in the Kombi, in the direction of the Baltic Sea. More gigs were lined up in Lübeck and Kiel. How – and whether – they managed without their drummer, Etienne never found out. The morning before the Bremen concert, Etienne had painted *Stunde Null* on the side of each drum. In red letters. When they drove away, he left his drums in the Kombi, let them go. Like a little family of refugees, those drums had made it from Pretoria to London to Berlin to Hannover and Bremen, and ultimately to the grim northern seas.

Once or twice thereafter, Etienne saw Frederick at a distance – in Oranienstrasse at dusk, or late at night in a bar. Each would half-heartedly lift a hand in greeting, twitch a corner of the mouth, quickly look away again. And once he saw Matthias and Christof. At a distance, in a crowd of people at an industrial gig. They didn't acknowledge his presence. Nor did Etienne make eye contact with them – Axel was with him. He knew Matthias and Christof wouldn't have thought much of the band. In his mind, he could hear their stern analyses, constantly interrupting each other: *Copycats. Johnny-come-latelies. Amateurs. Nothing's been the same since the Wendung. The industrial scene is fucked.* Etienne took his hand off Axel's neck, put it on his own heart. For a moment he wished he were there, between Matthias and Christof, feeling the heat of their shoulders. And that Frederick could bathe him again, put him to bed like a child. Or fiddle with his hands in Etienne's lap. That the four of them could write just one more song together in a freezing courtyard or on a snow-covered roof. Or could speed through the East German night in a black Kombi again, while they seduced him with far-fetched stories.

The disappearance of Etienne's three friends from his life has changed the city irrevocably. Their world – the Oranienstrasse factory with its echoes, the objects they would pick up in rail yards and recycle as instruments, the music writing sessions, the afternoon glow of their flat on Chamissoplatz, the late-night cafés they used to frequent – constituted West Berlin for Etienne. Now that he has lost them, each building looks different. Every street, every courtyard and every station.

On top of that, the tearing down of the Wall has robbed him of *his* Berlins, his two half-cities. Matthias and Christof would be justified in their grievances: the music scene isn't what it used to be. Everyone suddenly thinks they can grab a machine or saw or drill and make noise. Everyone thinks they can croak amid a shower of sparks and call it industrial music. And Etienne is no longer in the select company of the rats and cockroaches that used to slip back and forth freely through ghost stations' cracks as if through cloacae. Everything and everyone flows freely now; a secret border-crosser he is no more.

A year or so ago Etienne heard from mutual acquaintances that, although Matthias and Christof were still together, Frederick had withdrawn himself from them after the concert tour. As soon as they arrived back in Berlin, they dissolved Stunde Null. What had looked like the beginning of great things, there in the trampled field of tomatoes, turned out to be the moment when everything had started to fall apart.

'Huge swathes of indigenous forest were wiped out here in the 1960s and '70s,' the ranger explains, while taking them deeper and deeper into the plantations. They stop sporadically to unlock gates. He knows of places where there are anomalies in the geometric plantation patterns – rocky ledges, or the remnants of structures. 'I don't know *every* tree and clearing,' he says. 'These are large areas. But let's see what we can find.'

At their first stop, the rows of trees are interrupted by concrete foundations. Upon closer inspection the ranger shakes his head. 'Agricultural remnants. Old drinking troughs, perhaps. Or silos for feed.'

Etienne's mother pays him no heed, looks around. 'All the roads are seeming elsewhere. Everything is circling beyond the equator.' Her sentences sometimes start as comprehensible formulations, but then become derailed. Sometimes the constructions are clear on the surface but lack meaning. Sometimes one can extract meaning from the shuffled words, but, as soon as you start taking it as a private language with rules, rather than gibberish, you realise your mistake.

Dark clouds are amassing. Axel takes out a video camera, aims it skywards. Etienne had initially planned to film the trip, a record for his mother. At the last moment he decided to leave the camera in Berlin. He was surprised yesterday when he realised *Axel* had packed it. The ranger looks up too. Axel switches off the camera. They drive further.

The forest roads are indistinguishable. So too the rows of trees, plantations and sectors. Etienne has long since lost his sense of direction. They stop again. Another disruption in the plantation's patterns. The ruins they encounter were once stone enclosures for animals. 'Spaceship's nemesis,' Etienne's mother says and shakes her head.

At their third stop, she sniffs the air like a deer. As if the ground has suddenly caved away underneath her feet, she falls over. Soundlessly, on a thick carpet of needles. For a moment Etienne expects her to disappear under its surface, as if in quicksand. The illness's terror: first the words, then the balance. Axel is there first, helping her up. The ranger takes her other elbow. Her tears are flowing freely. Is she unsettled by the fall,

323

or has she recognised something? But how? There is no trace in this dead forest of the cool, secret cocoon of leaves that she had once described, of mossy children's swings, squirrels on a tin roof, birds flapping against filtered rays. Etienne holds out his palms. It has started drizzling. His mother stumbles back toward the vehicle, as if wounded. Axel helps her get in.

Etienne picks up the camera. He walks away, through the trunks, towards another clearing. He clears away some pine needles with his foot. And there it is: rusty steel emerging from concrete foundations. He squats, wipes away more needles. Four rooms are drawn in front of him, as if on paper. That's where he comes from too, this chunk of concrete. This invisible house. He lets the lens glide slowly across the concrete.

The heavens open. Rain pours down onto his shoulders. He switches off the camera, runs back to the vehicle.

They stop at a ford. When they crossed it earlier, there was a trickle of water. Now raging torrents are flowing by. Etienne's mother is mumbling something. He leans over to hear her above the rushing water. 'The lush thickets of blood,' is what she has to say.

The pickup gets stuck in the mud. The current tugs at the vehicle. 'We're too heavy,' the ranger says. 'You'll have to get out.' They stand there and get soaked while he is reversing with spinning wheels.

The storm keeps raging. The ranger is drinking beers with men in white coats. The only woman among the white coats is left to deal with Etienne, his mother and Axel. 'We rarely get rain this time of year,' she says. She is their guide, is taking them on a tour through the facility. Halfway through, Etienne's mother sinks into a chair in the staff tea room and almost immediately falls asleep. They leave her behind; the tour continues. The woman shows them two laboratories. In the first one there are dozens of plants in pots. Spatters of green against an expanse of white. There are test tubes and microscopes on long tables, pine needles and spores in Petri dishes. And shards of bark, trunk and root. Projects involving genetic modification and cloning, the woman in the white coat explains. Then she takes them to the plant pathology laboratory: microscopes, glass plates with fungi, stunted twigs, pale pine needles and speckled bark. In bottles on shelves, preserved beetles, worms and larvae are floating in fluid.

After they had been forced to turn back at the ford, the ranger brought them here for shelter: the government forestry research laboratory. Etienne wonders what his mother would make of these words. She hasn't said anything since their last stop in the plantations.

Outside it is still raining. The ranger reappears, interrupting their tour. They won't be able to drive back tonight, he explains. He will spend the night in the pickup. 'And she will help you out with a place to sleep.' He points to the researcher.

When the tour is over, Etienne goes to the staffroom to wake his mother gently. She looks up at the ceiling. 'Hostile seas,' she says. 'Fireflies are peeping holes in the night's crimp.'

The researcher leads them to a room with stacked beds and cheap grey blankets – probably accommodation for cleaners. Even in here one can smell the pine needles. The linoleum floors are polished to a high gloss. Their guide keeps lingering uncomfortably: 'Let me know if you need anything.' She is awkward in her role as hostess of sorts, clearly not used to considering others' needs. She leaves them on their own. Etienne feels disoriented. They sit in silence in the sharp light.

His mother holds out her hands. 'Broken knives and winter's harp.' Etienne gives up on the deciphering. The gap between what she is saying and what she wants to say is apparently widening. And yet, here and there he unexpectedly does understand something, or so he reckons. 'Cluttering clusters of hurt,' she now says. Pulsating with pain? Her hands are becoming infected, of that Etienne is certain: they are red and swollen around the wrists; the strips of improvised bandage are stained yellow. The plan was to wrap her hands with fresh strips when they returned to the mushroom factory, and then, tomorrow, to find a hospital in Pietermaritzburg. Now they are stranded on a laboratory island. And the rain isn't stopping. Etienne realises how hungry he is. He should have asked the researcher about food. Except for the mushrooms last night and a few rusks this morning, they haven't eaten in two days. His mother has fallen asleep in her clothes on one of the narrow beds. Etienne leaves Axel with her, wanders the corridors, randomly looking for something to eat. There isn't a soul around. The ranger is probably asleep in his truck. Where the researcher and her colleagues have gone is anyone's guess. The rain isn't sounding as loud against the panes. Etienne tries to look out through the staffroom's windows. All he can see is his own reflection.

Axel joins him. 'I am *so* hungry,' he says. He rummages around in a cupboard, finds some Marie biscuits. They sit down on plastic chairs, nibble in silence.

Biscuit and spittle mix cloyingly on Etienne's tongue. He looks at crumbs sifting onto the thin carpet around Axel's chair, shakes out a few pine needles from his trousers' turnups. Suddenly he smells mushrooms again. *Tastes* them. It is a guilty, uncomfortable flavour, like the meat of a human or favourite pet. Despite this, for the first time since that afternoon among the pulped tomatoes near Bremen two years ago, Etienne feels something loosening up in his chest.

Axel lies back in his chair. Etienne thinks of their silences in Berlin over the last couple of years. They had wanted to make a new beginning in West Berlin, in their Charlottenburg flat. They never talked about London, about the period during which they had been separated from each other. Or about the jail in Hannover, or the reason Axel had been there. Still not about Etienne's youth in South Africa. No word would ever be spoken about Axel's father or mother, about Ariel or the Benjamin film. Hardly anything about Irmgard. Never a word about Etienne's three friends who had driven away in their Kombi and left Etienne and Axel behind in a devastated tomato field.

Etienne often did think back to the accusation in Frederick's eyes when he climbed into the Kombi without saying goodbye. Of Matthias's unrelenting seriousness when he loaded the instruments. Of Christof's stiff neck, which he was scratching as if wanting to rip out his oesophagus. He sometimes thought of the months with Frau Drechsler and Nils, of the film school and the archive. He would sometimes dream of the ruin of a hospital on an island. He never visited Potsdam again, never looked up his old street in Prenzlauer Berg. Or his handlers, guides and subverters in the guise of Fraue Drechsler, Fuchs and Keller. He never set foot in the planetarium again.

He saw Nils once at a distance, a few months after the border posts had been flung open. It was on the Ku'damm, near the Gedächtniskirche. A bright, sunny morning. Nils was on the other side of the wide street. Etienne came to a halt, waited for Nils to catch his eye. He wanted to cross the road, but at that moment the traffic was too heavy. He wanted to ask Nils about his Japanese studies, about how it felt to be in the West. Etienne lifted his hand in a gesture of greeting. He wanted to tell Nils that his betrayal had been a trivial act, committed under the crushing weight of history, that he had forgiven him everything. He wanted to offer to help him. How raddled Nils looked. He was wearing East German shoes; that Etienne could see from afar. Nils pulled his head into his shoulders, kept his eyes on the pavement. Etienne let him go, spared him an encounter.

Etienne looks at Axel. In this stagnant air things that seemed impossible in the northern hemisphere suddenly feel possible. He sits forward. He is ready to start talking. He opens his mouth.

It catches him unawares when Axel beats him to it, and that, once he has started, he cannot stop.

Chapter 38

'How do you reckon you found Benjamin?'

Etienne frowns. He has to pry away his attention from the words whirling in his own chest. He listens to the pine needles blowing against the mirroring windows like sand, smells the chemicals from the laboratories.

'Benjamin?'

'The two film reels, I mean. *Berliner Chronik.*'

Pure luck? My dedicated – no, fanatical – *search?* is what Etienne wants to venture, but Axel's tone suggests *he* knows better. Etienne waits.

'Have you ever wondered about the clues appearing out of the blue? How unlikely it was that someone would come across your notes on forgotten noticeboards, or your obscure newspaper ads?'

A needle in all the world's haystacks, Etienne thinks.

'It was *me*, Etienne. I let you have that first clue in London, led you to the dying Ariel.'

Etienne scratches the chair's plastic armrest. 'Ariel? Surely you mean Bernhard Sauer.'

Axel shakes his head. 'It was Ariel himself who died there, in that building in Rotherhithe where you nicked the first reel.' He looks at Etienne in silence for a moment. 'Ariel was my grandfather.'

Etienne looks past Axel, to the window in which they are being reflected like two strangers. The wind is getting stronger.

He thinks of the tall tree that once burst through the window of an abandoned hospital. He hasn't ever told Axel that he worked out from the invisible text in Irmgard's diary that Ariel is his grandfather. It isn't that part of the disclosure that strikes Etienne. 'You are mistaken, Axel. The sick man's name was Sauer.'

Axel's smile veers between patience and condescension. 'Bernhard Sauer, indeed. Ariel lived under that name in England for decades. The alias under which he had fled from Germany. He never wanted his own name back.'

Etienne feels bewildered. Before long, he too will start talking gibberish, just like his mother. He wonders whether she is still asleep under her grey blanket. Are her dreams being derailed, just like her sentences? He should go and see whether she is all right – whether she is breathing, whether the self-consuming brain is making her shudder with epileptic shocks. But the mystery surrounding Bernhard Sauer keeps him in his chair.

Axel's voice is clear. 'I had visited him myself. A day before I sent you there. I had heard he was slipping away, had wanted to say goodbye.'

Outside the pine trees are blowing wildly. The corrugated-iron roof sounds like a crowd of people gnashing their teeth. For a while both of them just listen, looking at the window bulging in and out with the gusts of wind. Axel continues. 'There on his deathbed he mentioned the film reel for the first time, explained to me where—'

'So, you knew each other?'

Axel nods. 'For years, yes. But I never let on that I was his grandchild. That I had Irmgard's diary, or knew about the film. I had to get away from all that was familiar, I thought, had to start a life on my own, as someone without ties, without an origin. And, yes, I guess I was fooling myself. I subtly tried to sound him out over the years, but he never let slip a word about either Germany or Irmgard. I think he had wiped out his memory with sheer willpower. Other than the film reel, he hadn't brought anything with him from Germany. And never tried to make a film again.'

Etienne closes his eyes, imagines film melting into the cogs of a projector.

'Anyway, Ariel sent me to a closet. Inside it was a suitcase, inside that the reel. I decided to leave it there for you, locked in the sideboard. I tied a ribbon to the lock, took the key. Then I sent you.' Axel looks at the staffroom's blind windows again, at his and Etienne's doppelgängers sitting over there. 'I'm sorry about the group of mourners you encountered there, Ariel's fellow activists. I had had no idea they'd be there. I had just wanted you to meet *him*. My grandfather. Before he died. And for you to get your hands on the reel . . .'

Etienne feels half-perturbed, half-cheated. Moved too. Questions pile up in his mind. Too fast, too many. 'The second reel?' he blurts out. '*That* I found with great effort, after all. The whole bloody process with your father, with Volker . . .'

Axel stiffens. There is lightning in his eyes; his jaw muscles clench. Etienne likes it – it reminds him of the old Axel. But he knows how Axel can fall obstinately silent. And Volker's name now hangs between them.

Axel slackens again. 'Do you really think Irmgard's fifty-year-old diary, and a pretty aimless search in Berlin, mysteriously led you to the second reel?'

'Wait,' he says. 'I need to go and check up on my mother. Stay here. Hold that thought.'

Etienne walks swiftly down the corridor. Befuddled, he initially walks in the wrong direction. He turns around, finds the little room where his mother is mumbling in her sleep. In what way does her self-destructing brain affect her dreams? he wonders. Does it translate her confused sentences into poetry?

When he gets back to the staffroom, Axel has gone. The moment has passed; the floodgates will likely close again now. Etienne walks the corridors, calls out Axel's name in a loud whisper. He opens doors as he walks: offices, storerooms. Further down the corridor he can now see faint light. He walks briskly towards it. One of the laboratories' doors is open: Axel is there, inside, his back turned to the door, brightly lit. Etienne goes up to him, rests his chin on his shoulder, folds his arms around his abdomen. Axel is handling a fresh pine twig in a stainless steel bowl.

As if Axel has asked, he says: 'Everything's fine. She's sleeping. But I don't think much will remain of her in the days to come.'

It has stopped raining. The wind keeps blowing. 'The first thing that occurs to me when I think of *my* mother,' Axel says after a while, 'all that remains of *her*, is her coat sleeve brushing my cheek in the December Berlin air.' A vein in Axel's neck is throbbing against Etienne's shaved temple. His voice is vibrating in Etienne's skull.

'Tell me about your grandmother. About Irmgard.'

Axel smells the pine twig. It enters Etienne's nostrils too, the smell of camphor and mint, of dawn. 'I only know what my mother told me about her. And that too she had mostly heard from others.'

'I want to know everything.'

Axel sighs, starts telling. At some point in 1933, while they were rushing to finish the film, Irmgard had to decide whether she was going to flee Germany with Ariel. Her communist sentiments, and her collusion with Jews, weren't widely known; her exposure was limited. 'She was pregnant with my mother. Overnight she cut herself off from Ariel, as if they had never known each other. He fled, broken-hearted, left the country. She stayed. After that, she covered up her erstwhile collaboration with Schnur and other Jews and communists as well as she—'

'Was that why she, as a blind woman, had been given such an unlikely role on a film set? Because of her loyalties?'

'I guess so. Communists would surely have helped each other. Or perhaps Ariel had had his eye on her from the outset . . . Anyhow, after the war she very quickly made it clear that she had seen the National-Socialist light.' She became a Party member, Axel says, did everything that was expected of a woman who was loyal to the Volk. When things got tough during the war, and she had to keep herself and her baby fed and sheltered, she started helping to make propaganda films. For a while she worked as a production assistant on Leni Riefenstahl projects. Shortly after the war, when Riefenstahl was arrested, Irmgard disappeared. Her daughter Mariel, then nine years old, was left behind. Before her departure, Irmgard had arranged for Mariel to be adopted by a colleague of hers – one of Riefenstahl's cinematographers.

Etienne's eyes are burning (are the laboratory lights slowly becoming brighter?). It is the first time he has heard Axel's mother's name. Etienne rolls it around soundlessly on his tongue: *Mariel*. He carefully considers his next question. Each answer may be the last. 'Why was it necessary for

Irmgard to flee after the war? To just leave her child – your mother – behind?'

Axel shrugs his shoulders; his voice becomes quieter. About Irmgard's motivations, he can only speculate. Perhaps she was afraid she would be arrested herself due to her collaboration with the Nazis. But then why have Mariel adopted by another Riefenstahl collaborator? Perhaps she felt ashamed and guilty towards Ariel and her one-time Jewish friends. Although most of them must have died, or been dispersed to the four corners of the earth. Perhaps she felt her daughter would be better off in Germany, and without her. A refugee's life with a mother who had profoundly betrayed her father must hardly have looked ideal.

Etienne is standing next to Axel now. They are looking at specimens in Petri dishes, touching fragments of bark and root like hesitant scientists. How long – and how many detours – has it taken to arrive at this conversation? How far have they had to travel – to the distant south, and deep into the hinterland – before Axel found it possible to talk? Something is changing irrevocably between them here amid the flasks and clamps and microscopes. Etienne takes the pine twig, from which Axel has since stripped most of the needles. He fills a test tube with water, puts the twig in it.

He takes Axel by the hand, leads him out. They wander blindly back and forth in the dark corridor, repeatedly passing the locked plant pathology laboratory with its bottled insects: the borers, the egg-layers, the gnawers. Axel's disclosures are now flowing in an unbroken current. The reason for his sudden trip to Berlin, four years ago, was that his mother, Mariel, had just taken her own life. *That* was the news he had received by telegram that December evening in London. Two weeks earlier his mother had boarded a train and travelled north, to Kiel, where she had swum into the Baltic Sea and disappeared. Etienne pictures a head moving away, becoming ever smaller between chunks of floating ice. 'Nobody even reported her as missing. Least of all Volker.' Axel almost spits when he utters the name. 'It was the police who sent me that telegram. Only after she had washed up on the shore. They had had to search birth registers, had to force Volker to give them my address.'

Etienne shuts his eyes, sees a grey body washed up on a grey beach.

'When I arrived in Berlin, she had already been buried. A pauper's burial, at the state's expense. Volker wouldn't even pay for *that*.

'It was *he*,' Axel says. His jaws clench. 'Volker had killed her. Bit by bit. Over the years. Her life with him was a nightmare. Endless and unbearable.'

'What would he do to her?' Etienne asks cautiously. They are slowly walking down a pitch-dark corridor.

'What *didn't* he do . . .' Axel hesitates; it looks for a moment as if those are his last words for the night. 'Once,' he then continues, 'when I was small, he started going around the flat with a broom, smashing each of the smoke alarms on the ceiling. Then he tore the phone from the wall, crushed it under his foot. He locked me and my mother in the flat, soaked a rag in petrol, set it alight and threw it in through a window . . .' Axel is picking up the pace in the darkness; Etienne has to lengthen his stride to keep up. 'She did ultimately manage to extinguish it . . .' Etienne listens to Axel's footsteps. 'At other times he would throw her against the wall. Or push her face against the stove and turn up the gas until she started choking.' Then he slowly tells Etienne about his bleak childhood years.

How Volker had taken him to skinhead rallies as a boy, the vengefulness and violence when, in his teenage years, Axel started refusing to go. He absconded from home as soon as he could. At seventeen. First squatted in Berlin, then left for London when he was twenty. He left his mother in that man's hands. For *that* he can never forgive himself.

When, shortly before Christmas 1986, he arrived in Berlin from London and saw Volker for the first time after his mother's death, his first instinct was to kill him. It was too late to save his mother from his terror, but revenge was still to be had.

Axel stops, leans his back against a wall in the dark. Etienne gropes blindly towards him. 'I hadn't planned it that way, but, when I arrived at Volker's in Neukölln, I grabbed a kitchen knife and stormed at him. He was too fast for me, and too strong. He pushed me onto the floor, broke my arm. I hadn't inflicted so much as a scratch. The police were called; I was arrested and charged. The rest . . . well, that you know.'

Etienne's blood is pumping through him in cold currents. When he tries to wrap his arms around Axel, he hits a bare wall. Axel has slipped away in the dark. Etienne finds him near the laboratory. For a long time, they walk around in silence. When they pass the sleeping quarters, Etienne listens out for his mother's breathing.

Axel arbitrarily tries doors; one of them opens. Damp heat hits Etienne in the face. Axel closes the door behind them. Moonlight falls onto their faces through a glass roof. Etienne can make out the shapes of rows of saplings, like a miniature version of the plantations they drove through earlier. Needles glimmer like silver fur. It is a glasshouse, a nursery. A warm mist is pumped in from somewhere. Sweat starts trickling down Etienne's spine.

Axel's voice, when he continues, is softened by the humidity. His mother introduced him to *Berliner Chronik* early on. They didn't have a projector, but sometimes, when she came to tuck him in on winter evenings, he would ask to see 'pictures of the boy from the olden days'. Mariel would go and fetch the reel. Axel would insist that she tell the story of how Irmgard – *her* mother – used to show her the pictures in *her* bed. Then, as so often before, she had to explain how Irmgard had disappeared one day, how she had just left the reel on Mariel's pillow. Axel would then, as always, embrace his mother, pressing the air from her lungs, beg her not to go away too. She would assure him, over and over again. To calm him, Mariel would open the reel's case, just a little, so that he could sniff the vinegary smell. Then she would pull out a strip of film. 'Slowly, with a sly smile. She would tell me: "Look how your eyes are widening!" And I would laugh and say: "You know I can't see my own eyes. Look how big *yours* are!" She would then show me the frames against the light of the bed lamp, one by one. Just a shortish strip of film at a time, before she would wind it back and put the reel away.'

Over a period of years, Axel goes on, he and Mariel worked their way through the entire reel. She made up stories for each sequence. 'Because, face it, not much happens. You have to make it all up around the images.' Afterwards she always had to go and wash her hands. '"It is toxic," I had to hear every time. "Lethal." I wasn't allowed touch it myself.'

These evenings were the best times of his childhood, Axel says. Just he and his mother there in his room, in a cocoon of light.

Etienne and Axel are standing in front of a steamed-up glass door. Axel wipes a square clean with his palm, looks

337

out. The storm has passed. Etienne touches his damp hair; it is still raining in there. The pine trees are glistening outside, so too the soil.

'So, when we watched Ariel's first reel in London, it was the first time that you yourself had seen any part of the film *projected?*'

Axel nods. Etienne looks through the glass door. 'And how come you had Irmgard's diary in your possession?'

'When I left for London, my mother gave it to me.'

'Why?'

Axel looks out, shrugs. 'She didn't say. Perhaps she suspected . . . knew she would, at some point . . . She wanted it to be preserved, I think. As when Ariel had originally divided up the reels. To spread risk.'

Etienne's heart is in his throat. 'So, they *had* divided up the reels? Did your mother tell you that? And, if Ariel had taken one reel, and Irmgard another, which she then left for Mariel – who has the third one? *Are* there indeed three? Was the film ever completed?'

Axel opens the glass door, walks out into the night air, still fresh with rain smells. Etienne scurries after him. Was he too greedy; has he now frightened Axel off? They stop, feel the spongy ground underneath their feet, look at the moon emerging from behind the clouds.

'The first thing I did when I arrived in London was to look up Ariel. Earlier, when saying goodbye to me in Berlin, my mother had mentioned a name. "Ariel, your grandfather, who made this film, is now known as Bernhard Sauer. I don't know him, but he's in London." She had given me an address.

'I found Ariel – or Bernhard, as he introduced himself, and as I then called him – at that very address. I befriended him under false pretences. He was an activist, helping squatters who were subject to eviction. I pretended to be seeking advice on behalf of friends who were staying in a place that was to be demolished.

'We became good friends. And he was generous, over the years. Helped me to get the place in Bermondsey Street after I'd been kicked out of another squat. Later on he even helped pay for me to go to nurse's college . . .'

The stars are brightening; the last fleecy clouds disappear. Etienne enquires about the second reel, and the manner in which he found it. He doesn't mention Volker's name again.

'When my mother gave me the diary as I left for London, I asked her whether I could take the reel too, even though I knew it was her most treasured possession. She smiled. "You know it's poisonous. I'll keep it for you. Come back at some point. Come back for it."' For a while Etienne and Axel stand in silence. 'How it found its way to you? That *did* entail coincidence.' When he was released from jail, Axel goes on, he didn't have a penny to his name. In Hannover he started scouring the newspapers for work in Berlin and stumbled upon Etienne's advertisement about the film. He wanted to let Etienne have the reel. After his mother's death, Volker had obtained control over it. Axel couldn't bear the thought of engaging with Volker again, but it was his only option. He borrowed money from Horst and Ulrich, offered it to Volker to contact Etienne about the reel.

'You got in touch with *Volker* again? Rather than directly contact—?'

'A colossal angel. A shipwreck from the sun.' They both stiffen. It is Etienne's mother's voice, sounding clearly behind them. It is absorbed so swiftly by the pine trees that Etienne wonders whether he has actually heard it. But Axel looks around too. There is an open window hardly twenty steps away – the room where she is sleeping, apparently.

Etienne's urge is to go towards the voice. He turns around. Axel takes him by the arm. Etienne extracts himself from the grip, starts walking, though not towards his mother but into the plantation. He can hear Axel following.

Etienne walks fast and far, then leans against a trunk. Above them an owl is calling. She has my mother's voice, this owl, Etienne thinks. She is begging me for something. Or warning me. Axel catches up with him, gets his breath back. He continues his story, his voice now urgent. Before Axel handed over the money to Volker, he had made him promise not to tell Etienne Axel's whereabouts. 'I had wanted to contact you directly, but I couldn't. Everything was different, everything was wrong . . .' He pushes up his sleeves, holds out his ink-stained arms in the moonlight. 'Do you get it? What prison had done to me? My skin was scribbled on like the Berlin Wall. I constantly had septic sores on my back. I was penniless. I was living with Horst and Ulrich in that hole in Hannover, sniffing and injecting crap all day. I was borrowing more and more money from them, couldn't find work or pay them back—'

'But I could've done something, Axel, could have helped—'

Axel pinches his lips together, looks into the pines, as if spotting a nocturnal animal. His voice changes. 'You still don't get it.'

'Get what?'

'How angry I was?'

'Angry?' Then, softly: 'At me?'

'If you had said *yes*, that night in London, that *one* time in my life when I truly needed someone . . . If you had come with me to Berlin, you would've been able to help, would've stopped me. And I wouldn't have tried to kill Volker. And then none of this would've happened. *None* of it.' Axel pushes his sleeves down over his wrists, bows his head forward.

Etienne sits down on the wet pine needles, his legs half-paralysed. *How could I have known, Axel?* he wants to say. *How could I have recognised your cry for help if you didn't explain anything? It came entirely out of the blue, like a clap of thunder. And do you have any idea how constraining my circumstances were?* But what difference would it make?

Axel sits down too. He is crying. For a long time, they listen to the wind blowing through the pines. The damp seeps through to Etienne's buttocks. He is exhausted. If it weren't for the cold, he would fall asleep right there.

A long time passes before Axel takes a deep breath and goes on: 'It may sound strange to you. May surprise you. That I'm so angry.' He is speaking slowly, reluctantly. 'These are the kind of things that I told myself in jail. Or that the *needles* told me when I was lying in the dark, tattooing myself . . . It helped. To have someone to be angry at.' Each needle-prick like an ireful word, Etienne thinks. Each tattoo like a long, reproachful sentence. A body covered in ink tirades. Axel keeps nodding his head slowly. His voice is low. 'And yet. I wanted to lead you to the second reel. I didn't hate you.'

Etienne doesn't know what to say. Does Axel expect him to express gratitude? In the treetops above them, the wind is picking up. For a while, they just listen. 'What I struggle to get my head around is the lengths you went to to set up a treasure hunt for me. On such a scale. Across so many boundaries – cities, countries, political fault lines . . .'

'You overestimate me. I only pulled a few levers as and when

341

they presented themselves. But it's true that I did understand something about you. How necessary it was for you to search, to find. I knew how urgent your need was to exchange your childhood for something else. Frame by frame.' Etienne is startled. *You are mistaken about my project,* he wants to say. But he suddenly wonders: what is left behind when you cut out a part of your life like a tumour and try to replace it with light? 'Or perhaps I underestimate myself.' Axel lifts his chin, smiles weakly. 'You know how I like tricks, setting up installations. The bigger the scale, the better.' His smile becomes a grimace.

Etienne is wrapping pine needles around his fingers. *Whether I know you is doubtful, Axel,* he wants to say. But he turns towards the German. 'So tell it to me straight: *is* there a third reel? If so, where is it?'

Axel's voice is now clear and strong. 'When Ariel and I were whispering to each other shortly before his death, I called him "Ariel", rather than "Bernhard", for the first time. I told him: "Ariel, I am your grandchild, your daughter Mariel was my mother. Irmgard, your lover, was my grandmother." That was why he let me have the reel. I guess it wasn't reasonable to confront him with so much in that moment. I could see how it overwhelmed him . . . After I had fetched the reel, he urgently wanted to talk, but he was like a stalling engine. He could only grind his teeth, tighten his neck muscles.

'I asked him bluntly: "Where is the rest of the film? Is there more?" *Irmgard* is what he whispered. "She knows where it is. Find her. She was the one who divided the reels. Get the other two, put all three of them together. For the first time, there will then be a film . . ."

'Here's the thing, Etienne.' Etienne looks up in the half-light. Axel has never called him by his name before. 'For forty-five years, no one has known where Irmgard is or whether she's still alive. Logically she would have divided the reels among three people. Ariel clearly took only one. Irmgard too, and this she later gave to Mariel. Where the third one is? That only Irmgard knows.' Axel lifts his hand, almost touches Etienne's cheek, then drops his arm.

The air has a gleaming quality: empty and disinfected. Etienne looks at the steam rising from Axel's shoulders, as if he is dissolving. Axel starts coughing. It is a severe coughing fit; it seems as if it will never stop. Etienne thinks of all the silences, all the detours that have led them here. Axel finally catches his breath. They get up, start walking without a word. Not deeper into the rows of pines, but back to the laboratories' light.

Chapter 39

WHEN THE DATE of their departure from Johannesburg back to Berlin arrived, Etienne was reluctant to board a plane. His mother's oncologist couldn't say whether she had three weeks or three months left to live. 'These things are not to be foretold,' he intoned in a biblical-histrionic tone. It turned out to be three days. Etienne had hardly arrived back in Berlin when he received news of her death. Her hands had still been in bandages. To Etienne's chagrin, it was Frans Vermeulen who called him with the news. 'And nevermore a mother's caring hands will stir,' the imbecile declared.

Etienne didn't return for the funeral. There was nothing left for him in South Africa now; he would not travel there again. He made a copy of the video from their trip, sent it to Frans Vermeulen. Without any accompanying explanation. Etienne had never looked at it himself. It would contain nothing more than the soundless images of rain clouds, pine trees and the old foundations of a corrugated-iron house. Vermeulen could do with it what he would. He could play it at the memorial service that Etienne wouldn't be attending. He could bury it with her. Or he could throw it out with his rubbish.

When they got back from South Africa, it turned out they had left one of their windows in Charlottenburg open. The flat had been filled with fresh air in their absence, with the smells of spring. They decided to keep the window open all summer long – to let the breezes and the bumblebees in, to let ivy grow into the flat from the courtyard. They also resolved to find a place to start planting vegetables.

After Axel's night of revelations amid the test tubes and plantations, Etienne still had a lot of unanswered questions. And new ones kept cropping up. But, as far as Axel was concerned, the subject was closed: 'Now it's all about us. About who we will become. I'm going to make art again. You, music.'

When Axel takes a shower in the mornings, the sun shines into the bathroom. For the first time in a year, Etienne joins him under the lukewarm spray. He soaps up Axel's back and shoulders, over the tree tattoo and the grid of overlapping words and marks. Axel is becoming thinner again; his hip bones are starting to show. Sunrays filter through the ivy in the courtyard, casting green light onto his groin. There is now calm in their home, a new tenderness. That which had been burnt and engraved into Axel's skin has lost all meaning, and all power.

Once their flat was a grand bourgeois home. The ceilings have been crumbling for decades, the paint peeling. The two reception rooms are connected by double doors; each is large enough for a banquet. After they returned from South Africa, Axel set up his studio on one side. He is working on a new installation. As usual, Etienne doesn't ask questions about it; he does, however, see the materials that Axel is now trying out: rotting plants, ice, tufts of fur from species at risk of extinction. And bloody rabbit hearts, freshly slaughtered from their hosts. A friend of Axel who is a veterinary student supplies the fur and hearts. Axel immerses the hearts in salty solutions, tries to get the hearts to beat electrically. He also plays around with the camera, wants to incorporate video into the new work.

And now Axel needs butterflies. And they need to be alive. One sunny morning, they take a train to the Bodensee. They take videos of each other: shirtless, flying through the tall grass, nets in their hands. Etienne looks at the butterflies through the lens; they are flying towards the sun, outside time, intoxicated by the summer scents. Etienne finds it hard to think of them as *material*. Axel puts them in a butterfly cage, careful not to damage the wings. Etienne hopes he isn't planning to pin them on a board.

The second reel of *Berliner Chronik* is safely stored away, is no longer mentioned. The double doors between the two main rooms remain open. On Etienne's side, he is trying out a synthesiser, which he has bought second-hand. His ears are hungry again, but his hands are clumsy: it has been years since he last played the piano. All day long he experiments with the electronic sounds, while inconspicuously watching Axel working in the other room.

They could live here forever. The light can brighten and fade, the seasons can drift through the courtyard, their friends can come and go. So too the swallows overhead. To have Axel here with him will be enough.

The safer Etienne feels with Axel, the warmer the glow in these rooms, the more dangerous he can allow the music to become. He closes his eyes, translates what he sees. A pale green dawn in an icy region, columns of soldiers on a black highway, bodies piled up in a mass grave. As Etienne turns knobs and modulates frequencies and amplitudes on the synthesiser, the notes emanate from deeper and deeper inside a glacier – the sound of the forces bearing on the ice when the colossus shifts in infinitesimal increments. It is summer in Berlin, but the music is frozen. 'Black Ice', he calls his first electronic composition.

In the three months since their return from South Africa, they have burgeoned into guerrilla gardeners: on a bomb site down the street, they have started fertilising and planting. The site has high blind walls on three sides. First they cleared away the chunks of concrete and warped steel that they were able to lift and carry, then worked compost into the soil. They started with carrots and potatoes. Then came the beetroot and toma-toes. Sometimes city animals would dig up a carrot or two. Sometimes human animals would beat them to it, harvesting a few beets before Etienne could get to them, but such raids were rare.

The yield is good; ripe vegetables lie waiting in the warm loamy soil. After a morning's work in the flat, each on his own side of the double doors, they go out to harvest whatever is ripe and then return to cook. Vegetables in water, with a little salt. A Buddhist meal. They don't need much more. In the morn-ings, Etienne gets up early and cooks oats for Axel until they are gluey. They have stopped eating meat, stopped drinking alcohol. They are planting new crops: beans, sunflowers. Their days are becoming purer.

And yet: Axel is losing weight. Etienne can feel Axel's shoul-ders becoming sharper when he folds his arms around him or when they turn in bed at night. When Axel is asleep, Etienne fingers his ribs. And Etienne looks at him in the shower steam; he no longer looks like his dangerous London self. The oak tree on his back is fading: a winter tree now, shrouded by fog. The excess kilograms have melted away, and then a few more. His shoulder knobs are protruding. His palms are as dry as paper.

One morning Etienne confronts Axel over breakfast. They are sitting in the kitchen, looking out over the courtyard, at the crow's nest of bicycles in the racks below.

'Why are you becoming so thin?'

Axel looks at his coffee, shrugs his shoulders dismissively, coughs out the window. 'I am so busy with my project. I'm concentrating, not getting time to eat.'

That isn't true, Etienne wants to say. *We're eating, we're looking after ourselves. See how I'm flourishing.*

As far as Axel is concerned, the matter is closed.

In the mornings, when Etienne wakes up in their white bed, he smells grass and dew and flowers. But smells are never unambiguous in this city. Something is always hovering behind it. He turns to Axel. The sun is in his hair, which is now the longest it has been since Etienne met him. Etienne suddenly knows what is floating behind the scent of blossoms: the smell of injury, of a fresh wound.

Etienne yanks off the sheet, expecting something raw. There is no blood; their skins are unbroken. He studies his own body. He has become sturdier: his chest, so scrawny in his London days, is now muscular, his arms quite powerful. Axel is tall and skinny next to him. The rough ink marks on his skin are fading like forgotten graffiti on concrete.

The day before, Etienne noticed that Axel quickly gets out of breath. It was a perfect afternoon. They were working in the vegetable garden, digging and planting until blisters appeared

348

on Etienne's hands, until sweat ran down their sides. Axel, he saw from the corner of his eye, had to sit down every now and then, a little spade in his hands. They had their best harvest yet. Armfuls. Some of their neighbours in the street have recently started clearing and planting their own patches. A bartering market has been developing: beet for onions, carrots for artichokes. They take home a greater variety of things these days, enjoying steaming vegetable feasts. Everything they eat now comes from the gardens.

They drink black tea in the morning, sit in silence, their heads touching. After breakfast they follow the sun, from the kitchen to where it later streams into Axel's studio. Slowly, tentatively, he then starts working on his installation. These days, when he isn't fussing with his synthesiser, Etienne is allowed to watch Axel work. He may even sit right next to him. Etienne gets little tasks, as Axel's phalanx of helpers in London once did.

Etienne wakes up after midnight. Axel's sweat is soaking the sheets, despite the summer air drifting through the room like a cool sigh. Etienne tries to refresh him with damp cloths on his forehead and cheeks. He lies awake, listening to Axel's body. The food from the Berlin earth (this soil that is so sated with ash and bones) does not help to keep Axel healthy. Etienne lies wondering in the dark, trying to avoid the worst scenarios. Is Axel really eating too little? Does he need more protein? Red meat and poultry? Why is Etienne himself such a picture of good health, then?

When Axel's fever hasn't broken by morning, Etienne takes him to hospital. The doctor at accidents and emergencies diagnoses him with double pneumonia. They admit him.

The nursing staff insist that Etienne should leave, but he refuses. He overstays visiting hours, keeps vigil by Axel's bed.

'How pathetic of me,' Axel says. 'Pneumonia in summer.' He is overcome by an uncontrollable coughing fit. 'Fuck, here I go,' he says, laughing in between coughs, 'this is how it all ends.'

'Don't be silly,' Etienne says. 'We'll get you healthy and spry in no time. We'll grow more vegetables, drink even more water, get more sun, more exercise. We'll go and live in the countryside, where the air is cleaner.'

Axel smirks. 'In the deep East, yes. Near Leipzig or Dresden, I'm sure, one can pick up a patch of land for a song. Saturated with radioactive waste. With a vegetable garden where tomatoes glow in the dark.' Etienne feels relief at the spark of cynicism.

The next morning a doctor takes Etienne aside. 'He needs to be tested, your friend,' the doctor says. 'For that which he fears most. His immune system is compromised. I suggested it to him yesterday, but he refused. I will leave it to you.' He walks away, leaves Etienne behind in the corridor.

Etienne doesn't say anything to Axel. Three days later, he is discharged. Etienne goes to harvest a bag of vegetables. He buys a basket of other ingredients. He starts making soups, stirring wheat kernels and barley into them, and handfuls of herbs. He grinds oil-rich nuts, bakes breads.

He sees to it that Axel eats every day, tries to fatten him up. His body is making increasingly sharp angles nevertheless.

This is how they spend their time over the next month:

In the mornings they sit opposite each other at the kitchen

table. The days are sweet and generous, as Berlin summer days can be. They keep following the sun – or, on cloudy days, the light – through the bright rooms. They see the clouds drift by in each other's eyes. They listen to the pigeons in the courtyard. They let their breathing rhyme when they lie down in the evening, synchronise their turning at night. They never close the curtains, let the Berlin night smells drift inside. Sometimes they see glimpses of themselves in the panes of open windows, then laugh at the ghosts gliding over there.

They have forgiven each other everything, if there was anything to forgive. And they forgive each other in advance anything that may yet happen. They rarely see friends any more, mostly just the people arriving to plant vegetables in their neighbouring patches. They do not want for anything, do not need anyone else on earth. Etienne is alert to each of Axel's everyday acts. He looks at the little muscles in his forearm when he brushes his teeth, the wrists as thin as twigs. When Axel stands on the sunny side of a sheet when they are folding it together, he watches his transparent profile. He concentrates when Axel gulps down a glass of water: the turbulence of bubbles, the light playing on his fingers, the knuckles like pebbles, the beating Adam's apple.

After dinner they go for long walks, hand in hand. Around Schloss Charlottenburg, through Schöneberg's streets. They hardly hear the music emanating from bars, ignore the din of voices from cafés. They pay no heed to the furtive glances at the messy ink marks on Axel's arms. The city winds blow against their cheeks. They listen to the leaves, which will soon start to fall, and to the silences of the colder, higher currents.

They are spending more and more time at the guerrilla garden.

If you sit still for long enough, the late summer feels more intense here than anywhere else, and more intimate. Etienne pulls out the weeds that are coming up everywhere. Axel just watches. Etienne listens to Axel's breathing, mindful of signs of acceleration or slowing. His heightened attention makes him aware of other presences. Puddles of rainwater attract dragonflies from fountains elsewhere. They fly around, coupling in aimless, jerky trajectories above the water. Etienne wonders how the penetrator and penetrated synchronise their direction and the flapping of their wings. Or do they immediately regret their physical attachment, pulling in opposite directions until they uncouple violently? Mice scurry in corners. Ants navigate in long queues between chunks of concrete, sluggish in the rain-heavy air. 'Everything that lives is welcome here,' Axel says distractedly, his voice feeble. 'That goes for the gnats too, and the rodents, the carriers of disease.'

Their gardening neighbours look up when Axel speaks these words. They bring Axel handfuls of pumpkin and squash flowers. On the way back, Etienne pricks his ears for the buzz of human lives in the buildings above them. Everything sounds different now that he is making electronic music. He first has to recognise the human noises, then isolate them. He wants to strip the city, distil everything to something cleaner and simpler.

At home Etienne stuffs the delicate flowers with honey and cream cheese, but Axel's digestive system doesn't tolerate it. The rest of the afternoon he spends going back and forth between the toilet and his bed.

Their garden is lusher than ever. And beautiful: their sunflowers are in full bloom and there are bean blossoms too.

The yield is far more than they can use. They take some to friends and neighbours, take bowls of cooked vegetables – accompanied by beer – to give to alcoholics in a nearby park. They swill the beers, heads thrown back, mouths wide, then toss the vegetables under the bushes when Etienne and Axel start walking away.

Apart from the alcoholics, Etienne and Axel also feed the squirrels and pigeons on their strolls. A few crumbs are left behind for the rats. Late afternoon they sit in the guerrilla garden again. There is a new, rough-hewn wooden bench. They look out over the profusion of bean stalks, pumpkin leaves and beets. There is a host of new gardeners; a whole new community is forming here. On Saturdays some of them now erect tables, selling produce to passers-by. Etienne and Axel don't know all the people who are adding patches any more; there is hardly any space left. They sit there until dusk. Here and there someone is still half-heartedly digging or weeding. The last of them departs; just the two of them remain.

These days, Etienne always brings a blanket for Axel, for the evening chill. When he wraps it around Axel's legs (he waits until deep dusk, otherwise Axel is too self-conscious), Axel says, into the dark, rather than to Etienne: 'It was the best summer. I could not have asked for anything more.' He starts coughing; it takes a long time before he stops.

Chapter 40

ETIENNE IS CAUGHT unawares when he turns over the package that he has just picked up at the post office for Axel: the sender is Volker. He considers getting rid of it. What can be sent by Volker that won't cause anguish?

He does, after all, take it home. Axel looks at the sender's address, opens it without a word.

'My mother's things,' he says. There is a pile of envelopes, a diaphanous little scarf. Axel brings the scarf to his face, quickly sniffs it.

Etienne swallows. 'Why now?'

'I let him know.'

'Let him know what?'

'That the time is approaching.'

There is a high-pitched noise in Etienne's ears.

Axel continues: 'You want to deny it, but you know it as well as I.'

Etienne swallows, swallows again. He leaves the flat, walks to the vegetable garden. He starts digging wildly and blindly. How hard the soil was when they started, and how thoroughly and deeply have they fertilised it. The tears flow; he can hardly see what he is doing. When he is done, he realises he has dug out everything. Beets and carrots lie in the sun with deep gashes; some have split open. There are crushed, bloody tomatoes.

He returns in the dark. Axel is sitting at the kitchen table.

'You have closed it,' Etienne says. 'For the first time this summer.'

Axel looks at the closed window, as if he too is surprised by it. 'I had to. A bird flew in here. Earlier, while it was still light. I chased it out with a broomstick. It was bright: yellow chest, green and blue wings. The colour of summer elsewhere. I have it on video.' He gestures towards the camera, still lying on the table. 'A tropical bird. Probably escaped from a cage. Or *very* lost.' He looks up at the ceiling, and then out into the corridor, as if following the bird's trajectory.' Then he looks at Etienne. 'You know, Volker didn't teach me much. He did, however, once teach me a few names of exotic birds from the south. One evening we returned from one of the skinhead rallies he used to drag me to. He was so pumped up that he started thumping my mother without warning. When she lay on the floor, and had stopped whining and shielding herself, he lost interest and turned towards me. Broke both my hands.'

Silence rises from the courtyard. Not a plank in the wooden floor creaks. 'For weeks, while the bones in my hands were healing, Volker kept me out of school. One day he brought me a book about bird species. The first and only book in that house. He sat down next to me, we leafed through the pages together.' Axel looks at Etienne. 'I kept asking questions. As long as he was showing me bird pictures, I reckoned, he couldn't get angry. I was wrong. He became livid because I kept returning to earlier pages, kept asking the same questions. He flung the book against the wall, snapping its spine . . .

'The page facing upwards showed two tiny birds. Their names are all I can remember. A tomtit from New Zealand. And then the Cape penduline tit. From *your* world. The

355

smallest bird in Africa.' Axel shakes his head. 'But the bird that flew in here was something else.'

For a while neither of them says anything. Etienne clears his throat, points at the little pile of paper in front of Axel on the table. Sky-blue. A4 size. Typed letters, he can see from where he is standing.

'So, you had let Volker know that you . . . are ill . . . And then he sent your mother's documents.'

Axel nods. 'Letters, yes. And this.' He shows his hand. The little scarf is wrapped around his hand like a bandage. He brings it to his lips, smells it again and again, as if the scent is on the verge of evaporating.

Etienne starts with the letters that Axel has already worked through. From Irmgard, it appears, to Mariel. Written from Buenos Aires, where she is living. The letters start in 1959. The first few letters are addressed to *My Daughter*. The content of these letters is a disappointment. They read like a banal diary. Platitudes, Irmgard's daily life in Argentina: her cat, the prices of groceries, her noisy neighbour. An unsettling episode about her getting a trained guide dog. The dog is so useless that she has it put down after a few months. *I know I could have given it back*, she writes, *it could probably have been given to someone else on the waiting list. But it had to be punished.* Otherwise the emotional tenor is neutral. The glimpses of a doubt-ridden inner life that were discernible in the production diary are absent here. There are a few questions to Mariel – about where she is living now, whether she has a boyfriend yet. Etienne works out that Mariel must have been in her mid-twenties when the first letter was sent.

By the fourth letter, Irmgard begins with *My Daughter Mariel*. Ariel with an M in front of it, it strikes Etienne now that he sees it on paper. There are no longer questions; it is apparent that Irmgard hasn't been receiving responses to her letters.

Etienne reads faster, starting to work through the letters that Axel hasn't read himself. They exchange piles, slowly work through everything. It is the first time, Etienne thinks, that they are working through clues together, that they have equal access to information. It is the first time he isn't embarking on some dead-end search on his own or following a trail of crumbs that Axel has sprinkled. They read through the last few letters together – written in 1988, after Mariel's death. When they are done, their joint disappointment is palpable. There are no clues. Nothing about *Berliner Chronik*. Axel, Etienne then realises, might have been hoping for something else – personal revelations about his mother or grandmother. He suddenly feels guilty about his fixation on the film reels.

Something is bothering him, flickering just out of sight. He looks at the Berlin address on each letter again. It isn't Volker and Mariel's address in Neukölln, but he does recognise it: Herr Bösel's address near Alexanderplatz!

'Do you still have the envelopes?' Etienne wants to know. Axel listlessly points to the paper bin.

Etienne finds them. The letters are addressed to Mariel, although the address is Bösel's in East Berlin. In each instance, this address has been scratched out, and Volker and Mariel's address has been written in. Each letter carries both an Argentine and East German stamp. It had travelled from Argentina across the Atlantic Ocean to East Berlin, from where it was posted again to West Berlin. What a long paper route to deliver Irmgard's drab reports of her life in Buenos Aires into Mariel's hands . . .

'What,' Etienne wants to know, 'does this Bösel have to do with anything? Why were the letters sent via his address?' Did Bösel have the answer all along? he wonders. Had the secret of the third reel been right there, right in front of his nose, in that cheerless little Alexanderplatz flat? It makes him dizzy, all these answers that remain just out of reach. Etienne realises he has never told Axel about his visits to Bösel. He had dismissed it as just another false trail.

Now he recounts the story of his visits.

In response, Axel produces a sheet of paper from under the table. His voice is breezy. 'I don't think you've seen this yet. The first letter.'

Etienne looks at Axel, shakes his head in light rebuke. Once again, Axel has only released what should be the first piece of the jigsaw puzzle at the very end. Just when Etienne thought they had, for the first time, obtained equal access to the same facts. Is Axel addicted to leaving a trail for him to follow, to setting up labyrinths? To seducing him and then making him wait? Axel may be getting thinner and weaker, but his taste for riddles remains undiminished.

Etienne takes the letter from Axel. The date is October 1983. It is a letter from Irmgard in Buenos Aires, sent to Bösel's address. Not addressed to Mariel, but to a woman called Norna. A new name, although it vaguely rings a bell. Etienne looks quizzically at Axel. 'Norna?' Axel gestures with his head towards the letter. Etienne reads further. The letter is blunt, even brusque. *I know*, Irmgard writes to Norna, *that you may be astonished to hear from me after all these years*. Irmgard then makes clear that she isn't writing to explain anything or ask for any sort of forgiveness. She isn't writing to thank Norna for bringing up her child either. *It is you who should be grateful*

358

for having Mariel – a child's love is not to be taken for granted.
She wants to know how Mariel is doing. And Norna should
send her Mariel's address. It is her right as mother to contact
her daughter. If Norna won't help her, she will contact Bösel
directly. *Your husband and I were, after all, once in the best film
production team ever.*

Axel produces yet another piece of paper from below the
table, hands it to Etienne without a word. Etienne shakes his
head again; Axel smiles mischievously, feebly. It is a letter from
Norna to Mariel.

> *I include a letter from your mother, from Irmgard.*
> *She and I haven't been in contact for years. Since*
> *she entrusted you to me as a fragile nine-year-old,*
> *I have never kept anything from you. And hence*
> *I won't keep silent now about the fact that she*
> *wishes to contact you. I could give your address in*
> *Neukölln to Irmgard, or I could just forward her*
> *letters to you. Or I could let her know that you*
> *don't want to hear from her at all.*

'Apparently she wanted Norna to just forward Irmgard's letters,'
Axel says. 'Irmgard clearly never had direct contact with—'

'So, let me get my facts straight: Norna brought up Mariel
after Irmgard had left Germany? Norna and Bösel had a relationship? And Bösel had once been the *Berliner Chronik*
cameraman?'

Axel looks tired; his head is drooping. 'Norna was one
of Riefenstahl's cinematographers, I think I've told you this
before. And, yes, Bösel was indeed the *Berliner Chronik* cameraman. He wasn't Jewish, but nevertheless left Germany shortly

after Ariel. When he returned after the war, he looked up Mariel, who was in Norna's care, in Berlin. Perhaps Irmgard asked him to check up on her, who knows. In any event, this was how Bösel and Norna met, fell in love and got married. Bösel and Norna then brought up my mother. But when my mother was a young woman, when it was still possible to move relatively freely, she left with Volker for West Berlin. Norna and Bösel stayed behind in East Berlin. When the Wall was built, my mother and her stepmother were separated.'

Etienne lowers the letter. 'So, Mariel and her biological mother ended up on different sides of the Atlantic Ocean. And Mariel and the woman who had brought her up, on different sides of the Wall.' Etienne thinks for a moment, shakes his head. 'But Bösel was alone when I visited him. Twice. No sign of Norna.'

'Norna died in 1987, hardly a month after my mother's death. When Irmgard's letters to Mariel kept arriving at Bösel's address after Norna's death, he apparently kept sending them on to Neukölln, having lost his clarity of mind.' Etienne suddenly remembers where he has seen Norna's name before: written on a photo in Bösel's flat, the very flat where Axel's mother spent some of her childhood.

Etienne gets up. He wants to ask: *Are there more pieces in the jigsaw puzzle?* Every time he thinks the last piece has been found, it turns out the puzzle is bigger than he thought. But the time for such questions has passed. He can see how drained Axel is. He helps him to bed – his hand around Axel's waist, Axel's arm around his neck. Then he sits down alone in Axel's studio.

Etienne thinks of the letters, the distances between continents, the borders and silences. Of love and soundless violence.

Axel's breathing in the bedroom is hardly audible. Like the breath of a little bird.

At dusk the next day Etienne and Axel walk to the wooden bench by the vegetable garden. Axel is virtually weightless these days; his movements are like those of a sloth. When they sit down, the wall at the back – the windowless side of a block of flats – draws their attention. Overnight, someone has painted it black. The layers of graffiti that were there before have been wiped out. Right in the centre of the dark square is a white dot. From the bench, it looks no larger than the full stop after a sentence. In truth it probably has the diameter of a fist. Is it meant to depict approaching light? The fading sun? Is it just a spatter of bird shit?

The longer they look at the wall, the stranger its effect on Etienne becomes. One would have thought such a black wall would imply an occlusion, a dense veil. But it feels *deep*, like the ocean at night.

'Perhaps,' Axel says, 'I should colour myself like that. From my crown to my toes.' He holds out his arms in front of him, looks at the cordage of fading words on his grey skin. It is the first time since their night in Hannover three years before that he is drawing attention to it.

Something is written on the dark wall, Etienne notices. At the bottom, just above the soil. He gets up, walks over there. From the corner of his eye he can see the blanket slipping from Axel's knees. Axel gets up too, walks over and squats next to him. It exudes a gloom, the black paint, an enveloping fogginess. It is cool against the skin, and creepy. Etienne screws up his eyes to read in the half-light. He is expecting something weighty. German history encapsulated in a single word.

Something like *Trauer*, perhaps. Or *Gram*. But no. In tiny bright white letters it says: *Leuchtkäfer*. Firefly. He steps back, tilts his head, looks at the dot shining up there. Paint that glows in the dark. A needle prick of phosphor in the Berlin dusk.

Chapter 41

IT IS SWELTERING in the Buenos Aires airport. Etienne changes money at a currency bureau. In his pocket is everything that he had left after paying for a return flight, using his savings from moonlighting with Berlin bands. He has just about enough for two nights in a hotel.

He takes a taxi. It is full of dents; the driver is an oily character. On the way to the city, a tyre bursts. The little car veers over two lanes, comes to a halt on the narrow shoulder.

Etienne stands waiting on the dismal strip of land between the highway and sewage works. The sweating driver is changing the wheel. Every time a lorry drones past, the taxi totters and sways on the jack. Sewage fumes whirl around them.

After they had read through Irmgard's letters in Berlin, a deep exhaustion overcame Etienne. His obsession to find the last reel was waning; he could feel the fire in his chest burning low. To visit Bösel again would only require a U-Bahn ride to Alexanderplatz. The unspoken question was whether Irmgard might still be alive, and whether anyone would go and look for her in Argentina. Axel was too fragile to travel and Etienne couldn't leave him behind on his own.

The next morning, Etienne went to Bösel's flat. Confused, witless old Bösel. (Or was he in fact as cunning as a fox?) It was the first time since Etienne's departure from East Berlin, more than two years earlier, that he was back on Alexanderplatz.

There were new security doors in front of the building entrance. Etienne pressed the intercom. No response. He slipped in behind a resident. Upstairs he knocked on Bösel's door, then on his kitchen window. Nothing. He stood on his toes, tried peeking in, turned the doorknob. There was a cobweb in the corner of the door. Since the Wendung, it hadn't been unusual for flats in the East to stand empty.

One afternoon, two weeks later, Axel insisted: he wanted to go to the garden. Axel had been in bed for the last few days, with fluid dripping into him from a transparent bag. A nurse was now coming in three times a week. Axel's sheets still smelled of the previous day's sun, when Etienne had washed them and hung them out on the balcony. In the course of the morning, Axel had startled Etienne by addressing him by his *own* name a few times. 'Axel, please bring me some water.' Or: 'Axel, I have to go to the toilet.' When Etienne said: 'I am Etienne. *You* are Axel!' Axel chortled gleefully and rubbed his hands.

Etienne shook his head. 'It isn't wise to go out. Not in this weather.' There was something cold in the air; the clouds were moving in.

Axel tried to laugh, coughed drily. 'Wisdom, hey! What I would be able to do with *that!*'

Axel kept nagging until Etienne swaddled him in a blanket and carried him down the street. He was so light now, so light. All he wanted to do was to go and stick his hand in the soil. Etienne sat down on his haunches, with Axel like a pet in his arms. When Axel buried his hand under the clods, his body shuddered as if an electrical shock was shooting up out of the Berlin earth.

Back at home, Etienne laid him down. Axel was out of

breath, even though Etienne had been carrying *him*. Just cling-ing to Etienne with his lizard skeleton had drained him utterly. Everything made him weary now: uttering half a sentence, breathing.

The whirling clouds yielded only a few fat drops of rain. When the clouds had dispersed, Etienne dragged Axel's bed into the sunshine. Axel closed his eyes, angled his cheeks towards the light. Etienne thought of the sunflowers turning in unison in the guerrilla garden.

'You have to go,' Axel said, his eyes still closed. 'To Buenos Aires.'

Etienne sat down on his bed, vehemently shook his head. 'I'm staying right here.'

'I want you to go. Not for your sake, but mine.'

Etienne couldn't rely on his voice. 'I can't leave you here alone. You know that.'

He had a nurse, Axel insisted. And their neighbour, whose garden was next to theirs, would help to look after him too. Etienne looked closely at Axel. Trying to read him was like interpreting a deep river, or the currents of the sea.

Axel opened his eyes. 'The clouds are almost . . .' he said, then nothing else.

He fell into a deep sleep. They were spending their nights in separate beds now, to prevent Etienne from injuring Axel in his sleep. Axel would stay at home until the end, they had decided – no hospital or hospice. The nurse would show Etienne the ropes.

Etienne paced around the flat all night. Or did Axel want to find the last reel before it was too late? Did he expect it to contain a secret, expect that it would delay something, or fend it off?

The next day Axel once again insisted: Etienne had to go. Etienne obstinately pursed his lips. 'Under no circumstances.'

'Please,' Axel asked. He smiled wanly. 'Your last instruction from me. Your last clue, your final task.'

'Please,' Etienne said and turned away. 'You cannot send me away. Not now.'

'I'm asking you from my heart.'

'Is that what you want? *Really* want?'

'I have to feel the last reel in my hands before . . . I'll wait for you. You can fly back straight away. You only need two or three days. I'll be here when you return. I promise.' Etienne didn't ask: *What kind of control are you presuming?* Axel lay back against his pillows under the onslaught of Etienne's gaze, his smile fading. 'I'm not up to this, Etienne . . . I can't engage in a debate with you, or in battle. Not now.'

Did Axel want to spare him his deathbed? he wondered again. And, if so, should he give in? Would that be the ultimate sacrifice? To allow Axel to believe he was protecting Etienne? Etienne had to get out of the flat. He wandered the streets, sat down on the bench by the vegetable garden. Insects sank their little stings into strawberries and sucked up the sweetness. He couldn't linger, had to get back to watch over Axel.

Back home, he closed the bedroom door and phoned Axel's doctor. In a muted voice he wanted to know: 'How long will it still be?'

'Hard to say,' the doctor said. 'I would measure it in weeks, but that would be guesswork.'

He phoned the nurse too, who saw Axel more often. 'Perhaps a few more months,' she said and then had second thoughts. 'I give him two weeks, perhaps three.'

Once again, Etienne couldn't sleep, kept roaming through

the rooms. In the morning hours, while Axel was dreaming without a sound, he went out again, sat down in the park, among the sleeping alcoholics. When the sun dawned over the reeking bodies, he decided: if that was what Axel wanted, *really* wanted, and for whatever reason, he would do what Axel asked of him.

When he departed two days later, Etienne left a vase of sunflowers in each of the rooms. On either side of the bed, flanking Axel, were the nurse and the neighbour. When Etienne walked out the door, Axel and the neighbour were deep in conversation about seeds, about everything they were going to plant in the coming season.

Later, on the plane, high above the Atlantic Ocean, he thought of his and Axel's silences. Of the muteness from which a spark had originally sprung up between them. At first he had wished Axel would say more. Gradually he became used to the silences, started treasuring them. Over the last month, as Axel started shedding the kilograms and became more haggard, his sentences emerged more easily. As the crisis of the illness deepened, silence started displacing his words again. Only the cool ash of earlier conversations kept sifting down.

Etienne granted Axel the last few sentences. His final request, a few hours before Etienne's flight – in the early morning hours, both of them only half-awake – was for a Christmas tree. 'We have to get one this year, a pretty one. To decorate with lights, here in the flat.'

This one night Etienne had permitted himself to sleep next to Axel again. The body beside Etienne was now a parched seed. When Axel spoke, Etienne was still half-asleep, and flummoxed. It wouldn't have surprised him if Axel had instructed him to go and cut out dogs' hearts or collect material at a crematorium or sewage plant. To go and sift through rubble in a bunker or abandoned hospital, or search for something in the city's deepest entrails or among the detritus on its margins. But a Christmas tree? It was unimaginable that such an object could feature unironically in their home. And it was, in any event, still October.

'Promise,' Etienne mumbled. 'A tree. Before I leave.' He thought of perfectly cloned pines in South Africa, of plant fragments in a white laboratory. He slipped into half-sleep again, aware of his own weight, afraid that he would break Axel if he moved. When dawn broke and he opened his eyes, his first thought was that he had woken up next to a stranger.

The last thing that Etienne noticed when he walked out carrying a suitcase, while Axel was lying between his carers in the sunlight, was one of the rough prison tattoos on Axel's forearm. Only now, many hours later, in the sharp Argentine light, does Etienne remember that night's conversation and realise that he failed to keep his promise to bring home a Christmas tree. He can only hope that Axel's request had been made in a state of delirium and that he forgot about it immediately afterwards. Or that he understood that Etienne's promise had been made in the fog of sleep.

He wakes up at the break of dawn. He doesn't eat breakfast. Time is limited. He is just here for two nights; he needs to return to Berlin as soon as possible.

Here he is now: in front of Irmgard's door, in a dilapidated building close to his hotel. The lift is out of order; he takes the stairs. They look out onto a narrow courtyard. There is no bell by her front door. He knocks. Knocks again. Without a sound, the door swings open. There she is.

She looks more like a spider than someone's grandmother. Her hair is like the down on a fruit; her scalp is covered in sun blemishes. She comes right up to him, feels his face with both hands.

'Can I come in?' He speaks softly, as if his words – his very breath – could injure her. 'I'm here to discuss an important matter with you. The issue of—'

She steps back, lets him in. His eyes have to get used to the dark. The flat faces the gloomy courtyard. The thick velvet curtains are half-drawn. The smell of onions and turned milk makes him want to retch.

He stands in the centre of the room, turns around. 'I have to explain,' he says, 'why I'm here.'

She walks forcefully into a bookshelf, makes a little animal noise. A few books fall on the ground.

Etienne is too far away, but involuntarily stretches out an arm. 'Are you OK?' She ignores him, sits down. Etienne picks up the books, sits down too, on the edge of a chair. She smiles. Or rather, her mouth flattens into a lipless slit. Etienne explains: who Axel is, his own connection with him. And the saga of his search for *Berliner Chronik*. By this time, the story is smoothly polished. He can build it up in modular fashion, leaving out or adding parts depending on his listener. He speaks slowly, patiently.

When he is done, his blood suddenly starts pumping with deep red anger. He doesn't know why he is talking so gently to her. He would, in fact, like to wipe the imbecile smile from her face, punish her. 'You should also know,' he says, in a loud voice now, 'your grandson is dying in Berlin. Amid rabbit hearts and sunflowers. It was his last summer, his last planting season.' Etienne is surprised to hear himself cry.

Her smile does not change. She waits for Etienne to finish crying. Then they sit in silence.

His voice is lower again now. 'Do you understand why I'm here? Have you taken in what I just told you? If you want to do one thing for Axel, then give me the third reel. Or tell me where it is. I have to go back, to help him die.'

She giggles a little, spits something out. On her lap, slick with saliva, lies a Donald Duck figurine. It has apparently been in her mouth all along. She gropes towards it, puts it back in her cheek.

The wind has been taken out of his sails. She is in her dotage, hardly present. How does she manage on her own in this place? He looks around. Everything is well-organised; the smells suggest food is sometimes prepared here. She looks reasonably well looked after. There is a television and video cassette recorder, surely not for her own use. She must have a carer.

'Shall I try again, speak more slowly? My German isn't the best. Perhaps your own German is a little rusty? I don't, alas, speak Spanish.' She giggles again. The Donald Duck falls onto the floor. She feels around under her chair, whimpers. Etienne goes and picks it up. She puts it in her mouth, lets it protrude like a dummy. Etienne goes to the bathroom to wash his hands. Donald Duck is murky and slimy and has clearly been living in her mouth for a long time.

He switches on a floor lamp next to her chair. Do blind people switch on lights at night? For the first time he sees old bruises on her arms. In shades of yellow and green. A fresh blue contusion on her cheek. Is somebody abusing her? Or are her thoughts so far gone that her memory, and with that her ability to navigate, is wiped out every night? Does she bump into furniture and door frames every morning, which she has forgotten overnight?

Next to the bookshelf is a little desk. He switches on the reading lamp, keeps watching her from the corner of his eye. Her face follows his movements. She is sucking furiously on the Donald Duck.

On the little desk, in the glow of the lamp, there is a shiny black typewriter with a sheet of paper in it. The machine dates from the 1920s or '30s. On the right, above the keyboard, it says FILIA. Were the production diary's pages typed out on this keyboard? Did these keys and type levers make the invisible words that Etienne had to coax out of the paper fibres with a pencil? And is this the machine on which letters were written to Mariel, even after her death?

Etienne leans over. The date is 18 *December* 1989. A half-finished letter – her last? He catches sight of something stirring: when he looks down, he sees another page. It has fallen into the crack between the desk and bookshelf. Little flurries of air are drawn in underneath the front door, and the paper's edges are trembling.

He bends down, picks it up, holds it loosely up against the light. It is almost entirely black, with just the occasional sliver of white. The page is as thin as a butterfly wing. The corners curl inwards, as if on the verge of rolling the page into a scroll. When he brings it to his eyes, he instantly knows what must have happened. Every morning, after her memory has been wiped out overnight, she would be under the impression that there was a clean sheet in the machine, that she was starting a new letter. From scratch. The letters are so densely typed over each other that the ink covers the paper almost entirely, making it bleed into a single stain.

Who knows what she might have written here, against what she was railing or agitating, what she was lamenting or mourning? Which yearnings may have drowned in this ocean of ink, which love letters, missives of hate and revenge, or political manifestos? Which ravings, revelations, nuggets of wisdom, lunacies, confused utterances, clarifications, seductions or insults? Which nonsense-words and -sentences? Outpourings, perhaps, to Norna, Bösel, Ariel, Mariel. Or to the film production team of *Berliner Chronik*. To Leni Riefenstahl, or the Führer himself. Or, God knows, an dem Deutschen Volk or to the destroyed Jewry. To actors or famous film directors, to let them know how much she had enjoyed their films as a blind woman. To everyone she had known or never met: thousand-word letters to every human on earth. Everything that she had been unable, alone over decades in an Argentine flat, to say to someone. A black scream. History condensed on a page. A library on a single sheet of paper.

What grace, Etienne thinks, to be able to forget in this way. To be able to wipe out – overwrite – the daily histories with new sentences, to make everything that has ever happened sink back into the paper, into a vacuum of ink. To make all your predecessors' tracks disappear – and your own.

He carefully puts down the stained page, like an archival document. In places it is starting to disintegrate, like an old curtain. He looks at Irmgard, motionless in her chair, her lips a bloodless wound. He looks at his fingertips. They are stained grey.

He turns to the incomplete letter in the typewriter, pulls the sheet out. *Olympia*, it says in golden letters on the paper table. He sits down opposite Irmgard again. She is making smacking sounds while sucking on Donald Duck, like a child drinking from its mother. He reads. The letter is addressed to Norna. There is only one paragraph. It is clear and flawless, apparently written in a moment of clarity.

I am writing to ask, now that the Wall has fallen, that you should give the last reel of Berliner Chronik to Mariel. The reel that Bösel took when we all went our own ways in '33. Mariel must keep it and look after it. She already has the second reel. I will be writing to Ariel too (yes, I have his address in London, and it won't be the first time we correspond) and will ask him to send her the first reel as well. The whole film together again: the bones of a broken body. Perhaps Mariel has a child herself, someone to whom she could leave the film. The reels must never be separated again. If there isn't a child, she should give it to the archives. Although God only knows what was left in Germany's archives after everything had been blasted apart and the remnants plundered and carried away and divided and

Here it ends. The white space underneath the sentences is blotted with insect shit: the flies continued to write from the point where she had stopped. The typed letters are themselves deformed by tiny spots of excrement. They have been editing, the flies. Deleting and adding. A new, cryptic history, Etienne thinks. Determined by the insects. Addressed to the dead, for deciphering in the underworld.

He looks at Irmgard: sitting there, sucking.

These sentences were apparently written *after* the months of manic typing on the page that is so heavy with ink. When a gust had at last carried the black sheet to the floor, she must have realised there was no paper in the machine, must have replaced it. Or, who knows, perhaps her carer had decided it was time for a clean page.

He takes the page from the machine, holds it up against the light. There is a watermark: the colourless lines of an oak tree. There it hangs, majestically uprooted. Upside down. A kind of sob rips through him, settling in his chest, waiting there.

He turns the sheet upside down, the address now at the bottom. The tree is now upright, the text the wrong way round. Oak branches reach upwards like the fingers of someone drowning.

Chapter 42

WHEN ETIENNE WALKS back from Irmgard to his hotel, he thinks of Axel's art. Of the awe it used to inspire in him in their London days. He remembers the afternoons of sitting around in the Bermondsey Street backyard with Axel's acolytes, how they would all hold their breath for weeks on end. He recalls how the waiting would cause his blood to heat up.

As Etienne got to see more and more art in the museums and galleries of London and Berlin, the aura started waning. Axel tries too hard, he decided. His work either carries its heart on its sleeve or it is too obscure. What it lacks are simultaneous flashes of strangeness and recognition.

After Axel had restlessly experimented with materials for a while, in the weeks before Etienne left for Buenos Aires he'd started focusing largely on rabbit hearts. His friend the veterinary sciences student came to help set up the final installation. Only the three of them were present. Long gone were the days when the hordes would make their way up to a London attic. The vet-to-be brought a stainless steel bowl filled with fresh hearts. There were two video screens, electrodes and a buzzing electrical device. Axel sat in a chair, gave instructions. The hearts were serried in neat rows in an electrolyte solution. Electrodes were dipped into the fluid. One video screen showed a colourful tropical bird flapping about in their flat. The sequence kept showing in an infinite loop.

On the soundtrack, a cheerful chirping and tweeting. The other screen showed a frightened rabbit sniffing around in an all-white room. Intermittently the little animal was kicked by a man's foot in a shiny shoe. Coinciding with each kick, an electrical charge was administered to the hearts, which would beat violently once, and then continue shuddering for a while in an unsynchronised fashion. Some hearts stopped working after a while, like blown bulbs in a string of Christmas lights. After an hour or so, all the hearts would arrest and had to be replaced with fresh ones. Etienne stopped counting how many rabbits had had to die for the installation.

He arrives at his hotel. The cool interior is a relief; it is hot outside. He turns up the air conditioner, takes off his sweat-soaked clothes, strokes his shaven head and smooth body. He likes how strong and supple he has become. He thinks of the other materials Axel has been experimenting with in recent times: frozen flowers, his own blood and tears. Even night sweats wrung from a shirt – a few drops in a flask. When he became predominantly bed-bound, he compulsively started trying to tear his sheets into strips. He wanted to knot and plait the strips into voodoo-like dolls. But Axel's body was flickering like a candle flame, his fingers no longer up to these tasks. He sat upright in his bed, gave detailed instructions, which Etienne (at last again the helper and disciple) clumsily tried to execute.

Synthesiser sounds are suddenly playing in Etienne's ears. At first he thinks they emanate from another room. But no, they are inside his own skull. Quick, dry percussion. A thin note gradually flattening, then scratching with static. The image in his mind is that of a Finnish landscape. Ice, northern light, moonlight on the backs of steaming reindeers: his next synth composition.

Etienne suddenly feels deeply tired. The music in his head comes to an abrupt halt. He lies down, falls asleep.

He dreams he is standing next to a river in flood. His mother comes floating by. She has sunglasses on and is lying on her back, her feet sticking out of the water. She notices Etienne, smiles at him. 'Come and take a swim,' she says. 'It is lovely here in the grey waters of time!' He starts wading towards her. The water is icy. Something upstream draws his attention: a bloated cadaver. His father, he knows at once. It is floating towards him. He retreats quickly, pulls his feet from the water.

Downstream there is a weathered stone bridge, on which Axel is standing and waving. Except for the forceful oak's root tips curling around his neck, his skin is unblemished. Axel, he suddenly knows with dream certainty, was born with that tree on his back. The currents rise; the bridge collapses. Axel tumbles into the mist.

The alarm clock shows it is ten o'clock. Only when Etienne gets up and sleepily peers through the curtains does he realise it isn't evening, but morning: he has slept through an afternoon, evening and night. His flight departs in three hours. He washes his face, stumbles downstairs in a half-dazed state with a view to finding breakfast.

The concierge beckons him over. There was a phone call, the man explains in broken English. He hands over a note, which Etienne unfolds:

Time: 21h14
For: Etienne Nieuwenhuis

Room: 603
Message: Axel is dead

For a while Etienne keeps standing there without a word. He politely thanks the concierge, folds the note and hands it back to him.

He pays his bill, leaves his luggage at reception. He leaves the hotel, walks into the sharp sunlight. Everything is a shade of white. He walks through the streets, in whichever direction his feet take him. He encounters a grandiose entrance. He recognises it from pictures in the hotel brochure – the Recoleta cemetery.

He walks in through the gates, ignoring hawkers with maps showing famous people's graves. The cemetery is surrounded by office buildings. It is like a miniature city, a city within a city: paths like streets, graves like homes. Most mausoleums are ornate. He seeks out an unremarkable modern one, sits down on its step. The glass of the little door behind him is broken. A breeze is blowing from inside: a cool, musty draught on his neck. He rests his head against the black marble door frame, shuts his eyes.

The smell of meat enters his nostrils. He opens his eyes. Before him stands a sunburnt, wrinkled woman. She shoves a cardboard box of roast chickens under his nose. Etienne takes from his pocket the money that he had kept for a taxi back to the airport, pays her, lets her keep the change. She hands him a chicken with her bare hands. When she has gone, he starts eating. He doesn't have the slightest appetite, will *never* be hungry again. He eats messily and mechanically, defying his revulsion, ingesting the entire chicken. He chews and swallows, then picks morsels from his teeth with his tongue.

He suppresses his gag reflex. He licks the bones clean, stacks them neatly by his feet. He closes his eyes again, bangs his head against the marble until he feels dizzy.

On the inside of his lids, the black wall next to his and Axel's vegetable garden in Berlin appears. In a flash he is *there*, his nose pressed against the wall. His feet lift off the ground. Slowly he rises, until his eye is aligned with the bright spot.

It is a peephole, he realises. And there, on the other side – so close and yet not – Axel is standing. Alone and fierce. In a land of pure light, where, if Etienne were to join him, time's strongest winds could never blow them from each other's arms again.

Acknowledgements

Thank you to the University of the Western Cape for awarding me the Jan Rabie & Marjorie Wallace Bursary for 2014. This generous grant allowed me to write the novel full-time.

I am grateful to Pierre Brugman, Michiel Heyns and Marlene van Niekerk, who read drafts of the novel, and also to Fourie Botha, Beth Lindop and Fahiema Hallam of Umuzi. Thank you to Anne-Marie Mischke and Jenefer Shute for their editing, and also to my agent Rebecca Carter of Janklow & Nesbit. I am also indebted to Stevan Alcock and Evelyne Nerlich-Sinnassamy for patient conversations about life in (East and West) Berlin in the 1980s. Thank you to Deon and Marlene van der Westhuizen, in whose house in the Auvergne in France I wrote part of the book, and to Hannes Myburgh, on whose farm in the Eastern Cape in South Africa another part was written.

A few sources that I found useful:

Benjamin, Walter, 2006. *Berlin Childhood around 1900*. Belknap Press.

Benjamin, Walter, 2012. *Berliner Kindheit um Neunzehnhunderd*. e-artnow.

Bergfelder, Tim & Carter, Eric & Göktürk, Denis (eds), 2002. *The German Cinema Book*. Palgrave Macmillan.

Broadbent, Philip & Hake, Sabine (eds), 2012. *Berlin Divided City, 1945–1989: Culture and Society in Germany*. Berghahn Books.

Brockmann, Stephen, 2010. *A Critical History of German Film*. Camden House.

Eiland, Howard & Jennings, Michael, 2014. *Walter Benjamin: A Critical Life*. Belknap Press.

Funder, Anna, 2003. *Stasiland: Stories from behind the Berlin Wall*. Granta.

Gordon, Mel, 2006. *Voluptuous Panic: The Erotic World of Weimar Berlin*. Feral House.

Hauswald, Harald & Rathenow, Lutz, 2005. *Ost-Berlin: Leben vor dem Mauerfall*. Jaron Verlag.

Höhne, Günter, undated. *DDR Design*. Komet Verlag.

Lange, Karl-Ludwig, 2011. *Die Berliner Mauer: Fotografien 1973 bis heute*. Sutton Verlag.

Mascelli, Joseph, 1998. *The Five C's of Cinematography: Motion Picture Filming Techniques*. Silman-James Press.

Nooteboom, Cees, 2012. *Roads to Berlin*. Quercus.

Paris, Robert, 2013. *Entschwundene Stadt: Berlin 1980–1989*. Mitteldeutscher Verlag.

Reed, S. Alexander, 2013. *Assimilate: A Critical History of Industrial Music*. Oxford University Press.

Specht, Arno, 2012. *Geisterstätten: Vergessene Orte in Berlin und Umgebung*. Jaron Verlag.

Thompson, Frank, 1996. *Lost Films: Important Movies That Disappeared*. Citadel Press.

NEW FICTION FROM SALT

RON BUTLIN
Billionaires' Banquet (978-1-78463-100-0)

NEIL CAMPBELL
Sky Hooks (978-1-78463-037-9)

SUE GEE
Trio (978-1-78463-061-4)

CHRISTINA JAMES
Rooted in Dishonour (978-1-78463-089-8)

V.H. LESLIE
Bodies of Water (978-1-78463-071-3)

WYL MENMUIR
The Many (978-1-78463-048-5)

ALISON MOORE
Death and the Seaside (978-1-78463-069-0)

ANNA STOTHARD
The Museum of Cathy (978-1-78463-082-9)

STEPHANIE VICTOIRE
The Other World, It Whispers (978-1-78463-085-0)

ALSO AVAILABLE FROM SALT

ELIZABETH BAINES
Too Many Magpies (978-1-84471-721-7)
The Birth Machine (978-1-907773-02-0)

LESLEY GLAISTER
Little Egypt (978-1-907773-72-3)

ALISON MOORE
The Lighthouse (978-1-907773-17-4)
The Pre-War House and Other Stories (978-1-907773-50-1)*He Wants* (978-1-907773-81-5)
Death and the Seaside (978-1-78463-069-0)

ALICE THOMPSON
Justine (978-1-78463-031-7)
The Falconer (978-1-78463-009-6)
The Existential Detective (978-1-78463-011-9)
Burnt Island (978-1-907773-48-8)
The Book Collector (978-1-78463-043-0)

RECENT FICTION FROM SALT

KERRY HADLEY-PRYCE
The Black Country (978-1-78463-034-8)

CHRISTINA JAMES
The Crossing (978-1-78463-041-6)

IAN PARKINSON
The Beginning of the End (978-1-78463-026-3)

CHRISTOPHER PRENDERGAST
Septembers (978-1-907773-78-5)

MATTHEW PRITCHARD
Broken Arrow (978-1-78463-040-9)

JONATHAN TAYLOR
Melissa (978-1-78463-035-5)

GUY WARE
The Fat of Fed Beasts (978-1-78463-024-9)

NEW BOOKS FROM SALT

XAN BROOKS
The Clocks in This House All Tell Different Times
(978-1-78463-093-5)

RON BUTLIN
Billionaires' Banquet (978-1-78463-100-0)

MICKEY J C ORRIGAN
Project XX (978-1-78463-097-3)

MARIE GAMESON
The Giddy Career of Mr Gadd (deceased)
(978-1-78463-118-5)

LESLEY GLAISTER
The Squeeze (978-1-78463-116-1)

NAOMI HAMILL
How To Be a Kosovan Bride (978-1-78463-095-9)

CHRISTINA JAMES
Fair of Face (978-1-78463-108-6)

This book has been typeset by
SALT PUBLISHING LIMITED
using Neacademia, a font designed by Sergei Egorov
for the Rosetta Type Foundry in the Czech Republic.
It is manufactured using Creamy 70gsm, a Forest
Stewardship Council™ certified paper from Stora Enso's
Anjala Mill in Finland. It was printed and bound by
Clays Limited in Bungay, Suffolk, Great Britain.

CROMER
GREAT BRITAIN
MMXVIII